EXPEDITION OF EQUALITY

Paul R. Strickler

First Edition

PAGE PUBLISHING, INC.
Conneaut Lake, PA

First originally published by Page Publishing 2021

ISBN 978-1-6624-5916-0 (pbk)
ISBN 978-1-6624-5917-7 (digital)

Printed in the United States of America

Expedition of Equality starts in the year 3000 when a group of scientists travels to a new star system. Their only desire is to be able to experiment without government regulations. Over time, new societies are formed with their own philosophical beliefs. But once space pirates start to strike, a new universal police force is formed.

Follow the exploits of the spaceship Equality and its crew as they explore this strange new world while defending it from space pirates. Watch as they meet a clone of an infamous murderer, a clone who has also killed but who they quickly learn is the key to unraveling a mystery that puts every life in this bold new world at risk.

INTRODUCTION

"My name's Dolly, and I'd like to tell you a story" came a soft feminine voice echoing into a nursery.

In the nursery lay three babies and a large purple egg in one extra-large crib. The babies and the purple egg floated a few inches over the bed with a tether around their waists to keep them from floating off too far. Two of the babies wore blue onesies, and the third wore a pink onesie. All the onesies had the phrase "Geologists Rock" printed on them.

Dolly continued in a gentle tone, "This story is a story about where you got your names and how your namesakes became heroes."

One of the babies in blue began to cry.

Dolly said, "Shush now. They wouldn't want you to cry for them. Plus, this story has your godfather in it."

The crying baby stopped, then the baby in pink started to giggle and clap her little hands.

Dolly continued, "That's right. Whenever mankind is suffering with no hope of change, salvation, or survival, that's when your godfather or one of his clones somehow shows up, raining down death and destruction to bring hope back for the future of humanity. Even your namesake, Jake, didn't know whether to trust him or arrest him when they first met."

All three babies began to smile and clap.

Dolly whispered, "Don't clap too hard, little ones. Far more were lost than saved in this story."

CHAPTER 1

Mr. Jake

Jake awoke from his deep slumber, feeling proud that he beat his alarm clock going off. The sound of the beeping irritated him so. Whenever he tried to use music instead, he found himself sleeping right through it.

The day started out like any other day. Jake unzipped his sleeping bag then stood on his bed. His morning ritual was to make it into the bathroom (eight feet away) in a single jump. This might seem like an easy task for someone living in space without gravity, but it was in fact exceedingly difficult.

Jake's ceiling was ten feet tall. Jake himself was six-one. Jake had to stand on the very edge of his bed in a crouching position. His onesie was standard-issue blue. The magnetic souls clung to the bed, meaning Jake had to factor this into the force needed to make the jump. Moving too slow didn't count in his mind. Moving too fast would make the next push off the ceiling too difficult. More than once, Jake found himself crashing into the doorway. Adding to the difficulty was that the onesies weren't just a fashion statement. They restricted movement to build muscles in space.

Jake leaped to the ceiling then pushed off toward the bathroom as soon as he felt his brown crew cut hair touch. Jake, unfortunately, found himself coming in low and to the left. He quickly lifted his legs up then grabbed for the doorway, using it to reposition his landing. Jake felt his feet sink softly into the grass. After taking a quick glance to make sure he didn't mess up the wire mesh holding the soil and grass in place, Jake cheered, "Hell yeah, I'm good."

Jake got undressed and locked himself in the shower. The water pressure felt good as Jake relieved his bladder. There was warm air blowing down from above and suction from the floor to recover and filter the water for reuse. Once the shower was finished, Jake had to wait to be air-dried off before the door would let him out.

After finishing in the bathroom, Jake logged in to take care of his high school class work. Jake was a ward of Strum and Strum Inc. (S&S Inc.) ever since his parents died in an accident when he was five. Jake was seventeen now and considered as a well-adjusted emancipated youth.

Jake has always been a good student with a solid 3.5 GPA. Lately, his concentration has suffered. It seemed to only get worse the more time he spent with his supervisor, Stacy. Stacy was a twenty-one-year-old college intern working on her master's degree in botany with a minnow in geology. Stacy had the body of a goddess in Jake's mind. She was a five-five brunette with sun-kissed skin, a tiny waist, extremely ample bosom, the face of an angel, and pouty lips he couldn't help but long to kiss.

Around authoritarian figures, Stacy was shy and quiet as a mouse. Once out of earshot of such individuals, she became loud. Every other word out of her mouth was a swear word. Stacy was, without a doubt, the woman of Jake's dreams. He would do anything for her.

Jake got to work early in the hydroponics bay as he did most days. Stacy would already be there. The hydroponics bay was a massive room that grew the fruits and vegetables for the space station. Everything was bioengineered for accelerated growth, meaning crops were constantly being harvested.

Stacy, on this day, shocked Jake with her greeting. "What you gonna do without me, Jake?"

Jake's face became flush with fear as he asked, "What do you mean without you?"

Stacy smiled then answered, "I mean, I put my application in to join the Minnow. I might be leaving this solar system forever."

Jake had never gotten up the courage to tell Stacy how he felt. Now he feared he never would as he said, "That's great, Stacy."

Stacy exclaimed, "Fuck yeah, it is!"

Jake instinctively tried to discourage Stacy and asked, "Are you sure you trust that Carrie effect drive?"

Stacy shrugged her shoulder then said, "Well, the satellite from the first group should be returning tonight. If the Carrie effect drive doesn't work, we'll know then."

Jake said, "Yeah, maybe, but don't you find it odd that they only made enough of that Faraday metal for the shells of the expedition ships? It could have revolutionized travel right here."

Stacy giggled then said, "The government would never regulate that here. Traveling near the speed of light sounds great, but you can't stop. You're in theoretical math science. What happens if a ship traveling that fast hits Earth?"

Jake reluctantly agreed. "I know. That's part of the reason why so many scientists agreed to go. They want to be able to experiment however they want."

Stacy smiled then said, "Imaging what crazy shit they will come up with. The marijuana strains I can experiment with."

Jake asked, "Do you really think you can get there? I know the math makes sense. The faster you travel, the slower time moves, but do you really think it works that way?"

Stacy shrugged her shoulders then said, "We will see tonight. The ships that left four years ago should have sent back a satellite two years ago. Once we pick up its broadcast tonight, we will know if it works or not."

When Jake got home that evening, he watched the video that the S&S Inc. expedition did in fact send back. It was full of people looking out windows, exclaiming, "All we did was blink, and look how far we traveled! These are completely different stars!" There were also images of a baby named Joy, a baby that should have been two years old at the time the video was taken. The baby was, in fact, still a baby that barely aged a day.

Jake had never been interested in traveling to a new star system. He also had no real dreams of his own, and the thought of never getting to see Stacy's smile again brought pain to his heart. That night, Jake put in his application to join the SS Minnow.

A few days later, Jake was working with Stacy when her W2 (future version of a cell phone on steroids) beeped, indicating a new message. Stacy read the message then exclaimed, "I got the job!" Stacy then hugged Jake.

Jake was full of confused emotions at the moment. He had not heard back on his own application, nor had he told Stacy that he even applied. The feeling of warmth from getting to hold Stacy for the first time made his head spin on what he should say or do. Jake simply hugged Stacy back, unable to speak.

Stacy jumped back then said, "I only have ten days until I leave. I have to go put in notice." With that, Stacy was off.

A feeling of sadness started to come over Jake at the thought of losing Stacy. It was then that his W2 beeped. Jake received an interview with Captain Noem of the SS Minnow at 6:00 p.m. aboard the SS Minnow.

Jake googled Captain Noem. He read she was 103 years old (in the current photo, she looked maybe forty). She was five-eight with tan skin. She was of mixed descent (like almost everyone at this time) and a former member of the French military. She started out as a fighter pilot then transferred to the UN peacekeepers. Finally, she went with the money, joining S&S Inc.

Jake paused to look at the SS Minnow on his way to his interview. The Minnow was a massive oval-shaped ship almost the size of the space station he was on, although the Minnow was actually two ships. The bottom third of the ship was a second ship called the Tadpole. It was designed to be a passenger ship that could travel down to a planet's surface and back. Ships' built-in spaces were mostly made to stay in space. Their construction weight was far too heavy to ever go down to a planet then return.

Both the Minnow and the Tadpole had ion drives. The Tadpole also had plasma rockets attached to its sides for the extra kick needed to break the atmosphere. There were also port thrusters surrounding the exterior that released compressed gas for steering.

Jake was surprised to find Captain Noem waiting for him at the docks. She greeted him with a smile and shook his hand then said, "It's an honor to finally meet you."

Jake got confused. He wondered if she thought he was someone else.

The look of confusion was apparent on Jake's face, and this made Captain Noem smile. Captain Noem said, "You probably don't know this, but I served with your grandfather, Sergeant Jake, who you were named after, by the way. He gave his life-saving mine during the aftermath of the second Russell Arthur incident. Of course, that was long before your time. When I saw your application, I had to meet you. Can I give you the tour?"

Jake knew nothing about being named after his grandfather. All he knew about them was that they were deceased. Jake nodded yes, and they began to walk. Captain Noem asked, "Do you know the history of the Minnow?"

Jake replied, "It was the test ship for the Carrie effect shell. This ship gets placed in a perfectly circular shell made of Faraday metal. Ions get released, bouncing to and from one magnetically charged point. This causes the shell and everything in it to travel at near light speed in that direction. Something my science teacher says is mathematically impossible."

Captain Noem said, "That is mostly correct. Don't tell anyone, but this is actually the second test ship. They didn't find out about the shell traveling toward a magnetized point until after a malfunction. This is the second test ship."

Jake asked, "What happened to the first?"

Captain Noem replied, "Well, it had a stormfront battery powering it. So it's flying until it hits something."

They walked down the extended airlock, entering the Tadpole section of the ship. It seemed smaller somehow to Jake on the inside. The first room they walked into was the airlock with doors on either side.

Captain Noem said, "The door to the left leads to the engine room. The door on the right to the passenger cabin."

Captain Noem led Jake into the passenger section. The ceiling was eight feet tall with two aisles of double-row seating on each side. The chairs were above them as they currently walked on the ceiling. In space, up and down got a bit surreal.

There were vines growing on the walls, which was common on all spacecraft for fresh air. What was unusual was the fact that there was no grass on the floor or ceiling. Bioengineered shortgrass was standard on all ships. There was a door in the front, presumably leading to the cockpit, but there was no seeable way to enter the Minnow.

Captain Noem asked, "Wondering how to get to the Minnow?"

Jake replied, "Yes, actually." Jake thought there must be a way into the Minnow without having to go outside and enter through the cargo bay.

Captain Noem said, "Bob, we need to enter the Minnow."

A strong male voice responded, "Yes, Captain Noem." The ceiling then opened up, followed by the floor slowly rising, carrying them through the newly formed hole.

Jake had heard stories about how easily Faraday metal could be manipulated by magnetism. Actually seeing it in action was mind-blowing. Jake asked in more of a statement form, "This is Faraday metal, isn't it?"

Captain Noem answered, "Yes, it is. A strong magnet is basically pushing it up with an opposite attraction. It will only work in the weightlessness of space, of course."

Now inside of the Minnow, Jake could see the shortgrass covering the floors. They were now in the center of a courtyard, the heart of the ship.

Captain Noem said, "Toward the front of the ship on this level is the cargo bay with the bridge above that. To the rear is the engine room, which is also where the 3D printers are located. The ceiling here is fifteen feet tall with two levels of housing above them. Ceilings there are only eight feet high. A small medical bay is located right behind you next to the entrance of the Tadpole. The surrounding areas of the park have spaces for businesses. This courtyard is 2.5 acreage with a jogging trail around the outskirts. Half of the acreage is dedicated to our garden and hydroponics, where most of our food and medicine will grow. Harvests take place every two to three weeks, depending on the crops. Everyone is expected to pinch in, including the passengers. It's in their contract. There is a picnic area in the corner, and a jungle gym will be set near that before deployment. Along both sides of the ships are observation bays. There is a mess hall growing cells for the bio 3D printers. Do you have any questions so far?"

Jake asked, "Does this mean I have the job?"

Captain Noem smiled then answered, "If you want it."

Jake replied, "Yes, I want it." Then after a short pause, Jake asked, "What's the job?"

Captain Noem chuckled then replied, "Ah, the enthusiasm of youth. Well, your job is going to be everything. I have a limited crew with lots of passengers. You will need to learn every job and fill in or help out wherever needed. Your official title is floater. Think you can handle that?"

Jake smiled as he realized this meant he would get to work with Stacy occasionally. Jake answered, "Okay."

*****

On the day of departure, Jake was in his new room aboard the SS Minnow, unpacking the last of his belongings. All the crew quarters were on the second floor along the walls. They all had emergency exits built into the floor that dropped down into the courtyard.

The rooms themselves were all twenty by twenty with an eight-by-ten-foot bathroom in the corner. The walls were covered in vines while the floors remained bare. Grass could be placed later at the owner's discretion. For families, there were rooms with adjoining doors.

Captain Noem's voice came over the coms. "Welcome aboard the SS Minnow. I am your captain, Noem Sturgis. Departure will take place at 12:00 a.m. The time dilation field can cause some discomfort if you're awake. We ask everyone to try to be asleep for it. This is something we will all have to get used to for the next decade as we travel to our new home."

Most of the passengers did not heed the captain's warning. Everyone was teeming with excitement at the time, wanting to feel the rush that they thought for sure would accompany traveling at near the speed of light. This was not the case.

Once the ship took off, they were literally paralyzed for about five minutes. Even one's own thoughts felt sluggish.

Jake's first day on the job was spent assisting the doctor by passing out sleeping pills to extremely unnerved passengers and crew. The doctor reassured Jake and the patients that the feeling, however uncomfortable, was normal.

It wasn't until the last patient left that Jake had a chance to take in what happened. In the few minutes of paralysis, they had traveled well over two hundred light-years from Earth. The stars outside the ship were all new. The earth couldn't even be seen with the strongest telescope. Jake checked his W2, and there was a new link. It was a video from the second satellite the S&S Inc. expedition left behind.

Unlike the first videos from them, these videos had people freaking out over the paralysis during jumps (*jumps* being the new term used to describe traveling by the Carrie effect drive). Jake realized the company must have censored these types of videos in the first transmission. The reason they didn't this time was that there was no longer any point trying to hide it.

Jake was upset at this but not surprised. S&S Inc. had been good to Jake since his parents died. Yet they were still a corporation putting profit margins first. The fact Jake was assigned to the medical bay meant top officials knew about the psychological effect of this type of travel. Jake knew the reason for hiding it was to get funding. Tickets for this flight were presold at the cost of an average person's life's earnings. This was done to help fund the first expedition.

There was a discussion the next day about turning around. Captain Noem pointed out that by the time they could return to Earth, four years would have passed. The wealthy elite already gave away or sold their possessions before leaving. All their old jobs would have been filled. Their homes now had strange new families living in them. All this occurred in what seemed like five minutes.

The SS Minnow continued on its journey with Captain Noem's promise that the videos they sent back to Earth would be unedited. This way, any future travelers could make more informed decisions as to whether or not to make the journey.

Every night at midnight, a new jump took place. Each time they stopped, there would be a new satellite from the original S&S Inc. expedition. The satellite would be filled with personal videos, along with new astrological data used to plot the next course. The SS Minnow would download their own time capsule videos before the next jump.

As the years went by, Jake learned the basics of every department. He was never able to get out of the "just friends department" with Stacy. He did manage to have a few flings with one younger and one older passenger that never amounted to much. Oddly enough, Jake felt his heart belonged to his time capsule crust, Jemma.

Jemma was a cook's assistant aboard ship 2 of the S&S Inc. expedition. She was a short blond on the plump side but so full of energy in her videos. Jemma's videos were always just so sweet and adorable. Jake had a bedtime ritual of checking his links for new Jemma videos to watch before he fell asleep.

Jake made best friends with one of the passengers along the way. He was a boy named Calvin, who was twelve at the start of the trip. Calvin had a "runt of the litter" body type. His family won their tickets as a promotional prize. His family wasn't the kind to have the money for genetic tweaking most of the well-off pregnant women got. This somehow made the orphaned Jake feel a connection with Calvin.

Calvin was a wiz with computers and a practical joker who got Jake into trouble on more than one occasion. Among Calvin's biggest pranks was the time he hacked into and set all the ship's bathroom lights to flash SOS whenever someone flushed. Another time, Calvin had Jake play lookout as he swapped out a patch of shortgrass in a corridor with long grass they snuck out of hydroponics. For weeks, people would stop and stare, not sure what to make of it. Eventually, someone went to Stacy out of fear that somehow, the ship's air supply was at risk. They got scolded pretty good, but they felt it was worth it.

Along the way, Jake even got to play matchmaker with two of the female passengers, Amy and Jess. This hookup was one out of necessity for Jake. A wife (Jessica) caught her husband cheating. His mistress wasn't interested in leaving her own husband, who supported her sexual appetite. This left Jessica in need of new housing.

Jake was consoling Jessica, who was a couple of decades older than him, but with age-slowing medication, you wouldn't know. One evening, while consoling Jessica, things went further than Jake meant them to. This led Jake to push his friends, Amy and Jess, into moving in together in order to free up a room for Jessica, thus not forcing Jake to free up room for Jessica to move in with him.

Most free time spent on the journey was spent in the courtyard. There were all sorts of VR leagues set up as well as book clubs and talent shows. Considering most of the passengers came from money (with few exceptions like Calvin), everyone seemed to get along pretty well.

Jake also became close to Captain Noem over the years. He became her right-hand man in the decade they spent working together. Captain Noem became to Jake the mother he never got to have.

As it turned out, Captain Noem was not actually a woman who was easy to get to know. She had what was known as a resting bitch face. This made most feel as though she hated them, thus they kept their distance. However, whenever Jake was around, she made the effort to smile.

Jake learned over the years that Captain Noem was a fair captain who took the time to learn all sides of a situation before taking action. Although in a euchre game, she tended to be bold. Said she would rather lose on her terms than leave it to her opponent.

On the final few days of their journey, speculation ran rampant on what to expect when they finally reached their destination. The original S&S Inc. expedition had four ships and a four-year head start to build a space station for the passengers of the SS Minnow to move into.

Like the Minnow, each of the ships of the S&S Inc. expedition was designed to split apart. Only instead of two ships, they would break apart into four ships (AKA quarterships). Each of these quarterships was a third larger than the Minnow. Each quartership housed roughly a thousand people while the Minnow carried less than three hundred crew and passengers.

The passengers of the Minnow were excited to share the four years' worth of Earth news, music, and entertainment that the people of S&S Inc. expedition had missed out on. They were also excited to finally meet all the people from the videos they had been watching these past ten years. Jake especially so to meet Jemma.

Jake was twenty-seven now, and he knew Jemma would also be twenty-seven. To Jake, this was an indicator of fate. He found himself hoping Jemma would be at the welcoming party for the Minnow.

Over the years, Jake found his contact lenses to be his most important piece of gear. While working, he could ask someone a question regardless of where they were on the ship at the time. He could then share his link with that person, allowing them to see through his lenses. That way, the person could see exactly what Jake was asking about in real time. Once you had access to someone else's feed, you could even use zoom features and playback. Time limits were preset by the user before sharing the link on how far back viewers could go (standard preset was one minute).

On the night of the last jump, no one could sleep. Even knowing that staying awake meant enduring that horrible feeling of being paralyzed, almost everyone was awake. Before the jump took place, Captain Noem opened a link to her W2 live feed for all passengers and crew. This would allow everyone to witness first contact with the S&S Inc. expedition.

Everyone was fully expecting to be welcomed by the owners of S&S Inc., Carrie and Stan Strum. What they saw instead, no one could have anticipated.

What the Hell

The bridge of the Minnow had five seats, two in the front for pilot and copilot. There was one along each side with consoles displaying the ship's functions. One station was for external and the other for internal sensors. The captain's seat sat in the middle.

Captain Noem asked Jake to be on the bridge with her during the first contact. Jake was honored and jumped at the chance, even though it meant standing in the corner.

Jake had to endure the paralyzing effect of time dilation many times over the past decade. The feeling of helplessness it brought was something he never could get used to. Jake always found himself squeezing his butt cheeks together to help cope. This was based on a tip from Calvin: "Squeeze your butt cheeks together before the jump like you're in prison and just dropped the soap. It helps." Jake didn't actually find this to be helpful, but it was better than doing nothing. Jake clenched his butt cheeks for the final time. The paralyzing effect came and went.

Captain Noem ordered, "Crack the shell."

Fourteen poles were attached to the Minnow that extended to the Faraday shell. These poles were used to transfer electrical currents and ions to the shell for jumping. They also allowed manipulating the shell to open it. This had to be done to see out and scan the area after each jump.

As the shell opened for what would be the final time, they could see nothing but dark open space at first. The ship was still traveling at speeds in excess of 1000 mph but slowing. The Minnow immediately picked up dozens of new links arranged by closest location. There were three links about the same distance apart straight ahead (two hundred thousand miles away) in the middle of space.

Captain Noem asked, "Bob, can you get me visual on the nearest link's location?"

Bob, the ships AI, responded, "At current speed, it will be two hours before I can give you a visual."

Captain Noem asked, "If you can't give visual, how do you know their location and distance, Bob?"

Bob replied, "There are two satellites between SS Minnow and that location giving a GPS [galactic positioning system] signal. There is an incoming three-way transmission from that location. Would you like it on screen?"

Everyone in the room got excited, thinking this must be Carrie and Stan Strum there to welcome them.

Captain Noem answered, "Yes, Bob."

Nothing could have prepared them for what they saw next. On the left third of the screen was a woman wearing a black suit of armor with random red stripes and an odd shimmer as if it were covered with glitter. The woman herself looked to be in her thirties (with age-slowing treatments, it was impossible to tell by looks). She had dark tan skin and a scar that went from just above her left eye across her lips down to the base of her chin.

In the center screen was a teenage boy wearing a Metallica T-shirt over a yellow onesie. He was a slender and lanky blond with a very long and pointy nose. Add in his pointy dimpled chin, and he almost looked like a comical cartoon character.

On the right screen was the most disturbing sight. It was a man wearing a yellow metal suit with black stripes. His suit didn't shimmer like the lady's on the left did. The disturbing quality of this man was that he appeared to be covered in short black fur. There were no apparent animal features like pointy ears or whiskers. He simply appeared to be a man covered in black fur, wearing gold hoop earrings.

The teen in the middle spoke. "It's an honor to finally meet you guys. You are the inspiration that got here. I've watched all your time capsule videos so many times over the years. I feel I know you. Well, everyone here has watched them actually. I mean, they have been on the most viewed list here multiple times in the past ninety years. You guys are famous." The teen paused for a moment to take a breath before continuing, "My name's Harry Strum, by the way. Grandson of Carrie and Stan Strum."

Jake thought about how this was possible. Their signal couldn't have gotten here ninety years before them. The magnetic void between star systems jams signals. Besides that, the S&S Inc. expedition was only supposed to be four years ahead of them…unless something went wrong. Was the fur-covered man an alien?

The head pilot, Jesus, said, "That can't be Harry Strum. It looks like him, but then he couldn't have aged. Unless he's a clone."

Jake thought, *Jesus, king of useless knowledge, comes through in a pinch.* Jake quickly googled Harry Strum. Jake found Harry Strum, and the likeness was unmistakable. Harry was fourteen when SS Minnow left Earth and was supposed to still be there.

Harry explained, "It's me. The one and only. We can get to my eternally youthful transformation later. Let's start the story from the beginning, shall we?"

Captain Noem interrupted with a stern tone, "How many years has the S&S Inc. expedition been here?"

Harry answered, "It was not my fault. I had no idea what my grandparents had planned. If I had, I would have adjusted the Carrie effect field to their settings."

Captain Noem repeated in a sterner tone, "How long?"

Harry continued to hesitate answering the question.

The woman with the scar answered instead. "It's the year 500 here. That's five hundred years since the S&S Inc. expedition landed. Stan, Carrie, and all the original expedition members are long dead now."

Harry shouted, "Hey! You agreed to let me do all the talking until they were up to speed."

The woman snarled then said, "Get on with it then."

Harry explained, "My grandparents were so paranoid about government oversight that they altered the data on the time dilation field. They wanted to ensure no one would show up and try to interfere with their work." Harry raised both his hands then said, "I know what you're thinking. If they altered data, how did this fine-looking young man get to stand before you? Well, this fine young man also happens to be a bit of a thief. My parents forbid me from joining my grandparents' expedition. I was still too young to join you guys when you left. After your satellite reached Earth, everyone freaked out. No one knew about the paralyzing effects that came with traveling by the Carrie effect drive. My grandparents hid this from everyone. All future expeditions were immediately canceled. I wasn't about to give up on my dream to join you all here. So I commandeered a prototype vessel, a small one-man ship that kept its passenger in a medically induced coma for the journey." Harry got extra proud and cocky as he said, "My ship was slightly faster than yours, so I was able to beat you here."

The fur-covered man said, "I wouldn't boast about what you did. You almost died. It took us six months to rehabilitate what little was left of your body. If anyone else had recovered your vessel first, you surely would have died."

The scarred woman got enraged and exclaimed, "We could have cared for him just as easily and effectively!"

Harry shouted, "I'm not done talking yet!" Harry shook his head then said, "The charming lady is Tanis of Juliet. The furry man is Colt of Romeo. Apparently, during my grandparents' trip here, there was a bit of a falling out."

Both Tanis and Colt started to speak, but Harry quickly stopped them, shouting, "I will tell the story! Don't make me mute you!"

Tanis roared, "Try it and—" Harry hit mute.

Colt laughed and then said, "That's the way to han—" Harry muted Colt as well.

Harry continued, "As I was saying, there was a falling out. Apparently, my grandfather was a bit of an egotist who couldn't handle all the praise my grandmother, Carrie, was receiving for discovering the Carrie effect shell. My grandfather claimed that since it was discovered by complete accident, she deserved no credit. Well, it turns out it's not a good idea to piss off your top engineer on a space-time dilation journey. Grandma Carrie decided she wanted a break from Grandpa Stan, and she slowed his ship's Carrie effect drive. Grandpa Stan arrived six months after everyone else. As you can imagine, this caused a bit of a rift. Not only between my grandparents, but everyone had friends and acquaintances that they were cut off from for six months. Not to mention Grandpa Stan's ship was the head medical vessel that produced most of the drugs and medicine for the convoy. The rift created back then continues to this day."

The left screen changed from showing Tanis to displaying an image of two other spaceships. The closest spaceship appeared to be a small vessel with a block shape to it. It was painted with bright alternating colors of red, yellow, and purple. The other space ship looked much bigger with a flying saucer shape to it. This ship had images of a bear roaring painted on it.

Harry cursed, "Fuck me!"

The left screen showed the small middle ship suddenly being propelled into the larger saucer-shaped ship. The center screen showed Harry being half knocked out of his seat.

Harry screamed, "Unmute!" Then after a moment to readjust himself in his seat, Harry said, "Happy now, you crazy bitch!"

The saucer-shaped spaceship (after it stopped flying back from being hit with Harry's spaceship) deployed eight small jet-shaped ships. Colt screamed, "You'll pay for that!"

The left screen returned to an image of Tanis, who replied, "Bring it, furball."

Jesus said, "Captain, it was a projectile fired from Tanis's ship that struck Harry's vessel. By Bob's calculations, it had to have been fired from a rail gun. You might want to consider changing course, Captain."

Captain Noem appeared to ignore Jesus as she watched Harry trying to calm down Tanis and Colt.

Jake did what he knew Captain Noem was doing. He used his W2 to replay the footage of the projectile hitting Harry's spaceship to learn how it survived.

Jake saw that when the projectile reached Harry's vessel, it appeared to strike a shimmering shield that was pushed inward like pressing your finger down on a balloon. The ship was sent flying but didn't actually get struck by the projectile. When Harry's spaceship then struck the saucer-shaped spaceship, both ships displayed the same balloon-style shielding.

Harry shouted, "Both of you return your jet arms or I will escort the Minnow to the outer rings, leaving you two here to play patty-cake!"

Tanis and Colt reluctantly agreed.

Captain Noem didn't show it, but Jake knew she was now nervous. She had realized they had the power to take the Minnow by force if they wanted to.

Captain Noem kept her poker face as best she could and asked, "What is to happen to my passengers and crew?"

The center screen changed to show a blue planet with two moons orbiting it. Calvin answered, "This is Titan. There are six rings that make up this star system we have named Einstein. I'm in the fifth ring while you're currently in the sixth ring nearing the fifth ring. Titan is located on the second ring. Miles wise, Titan is about the same distance from this sun as our Earth is from our sun. Only Titan is bigger. In fact, the gravity is so heavy, there's no going down and returning to space. The moons of Titan are where most of the scientists decided to settle after they arrived. Grandma Carrie obviously had first pick getting here before Grandpa Stan. She chose the ore-rich moon she named Juliet. Then, as if to tell Grandpa Stan where the doghouse was, she named the other moon Romeo. That's where Grandpa Stan's ship settled."

Captain Noem asked, "Which of these moons are we headed to?"

Harry replied, "Neither." The center screen now changed to show what looked like a quartership from the S&S Inc. expedition, although the outside was covered with bright graffiti in multiple styles. Also, the top of the ship carried a large metal plate built on top of it, with dozens of ships like Harry's parked on it. Harry continued, "This is SS Middleman. It orbits between the two moons. This is where the trade takes place between the two moons, and sometimes the outer rings." The center screen returned to showing Harry, who continued, "This is where your passengers will go. Now there is a matter of a fee."

Captain Noem went from resting bitch face to intentional bitch face and asked, "What fee? Every passenger has already paid a fee. It's called a ticket."

Tanis spoke with a snarky pitch to it. "The people you had a deal with are long since dead."

Colt jumped in and said, "Calm down, Captain Noem. Money here is no longer based on your vid coin, I believe you called it. Currency is now based on Faraday particles. FP for short. You have a massive fortune with that Faraday shell you to get here."

Captain Noem asked, "Why is Faraday metal the basis of your economy?"

Tanis corrected Captain Noem. "Faraday particles, not metal. Faraday metal gets ground down to the size of a grain of sand. If you notice the shimmer on my armor, it's actually Faraday particles."

Colt scoffed. "What a waste of such precious metal."

Tanis began to speak an insult when Harry cut her off. "Anyways! The process to make Faraday metal was a corporate secret left behind in our old solar system. Captain Noem, your Faraday shell is quite rare and valuable. If you agree to it, your Faraday shell will be taken and processed. The proceeds of which can be divided up among you and your passengers."

Tanis added, "Minus processing and retrofitting fees."

Jake knew Captain Noem never considered herself the owner of the SS Minnow. Jake thought, *She would never, in normal circumstances, consider selling something that wasn't hers. Right now, she's looking for leverage to ensure the safety of everyone on board the Minnow.*

She's worried after seeing a rail gun, which has the impact force of a ballistic missile, being fired so casually. Then it's blocked with no more lasting effect than getting a slap on the back. Captain Noem must be worried about what happens next. She may even be considering turning back to Earth.

Captain Noem asked, "Do I get time to decide?"

Tanis replied, "No."

Harry and Colt yelled at Tanis, "Yes, they do!"

Colt scolded Tanis, "You know full well we still have a week's travel until we get back to Middleman. Don't give grief to this poor woman who has just had her world turned upside down."

Harry spoke to Captain Noem, "You and your crew should already have access to our cloud. Please take your time and research Einstein. Your passengers can even start looking for homes, jobs, or sign up for evocation classes."

Captain Noem asked, "Do you still honor the People's Declaration of Rights here?"

Colt answered, "It's been our bedrock as our society has grown."

Tanis snarked, "For Juliet, it has. The hell it has for Romeo! Are you forgetting about the quad sisters?"

Colt replied, "That has been cleared up. They have always been free to do what they like."

Tanis replied, "After they sued your asses. On Juliet, we truly honor the People's Declaration of Rights."

Now it was Colt who scoffed. "Your people don't even have the right to leave their homes without wearing power armor."

Harry screamed, "Enough already! Save the politics for another time."

Captain Noem asked, "What was this about retrofitting Tanis mentioned earlier?"

Tanis answered, "You can't hunt pirates unless we upgrade your ship. Don't bother looking for a better price. Our government already agreed to a discount, and you won't find better engineers in all of Einstein."

Jake was already connecting to the new internet. According to the article he pulled up, pirates started raiding cargo vessels a few years ago. Because each sector of space had its own police force that couldn't cross into other sectors of space, catching the pirates had been difficult, to say the least.

Harry scolded Tanis, "That's not how you offer someone a job!" Harry lowered his tone then asked, "Captain Noem, you are ex-United Nations. This makes you the only person on this side of the known universe qualified to help. No government here trusts the other governments. You, Captain Noem, are an outsider with an irreproachable record that we have all read. We would like you to recreate the UN here. If you accept, you will be in charge of the Einstein system's law enforcement."

*****

The SS Minnow continued on course to rendezvous with Harry, Colt, and Tanis. Jake researched FP along the way. He learned that by using Faraday particles instead of a solid metal, they could create a much weaker Carrie effect ion drive. This did require the particles to be gathered together to form a ring around the ship, thus removing the shielding effect when activated. The speed achieved, although nowhere near as fast as a solid shell, was still multiple times faster than the standard ion drives.

Everyone was given the time to sleep and spend the next day researching the new Einstein system before gathering in the courtyard the next evening for a town hall-style meeting.

Jake arrived in the courtyard, surprised to see how excited the passengers and crew were about this new twist to their journey. Jake realized he shouldn't be so surprised. After all, every crew member and passenger on board (except those who started the journey as kids) came here to discover a new world. That's exactly what they were getting.

Calvin ran up to Jake then said, "Dude! They have dinosaurs on a planet called Chronos. Real live dinosaurs."

Jake smiled and replied, "That's crazy."

Calvin continued, "That's nothing. I have been getting so many friend requests from hotties. Oh! The games they have here. Thread the Needle and King of the Hill. This place is wild beyond belief."

Jake was an avid historian. He knew ever since the People's Declaration of Rights was signed into law in the early 2100s, war became extinct. Instead, people took their competitive natures to focus on creating the most insanely dangerous yet completely safe competitions they could come up with. Apparently, that spirit was alive and thriving here in Einstein.

Captain Noem stood on the entrance to the Tadpole. The Faraday metal pad under her feet began to lift her into the air, creating a makeshift podium to speak from. Her voice echoed over the PA system throughout the Minnow. "It has been an honor serving you all. This journey is not ending as we expected it to. I appreciate most of you taking this news not only in stride but embracing what may come next for you. You all have become like family to me, and I wish you all the best in your future endeavors." There was a pause as people cheered and clapped. Captain Noem continued, "To help ensure all of you are safe in this new world, I have decided to take the offer to head what will be called the Einstein Protection Force. EPF for short."

There was another round of applause. Someone shouted, "I'll fight the pirates!"

Captain Noem said, "No members of this crew signed up for this new mission, and none will be expected to join. When we get near SS Middleman, the passengers will load onto the Tadpole for transport to Middleman. It's going to take a couple of trips, so we will be going alphabetically. The rest of the crew shall stay with the Minnow for the journey to Romeo. Once there, you will have completed your contracts and are free to continue with your new lives."

To Jake's surprise, Calvin shouted, "What about us who want to stay and help you fight the pirates?"

Suddenly, the room got silent. Coming from Calvin, his words sounded like a joke. Yet many were thinking the same thing after living together for a decade.

Captain Noem responded, "Calvin, you're not even a member of this crew."

Calvin replied, "I've been aboard this ship for a decade and been in every computer system. That makes me crew."

Now everyone laughed.

Captain Noem kept a straight face and said. "Everyone on board is aware of your computer hacking antics. That doesn't make you crew." Calvin looked like he was about to argue the point when Captain Noem continued, "If you want to become a member of the new crew, you will have to put in your application like everyone else."

Jake couldn't help but smile. Captain Noem just filled out a letter of recommendation for his resumé the month prior. Jake loaded his resume into his W2 and sent it to Captain Noem then and there.

Captain Noem's W2 beeped, and a small smile creeped across her face as she looked at her W2. Jake must have not been the only person with this idea as Captain Noem's W2 continued to beep with new email notifications.

The day of separation came with Jesus piloting the Tadpole. When Jake asked him if he was returning, Jesus replied, "I'm a lover, not a fighter. Keep your head down and stay safe, kid."

Right after Jesus departed, Harry Strum arrived through the cargo bay. He was joining the Minnow crew as the Einstein interrelations expert.

Jake greeted Harry and escorted him to the bridge to meet Captain Noem in person. As they walked, Jake asked, "I take it Colt is part of the plushy race I read about?"

Harry, who was wearing a red onesie with a T-shirt that had a picture of a TV with a smiley face in it, answered, "Stupid scientists. Of all the things they could do without big brother watching over them. The first thing the gene-hacking weirdos do when they get settled on Romeo is clone a new race of people with fur. Inconceivable! I would have gone for three-breasted women. Now that's a race worth creating."

Jake asked, "Have you really been here a hundred years?"

Harry, who stood six-six, looked down at Jake with his youthful smile and answered, "Sure am. The one thing the Romeo scientists got right is a pill called 15 for Life. It reverses the aging process, making you a teenager again. As a bonus, I didn't lose the growth spurt that I got when I woke from my coma. On the downside, if I ever stop taking it, I die a horrible death."

Jake exclaimed, "What?"

Harry said, "Yep. Miss more than a couple of days and death is irreversible. Your body gets riddled with cancer. Of course, you can't get on it in the first place if you have ever been on an age-delaying medication. You have to make a choice. Age slowly or not at all."

Jake said, "Yeah, but what happens if something happens to the pills? It's instant death."

Harry said, "Not many people are on the pills. Just a few thousand. They can't be mass produced, you see. You also have to be a resident of Romeo living on the moon. I'm an exception due to being the only Strum left in Einstein."

Jake asked, "Why didn't they get on it?"

Harry answered, "The pill only got developed a couple hundred years ago. They were both dead by then. Once you hit 150 on age-delaying medication, you're at high risk of aneurysms. You also can't get on 15 for Life if you have ever been on age-delaying medication. There's a long waiting list to get on 15 for Life."

Jake asked, "Why didn't your grandparents clone themselves?"

Harry answered, "They were on earth during the second Russell Arthur incident. Almost no one from that era got cloned. Most stopped taking age-delaying medication altogether. My grandparents were a rare exception to stay on it."

They reached the bridge, where Jake introduced Harry formally to Captain Noem.

Harry shook Captain Noem's hand then said, "Let's head to Juliet. You are all in for one heck of a culture shock, and I can't wait to see your reactions."

Juliet

Jake googled Juliet to learn that the moon named Juliet was covered by three large dome cities that extended far underground. Each of the domes were constructed with a solid metal shell that had a ten-mile radius. According to Google, there were African planes artificially created underneath each dome. The Juliet citizens didn't live on these planes. Instead, their homes and businesses were constructed deep underground.

Jake sat on the bridge of the Minnow in the pilot's seat, taking over Jesus's spot. Captain Noem sat in the captain's seat, and Harry sat at the interior sensor's console.

Harry pointed out the window then asked, "See the domes?"

Jake looked down at the domes. They looked as if there were different colors of lightning shooting off them. Jake asked, "Is the lightning a byproduct of the environmental settings or something?"

Harry laughed then said, "Look closer."

Jake wanted to ask Bob to zoom in on the main screen, but that would be against landing protocol (due to the fact that the main screen was the bridge's windows). Instead, Jake used his own W2 contact lenses to zoom in. Jake's jaw dropped as he saw people on the domes wearing the black power armor with red stripes. These people were holding glowing swords in one hand while firing lightning bolts at each other with their other hand. It looked like a real-life VR game.

Jake asked, "What is that?"

Harry chuckled then answered, "That's a game called King of the Hill."

Captain Noem said, "Bob, zoom in. Main screen." The bridge's windows were replaced with the image of dozens of players battling to become king of the hill.

Harry explained the game. "They're using what's known as spider pistols to produce the lightning. Spider is a nerd term used to describe horizontal lightning. The color of the lightning discharged varies based on charge time. Yellow has the shortest charge time. Purple is the strongest a spider pistol can produce. Now spider cannons like the one that will be attached to the Minnow can fire white lightning when at full charge."

Jake asked, "What's the point of this game?"

Harry answered, "You have to think of Faraday particles like grains of sand. When sand gets struck by lightning, it turns to glass. When FP gets hit with lightning, the heat from the lightning causes the FP to lose their ability to hold an electrical charge for about twenty-four hours. The spider pistol is the most practical weapon we have that can break down a FP shield. When a player gets struck with a lightning bolt, all that happens to them is that they lose FP. One hit and you're out of the game, for safety's sake. Taking a hit without an FP shield causes heat damage to your power armor and a chance that the electricity will stop your heart."

Captain Noem asked, "And the swords?"

Harry answered, "They're called sawswords. Miners call them can openers. They were created as a miner's tool to survey asteroids. The blade is one foot and three-fourths long, four inches wide and two inches thick. It also weighs about fifty pounds in gravity, so an exoskeleton is required to wield one. They all have diamond chainsaw link chains that come in the color of the buyer's choosing. They will cut through just about anything. The internal working of the sawsword got a redesign over the years to act like a lightning rod. It can be used to block lightning bolts your opponents send your way. It should go without saying that it is extremely frowned upon to use your sawsword to hack off anyone's limbs."

Jake asked, “How is that a miner’s tool?”

Harry replied, “They use it to slice into an asteroid. The dirt that gets kicked up is then analyzed by your W2 contact lenses. Quick and efficient.”

Captain Noem asked, “What’s the point of this game?”

Harry answered, “It’s fun and lucrative. There’s a platform on the top of the dome. Stand on it for a minute to win. The winner of the game gets half of all the FP lost during the game. The other players get 10 percent of every takedown they had as a bounty prize. The remainder gets divided up evenly and distributed among the losers as a consolation prize. Even when you lose, you can come out ahead. Team ups and backstabbing are common practices that make for good streaming entertainment the next time you are looking for something to watch.”

Jake landed the Minnow next to the dome city of Nickola Tesla. This was where the Minnow would be getting its upgrades while the Tadpole was with the Juliet people for its upgrades.

The Minnow was met on the landing pad by a small group of Juliet people all wearing the black power armor with red stripes, and they were carrying crates with them. Once they landed, this group began to load these crates into the Minnow’s cargo bay.

Jake asked Captain Noem, “What’s in the crates?”

Captain Noem answered, “It’s law here that no one can enter a dome city of Juliet without wearing power armor.”

Jake exclaimed, “We’re getting power armor!”

The remaining crew of the Minnow got split up into pairs for their power armor training. During the pairing process, Stacy called dibs on Jake. The two exited the Minnow with their instructor, a Juliet named Frank.

Frank was a large stout Black man standing six-four. He was bald with the exception of a long ponytail wrapped around his neck. Frank had a police officer air about him. He was always standing straight with a serious look on his face, never talking unless he had to. When Frank did speak, his words were carefully chosen.

The landing pad where the Minnow parked was rather desolate. There were streetlights and some sort of thick stickers on the ground to mark parking spaces. The dome was in clear view, but to Jake's disappointment, there was no King of the Hill match taking place.

Jake immediately noticed his visor was clear while Stacy's had a greenish tint to hers, and Frank's was tinted blue. Jake wanted to know if he could change his visor. Jake said, "Bob, call Stacy."

Before Stacy could answer, Frank's booming drill inspector voice echoed in Jake's helmet. "The power armor is automatically linked to one another for this training. Power armor can also auto link to anyone you stare at and try to speak with. Although these settings can be altered under your personal setting screen on your W2. While your W2 is under your power armor, an image of it can be produced and used whenever you want." An image of a W2 appeared on Frank's left arm. Frank typed into it for a moment then continued, "You will now note a shimmer a half inch off your power armor. This is your FP shield. Think of this barrier like two magnets with the same attraction trying to be pushed together. This barrier will absorb impacts while the power armor itself can amplify your strength tenfold. There are strength limiters in place to keep you from accidentally ripping someone's arm off. To get used to what your power armor can do, I want you and your partner to stand five feet apart."

Stacy and Jake stood on the open landing pad five feet apart, staring at each other. Jake squeezed his arm. Through touch sensors, Jake could feel the Faraday particles shift under his fingers. No matter how hard Jake squeezed, he couldn't get his fingers or the Faraday particles to touch his power armor. Jake then attempted a small jump to test the gravity.

Stacy yelled, "Where the hell are you going, Jake?" as Jake floated ten feet into the air.

Frank said, "The gravity on Juliet is weak. Be careful."

As Jake started to come back down, Stacy asked, "What happens if someone jumps too high? Do they just float off into space?"

Frank answered, "Power armor has emergency pressurized gas thrusters in case of emergency." Jake landed, his face red with embarrassment. Frank said, "Now I want the two of you to run at each other and chest bump."

Stacy and Jake did as they were told. The FP shield absorbed the impact, so they felt nothing. It was like they just chest bumped a giant mattress that pushed them gently back afterward.

Frank said, "Now back up to fifteen feet and repeat. Only this time, run harder."

Stacy and Jake again did as they were told. This time, they had a brief chance to feel the power of the power armor as they reached incredible speeds. The attempted chest bump this time was awkward, as their timing was completely thrown off. Both Stacy and Jake ended up laying on the ground, but still, neither felt the impact.

Stacy said, "What the fuck, Jake" as she picked herself up off the ground.

Jake replied, "You didn't do any better."

Frank said, "Make it forty feet this time."

Jake and Stacy did as they were told. As they started to run at each other, Stacy shouted, "Run faster, pussy!"

This time, their timing was perfect. The force of the impact was enough to send them both flying backward in a high arc. Each landed farther back than where they started.

Stacy screamed, "That was awesome! Let's go again from even farther back."

Frank said, "That's enough. We still have a welcoming party to attend."

Stacy repeated, "Party? Like alcohol?"

Frank nodded yes.

Stacy screamed, "Party!"

Frank then escorted them to an underground airlock that led to Nickola Tesla City under the dome. Once inside, they walked down a large tunnel with walls covered in lonadescent cherry blossoms.

Frank's visor lifted up, and he said, "You can raise your visor by going into the power armor options on your W2 or just use verbal commands. Don't worry, the visor will auto close if anything gets too close to your face."

Stacy said, "Visor up."

Jake looked up his options menu, setting it to auto open in a breathable atmosphere.

As they rounded a corner, Jake asked, "What could get near our faces?"

Just then, Jake froze in his tracks as he saw a large lion standing just ten feet in front of them. Jake's instincts told him to turn and run back to the airlock for safety.

Stacy was walking just behind Jake. At the sight of the lion, she shoved Jake to the side, screaming, "I want to pet the lion!" The lion took off running with Stacy giving chase, yelling, "Get back here, kitty!"

Frank gave chase to Stacy, yelling, "Be careful not to hurt the lion!"

Jake stood there, muttering to himself, "What just happened?"

Jake discovered the underground city to be far larger than the pictures he found online showed it to be. The city was large enough to hold five-story buildings, of which there were many. The ceiling showed bright with artificial light. There were dirt roads lined with magnetic strips, but there were no vehicles in sight. Instead, there were running lanes as everyone used their power armor to run to where they needed to get to. The magnetic strips allowed people to run without accidentally sending themselves flying in the weak gravity.

Jake was amazed to see birds flying about. He noticed multiple breeds from killdeer to bald eagles. Jake lost Stacy and Frank, but the com was still open. Jake asked, "Do all these birds live here?"

Frank answered, "We leave doors open to the dome above. Any animal that wants to come down to visit can do so. You have nothing to fear as long as you keep your power armor on."

Stacy said, "I never want to leave this place."

That night, there was a celebration in the streets to welcome the Minnow crew to Juliet. Jake found that Harry wasn't exaggerating when he said everyone watched their time capsule videos. Even though Jake only made a couple of videos himself over the years, everyone seemed to know who he was. Jake quickly found this off-putting. He didn't like strangers thinking they knew who he was. It also didn't help that on Juliet, instead of shaking hands, the standard greeting was a shoulder bump. Jake couldn't walk three feet without someone ramming into his shoulder. To add insult to injury, the power armor hid the curves of all the women, so even when a beautiful woman shoulder bumped him, he couldn't tell.

Calvin didn't have the same issues Jake did. He quickly made new drinking buddies, discussing code and modern hacking techniques. Stacy was busy making new friends with whoever handed her her next drink.

Jake noticed Captain Noem slip out of the party early. Jake knew that she had been obsessed with catching up on the political climate of Einstein. Jake imagined figuring out how to structure the new EPF was weighing heavily on her mind.

Jake himself didn't feel much like drinking. He had plans to meet up with Frank the next morning for power armor combat training. Jake stayed at the party long enough to play wingman for Stacy. Jake kept the random dirtbags off Stacy until she found one she liked. After that, Jake slipped off to bed.

Jake awoke in his hotel room, attempting to unzip his sleeping bag. After a minute of failing to locate it, Jake laughed then said to himself, "You in gravity, stupid. No sleeping bags here."

Jake got ready that morning, enjoying almost every little thing about being in gravity. Even getting dressed was a different experience with gravity pulling everything down. Eventually, Jake finished and headed out to meet with Frank outside the dome.

As Jake exited his hotel room, he saw a person in power armor exiting Stacy's room. Jake stared at the person, wondering if it was the man Jake left Stacy with the night before. His back was to Jake, so Jake couldn't see his face. Suddenly, to Jake's surprise, an image of the man he was thinking about appeared in the bottom of his W2 contact lenses. Jake jumped back, startled. Jake then smiled at himself when he remembered Frank saying something about how staring at someone in power armor long enough would activate a link.

Jake decided to stop by Calvin's room to see if Calvin wanted to join him and Frank. Captain Noem had told Jake that she was going to accept Calvin as a member of the new crew in the tech department. Jake didn't see the harm in Calvin getting basic combat training just in case.

Calvin had given Jake his spare key just in case he locked himself out. Jake entered Calvin's room without bothering to knock. Walking into each other's room had become a common habit between the two friends over the years.

Jake entered to find Calvin on the floor, sleeping. He was sandwiched between an overweight man and what he hoped was a tall lanky woman. Jake quickly noticed a multitude of sex toys strung about the room. Jake quickly and silently exited the room. That was the last time Jake ever again entered Calvin's room without knocking.

Thirty minutes later, Jake met up with Frank outside the dome on the barren moon. For various reasons, it was forbidden to discharge spider pistols inside the dome. Jake was happy to see a King of the Hill match was taking place. Although from the ground, Jake couldn't see much.

Although it was just Frank and Jake this time, Frank continued to speak with his drill instructor voice. "This is your spider pistol. It is a delicate piece of equipment that you are to protect at all costs." Frank was holding out his spider pistol.

This was the first time Jake got to see one up close. Jake did have one in his holster attached to his leg. However, it was locked in place. The spider pistol looked like a Desert Eagle handgun, with the exception that the base of the handle had an extension in the shape of a thick arm brace. The arm brace extended all the way to the bottom of the elbow.

Frank continued, "This spider pistol is in fact a converted stormfront battery that also powers your power armor."

Jake immediately jumped back from Frank upon hearing this. Jake exclaimed, "What!"

Frank said, "I take it you know what that is?"

Jake started staring down at his leg, where his own spider pistol was residing, then said, "Everyone wearing power armor has a stormfront battery? Even the kids? The city has an atmosphere. That's illegal and extremely dangerous. Don't you know about the first Russell Arthur incident?"

Frank replied, "We know about the incident. We also know about the Hindenburg. Yes, inside the spider pistol is an artificial atmosphere with hundreds of thousands of miniaturized ice particles. These ice particles are constantly rubbing against each other to create lightning just like in the skies of your old Earth or here on planet Zeus. The atmosphere inside this spider pistol is a constant negative three thousand degrees. Every ship in Einstein, including your Minnow that you used to get here, has a stormfront battery as its power source."

Jake said, "Yes, in outer space. Not in an environment like inside the dome. What if a single spider pistol gets damaged?"

Frank replied, "It's good you understand the importance of protecting your weapon. If you ever fail to protect your weapon, get away from it. Whether it be in atmosphere or not. The contents of the spider pistol will damage your power armor. Is that understood?"

Jake replied back, "Clear, sir, but…"

Frank explained, "Even if every spider pistol in the dome broke at the same time, it still wouldn't be enough to replicate the first Russell Arthur incident. You can rest easy."

Jake did feel better at hearing that. Jake said, "Good to know, sir."

Frank said, "The spider pistol powers your power armor, so keep it in its holster whenever possible. Without it, your reserves will run out in a matter of hours, depending on how active you are. Now your spider pistol is on your left. That should mean that you're right-handed, correct?"

Jake replied, "Right-handed, sir."

Frank paused to type something into his W2 then said, "You can now draw your spider pistol. Hold it in your left hand."

Jake didn't understand but did as he was told. Jake was surprised to find the FP react so as to let the spider pistol extension fit flush against the metal of his power armor.

Frank picked up a sawsword that had been leaning up against a large rock and presented it to Jake.

Jake took the sawsword into his right hand, remembering Harry saying that it weighed fifty pounds. The handle was large enough to use two hands to hold it, but Jake wielded it easily with just one hand. At the top of the handle, extending into the guard, was an upside triangle. Jake thought this was most likely where the motor of the chain was located. The chain itself was constructed with bloodred diamonds.

Frank said, "I give all my trainees sawswords with bloodred diamond chains. Do you know why?"

Jake replied, "No, sir."

Frank said, "Because I don't want you distracted when your sawsword inevitably turns red from the blood of your enemies."

Jake replied, "Sir, yes, sir."

Frank now drew his sawsword. Jake could see the blades start moving but couldn't hear anything. Without atmosphere, sound couldn't travel. Frank took a swing at the rock Jake's sawsword was leaning against. The rock practically exploded as the sawsword's chain tore it to sunder.

Jake whispered, "Cool!"

Frank now calmly approached Jake. Before Jake realized what was happening, Frank swung his sawsword at Jake, striking him in the arm. The second the bloodred diamond chain touched Jake's FP shield, he could begin to hear the humming sound of the sawsword. Jake looked at his arm in disbelief. The sawsword was stopped by his FP shield. The FP were spinning wildly under the bloodred diamond chain links, but never allowing the deadly chain to pass through.

Frank pulled back his sawsword and sheathed it. Frank said, "As you can see, your FP shield will protect you as well as your opponents from sawsword strikes. This is why you have a spider pistol. One shot will nullify a large amount of your enemy's FP, allowing you to strike with your sawsword while there's an opening." Frank's tone finally softened to a normal decibel. "Now hold your sawsword in front of you like a shield, keeping the flat of your sword facing me. Then place the tip of your sword over your left shoulder."

Jake did as he was asked.

Frank said, "Good, now half raise your spider pistol. Keep it aimed at the ground while letting your enemy know that you're ready to roast him if he tries anything. Never point your spider pistol at anyone unless you're going to fire it."

Jake again did as he was asked.

Frank said, "That is the proper stance for one in combat. If you see an opening, you raise and fire your spider pistol. Otherwise, you stay prepared to block." Frank quickly raised his spider pistol, firing a yellow lightning bolt at Jake.

Jake stared in amazement as his sawsword absorbed the yellow bolt of lightning. Jake's sawsword slowly began changing colors from dull black to light red.

Frank sheathed his weapons then walked to a spot sixty feet away from Jake. With his back still turned to Jake, Frank said, "Shoot me."

Jake stood there, hesitating.

Frank shouted this time, "Shoot me!"

Jake did as he was told. He raised his spider pistol at Frank and pulled the trigger. Using his left hand felt awkward. Jake was first surprised at the lack of kickback from releasing a lightning bolt. More surprising was the color of lightning. Instead of yellow like Frank's spider pistol, Jake's spider pistol produced pink lightning. Even more disappointing yet was the fact that Jake's pink lightning only went a few feet then fizzled to the ground.

Frank explained, "The spider pistol has a range of about fifty feet. It has to have a target to hit. If there is no target to hit. the lightning fizzles. This auto hit effect is why you use your off hand to shoot. You don't have to be very accurate to hit your target." Frank walked toward Jake with an evil grin on his face then said, "Now let's start your training in earnest."

After a month spent training with Frank, Jake got pretty good with the sawsword and spider pistol. Frank and Jake even became friends. Jake was truly excited to learn that Frank would be joining SS Minnow as the new head of security.

After their last day of training, Frank asked, "Only one day left before we ship off. Are you going to try to win some FP before you leave?"

Jake muttered to himself, "King of the Hill." Then with a stronger tone, Jake asked, "You think I'm ready?"

Frank answered, "Tomorrow's your last chance to find out if you're ready or not."

Jake said, "Harry said there can be backstabbing in the game. Would be better to play with someone I could trust to watch my back. What are you doing tomorrow, Frank?"

Frank laughed then said, "Bad idea, Jake. Do you see how much denser my FP shield is than yours?"

Jake had never really paid attention to that before, but now that Frank said it, Jake could tell the difference. Frank's FP shield was far denser than Jake's. Jake asked, "Where can I buy more FP?"

Frank answered, "You don't. Extra FP can only be earned by playing King of the Hill. You're not allowed to enter a match with less than what you last finished playing with. In the beginner's racket, where you want to start. Shooting me with even a weak yellow lightning bolt would easily earn them ten times more FP in the prize pool than shooting anyone else with purple lightning. No, Jake. Me playing with you would just put a target on your back. Everyone versus us."

Jake added, "The risk reward would also suck for you. I understand."

Frank said, "Your FP count doesn't determine how good you are. Play and the advantage will be yours because everyone will underestimate you. Take advantage of that."

Jake took Frank's advice and signed up for the next day's morning match.

Jake signed up for the beginner's match, which took place outside the Elon Musk dome. To play, Jake had to download an app to his W2. The new app told him where to go to start his match. Jake got to the location with no other players in sight. The dome started out like a wall going straight up for a quarter of a mile. Fortunately, the wall was covered with handholds and footholds like a climbing wall would have.

Jake's app beeped, signaling the start of the match. Jake quickly started to climb the wall. This was Jake's first time climbing, and he was enjoying it. Between the light gravity and extra strength from his power suit, Jake was flying. Jake was enjoying it so much that he got caught off guard when the wall started to ebb inward. Jake quickly bent forward, reaching toward the wall. In his rush, Jake overreached and ended up accidentally pushing off the wall instead.

The light gravity made it take a while for Jake to hit the ground. With the only thing bruised from the fall being Jake's pride, he quickly restarted his climb. This time, he paid attention to the wall when it began to ebb inward. Taking his time, Jake made it where he could start to walk across the dome's top.

Jakes King of the Hill app began to beep. Jake looked at his W2 to see a person wearing power armor standing on a platform. There was a counter below the person with a one-minute countdown.

Jake said, "Bob, zoom in." Jake zoomed in to see that the person on his W2 screen was the same person standing on the winner's platform miles away from where Jake was standing. There was no one near the platform that Jake could see. Jake looked around to find people standing next to each other with their weapons drawn, but no one was fighting.

After a moment of staring at these people, a link opened up in Jake's W2 contact lenses. Jake said, "Bob, open link to Iceman and Coco."

"Get off the platform, you fucking idiot!" he blared into Jake's helmet. The guy on the buzzer wasn't paying any attention to them. Most likely he had his comms muted. Jake checked his app to see zero being displayed in the prize pool as the buzzer ending the match sounded.

Jake muttered to himself, "Newbie must have run straight to the platform without even thinking. He won nothing and wasted all of our mornings."

Jake was about to turn around and jump back off the dome for a second time when he noticed a group of people converging on the winner. The winner could do nothing as the small mob each took a limb and started swinging the winner back and forth, building up momentum. Jake opened a link to hear a man screaming in the background as the mob counted, "Three, two one!" The mob released the winner, who went soaring into the air. Jake had no doubt that the winner was going to easily clear the dome.

It was almost three hours until the second beginner's match started. Jake was determined to get redemption after his first debacle. Jake even took the time to set up auto open chat links and add a call sign. Jake went with Argyle. Argyle was the name of the limo driver in his favorite Christmas movie growing up, and it always struck Jake as cool.

The early match only had thirty players. This later match was up to seventy-four players. Jake was getting excited at the impending action, even if he still couldn't see any other competitors waiting to start the climb.

With just seconds to go before the start of the match, Jake received a text message on his W2. The message was from Captain Noem that read, "Don't fall off this time."

Jake said to himself, "I didn't even know that she knew I was competing."

The buzzer rang to start the match. Jake started his climb, feeling more embarrassed than when he fell off the wall in the morning match.

Jake reached the top easily this time. He immediately surveyed the area, not wanting to charge the platform and risk repeating what happened in the earlier match. Jake didn't care for the idea of being tossed from the top of the dome.

The first person Jake saw was to his right a half mile away with the call sign "Little Finger."

Jake headed in that direction and asked, "How's it going?"

A soft female voice replied, "Not dead yet." An image of a young woman with a cute freckled face appeared in Jake's W2 contact lens.

Jake suddenly found his heart beating faster for a different reason. Jake said, "It's my first time playing. How about you?"

Little Finger responded, "I've played once or twice. Care to make a team up? You watch my back, I watch yours. After we win, you can buy me a drink?"

Jake answered with a nonchalant voice, "Yeah, we can do that."

Little Finger and Jake slowly moved up the dome while moving closer to each other. Jake made a conscious decision to keep a sixty-foot gap between them just in case she wasn't what she seemed.

Jake didn't want to risk embarrassing himself in front of Captain Noem twice in one day.

The closer to the top they got, the more people they could see. Little Finger suddenly said, "I have three hostiles headed my way."

Jake looked over to see three people with no call signs spreading out and approaching Little Finger. Jake moved quickly back down the slope, keeping the sixty-foot distance from Little Finger before cutting across to cut off the lowest of the approaching men.

Little Finger shouted, "Get back here, Argyle! You coward! You promised me to watch my back!"

Jake replied, "Stall!"

Jake moved as quickly as he could on the uneven surface. Jake finally reached his opponent, who had the higher ground. Jake decided his best chance was a move Frank taught him during training. Frank called it the bushido.

Jake approached with his spider pistol drawn, pointing at the ground in front of him. Jake's right hand was on the hilt of his sawsword that was still in its sheath on his left side. Jake's opponent had his weapons drawn, his spider pistol aimed at Jake.

Jake's opponent was in no hurry to shoot. Jake could see that all three of his opponents had images of wolves on their visors. Jake continued his approach, getting within ten feet when he saw it. The sawsword arm of his opponent twitched in preparation of firing his spider pistol. Frank had told Jake about this tendency and made him practice daily to get rid of it.

In that moment, Jake dropped to one knee while twisting his body sideways and pulling, but not completely drawing his sawsword to block the incoming lightning bolt. A green lightning bolt did strike Jake's sawsword, but by that time, his opponent was already defeated. While Jake moved to block, he also fired his spider pistol at his opponent's foot. Jake successfully completed Frank's bushido maneuver.

Jake wasted no time dropping his hot sawsword back into its sheath then pushed past his opponent. He moved on to the next two who were trying to flank Little Finger. The two men both had their spider pistols aimed at Little Finger, but their sawswords were still sheathed. Little Finger also had her spider pistol drawn, but not her sawsword.

Jake immediately stopped moving forward. He was right at the fifty-foot threshold from the nearest opponent. Jake asked, "These guys with you, Little Finger?"

Little Finger replied, "Nooo, of course not. Now get over here, Argyle."

Jake now heard another voice over Little Finger's comm. "Be careful. The way he took out Ed. This guy's a pro."

Jake took a step back.

Little Finger's visor suddenly changed from clear to an image of a beautiful purple-skinned woman wearing a miniskirt. The purple image had fangs and claws with blood dripping from them. Little Finger said, "Let me shoot you, and I'll still let you buy me that drink after the match."

Jake turned and ran toward the next closest person, shouting, "Bob, cut off the link with Little Finger!" Jake needed time for his spider pistol to recharge and to figure out a way to even the odds.

One mile away was the call sign Iceman that Jake remembered seeing in his early morning match. Jake said, "Iceman, you copy?"

Iceman replied, "I copy, Argyle. Don't believe we've met before."

Jake replied, "This morning was my first match, if you can call it that."

Iceman laughed then said, "Yeah. That was a waste of a morning. Gotta ask, Argyle. Those three behind you, they with you or after you?"

Jake replied, "I wouldn't be running this fast if they were with me. Any chance you'd be willing to even the odds a little?"

Iceman replied, "I'd like to help, but two on three ain't much better. That considering you know what you're doing."

Jake replied, "I was thinking you make it look like you're backing off. I run down and past you, keeping them at the edge of that fifty-foot mark."

Iceman finished Jake's sentence, "Then I pick off the last person."

Jake said, "That's the route I'm running either way."

Just as planned, Jake ran toward the bottom side of the dome, keeping Iceman about fifty feet to his left. Jake even slowed down a bit to keep his pursuers from giving up. The only thing Jake didn't expect to happen was seeing Iceman fire purple lightning (the strongest lightning bolt a spider pistol produced). Not only did Iceman take out the player, but he added three times as much FP with his takedown than Jake did with his. Downside for Iceman was that he would have to wait three minutes before he could fire another lightning bolt.

Little Finger looked back at Iceman and said, "We'll remember that."

Jake pivoted, charging back at his last two pursuers. Little Finger fired a green lightning bolt at Jake that he easily blocked. The other man froze suddenly, fearing that they were surrounded.

Jake never stopped charging, wanting to fire point-blank at Little Finger. That's what Jake did as he passed by, first striking her sawsword with his to knock it out of the way before firing a yellow lightning bolt.

As Little Finger was eliminated, the buzzer sounded, and the one-minute countdown began. Jake was still six miles from the platform with no chance to do anything about it.

Iceman said, "Don't fret. Still one minute left to take out this guy."

The last of Jake's pursuers with the wolf image on his visor began to run, but so did Jake and Iceman.

Jake said, "Purple lightning is powerful, but you'll never catch me using it."

Iceman asked, "Why's that?"

Jake's spider pistol signaled it was recharged, then Jake said, "Because it takes too long to recharge." Jake fired his yellowing lightning bolt, taking out his last opponent.

Iceman replied, "Fair enough." Then he fired a purple lightning bolt at Jake as the buzzer sounded, ending the match.

The New Crew

Stacy, Jake, and Calvin left the dome city to return to the landing pad where they left SS Minnow. They were all excited to see what new renovations were made to their spaceship.

What they found on the landing pad instead of SS Minnow was a spaceship that had *Equality* written on a large rectangular block attached to the side of the ship. This block extended the length of the ship, slimming down to what appeared to be a barrel at the end. The barrel stopped just short of the bridge.

Calvin stated, "That's a rail gun."

Stacy asked, "Is this supposed to be the Minnow?"

Jake answered, "If you ignore the rail gun, it's the same shape as our Minnow."

Stacy, Calvin, and Jake stood looking around and wondering what was going on when Captain Noem exited the ship via the cargo ramp out of the front of the ship. She walked over to the three of them and asked, "What are you all waiting for?"

Jake asked, "So this is the Minnow?"

Captain Noem replied, "It's Equality now. Deck two has been altered, adding a state-of-the-art hospital and holding cells in the rear. Crew quarters are still on the second deck, but you'll have to check with Bob to see if you had to get moved. Deck three housing will be primarily reserved for entrepreneurs that will be opening up businesses in the courtyard."

Calvin asked, "Is it wise to bring civilians with us pirate hunting?"

Jake answered, "The pirates haven't killed anyone. They primarily target cargo ships with Carrie effect drives, typically leaving mini stormfront batteries converted into spacemines in the cargo ships path. If the cargo ship tries to stick around a day to recover its lost FP, jet arms with spider cannons show up, forcing them to run. If they want the cargo instead of FP, they use spider cannons to disable the ship. Still, no one has been seriously injured yet."

Calvin asked, "How are they getting spider cannons? Those types of weapons have to be registered, right?"

Jake quickly answered, "Spider cannons are just modified stormfront batteries. Every ship has one."

Calvin exclaimed, "Seriously! That's what that is?"

Stacy changed the subject. "As the new head botanist, I have to ask Captain Noem, does the hospital getting moved mean I have more room for planting?" she asked.

Captain Noem answered, "Yes, it does. However, they have already used up some of the space to add apple trees."

Stacy replied, "That's awesome."

Jake now changed the subject. "Did they change the Minnow's name?" he asked.

Captain Noem replied, "Nope. That was all me. Couldn't go around chasing pirates in a ship called the Minnow. Equality is a name that should help get the people on our side. That's the first thing they teach us at the UN. Make certain the people know you're there for them."

Jake said, "That's the reason to bring vendors with us. Show the people we aren't just a military powerhouse to fear."

Calvin said, "You also can't chase pirates in a ship called the Tadpole. Can I rename it if you haven't already?"

Captain Noem replied, "I thought I'd leave that up to my new first officer, actually."

Jake was taken back by this new information. He hadn't realized he'd have to start reporting to someone else. Jake asked, "Who's the new first officer? They must be from Romeo since you're head of security is from Juliet, right?"

Captain Noem answered, "Well, I don't think you're from Juliet, Jake."

Jake stood there, stunned, while Calvin shouted, "No! Jake sucks at names. Just let me pick the name instead. I want something cool, like Viper."

Stacy hugged Jake and said, "Congratulations, Jake."

Jake was surprised, to say the least. At the same time, thoughts of what to rename the Tadpole went through his mind. He wanted to follow Captain Noem's example to give a name that reassured the people that they weren't warmongers. That kind of tactic only perpetuated hate and violence. The name that came to Jake's mind was from his favorite sci-fi show. The show was actually the most rebooted TV show in history.

Jake looked at Captain Noem then said, "Serenity."

Calvin sighed. "I knew you'd pick something stupid."

Stacy punched Calvin in the arm. The extra strength Stacy had from her power armor sent Calvin flying five feet and knocking him to the ground. Stacy pretended she did it intentionally and said, "I like the name."

Captain Noem looked at Calvin on the ground and said, "I like it as well. Now let's get to the courtyard to introduce you all to the new crew."

The courtyard was full of familiar and unfamiliar faces. Most of the familiar faces to Jake came from the engineering department. Engineer Emily Dean, thirty-four, ex-military. She was here with her husband, Randolf, who was an accountant, and their son, Johnny, who was now fourteen. Jake recalled they had a family ride or die motto.

There was also Ron Dutton, fifty-two. His wife and two girls were on SS Middleman. One of the chefs stayed, but Jake only knew him by his nickname, Chef. There were a few former passengers who ran businesses like a hair salon and apparel shop, but Jake couldn't recall their names. Harry and Frank were there as well. The rest Jake didn't recognize.

Captain Noem stood on the raised platform from Serenity to speak. "Welcome aboard SS Equality. The job of everyone aboard this vessel will be to bring the citizens of Einstein closer together. To get them to bury old bitterness toward one another and start fresh. That mission starts right here on Equality. Every new sector of space we visit, we will be picking up new crew members and new vendors, turning Equality into a melting pot for Einstein. That process starts right here with you in Juliet. First, let me introduce our new head of security, Frank of Juliet."

Jake learned they no longer used middle or last names. Instead, they used a person's birthplace as sort of a last name. The same way a search engine would work.

Frank stepped forward then back again.

Captain Noem then said, "Filipe of Juliet, our new head mechanic. He's only twenty-two, but he's an expert on our new Carrie effect drive."

Filipe raised a hand and waved briefly.

Captain Noem said, "Last of the new crew members from Juliet is Tie, our weapons expert."

Tie gave a slight bow.

Captain Noem went on to introduce some vendors. After that, she said, "Stopping the pirate attacks is our secondary objective. That sounds odd, I'm sure, considering the pirate threat is why the EPF is being formed. Don't get me wrong, we will hunt them. But pirates can always return as long as the people are divided. One culture will always hate another that it doesn't understand. Einstein has grown at a rapid pace, creating new cultures that have lost touch with one another. This ship, with your help, will become the melting pot that shows the star system Einstein how to get along in peace. A shining example of how to treat other cultures. Just as President Taylor did on Earth with the signing of the People's Declaration of Rights in 2102. Sustainable peace can be obtained as long as we work together."

Jake started a slow clap that everyone joined in on.

After the applause died down, and while still blushing, Captain Noem said, "Thank you all. And thank you to our new first officer, Jake."

There was another round of applause for Jake. Frank even walked up to Jake and gave him a shoulder bump with pride.

The next stop for Equality was SS Middleman to meet up with the newly named Serenity. During the journey, Tie asked Jake to meet him in the courtyard to run battle simulations. The two sat at a picnic table under one of the new apple trees.

Tie said, "You probably saw the rail guns on the way in."

Jake replied, "I saw one of them. Kinda hard to miss."

Tie asked, "Do you know how they work?"

Jake answered, "Magnets and a butt ton of electricity."

Tie smiled and said, "Yes. You probably weren't able to see it, but there is a large turntable on the top of Equality. It houses the only triple-barrel spider cannon currently in existence. The spider cannons also power the rail guns. Meaning you can only fire one or the other. Do you happen to know how fast a rail gun shell travels?"

Jake thought for a second before answering, "What is 36,000 mph."

Tie said, "I'm impressed, Mr. First Officer. Frank had me watch your King of the Hill match, by the way. You did great until you dropped your guard at the end."

Jake replied, "Yeah. That was my bad. I still broke even at the end with the three bounties I collected."

Tie said, "You understand the principle of how the spider cannons work. That's what really matters."

Jake said, "I think so. What's the range on the triple-barrel spider cannons? I imagine it's farther than fifty feet."

Tie answered, "Just under half a mile, actually."

Jake asked, "There is no range on the rail gun, right?"

Tie replied, "No, but if the target's too far away and mobile, they can just dodge the shell. Well, depending on what you use. There are two types of shells. The standard, which is cylinder-shaped, six feet in diameter, three feet in length. The second type of shell is called scatter shot. Same size but breaks up by design to strike multiple targets."

Jake said, "I want to see that one in use."

Tie replied, "All right, buttercup. Let's hit that simulator and you fire all the scattershot you want."

Five miles away from Middleman, Jake was piloting Equality when a call came from the now named Serenity.

Jake, who was alone on the bridge. Said, "Bob, put the call on the big screen." To Jake's surprise, Jesus was on the other end of the call. Jake asked with glee, "What the hell are you doing back? What happened to 'I'm a lover, not a fighter?'"

Jesus replied, "Yeah, yeah. Grant me permission to merge and you'll understand why I'm back. What happened to everyone? Don't tell me they trust you to be alone on the bridge."

Jake replied, "I'm almost offended by that. We're down to a skeleton crew for now. Everyone gets alerts sent to them if anything interesting comes up."

Jesus said, "I saw pictures of the remodel. Can't believe more people didn't want to stay."

Jake replied, "Oh, they did. Unfortunately, Captain Noem needs to make room to fill the ship with citizens from across Einstein. We are to become a melting pot, in her words."

Jesus said, "Just make sure she doesn't give away my spot, kid."

Captain Noem walked into the bridge and said, "That's First Officer Kid to you, Jesus."

Jesus exclaimed, "No shit! Pardon my French, Captain."

Captain Noem replied, "I'm from France, Jesus. That wasn't French. Good to see you again."

Jesus smiled then said, "Good to see you too, Captain. Thanks for having me back."

Captain Noem replied, "Don't thank me yet. Tie, the new weapons officer, wants you and Jake in the simulator with him four hours a day starting yesterday."

Jesus sighed. "Well, at least I'm not suffering alone. Requesting permission to merge?"

Captain Noem asked, "Everyone with you?"

The image on the bridge's main screen changed to show Serenity's passenger cabin. Among the passengers were four identical blond bombshells wearing yellow Juliet power suits with black stripes. Jake instantly knew why Jesus changed his mind about staying with them.

Captain Noem said, "Permission granted."

There was another introduction ceremony in the courtyard. Among the new members was Dr. Helix of Romeo, a middle-aged plushie with orange fur. Next was his nurse, Irene of Romeo. Irene was accompanied by her husband, Zac of Romeo, who was to be the ship's field medic. Irene looked a little older than Zac, so Jake peeked at their personal file out of curiosity. Jake discovered Irene was 102 while Zac was only seventy-two. Both looked to Jake to be at different ends of the forty spectrum.

Irene and Zac were accompanied by their eight-year-old daughter, Clair of Nowhere. Clair was a plushie with white fur born on a small spaceship. Anyone not born in a city or quartership got the designation nowhere. According to their file, Irene and Zac adopted Clair when she was just a baby.

After them, there were the quadruplet sisters—April, age twenty-five; May, age twenty-four; June, age twenty-three; and July, age twenty-two. They were and were not sisters. All four were clones made for the ultimate nature versus nurture experiment. Each clone was born a year apart. They were placed with different families in different cities of Romeo to be observed.

The eldest, April, learned of this when coming of age. April took great offense to being used as a lab rat. She located her sisters then sued Romeo to gain guardianship over them. Their court case made them famous for human rights against immoral science. The quad sisters all joined the Romeo military after that to continue the fight for people's rights. This made them the perfect security force for SS Equality.

*****

The first meeting between Frank and his new security team was a tense one. They met in the cargo bay so Frank could give them instructions on their new Juliet black power armor with red stripes and FP shield.

Frank spoke in his drill sergeant voice. "I don't care that you're Romeos. You have now upgraded from your inferior power suits to the superior power armor. That now makes you one of the elites."

One of the sisters began giggling uncontrollably.

Frank walked in front of her and asked with an angry tone, "What's so funny?"

Another sister stated, "You saying we are now one of the elites."

A different sister stated, "Or you saying that power armor is superior to a power suit."

The last sister stated, "Or both."

Frank was flustered. Never had he been spoken to in such a disrespectful manner. Anyone in the know just looking at his dense FP shield would know he was not a man to be trifled with. Frank moved in front of the quad sister to his far right who was the last to speak. Frank stopped and stared at her for a moment before shouting, "Step forward and state your name!"

The quad sister at the opposite end used her W2 to shut off her FP shield, causing her FP to start floating off. She then stepped forward, sending many FP flying, and said, "My name's April. This is the first and last time we wear crappy power armor. So there is no confusion going forward. I lead this squad. You just give me our missions then stay the hell out of our way."

Frank shouted, "Is that so!"

April said, "Last thing. You get no respect until you can tell us apart." April stepped back in line.

The three remaining sisters shut off their FP shields at almost the exact same moment. Another sister took three small steps forward, again sending FP flying. Then she stated, "I'm May. What she said." May took the same three small steps to get back in line.

Frank noticed while May was stepping forward that the other three sisters shuffled their position like a shell game. Frank kept his eye on April, assuming she was going to be the objective in this little farce.

Another sister stepped forward, displaying catlike claws that shone with small sparks of green lightning, then said, "My name's June. These nails are from my superior power suit. They were a bitch to get attached to this shitty Juliet power armor. These claws scoop away FP like a shovel in dry sand. Piss me off and you'll find out just what these babies can do."

Frank was enraged. It was sacrilegious to tamper with power armor. Frank almost lost his focus to the point where he lost track of April as the sisters shifted again.

The last sister stepped forward then said with a cheery voice, "Hi, Frank. My name's July. I'm the youngest but also the best at martial arts." July, like the other sisters, only stood five-six. July had to stretch to be able to throw her closed fist at Frank's head.

Frank was never one to be caught off guard. He leaned to the side to avoid the punch easily. What Frank couldn't have been prepared for was July opening her closed fist right next to Frank's face. July was also wearing the catlike nails aglow with green lightning flickering off them. When July fully extended her fingers, there was a bright flash of green light that momentarily blinded Frank.

When Frank regained his sight, the sisters were standing in line next to each other. In perfect unison, they asked, "Which one is April?"

Frank was so mad he could almost see red. These four little girls were playing him for a fool. Frank had already instinctively reached for his spider pistol and sawsword. Frank took a deep breath to calm down and think. Frank stood up straight, moving his hands away from his weapons. Frank knew attacking was pointless. He fought enough battles to know when he was outmatched. These women didn't hesitate to sue their own government; they won't be going anywhere. Frank decided the only thing he could do was play along.

Frank started at the far left then moved right, taking a moment to stare at each sister as he went. They all had their blond hair pulled back in a ponytail cut the same length. All physical features were the same. Frank got so close he could smell that they even wore the same deodorant. Frank finally stopped on his second pass by the sister second from the left. Frank stared deep into her eyes. This was the longest Frank ever stared into anyone's eyes. Frank suddenly felt his anger melt away, even forgetting where he was for a second.

Frank pulled back suddenly then casually stated, "You're April."

April got a furious look on her face as she asked, "How did you know?"

Frank stated smugly, "Your eyes. Strong and deep. There's no way for them to blend in with your sisters."

One of the sisters whispered, "It's more like April's crow's feet couldn't blend in." The other sister giggled.

April didn't hear her sister's remark. April blushed then said to Frank, "Whatever. Girls, collect the FP then get your Romeo power suits and jetpacks on. We have space combat training to get to."

*****

Jake stopped in the medical bay to check on Dr. Helix. The medical bay was spacious and very open. The room was designed to hold up to thirty patients, but beds weren't deployed until needed.

Jake asked, "Everything to your liking, Dr. Helix?"

Dr. Helix was grinning from ear to ear and said, "This is amazing." Dr Helix pointed at what looked like a tanning booth along the wall.

Jake asked, "What is it?"

Dr. Helix replied, "A time dilation pod. One of only five in existence due to how long Faraday metal it takes to make. With this, someone who needs a month to recover can be healed within minutes. It's amazing technology. Simply amazing."

The small plushie girl, Clair, walked up to Jake then said, "Hi, my name's Clair."

Jake looked down smiling and said, "How do you do? My name's Jake."

Clair said, "My fur's white, not orange like Dr. Helix's. That makes my fur softer. Here, do you want to feel?" Clair pulled back her pink and yellow striped onesie sleeve and raised her arm up to Jake.

Jake was stumbling on his tongue, not sure what the appropriate response was.

A lady's voice came from the far side of the room. "It's okay. She likes to be petted."

Jake turned to see Clair's mother, Irene. Jake then reached down and petted Clair's arm and said, "That is soft."

Clair proudly stated, "I told you so."

Dr. Helix said to Jake, "I don't like to be petted. Don't try."

Zac snuck up on Dr. Helix and began to scratch him behind the ear. Dr. Helix got a big smile on his face before pulling away and yelling, "Stop that!"

Zac said, "You know you like it."

Dr. Helix retorted, "I do not!"

Clair giggled and said, "I saw you smile."

Dr. Helix said, "I did not." Then he raised his head in the air, stomping off comically to make Clair laugh.

Zac shook Jake's hand and said, "I'm Zac, and that's my wife, Irene. Pleased to meet you, Jake."

Jake replied, "Good to meet you all. You have a lovely daughter."

Irene said, "Clair makes life worth living."

Jake said, "May I ask a question? It may be personal. I'm not sure."

Zac said, "Ask whatever you like. You may or may not get an answer."

Irene exclaimed, "Zac! Jake, you have to ignore Zac. He thinks he's being funny. We can tell you whatever it is you want to know."

Jake asked, "You guys are on age-delaying meds, right? Now doesn't that mean you can't get on 15 for Life?"

Irene said, "Is that all? That's not personal at all. Here I thought it might be something interesting."

Zac said, "The list is long to get on 15 for Life. Not to mention you have to go through normal aging."

Irene added, "I'm 102. My body's that of a fifty-year-old. I feel ancient now. I mean the aches, and I can't even eat what I used to. The medication didn't stop menopause either. They say it makes the systems milder. I say they're full of s-h-i-t. I don't even want to imagine what it would be like to have to feel my age. Heck, Zac would have never asked me out if I looked my age."

Zac nodded and said, "True."

Irene said, "Hey!"

Zac said, "What? You were seventy when I met you. You know I love you."

Irene walked over and kissed Zac then said, "I know, but next time, hesitate a little. Make me feel eighty again."

Zac replied, "Yes, dear." Then he gave Irene a quick kiss.

Clair said, "Not again," while rolling her eyes.

Zac looked at Jake then said, "I'm a field medic. I've seen plenty of lives cut short. Why age normally and make life harder for a benefit of eternal youth that may never come?"

Irene added, "It's not natural anyway. Honestly, life gets old as it is. Eventually, you see it all. One of the reasons we adopted Clair is because it gives us a chance to see life through fresh eyes again. Clair really does make life worth living. Do you have someone special in your life, Jake? Think you might want kids?"

With that, Jake said, "Thank you. Forgot I have a training session with Tie. Nice meeting you all."

First Mission

After spending a couple of days near Middleman for team building exercises and stocking up on supplies for their first mission, Equality headed off to rendezvous with the quartership Alpha Mining along the fourth ring.

Equality's mission was to deliver 3D printing material needed for an expansion project. While there (besides recruiting for Equality), Captain Noem was to create the first volunteer EPF patrol group. The volunteers would help out with patrolling shipping routes and battling the pirates when necessary.

Jake didn't mind traveling by the new Carrie effect drive one bit. It was slower, but you could still travel from one ring to another in the course of a day. With the new system, there was no longer the horrific paralysis to contend with. You also were no longer cut off from the internet while traveling. Even when the FP shield was active, an antenna was deployed to receive and send signals.

Shortly after passing the sparsely populated planet Icarus, Equality received a distress signal. Captain Noem listened to the call then said, "Bob, shut down the Carrie effect drive. Red alert."

Red alert allowed all officers and security personnel to link into the captain's feed to see exactly what was going on. Captain Noem replayed the distress call for them to hear.

"Hi, is anyone out there?" came a woman's voice.

Captain Noem replied, "This is Captain Noem of the SS Equality. What is your distress?"

The woman responded, "Thank God! I'm a miner. I got dropped off here in a bucketship to survey this large asteroid. I left my ship, and a big rock came flying in and hit it. My bucketship got sent flying, and I need help getting it back."

Jake and Tie were already on the bridge with Captain Noem. Harry and Calvin entered the bridge with Harry saying, "A bucketship is what I was flying when we first met. It's a one-man vessel mostly used by miners."

Calvin said, "The signal is four thousand miles away in a small cluster of asteroids. Tell you in a minute."

The woman asked softly, "You will help me, won't you?"

Captain Noem replied, "We can't get a visual from your signal. Why is that?"

The woman responded, "Sorry." An image appeared on the bridge's main screen of a young woman's innocent-looking face inside of a space helmet. She said, "Had it set to audio only to boost the signal. You have no idea how close I came to eating applesauce. Please tell me you're going to help me."

Harry said, "Captain, that girl is far too cute to have to eat applesauce. We need to help her."

Frank said over the comm, "It could be a trap."

Tie added, "Applesauce isn't that bad."

Harry asked Tie, "Have you ever had to eat applesauce?"

Tie replied, "No, but I hear it's flavored."

Jake said, "I'm guessing this applesauce isn't made from apples. What is it?"

Calvin said, "Facial recognition says the girl's name is Samantha of SS Expedition. Currently employed out of Alpha Mining. Doesn't say which crews she's with."

Harry answered Jake's question. "Miners are set out into space with miner's suits. A miner's suit is just heavy cloth with some exoskeleton gear. In case of an emergency, it can reprocess your waste with some powdered nutrients added. The texture is supposedly like applesauce."

Jake said, "I knew I was going to regret asking."

Calvin said, "I can confirm a small ship is floating away from Samantha's position."

Captain Noem asked, "Jake, what would you do?"

Jake was completely caught off guard by the question, but he had already been surmising what Captain Noem was going to do. Jake answered, "Not helping isn't an option. We'd risk ruining our relationship with Alpha Mining before we even got there. Send in Serenity with Equality staying one mile back. Believe you assigned April and June to Serenity during red alerts. Have one of them fly out with a jetpack once Serenity gets close. Check out her bucketship for traps. If it's all clear, send it back. We keep our distance the whole time, watching for an ambush."

Captain Noem said, "You heard the man. Serenity crew, get prepped. Jake, set course using ion thrusters only. I don't want to find a spacemine the hard way. Slow Equality down once we reach a distance of five hundred miles. That's when we separate."

Harry said, "Don't worry, Samantha. Equality is on the way."

*****

Jesus separated Serenity from Equality with his standard away crew onboard. This included security personnel April and June, as well as engineer Emily and field medic Zac. Everyone was still connected to the red alert system to communicate with Captain Noem and authorized Equality crew.

Jesus whispered to himself, "She better have a hot body to go with that pretty face. And very, very grateful."

Serenity stopped a fourth short of Samantha's bucketship. June deployed out the airlock using her jetpack to travel the rest of the way. June circled the bucketship, not much larger than a compact car, stopping to stare at a dent in the side. June said, "Looking like her story checks out."

Filipe said, "I don't see anything off, Captain."

Captain Noem said, "Go ahead and start pushing it back, June."

Jesus whispered to himself, "Yes! Not a trap. Now let her be hot." Jesus nudged the controller so Serenity would start drifting toward Samantha to give Jesus a better view of the damsel in distress.

Captain Noem said, "Samantha, we have your bucketship headed your way."

Samantha squealed, "Thank you so much. Will I get to thank you in person?"

Captain replied, "Afraid not. We need to be getting underway to make an appointment."

April said, "To be safe, Captain. I would like to have June stop sixty feet short. Momentum can carry the bucketship the rest of the way."

Harry said, "Wait, you want that girl to what? Catch her ship?"

June said, "I am going to set the bucketship down before returning." That's what June did. She set the bucketship down on the large barren asteroid Samantha was standing on. June waved to Samantha before jetpacking back toward Serenity.

Jesus said, "Samantha, we'll be at Alpha Mining for a while if you want to buy us, or me, a drink."

Samantha asked with a now sultry tone, "How will I know what you look like to buy you that drink?"

Jesus could see Samantha's outline. She was holding what looked like a stick Jesus assumed was some sort of a mining tool. Samantha was short and stout with a chest plate outline Jesus found appealing. Jesus pushed Serenity in closer, nudging the nose down so Samantha could get a look at him. Jesus said, "Name's Jesus, the pilot of Serenity who came to your rescue."

April entered the cockpit then asked in an angry tone, "What the hell do you think you're doing?"

Jesus replied, "Don't worry. Samantha's harmless."

Samantha was climbing on top of her returned bucketship. When she reached the top, Samantha jumped straight up. Without gravity, she continued to soar ever higher. Once Samantha reached her desired height, she raised the stick she was holding, pointing it at Serenity. Samantha whispered, "Pleased to meet you, Jesus. My hero." Then she pulled the trigger on her stick.

*****

Samantha sat on a small asteroid, leaning against her bucketship and cursing her life. Samantha grew up on the SS Expedition, a quartership whose original mission was to survey the planets of Einstein. This later allowed the other quarterships to deploy their assets in the most efficient manner. After that, the SS Expedition became the only quartership to have the new Carrie effect drive installed. This helped out tremendously in getting new colonies set up.

Samantha was happy there while she was a child. At sixteen, she had a fiancé that her parents adored. He was a twenty-year-old scientist who was going places. Then for Christmas, Samantha went to his apartment to cook him Christmas dinner. Against Samantha's will, her then fiancé decided they no longer needed to wait until their wedding night to consummate their vows.

Samantha ended things afterward. Her parents were furious with her for it. They demanded Samantha take him back or move out. Samantha left, staying with an older girlfriend at first. A few nights later, this friend took Samantha to a party where she told Samantha, "That asshole gave you a gift. From now on, you get to fuck whoever the hell you want."

The next two years were a blur to Samantha—just fragmented memories of alcohol and drugs mixed with flashes of wild sex orgies. During that time, SS Expedition decided to continue its original mission of exploring new planets. They left the Einstein star system to explore the Taylor star system.

Samantha had no interest spending her life on a ship filled with people who let her down. Samantha left SS Expedition, surviving by stealing and sleeping with whoever got her stoned that day. These choices eventually landed her with the pirates.

For the past eight months, Samantha had served with the pirates. Most of it was a blur. Samantha always had memory issues when it came to people and events. Now whenever she woke up with the slightest of hangovers, the previous night's events were a blank. Samantha always woke up with a hangover.

Two days ago, Captain Spike gave Samantha a rail rifle and power backpack. He told her to start practicing because he had a job for her. In two days of practicing, Samantha hadn't hit the target once. Samantha told Captain Spike that before he dropped her off on the desolate asteroid.

Captain Spike told her, "You sit here and put out a distress signal. When a ship comes to rescue you, it will have its FP shield up. You, Samantha, are to shoot off that ship's antenna. I promise you won't miss when the time comes." Samantha felt reassured by Captains Spike's words.

For seven hours, Samantha sat there waiting until finally, someone answered her distress call. "This is Captain Noem of the SS Equality. What is your distress?" Samantha quickly got up, punching her bucketship so hard that she put a dent in it as the bucketship flew off into space.

Samantha played the part of damsel in distress perfectly, but they were being super cautious. They even split their ship into two. Samantha didn't realize that was actually a thing. Still, there was one ship with an antenna she could shoot. She just needed the ship to get closer and lower so she could hit the antenna on top.

Samantha was trying to come up with a plan when she heard, "We'll be in Alpha Mining for a while if you want to buy us, or me, a drink."

Samantha thought, *Thank you, Jesus. Literally*. After a little flirting, the pilot was doing exactly what she needed him to do. He was moving Serenity into position for her to shoot off its antenna.

Samantha still needed a better angle for the shot, so she climbed on top of her bucketship. Still needing more height, she leaped straight up. To make the shot more difficult, she had to strike the antenna just above the shimmer of the FP shield.

Samantha remembered Captain Spike's words: "I promise you won't miss when the time comes."

Samantha was filled with such confidence that she even said, "Pleased to meet you, Jesus. My hero" before she pulled the trigger.

Her bullet struck true, snapping off the foot of the antenna that was sticking out above Serenity's FP shield.

Samantha was so happy she actually made the shot that she didn't realize she was still floating helplessly into space. That quickly changed when she saw the SS Equality approaching. Samantha hit her miner's space suit thrusters to head back toward her bucketship, but she was too slow.

*****

Calvin exclaimed, "We just lost contact with Serenity! There are twenty small heat signatures that just appeared thirty miles straight ahead. They're moving this way, Captain."

Harry said, "They're droid jet arms."

Jake said, "Bob, emergency recall message." Floodlights on the hull of Equality began to flash Morse code to Serenity. Jake quickly accelerated the Equality toward Serenity then said, "Tie, ready a scooter shot and drop the recoil dampener to 50 percent. We're going to need to make a quick turn."

Captain Noem went over the ship-wide comms then ordered, "Brace for impact, everyone."

Tie got excited and said, "I'm really starting to like you people."

Jesus's voice came over the comms. "We're back, Captain."

Captain Noem said, "Good to hear your voice, Jesus. Everyone on Serenity, brace for impact."

Jesus exclaimed, "They're shooting at us?"

Tie replied, "Nope. We're shooting at them. Scatter shot loaded with recoil field lowered to 50 percent."

Harry stated, "Not answering hails. Definitely drones."

Captain Noem said, "Fire!"

Jake interrupted and yelled, "Not yet, Captain! Bob, open cargo bay doors. April, May, I have a guest coming your way." Jake then accelerated Equality toward Samantha, who was trying to get back to her bucketship.

Jake scooped Samantha up while her bucketship got struck by Equality. Samantha's bucketship was once again sent hurtling into space.

Jake said, "Bob, close the bay door. Tie, you know what to do."

The moment the bay door closed, Tie fired the rail gun. The recoil of the shot with the intentionally weakened recoil dampeners spun Equality into a quick 180-degree turn. Jake immediately fired Serenity's plasma rockets to get more distance from the remaining jet arms.

Tie stated, "The scattershot took out a dozen jet arms."

Calvin said, "Another twenty heat signatures just lit up."

Tie asked, "Run or fight?"

Captain Noem replied, "We have a mission to transport needed supplies. If we stay and fight, there's no telling how many more surprises the pirates have planned for us. Besides that, Jake caught us a prisoner to interrogate. Let's just outrun them."

Jake replied, "Not a problem, Captain."

*****

May and July were in the cargo bay holding double hand cannons (large antivehicle spider pistols with a backpack power supply). They were awaiting orders for deployment to fight the incoming pirate jet arms when they heard Jake say, "July, May, I have a guest coming your way."

Moments later, the cargo bay doors opened. Thirty seconds later, Samantha was scooped up, making her grand entrance by bouncing off the floor then getting herself magnet locked against the back wall.

May and July approached Samantha, taking flanking positions.

Samantha looked at one sister then turned to look at the other sister. Samantha asked, "How hard did I hit my head?"

The ship violently spun then stopped suddenly. The sisters' power suits automatically stiffened and increased magnetic locks to the floor for the maneuver. May and July still felt the maneuver.

May was the first to recover after the ship stopped spinning. May pointed her hand cannons at Samantha and said, "Don't move."

July also raised her hand cannons then said, "Yeah! What she said."

Samantha, still magnet locked to the wall, had no choice but to not move. Samantha licked her lips then said, "Twins! Please tell me you're both going to strip-search me."

Captain Noem said over the comm, "Take Samantha to a cell. I have questions for her."

After the cargo bay was pressurized, Samantha was in fact stripped and scanned. Samantha was smiling the whole time.

*****

Captain Noem waited a while before checking on Samantha. She wanted Samantha to stew a bit before her interrogation started. When Captain Noem was ready, she asked Jake to join her. They were met outside the holding cell section by Dr. Helix and Zac.

Captain Noem asked, "What's up, guys?"

Dr. Helix replied, "We understand you are going to be interrogating the prisoner. I took the liberty of making a truth serum syringe. Zac is here to administer it if you would like to use it."

Captain Noem asked, "Does it really work?"

Dr. Helix answered, "It's 100 percent effective with no side effects. I personally tailored this shot to Samantha's DNA that I pulled from her file."

Captain Noem asked, "Is it legal?"

Zac answered, "It's standard use in court on Romeo. There isn't much in the way of trials in this era. The accused does need to consent or have a judge issue a warrant. At least that's how it works back on Romeo. I don't know what the law is out here."

Captain Noem replied, "We'll hold off for now."

Dr. Helix said, "As you wish, Captain. It's ready any time should you change your mind." Dr. Helix and Zac left.

Captain Noem and Jake entered the holding cell area to find Frank with one of the quad sisters standing guard.

The holding cell section consisted of four cells, two against each wall parallel to one another. Three of these cells were constructed of metal bars. The fourth was a padded soundproof cell for the suicidal or just obnoxious detainees.

The back walls of all the cells were constructed of Faraday metal. The wall could shift to deliver food or drink without anyone ever having to enter. There were even voice command screens that could be shifted in and out of the wall for detainees staying awhile.

Frank said, "We examined Samantha's gear. She shot off Serenity's antenna with a back powered rail rifle. I've never seen this type of weapon before. No other weapons were found on her person. Her space suit was a standard-issue Teflon weave with air and refuse recycling. Her W2 was a burner. No data could be recovered. Her exoskeleton was damaged, but Filipe believes it's been that way for a while. Samantha made that shot without mechanical assistance. You shouldn't get too close to her, Captain."

Captain Noem said, "Thank you, Frank. Would you two mind giving us the room?"

Frank and the quad sister bowed to Captain Noem then exited the room.

Jake still had no idea how to tell one quad sister from another. He wondered if Captain Noem knew how to tell them apart yet.

They approached Samantha's cell. Samantha was laying on her cot along the back wall. Captain Noem introduced them. "I'm Captain Noem. This is my first officer, Jake."

Samantha stood up. Jake was immediately taken aback by Samantha's beauty. Her straight red hair was just long enough to caress her milky white shoulders. She stood five-four with a stout body. She had a couple of extra pounds on her, but they were all in the right places.

The onesie Samantha wore was unlike any Jake had seen before. It was green with a large purple stripe around the midsection. It had no sleeves, and the top section looked like a tank top exposing more skin than Jake was used to seeing. Even her breasts weren't constricted as her ample cleavage was fully exposed.

Samantha slowly strutted to the front of the cell then said, "A woman in authority is very attractive, Captain Noem."

Captain Noem ignored the remark and asked, "Where are the pirates headed?"

Samantha giggled then answered, "I don't know what you're talking about."

Captain Noem spoke in a deeper voice. "The pirates that attacked us. Where are they headed? Do you have a home base of operations?"

Samantha strutted back to her cot, giving her butt an extra wiggle as she went. Samantha said, "I was the victim. I asked you for help, and you kidnapped me." Samantha sat back down on the cot, throwing her arms against the back wall and pushing out her chest. Samantha dramatically said, "Now I'm at your mercy, my captain!"

Captain Noem angrily stated, "This is not a game."

Samantha licked her lips then said, "Oh! But it could be. Just ask Jakey there to leave." Samantha stared at Jake for a moment then smirked. "On second thought, he's kinda cute. Jakey can stay." Samantha slowly started to pull the straps of her onesie down.

Captain Noem stomped off in a rage. Jake reluctantly followed while peering back to see if Samantha really was going to drop her top.

Alpha Mining

Upon Equality's approach to SS Alpha Mining, Captain Noem, Harry, and Jake were on the bridge of Equality.

Harry said to Jake, "The Alpha Mining quartership itself was transferred into a giant ore-processing plant. It processes 80 percent of all the industrial steel in Einstein." Harry pointed out the bridge window at a large saucer-shaped spaceship. Harry said, "That's a mothership. Most have Carrie effect drives and FP shields. They come with docking ports for eight bucketships or jet arms. That's where jet arms get their names. The jets are the arms of the motherships. Get it?"

Jake said, "Yeah, I got it. They look like the old F15 fighter jets."

Harry agreed. "Yes, they do. Union laws say the jet arms have to be piloted manually, but as you've seen, they can also be flown remotely or preprogrammed. Get caught mining with anything but manned ships, and you not only forfeit your pay, you'll also get banned from Alpha Mining."

Jake said, "So the pirates are banned from here then."

Captain Noem answered, "Supposedly, the pirates have never tried to do business here."

Harry asked, "See that giant rotating asteroid cluster up ahead?"

Jake answered, "Couldn't miss it."

Tie said, "That's Alpha Mining."

Jake replied, "What? Aren't we supposed to rendezvous with a quartership?"

Captain Noem said, "You need to read your briefings more closely, Jake. SS Alpha Mining was converted into an ore-processing plant like Harry just got done telling you. For us, the quartership is nothing more than a docking point to enter the asteroids that were converted into space stations."

Calvin asked, "Why are the asteroids spinning like that?"

Jake answered, "Centripetal gravity. I read some of the reports."

Harry said, "Whenever they mine out a large enough asteroid, they convert it into a space station. The space stations click together like Legos that can be relocated over time to best serve Alpha Mining's needs. It's definitely been rearranged since last I was here. One of those big rocks holds the largest casino in Einstein. Space Vegas."

Jake immediately asked, "Do they have Texas hold 'em?"

Captain Noem said, "Don't get too excited just yet. We don't have permission to dock until tomorrow. They are preparing a parade for us."

Harry bragged, "They threw me a parade the first time I came here eighty some years ago."

Captain Noem said, "You gentlemen are dismissed for the rest of the day. You earned a rest before tomorrow's celebrations."

*****

That evening, Jake was in the courtyard going for his evening run when he looked over to see Frank and one of the quad sisters sparring. Battle suit training of any sort was banned in the courtyard out of fear of tearing up the metal mesh holding down the soil. Instead, Frank was wearing a black kimono with red stripes. The quad sister was wearing a yellow kimono with black stripes. Both were wielding bamboo swords.

The other three sisters were gathered in the center of the courtyard. When they saw Jake, they waved for him to join them.

Jake wandered over, doing his cooldown walk. With his cool voice, he said, "Hi, ladies."

One of the sisters said, “Hi. I’m June. I was on Serenity when you sent the Morse code calling us back. Quick thinking.”

Before Jake could say anything, another sister said, “Yeah! I’m May, and this is July. We’re less grateful, seeing as how your batshit crazy flying sent a woman flying at us. What if Samantha hit one of us?”

July said, “Whatever, May. He’s the reason Samantha’s on board. I saw you blushing when she was hitting on you.”

May yelled, “Liar!”

July continued, “I also saw you during the strip search. You put your hand between her legs then smelled your finger.”

May screamed, “Lying skank!” May pulled back her arm to punch July, who started to run off and giggling. May gave chase, screaming, “Take that back!”

June said, “Sorry about my sisters. I hear Frank taught you how to fight with a sawsword and spider pistol.”

Jake found himself hoping June hadn’t watched his King of the Hill matches. Jake answered, “He did.” Jake wanted to quickly change the subject, so he asked, “Are Frank and your sister sparring or fighting? It looks intense.”

June replied, “Who knows. Those two haven’t been apart for more than a couple hours since they met. They constantly make up excuses to see each other. Wish they’d just get a room and get it over with already. April is technically my mother, by the way. She likes to act like it too.”

Jake said, “I did hear about her adopting you and your sisters.”

July said, “We got a little off topic. I wanted to ask you if you wanted to learn how to use some Romeo weapons. My way of saying thanks for earlier.”

Jake replied, trying to act nonchalant, “Sure.”

June said, “Cool. Meet me in the cargo bay at eight a.m. Make sure to wear your power armor.”

Jake walked away, trying to hide his excitement as inside his head, he was shouting, *I got a date with a quad sister!*

*****

Stacy received a message from Harry to meet him at 11:00 p.m. in the courtyard by the pickle patch. Stacy always felt a bit weird around Harry. She constantly had to remind herself that he wasn't a teenager like he looked like.

Stacy arrived at her destination in the courtyard with only the occasional dim light around the jogging path to see with. The original designers of Equality wanted as much normality as possible for the residents on their decade-long journey.

Stacy heard Harry call out, "Over here!" Stacy turned to see Harry standing next to a TV screen. Stacy wondered where Harry got the TV from as she walked over. When Stacy got close, she noticed that the TV was on a metal table. Stacy recalled seeing a bare spot there since the remodeling.

Stacy asked, "Where did all this come from?"

Harry replied, "It's retractable from the floor. This was installed on Juliet to be used as a conference table for officer meetings. Captain Noem has not yet seen it fit to bring it up, but I thought that was a waste."

Stacy asked, "Are you going to get in trouble for using it?"

Harry replied, "Of course not. I am an officer after all."

Stacy replied, "A teenage officer."

Harry replied, "I'm over a hundred."

Stacy said, "That is so creepy."

Harry replied, "Haters gonna hate."

Stacy said, "That's something Calvin says. Don't let him rub off on you. One Calvin's all I can take."

Harry said, "I won't. The reason I asked you here is that I made a video today. I wanted your opinion before I broadcasted it." Harry handed Stacy a sports bottle labeled margarita then said, "To get you in the right frame of mind."

Stacy took the margarita bottle from Harry then said, "You're starting to grow on me, Harry."

Harry said, "Bob, can we get a couple of seats?" Two chairs started to form out of the floor. Harry said, "We need cupholders, Bob. Work with me here." Cupholders slowly formed in the chairs' armrests.

Stacy sat down, took a hit of her margarita, then asked, "What are we watching?"

Harry replied, "I made a video of the pirate encounter from this morning using the ship's security cameras. Thought it would help with the recruitment drive. Captain Noem has stated several times we need to win the hearts of the people."

Stacy asked, "Am I in it?"

Harry seemed a bit confused for a second by the question. Harry stated, "You weren't in the battle."

Stacy replied, "I was on the ship that got attacked by pirates."

Harry thought for a second then said, "That's brilliant. I can add a more human touch if I cut in passengers' real-time reactions to the battle."

Stacy said, "Do that later. Start playing what you got."

Harry hit play. The video was narrated by Harry explaining the failed trap set by the pirates. Then it showed Equality destroying multiple jet arms with a single shot.

Stacy said, "Nice. How are you going to get people to watch it?"

Harry replied, "I have a hundred thousand followers."

Stacy nodded then said, "That'll do it."

*****

Jake entered the cargo bay wearing his power armor like asked. His excitement for his morning date quickly turned to disappointment when he found all four quad sisters were waiting for him.

All four sisters were wearing the yellow power suit with black stripes that lacked a FP shield by design. One of the sisters (Jake still couldn't tell them apart) said, "I hear you're pretty good at fighting like a Juliet."

A different sister whispered, "I wonder who she heard that from?" Three of the sisters began to giggle.

The first sister to speak—Jake was now convinced it was April, and the one making the remark was July—continued ignoring her sisters. "The power suit of the Romeo people render that fighting style useless. Our power suits are constructed like the sawswords. Designed to absorb lightning."

Jake asked, "Doesn't it still get hot?"

April answered, "A single standard shot won't be noticed. The W2 cooling onesie is more than enough to compensate. Taking several hits or a shot from something more powerful like a spider cannon would cause damage. Seeing as how spider pistols need time to recharge, they're a complete waste in single combat. Sawswords can cut through power suits. However, power suits are also more agile than power armor."

Jake was noticing for the first time that the sisters were all wearing belts that held what looked like darts. Jake stared at April's belt then said, "Power armor can't shoot you, but you still need to shoot power armor to get past the FP shield. Does that on your belt do something to give you an edge?"

All four sisters began to smile as if Jake said something funny. April said, "Because our suits don't waste electricity to power an FP shield." All four sisters suddenly performed jazz hands that gave off a blinding flash of green light.

Before Jake knew it, he was on the ground with his left arm being pinned behind his back by one of the sisters. Jake's right arm was being extended and held down by a second sister. Jake struggled to free himself to no avail.

A third sister bent down, dangling what looked like a good-sized throwing dart that she pulled out of her belt. What Jake found odd was that the tip of the dart was only half an inch long.

The fourth sister stood over Jake and said, "This is a drill dart. It's filled with saline and nanites. This little darling will knock out any animal regardless of size or species. They will stay knocked out for eight hours or until the nanites are deactivated." April now started to walk the room and continued, "I know what you're thinking. Your precious FP shield will protect you."

The sister dangling the drill dart in front of Jake suddenly stood up. She then held the drill dart over Jake's extended arm. She then swung the dart back and forth three times before stopping and dropping the drill dart onto Jake's arm.

Jake saw the drill dart stop short of his power armor. His FP shield did its job. To Jake's amazement, however, when the drill dart hit his FP shield, a tripod of arms flung out of the drill dart. These small arms looked to be supporting the drill dart in place. Jake noticed the needle of the drill dart was spinning, but his FP shield was still keeping it away from his power armor.

April explained, "Those little arms sticking out of the drill dart are powerful magnets covered with a very sticky substance. This holds the drill dart in place to just about anything it hits. The drill dart then starts to drill, penetrating power armor in as little as thirty seconds. Don't worry if you use a drill dart in space. It forms an airtight seal as long as you don't try to remove the drill dart after it penetrates a suit."

The sister who dropped the drill dart now bent down and removed the drill dart. She then dropped and removed the drill dart two more times before putting it back away into her belt.

Jake felt a wave of relief come over him as May—since he didn't notice any of the other sisters have a compulsory condition, Jake assumed it was her—put the drill dart away. Jake said, "So you shoot with the spider pistol to create an opening in the FP shield. Then use the drill dart to disable your opponent."

All four sisters began to laugh again. This sent a chill down Jake's back. He found himself wishing he kept his mouth shut at least until they let him off the cargo bay floor.

April walked toward Jake and said, "That blinding flash from earlier."

May kneeled down by the far side of Jake's extended arm. She then revealed a set of catlike claws that shone with flickers of green lightning. May waved these claws back and forth in intervals of three over Jake's arm.

April said, "FP is money. You wear that pretentious power armor out in the outer rings. You risk someone." May sunk her claws into Jake's FP shield, scooping out a fair amount of FP. April never stopped talking. "Walking past you and collecting a nice payday. Not to mention how disrespectful it is to walk around flaunting your cash. Some of the people you meet will be struggling just to get by while there you are, walking around with rent money for a year just floating around your body."

Jake said, "I never thought about it like that."

April said, "Just to point out how useless that armor is." She pulled a drill dart out of her belt.

May removed another large scoop of FP from Jake's power armor. April then dropped her drill dart into the newly formed gap.

Jake watched helplessly as the tripod deployed. Jake could hear the drill drilling into his power armor. Jake watched as his remaining FP shifted to enclose the gap May's green lightning claws made. This did nothing to stop the drill dart from penetrating his power armor.

*****

Jake awoke in the medical bay. He felt as though he had just been asleep for a week. Dr. Helix was standing over Jake and said, "You're awake."

Jake asked, "How long was I out?"

Dr. Helix answered, "Only an hour. Your power armor had to be taken down to engineering for repairs. The quad sisters said there would be a power suit sent to your room in case you needed something in the meantime. Although, if you're headed to Alpha Mining for the celebration, I should remind you all power attire and weapons are not allowed on the station."

Jake said, "Thanks for reminding me, Doc. I'm late." Jake began to get out of bed.

Dr. Helix said, "Before you go." Dr. Helix reached behind him and picked up an ammo belt filled with drill darts that he handed to Jake. Dr. Helix said, "The sisters also wanted you to have this. They asked for me to tell you that you should know how to use these now."

Jake took the ammo belt and said, "I think I get the gist of them now."

Jake's W2 beeped with a call from Stacy. Jake hit the answer button, and Stacy immediately shouted, "Where are you? We're going to be late for our parade!"

Jake, still groggy, replied, "I'm on my way." Jake then double tapped his left wrist with his pointer and middle finger. (This was Jake's visual signal to his W2 to end a call.) Jake asked, "Am I good to go, Doc?"

Dr. Helix replied, "You will feel groggy for another hour. You should be fine after that as long as you avoid any more training accidents."

Jake thought, *Yeah! Training accident.* he said out loud, "Sure thing, Doc."

Jake stopped at his quarters to drop off his new drill dart belt. He also needed to dress more appropriately for the parade. The EPF didn't yet have an official uniform, so Jake tossed on blue jeans and a flannel shirt over his onesie.

Jake got to the courtyard to find Captain Noem standing with Frank and the quad sister, waiting for him.

Captain Noem stated, "You're late."

Jake walked toward the quad sisters and replied, "Must have overslept."

The quad sisters began giggling over Jake's response. Jake noticed Frank staring at the far left sister and raised an eyebrow. The far left sister saw this then quickly typed a message into her W2. Moments later, Frank received a message on his W2 then nodded in understanding toward the sister.

Jake and Captain Noem left Equality through the airlock in Serenity, which was currently connected to the quartership Alpha Mining. Once inside the quartership, Jake was instantly hit by the heat. The interior of the quartership had been conferred to massive furnaces for smelting metal. Although the cargo bay was cut off from the furnaces, the heat still seeped through.

Jake was surprised to see a small line of patients on gurneys waiting to be brought aboard Equality. Jake asked, "What's going on?"

Captain Noem answered, "Our medical bay has a time dilation pod. A rare piece of medical equipment. They only have one here for 150,000 residents. Dr. Helix will be seeing patients here and everywhere else Equality travels."

Jake said, "Dr. Helix mentioned something about the pod speeding up treatments. I don't actually understand how slowing time speeds up treatment."

The captain replied, "It wouldn't. The pod accelerates time."

Jake exclaimed, "How?"

Captain Noem replied, "Simple answer I was given is they have two magnetically charged points in the Faraday metal instead of one. It works, is all that matters."

Jake said, "That's crazy." The two of them then continued to the next airlock where the rest of the crew were waiting for them.

The Equality crew was met by the mayor of Alpha Mining. She was a polite older lady who had a couple of twelve-seat party bikes waiting for them. Stacy was the first one to jump on and grab a drink.

They rode the party bikes to the next airlock, where they saw dozens of parade floats were waiting for them to get started.

There were floats from multiple groups and businesses, including schools with a superhero theme, manufactures with their logos, and even a plushy pride parade.

As the parade traveled from airlock to airlock, Jake learned none of the stations were constructed the same. Some were just large tunnels with sidewalks and entrances to buildings built into walls. Others were completely hollowed out with nothing but trees or acres upon acres of crops. Others still would look like a city with paved roads and three-story-high office buildings. There was even a suburbs station with houses and white picket fences.

On many of the office buildings, there were advertising billboards built into them. On these billboards, playing on a loop, was Harry's video of Equality fending off the pirate attack.

Stacy screamed, "That's me!" She pointed at one of the billboards. Stacy yelled at Harry, who was sitting across from her, "You did put me in it!"

Captain Noem was also on the party bike and asked, "You did this, Harry?"

Jake couldn't tell if Captain Noem was mad or impressed. Her resting bitch face made here difficult to read.

Harry answered, "I thought it might help with recruitment." Harry waved to the crowd lining the sidewalk who gathered to watch the parade then said, "I think it's working."

The parade ended with mobs of people, including other float members, coming up to the Equality crew asking for selfies. This lasted over an hour. Afterward, the crew was left sort of standing around, wondering what to do now. Captain Noem slipped out early, saying she had business to attend to. This gave the crew (who were already feeling pretty good from the alcohol) free rein to do as they pleased.

Suddenly, Harry shouted, "This way, minions!"

Tie asked while following behind, "Where we going, master?"

Harry screamed, "Space Vegas, baby!"

*****

Other than a brief trip to hand off Samantha to the Alpha Mining authorities for pending charges, Frank and the quad sisters stayed behind on Equality to serve on guard duty. Although most of the crew were gone, the courtyard shops as well as the medical bay were actively open to the citizens of Alpha Mining during the day.

Once business closed for the day, May, June, and July were allowed to go explore Alpha Mining while April and Frank remained on duty, walking the empty courtyard.

Frank commented, "One of us really should have gone to keep an eye on your sisters."

April replied, "You knew the terms of the wager when you accepted. I won, so we are spending this stop aboard Equality without my nosey sisters about. If you had won, then I would have let you take me to dinner on Alpha Mining."

Frank stated, "You didn't play fair. Had I known—"

April interrupted Frank. "The first person to give in to temptation lost. Them were the rules."

Frank replied, "You used hot wax. That may be acceptable tactics on tactics on Romeo, but—"

April cut Frank off and said, "Careful, Frank. Otherwise, I might remember you're Juliet. Besides, I don't recall you complaining at the time."

Frank smiled then said, "No, I didn't." Frank then pulled April in close and kissed her.

April pulled back after the kiss and said, "Frank, there could be people around."

Frank replied, "Let them get their own woman."

April replied, "You think I'm your woman?"

Frank quickly decided to change the subject by asking, "What was up with that oversleeping comment by Jake earlier? You said you would tell me later."

April giggled then answered, "We gave Jake a tutorial in drill darts."

Frank laughed then said, "Hope you don't intend to give me that same tutorial."

April got up on her tippy-toes then said, "I need you awake" before kissing Frank.

*****

When Harry and his minions reached Space Vegas, they split up. Stacy went to the casino's dance club, dragging Tie with her. Jake saw a sign for a Texas hold 'em tournament. He convinced Calvin and Harry to join him in entering it.

The tournament was a monthly event drawing in a hundred plus players. The tournament was labeled a freezeout tournament. Meaning once you were out of chips, you were out.

Jake started at a table with nine other players. He was seated next to a large seven-three Black man with dreadlocks. As they played, Jake learned the man's name was AJ. AJ was in a conversation with others at the table, discussing his new career as an MMA fighter.

AJ said, "I go pro next month. Right now, I'm 5-0 with all five wins being first round knockouts."

Jake was in a hand with AJ immediately following this comment. AJ raised after the flop. Jake, who had already checked (hit two small pairs on the board), now tripled AJ's bet.

AJ looked down at Jake and, with a stern voice, asked, "You messing with me?"

Jake had already been knocked out once today and wasn't looking forward to it happening again. Jake softly answered, "No."

AJ started to laugh while throwing his cards in to indicate a fold. AJ said, "Just messing with you, man. I only fight in the octagon."

A sense of relief came over Jake. As the tournament continued, Jake found most everyone was like AJ—good souls just living their lives.

As the tournament progressed, Jake held his own while Harry and Calvin got eliminated. Jake eventually made the final table with nine other fresh faces. Three seats to Jake's left sat an older heavyset Black woman named Davinie.

Jake noticed Davinie playing tight. To take advantage of this on Davinie's big blind (when she was forced to put chips in the pot), Jake would raise regardless of having good cards or not. He did this knowing Davinie would fold, forfeiting her chips.

Jake did this three times in a row. After the third time, Davinie folded then said to Jake, "I'm watching you, boy. Keep doing it and see what happens."

The table all chuckled at Davinie's remark.

The very next hand, Jake was dealt the best starting hand in the game—pocket aces. There was a raise, a call, then another raise four times larger than the unusual raise. Jake felt this raise was high enough to chase out the other players. Jake wanted to shove all his chips into the pot right then, but he knew that would tell his opponent what he had, causing him to fold. Jake played it cool and hesitated before calling.

The flop came 4 of clubs, 7 of spades, 10 of clubs. It was a good flop for Jake since he believed his opponent had pocket Jacks or better based on his preflop raise. This meant his opponent would raise big to keep Jake from trying to outdraw him.

Jake's opponent was an older man wearing all black. He looked like someone who spent a lot of time at the table. Jake got excited at the thought of knocking him out of the tournament.

Just as Jake predicted, his opponent made a large bet. It was a larger bet than Jake expected, placing well over half his chips now into the pot.

Jake was excited knowing he was about to knock this player out. "All in," Jake announced with pride.

His opponent didn't hesitate to say, "Call."

Jake flipped over his pocket aces with a rush of excitement flowing through him.

His opponent laughed and said, "Good hand." He flipped his hand over.

Jake looked to see what card he would have to avoid to win. Jake began to laugh as he saw his opponent also had pocket aces. Jake repeated back to the man, "Good hand."

The dealer placed the turn and river cards on the board. Jake reached in to take back his last bet to make it easier on the dealer to chop up the pot.

The dealer said very loudly, "Sir! What are you doing?"

Jake got a perplexed look on his face then replied, "Taking back my bet. Why?"

Davinie shouted, "You lost, fool!"

Jake looked down at the board, trying to understand what they were talking about. The turn was king of clubs, and the river was the 2 of clubs. Jake looked at his aces to see neither was the ace of clubs.

Jake looked at the winning player in disbelief. The winning player, in return, shrugged his shoulders and said, "Runner, runner, nothing funner." He then began to rake in his winning chips.

The dealer said to Jake, "He has you covered, sir." Meaning Jake was eliminated.

As Jake walked away, he heard the elderly woman Davinie yell, "Karma's a bitch!"

*****

The next evening, Captain Noem held another introduction ceremony for new crew members. Before the ceremony, she sent Jake a message, requesting he join her on the bridge.

Jake entered the bridge to find Captain Noem sitting in his pilot's seat. Jake asked, "What's up?"

Captain Noem gestured to the captain's chair then said, "Have a seat."

Jake felt a sudden feeling of foreboding as he sat in the chair. Jake said, "This sounds serious."

Captain Noem said, "I won't be leaving Alpha Mining. I have to stay here to build the EPF. I need to secure ships and personnel. The Equality is still the flagship of the EPF. I need someone I can trust to be in charge. Jake, I need you to become the captain of SS Equality. Will you accept?"

Jake was in shock. He hesitated before he answered, "Of course, Captain Noem. Whatever you need."

Captain Noem said, "You're the captain now. I had to give myself a promotion to admiral."

Captain Jake said, "Admiral Noem. I like it. Do I get a new pilot?"

Admiral Noem answered, "I got you an interesting pilot if she works out. I also found you a lawyer to serve as first officer. Someone I think I can trust to keep you from starting any interplanetary incidents in my absence. They should be waiting in the Serenity section for me to introduce them."

Admiral Noem and Captain Jake left the bridge to go to the courtyard for the introduction ceremony. Once there, they stood on the platform from Serenity that lifted them a couple of feet into the air so Admiral Noem could address the crowd.

The admiral said, "Thank you all for coming. As you know, we are continuing to recruit. Thanks to Harry's video, there is no shortage of candidates. The EPF already has a patrol mothership named Eagle One to help. Well, as soon as I sort through the applicants to pick a crew anyways. Because of this and so many other aspects that need to be addressed to form the EPF, I will not be able to continue traveling with you on Equality. I will instead be remaining here on

Alpha Mining to create the EPF headquarters. So my first introduction of the day is Captain Jake."

The crowd was stunned and silent. Only a few faint whispers were spoken for a moment. Finally, Calvin broke the silence and shouted, "Hail Captain Jake!" Others quickly joined in with clapping and cheers.

Once the applause calmed down, Admiral Noem whispered to Jake, "You should say something, Captain."

Captain Jake stepped forward then said, "Thank you all. It's now my privilege to introduce you all to our new leader, Admiral Noem." There was instantly an even louder round of cheers. Once that died down, Captain Jake said, "Titles have changed, but she's still the boss." The crowd laughed.

Admiral Noem said, "Thank you all for that." The platform lowered, with Admiral Noem and Jake stepping off as it lowered into Serenity. Admiral Noem announced, "To replace Captain Jake as first officer, I have asked a very distinguished and knowledgeable attorney to help us out." The platform raised back up, carrying a bigger short elderly Black woman. Admiral Noem said, "Please welcome Davinie of Alpha Mining."

As the crowd gave Davinie a warm round of applause, Jake's jaw dropped, recognizing Davinie from the previous night's poker game.

Davinie took one look at Jake then said, "I'm gonna enjoy teaching you what happens to people who go around picking on little old ladies. Karma's a bitch."

Davinie stepped off the platform as it lowered back down into Serenity. Admiral Noem announced, "Some of you have already met our new pilot."

Jake now wondered who the new pilot was. Jake thought, *The crew as a whole hadn't met that many people. Unless it's someone from the journey from Earth*. A list of possible candidates flowed through Jake's mind.

The platform began to rise. Jake could see the person had red hair down to their shoulders.

Admiral Noem announced, "Please welcome Samantha of SS Expedition."

Beta Mining

After the introduction of Samantha, the crew wanted to know how a pirate could become a new member of the EPF. Admiral Noem escorted the officers and Samantha to the conference table for Equality's first officers' meeting to explain.

The conference table was round and adjustable to accommodate varying numbers of people. It also had three curved TV screens that formed a circle at the center of the table.

As everyone else adjusted their seats to their own person settings, Frank stood staring at Samantha with hatred in his eyes.

Admiral Noem said, "Take a seat, Frank. Please." Once Frank sat down, Admiral Noem explained, "Samantha here was planted with the pirates by the Alpha Mining government. She served with them for the past six months."

Frank sighed with relief then said, "So she's an undercover officer?"

Samantha half keeled over with laughter then said, "Hell no!"

Frank's look of anger returned as Admiral Noem explained, "Samantha has had a colorful past. That past landed her in trouble with the Alpha Mining law enforcement. To avoid a rehabilitation center, Samantha agreed to go undercover. Now she will be joining us as our pilot and pirate expert."

Frank said, "All right, expert, what can you tell us about the pirates?"

Samantha shrugged her shoulders then answered, "Not much. Captain Spike is the leader. He assembled his first mothership out of salvaged junkyard parts. He slowly built a crew. Then three years ago, he set off for the magnetic void between this star system and the Taylor system. Said it was getting too crowded here, so he was going to go construct his own space station. Next thing you know, he's back recruiting. Offers anyone who joins him a new home with all the amenities Einstein has to offer. Without restrictions."

Harry asked, "What amenities?"

Frank answered, "Stuff like spacemines and backpack powered rail rifles."

Samantha said, "Those, and stuff like 15 for Life."

Dr. Helix exclaimed, "That's a lie!"

Samantha replied, "I don't think so. Captain Spike and his crew all looked like teenagers to me."

Calvin said, "According to records, Captain Spike is sixty-four." Captain Spike's picture appeared on screen. He looked to be about forty with dark hair and bangs. He wore an eye patch over his left eye.

Davinie said, "That's too young to be on it by Romeo standard. You have to reach seventy."

Dr. Helix said, "She's lying. That picture is dated three years ago. That means he was on age-delaying medication, so 15 for Life wouldn't even work on him."

Admiral Noem said, "The Alpha Mining authorities assure me Samantha was debriefed with truth serum."

Dr. Helix said, "Even if she's not lying, it's not possible."

Captain Jake said, "We find Captain Spike, and you can ask him yourself, Doc."

Dr. Helix said, "Still. You can only be on the drug if you live on Romeo."

Harry coughed very loudly.

Dr. Helix corrected himself, "Unless you're the only living relative of the founders of Einstein."

Harry said, "It is a death sentence if they stop taking it. Do we know how they're getting the pills?"

Samantha answered, "No clue. Ship got put in lockdown whenever we met with another ship. Drop points are never at the same place twice."

Calvin said, "If they can use 15 for Life even though they were on age-delaying medication, couldn't they have also found a way to not die if they stop taking it? Maybe they only need one pill."

Dr. Helix said, "That's impossible. The greatest minds of Einstein have been working on the problem for nearly two hundred years."

Davinie added, "Even the godlings haven't been able to crack it."

Captain Jake asked, "What are godlings?"

Harry answered, "Arrogant pricks."

Calvin said, "They make the best puzzle games."

Dr. Helix said, "They are a genetically engineered race."

Harry added, "Purple hermaphroditic race on the outer rings. Genetically engineered to survive on a planet out there."

Dr. Helix said, "All with IQs over 200 in addition to incredible strength. They could conquer Einstein in a day if they felt like it. That's why they were also created with a lack of aggression and a very sympathetic nature. Everyone in Einstein goes to them when they have a complicated problem."

Frank said, "Juliet doesn't ask them for help, and we wouldn't be easily conquered."

Admiral Noem said, "Captain Jake, do you have any questions?"

Captain Jake asked, "How many ships does Captain Spike have?"

Samantha replied, "I don't know. The one I was on was brand-new."

Calvin said, "According to records, Captain Spike left Einstein with twenty-four jet arms, three bucketships, two cargo vessels, and two motherships."

Frank said, "We saw at least forty jet arms. One mothership has docking bays for eight, but more can be attached to the hull for transport."

Admiral Noem said, "Raiding has been good for them. No telling how many ships they have now. Outer rings aren't big on keeping records of financial transactions, I'm learning."

Calvin said, "Most motherships are marked with an identification symbol. Captain Spike's is two women kissing while sitting on the shoulder of a robot. I like this guy's style."

Admiral Noem cleared her throat loudly.

Calvin reiterated, "His taste. Not his whole raiding thing."

Admiral Noem said, "Your next mission will be to go to the quartership Beta Mining on a humanitarian mission to deliver food. While there, consider yourselves ambassadors and carry on appropriately. Harry, I would like you to start an official news podcast from Equality. Let the people know what we're doing to help them. Nothing that will give your position away until you arrive. No helping the pirates set up another ambush."

Harry replied, "I can do that."

Admiral Noem looked at Captain Jake and said, "Come back in one piece."

*****

The quartership SS Beta Mining was also located along the fourth ring orbiting at the opposite end of Einstein. It was parked on an artificial moon of the gas giant planet Zeus. The artificial moon was created with worthless rock left behind after mining and is now large enough to have its own gravitational pull.

Captain Jake sat alone on the Equality bridge as they entered Beta Mining's sector of space. Jake immediately cut off the Carrie effect drive, slowing Equality to obey local speed limit laws.

Even from tens of thousands of miles away, Captain Jake could see the lightning bolts flash in the blue planet Zeus's atmosphere. Jake stared at Zeus, mesmerized by the lightning until his W2 beeped.

Jake checked his W2 to see it was an alert for an incoming object. Jake asked, "Bob, what's incoming?"

A feminine voice responded, "Bob's gone, sugar. You can call me Dolly." The main screen changed to show a bucketship leaving the moon's surface. Dolly said, "This ship is on an intercept course with us, sugar."

Jake now recognized Dolly's voice to be Dolly Parton, an ancient singer and actress from Earth. Jake said, "That bucketship is only just leaving the moon, Dolly. Unless it has a Carrie effect drive, it won't reach us for hours. Plenty of time to change course. Why the alert?"

The screen changed to show a naked man in a bucketship cockpit. The man had pasty white skin covered in sweat. He was screaming, "Shake'n bake! Shake'n bake!" repeatedly. In the corner of the screen was an image of a plushy with tiger print fur wearing a blue onesie with an exoskeleton suit.

The plushy was saying, "Calm down and get back here."

Jake said, "Good call, Dolly. Check our path. If it's clear, I'm going to kick our Carrie effect drive back on for a second to cut down on arrival time. I want to get there before that guy ODs or does something stupid."

Dolly replied, "Coast is clear, sugar."

Captain Jake activated the Carrie effect drive then immediately deactivated it.

Dolly said, "Equality has just been issued a citation, and our mining license has been suspended until our hearing. I'm sorry, sugar."

Captain Jake replied, "Not an issue, Dolly. We aren't here to mine. Issue a yellow alert, Dolly. I need my crew."

Davinie shouted over the comm, "What the hell did you just do? We're supposed to be here to enforce the law, not break it!"

Stacy's voice came over the comm. "What did you do, Jake? And why are you watching porn?"

Jesus added, "The question is, why is Jake watching gay porn? I didn't know you swung that way, Captain."

The door to the bridge opened. Calvin stood outside and asked, "Are you decent, Jake?"

Captain Jake asked, "Why is Bob now Dolly?"

Calvin replied, "New captain, new AI. Dolly's fitting since we have clones on board. The first cloned sheep was named Dolly, after Dolly Parton."

Tie walked up behind Calvin and asked, "Is he decent?"

Captain Jake stated, "I'm not watching porn. Let's get serious, people. Looks like this guy is flying a bucketship on a potential intercept course with us. I tapped on the gas to get us to him sooner."

Calvin, Tie, Harry, and Samantha entered the bridge and took their seats.

Samantha said, "I know I'm new here, but if someone's trying to ram us, Why are we getting closer? Or do you guys just like getting rammed?"

Tie ignored Samantha and said, "I can disable the bucketship with a shot from the triple barrel. But it's already charged for white lightning, which would cook him alive inside that thing. I'd need to release a charge so I can reset to a lower setting."

Calvin whispered to Samantha, "I like getting rammed."

Samantha whispered back, "Don't care."

Dr. Helix said, "I wouldn't advise that, Captain. In his altered state of mind, he might try to exit the bucketship if you disable it."

Captain Jake said, "Let's see how good you are, Samantha. Need you to drop shields and use thrusters to match speed with his bucketship. Keep it right in front of the cargo bay doors."

Samantha replied with a cocky tone, "Consider it done." Then she added in a sultry tone, "Let me know when you want me to put it in."

Captain Jake blushed slightly then said, "April and June, please join your sisters in the cargo bay. Need two of you to jetpack over and place welding clamps on the bucketship's hatch. We need to keep him from getting out until he's got air to breathe. Disable the ship with hand cannons after that so we can bring it aboard."

Davinie's voice came over the comms, scolding Jake. "Don't you dare think of interfering without getting permission. We just got here, and you have already caused us to get a citation. Your job is not to get this crew arrested."

Captain Jake hadn't even considered getting permission to help. "Will do, Davinie. Thank you for watching out," said Captain Jake in a sincere voice.

Harry said, "You're patched in, Captain."

Captain Jake said, “This is Captain Jake of the SS Equality representing the EPF. May we be of any assistance?”

The bucketship pilot continued to head bang as if listening to music. The tiger print plushy replied, “I’m Tigger head of security for Beta Mining. Assistance would be appreciated.”

*****

The plan went off without a hitch, and the bucketship was brought aboard Equality. Per Tigger’s request, they left the bucketship sealed. Once they landed on the artificial moon, a recovery team collected the bucketship to get it inside for unsealing.

Once they docked with the Beta Mining quartership, Tigger was waiting to greet them. Tigger said, “Thank you for your assistance.”

Captain Jake replied, “That’s what we’re here for.” Captain Jake was taken back to see that Tigger was only five-two. Captain Jake was accompanied by Dr. Helix, who also greeted Tigger.

Tigger said, “I understand you’re here with a fresh supply of material for our 3D meat printers.”

Captain Jake replied, “As well as fresh cultures for growth, and our head botanist has some gear she thinks can help improve your yields from your hydroponics bay. She’s gathering the gear now.”

Tigger said, “That sounds great.”

Dr. Helix asked, “Do you have any idea what that man was on?”

Tigger lowered his head and averted his head when he answered, “That’s up to our doctors to decide.”

Dr. Helix said, “I will head there now.”

Tigger quickly repeated, “Our doctors got this.”

Captain Jake said, “We were headed to the hospital on different business. We have a time dilation pod. Dr. Helix has a meeting at the hospital to schedule appointments while we’re here. We want to help out in every way we can to promote the EPF.”

Tigger said, “In that case, let me give you the tour of Beta Mining on the way.” Tigger led them into the lower courtyard.

Beta Mining was designed much like Equality, except on a far larger scale with multiple courtyards on different decks. The lower courtyard was full of both giant oak trees and weeping willows. The courtyard was also filled with what looked like college kids smoking pot and playing hacky sack.

Tigger stated, “Beta Mining has four docking bays plus two large hangar doors left open at all times. Bucketships freely come and go in high volume. Seventy-five thousand residents in this sector of space. Most living on motherships parked across our moon that is getting bigger every day. Right now, we are only at a fourth G, but we hope to be up to a third G by the end of the solar cycle.”

Captain Jake asked, “What’s up with all the kids?”

Tigger proudly stated, “Beta Mining has the largest college in the outer rings. We also have the largest shops in this sector of space, should you need anything.”

As they walked to reach the hospital and the second floor, Captain Jake sent Dr. Helix a message that read, “Discover what was wrong with that pilot if you can. Something feels off.”

Once they reached the hospital, Dr. Helix went inside while Captain Jake continued receiving his tour from Tigger.

*****

Stacy took Calvin with her to the hydroponics bay of Beta Mining to help carry supplies. Upon arrival, Stacy said to Calvin, “No wonder they have trouble feeding everyone. Half their crops are marijuana.”

“You can buy food anywhere. You can only trust the quality of pot you grow yourself” came a voice from behind them.

Stacy turned to see Brett, a fellow botanist she had been video chatting with. Brett looked to be in his thirties. He was tall and slender. He walked with a slight hunch as he approached Stacy and Calvin.

Stacy stated, “I like pot more than the next person, but this is ridiculous, considering you have to have food shipped in.”

Brett explained, “Miners travel in space for weeks at a time trying to find a decent asteroid to bring back. My marijuana is the only thing that gets them through. It's also used to make so many other things that it is truly necessary for our survival."

Calvin asked, "Where can I set these down?"

Brett asked, "What is it?"

Stacy answered, "What I told you I was bringing. The latest version of the high-pressure sodium and metal halide hybrid bulbs. They can increase your yields by a tenth. You need to start laying off your own product, Brett."

Brett said, "Follow me." He led them into a smaller room where he pointed at an empty table and said, "You can set them there."

Stacy looked around then exclaimed, "You're growing pot in here too!"

Calvin said, "I'm going to leave you guys to talk shop." Calvin left the room.

Brett started to roll a joint and said, "This is where I grow the specialty stuff."

Stacy replied, "This is where you should be growing the rice and grain."

Brett stated, "Don't knock it till you try it." He handed the joint to Stacy.

Stacy said, "It can't possibly be better than starvation" as she took the joint. Brett pulled out a lighter, lighting the joint for her. Stacy took a hit then stated, "I stand corrected."

Brett smiled then said, "Think that's good? There's a party tonight with something called heaven's bliss. Makes the pot you smoke afterward so much better."

Stacy took another hit then asked, "When do we leave?"

*****

Captain Jake returned to Equality and headed straight for the conference table to send a report of the day's activities. Jake said, "Bob. Sorry, Dolly. I need to send an encrypted message to Admiral Noem."

Suddenly, there was a shimmer surrounding the conference table area. Dolly said, "Sound barrier deployed. Ready to record when you are, sugar."

Captain Jake was about to start when Dolly said, "Sugar, Dr. Helix is outside."

Captain Jake turned to see Dr. Helix standing outside of the sound barrier. Captain Jake asked, "Dolly, is it all right to pass through the sound barrier?"

Dolly replied, "It's perfectly safe, sugar."

Captain Jake waved for Dr. Helix to come inside.

Dr. Helix entered and said, "I'm sorry to disturb you, Captain. I thought you would want to hear what I learned right away."

Captain Jake replied, "Can't wait to hear why Tigger didn't want you examining that guy."

Dr. Helix answered, "I think it's because there's a new drug that doesn't exist."

Captain Jake said, "Come again?"

Dr. Helix explained, "They call it heaven's bliss. It's like an amplifier for whatever other drug you take. Think of it as adding a pill to a beer to triple its alcohol content without changing its flavor. The drug itself is not addictive, but it makes getting hooked on whatever else they're taking that much easier. Now they're starting to find cases like Kevin, who is currently in a vegetative state. Kevin's brain damage may be temporary, but it's too soon to tell. They don't know how heaven's bliss works. It has supposedly been around for months now, but they can't get their hands on a sample of the drug to test it. Until they do, the drug doesn't officially exist."

Captain Jake asked, "How is that possible? Is truth serum banned out here?"

Dr. Helix answered, "I asked about that. They say if used, the truth serum erases the patient's memory to a week before they started taking heaven's bliss. I've offered the use of the time dilation pod for Kevin. Kevin was the name of the individual in the bucketship. Accelerating time may be the best way to flush heaven's bliss out of his system to see if he regains brain function. I can't say more without a sample of the drug."

Captain Jake whispered to himself, "If anyone can get a sample of an illegal substance, Stacy can."

*****

Stacy and Brett arrived at a rave party in the education sector of Beta Mining. The building hosting the rave was a college dorm for Beta Mining students. The dorm was blaring music and had flashing neon lights as they approached.

Brett said, "Heaven's bliss is completely organic. It's an implant that gets injected into the back of your neck. Completely painless."

Stacy replied, "You had me at organic. Where do I get this injection?"

Brett pointed at the bouncer holding an injection gun. As they approached, Stacy got a call from Captain Jake. Stacy pressed ignore then got her injection.

Stacy walked into the dorm, screaming, "Where's my drink, bitches?"

As someone handed her a drink, Stacy received a text message from Captain Jake that read, "I need you to get a sample of a new drug called heaven's bliss for Dr. Helix. DO NOT TAKE!"

Stacy was laughing as she typed her reply. "If I get you this drug, I want animals for the courtyard, and NO QUESTIONS about how I got the drug. I'm no narc."

Captain Jake replied, "Fine."

Stacy shouted at Brett to be heard over the blaring music, "How long does this implant last?"

Brett answered, "It will dissolve into your system over the course of a week." Brett handed Stacy another joint.

Stacy said, "Perfect." Then she took a hit of the joint and shouted, "Holy fucken cock sucker, does that make a difference!"

*****

The next morning, there was an officers' meeting at the conference table aboard Equality. Captain Jake started the meeting by saying, "Good morning, everyone. Harry, Admiral Noem says to tell you she likes your news feed. Keep up the good work."

Harry replied, "Thank you. I thought the footage of saving that bucketship was priceless."

Captain Jake then asked, "Dr. Helix, any news on Kevin?"

Dr. Helix replied, "He just arrived for treatment before this meeting started. Nurse Irene is prepping him as we speak."

Captain Jake turned to Stacy, who looked like she was suffering from a massive hangover, and asked, "Were you able to get that sample?"

Stacy asked, "Do I get animals for the courtyard?"

Captain Jake replied, "Already said yes."

Stacy answered, "Then yes, I got it."

Dr. Helix asked, "You aren't talking about heaven's bliss, are you?"

Stacy replied, "That's the stuff."

Dr. Helix said, "Give it here."

Stacy replied, "Can't."

Captain Jake's tone turned stern. "Stacy!"

Stacy explained, "It's in the back of my neck. I can't just rip out an implant."

Dr. Helix jumped up and quickly walked around the table to Stacy. He then grabbed Stacy by the arm and said, "You're coming with me to the medical bay right now. Do you have any idea how dangerous heaven's bliss can be?" Dr. Helix began to drag Stacy away from the table.

Frank asked, "What's heaven's bliss, and where did Stacy get it?"

Just before being dragged through the sound barrier, Stacy screamed, "I'm no narc!"

Davinie looked at Captain Jake with a look of disgust on her face then asked, "You wouldn't be stupid enough to sanction a black ops operation on Beta Mining now, would you?"

Captain Jake looked back at Davinie with a "deer in the headlights" look on his face. Jake hadn't thought of it like that. Jake began to answer, "I—"

Dolly interrupted, "Sugar, Tigger of Beta Mining is here to see you. He's waiting in the Serenity section."

Captain Jake said, "Ask him to come to the courtyard. I'll start walking there now. Calvin, get rid of the sugar. Joke's over."

Calvin replied, "I'll get right on that, sugar."

Captain Jake said, "Meeting adjourned."

*****

As soon as Tigger saw Captain Jake approach, he started to walk toward Captain Jake, shouting. "Why is Kevin aboard Equality? I told you our doctors would take care of this!"

Captain Jake reached Tigger, but before he could say anything, he heard, "Take care of what exactly?" Captain Jake turned to see that Davinie had followed him.

Captain Jake wasn't prepared to be scolded on two fronts as he answered, "I told Tigger yesterday that our Dr. Helix would be taking patients who could benefit from our time dilation pod. Kevin's doctors thought it might be beneficial to use our pod to age Kevin to try and get the heaven's bliss out of his system."

Tigger shouted, "That drug is a myth! It doesn't exist."

Captain Jake replied, "We have a sample."

Tigger's demeanor immediately changed as he softly replied, "What?"

Captain Jake explained, "It's an implant injected into the back of the neck. That's why you couldn't find any pills. Our Dr. Helix is removing it from a patient right now. I was just headed that way, if you care to join me."

Tigger said, "Yes, please."

Davinie said, "I need one moment with my captain." Davinie pulled Captain Jake to the side then angrily whispered, "You did authorize a covert mission in Beta Mining jurisdiction without their knowledge or permission."

Captain Jake whispered, "I wouldn't—"

Davinie cut Captain Jake off. "You may get away with it this time, but don't think that makes you right. You got lucky. Luck always runs out, then everyone suffers. Remember that." Davinie angrily walked away.

*****

Captain Jake and Tigger entered the medical bay to find Dr. Helix cursing. He and Irene were staring at a stand next to the examination table where Stacy was sitting and also staring in wonder at the stand.

Captain Jake asked, "What is it, Doc?"

Dr. Helix was too upset to talk, so Irene answered, "As soon as the doctor exposed the implant to air, it began to disintegrate. The doctor couldn't save the sample."

Tigger was clearly upset as he said, "So there's still no proof that heaven's bliss exists. Wait, what about Kevin? Doesn't he have an implant?"

Dr. Helix recomposed himself then said, "Kevin does have implant marks on the back of his neck. I checked as soon as I got back. Unfortunately, the implant is gone. After seeing this one disintegrate, I believe they are smart implants designed to self-destruct if discovered. That may be what caused Kevin's current condition."

Captain Jake said, "You tried, Doc."

Dr. Helix said, "I will still be aging Kevin a week, scanning his brain as he ages. If that doesn't get him out of his vegetative state, I can try gene therapy. Once Kevin can answer questions, you may be able to learn more about heaven's bliss."

Tigger looked at Stacy and asked, "Who gave you the implant?"

Stacy replied, "Jake promised me I wouldn't have to tell if I got it for him."

Tigger turned to look at Captain Jake, who responded, "I did promise her, and I don't renege on a promise. I can tell you that she got it aboard Beta Mining. You have security cameras, don't you?"

Tigger smiled and said, "Yes, I do." Tigger turned to shake Dr. Helix's hand and said, "Thank you, Doctor. This is more information than we have ever had." Tigger then turned to Captain Jake and said, "Thank you too, Captain. I'm sorry for my behavior before. Beta

Mining has a reputation in Einstein of being nothing but stoners. Letting Einstein know that we're suffering from an epidemic caused by a drug that doesn't exist would make us a laughing stock."

Captain Jake said, "We'll keep it quiet until we learn more."

Captain Jake escorted Tigger out of the medical bay. Once they were out of the room, Stacy asked Dr. Helix, "That implant isn't really what turned Kevin into a vegetable, is it? I was told it was all organic."

*****

After Captain Jake escorted Tigger to the airlock, he met up with Samantha in the mess hall. Captain Jake figured if anyone knew about heaven's bliss, it would be her.

Captain Jake sat down next to Samantha and said, "I need to ask you something."

Samantha replied, "I don't sleep with my captains. You waited too long to ask."

Captain Jake replied, "That's good to know, I guess."

Samantha said, "Of course, if you give me enough tequila, I might forget about my rule."

Captain Jake replied, "I'm not here about sex. Do you know about a drug called heaven's bliss?"

Samantha replied, "Never heard of it. What's it do?"

Captain Jake answered, "It's an implant that goes into the back of the neck that amplifies any recreational drugs you take."

Samantha said, "Now I want this implant."

Captain Jake said, "So the pirates aren't behind it?"

Samantha finished the last of her food and got up from the table, answering, "Not that I know off. Anything that advanced was probably made by those genetic freaks on Chuck Norris."

Captain Jake stood up and asked, "Chuck Norris?"

Samantha said, "Yeah. It's on the outer ring. Air's not breathable for us humans. There's a purple race of people that live there."

Captain Jake said, "Godlings. I've heard of them."

Samantha nodded yes and said, "That's them. Anything on the cutting edge of science, they'll know about it."

Captain Jake said, "Thanks for the info, Samantha."

Samantha said, "Remember what I said about tequila." She slapped Captain Jake's butt as she walked past him.

*****

Captain Jake returned to the medical bay a few hours later to check on Kevin and Stacy (Dr. Helix insisted Stacy remain for observation). Upon entering, Captain Jake found Stacy, Irene, and Kevin in conversation. Captain Jake said, "I see Kevin's doing better."

Dr. Helix replied from the other end of the room, "He can speak a little now. Afraid his IQ isn't what it used to be. I would like to keep Kevin on board for a while for observation, and perhaps another round of gene therapy."

Captain Jake asked, "What does his family say?"

Dr. Helix answered, "Nothing, I'm afraid. Appears Kevin has been suffering from a drug problem for a while. His parents wrote him out of their lives years ago."

Captain Jake walked over to Kevin and asked, "How's it going, Kevin?"

After a moment of silence, Irene answered for Kevin, "Kevin has two beautiful women doting on him. He's happy as a pea in a pod, aren't you, Kevin?"

Kevin smiled back at Irene then said, "I'm Kevin."

Captain Jake asked, "Kevin, would you like to stay with us on Equality for a while?"

Kevin pointed at Stacy and said, "Irene."

Irene said, "No, I'm Irene. That's Stacy."

Kevin repeated, "Stacy."

Stacy looked at Jake then said, "This could have been me, Jake. He's staying."

Captain Jake nodded in agreement.

Chuck Norris

Upon leaving Beta Mining, Captain Jake held an officers' meeting. Captain Jake said, "Our next destination is planet Chuck Norris along the sixth ring."

Filipe immediately asked, "Are we getting easy airlocks installed?"

Captain Jake replied, "I don't know what that is."

Filipe explained, "Easy airlocks are a second airlock attached to the entrance airlock. They can extend out like an accordion to connect ships at a greater distance apart."

Frank added, "Also less safe. That's why they're not allowed in the inner rings."

Harry said, "We're not in the inner rings. They're necessary in the outer rings since most shops and restaurants are converted motherships. We should also add one to the cargo bay."

Frank agreed. "That would be safer than having to let bucketships park inside our cargo bay for people to visit our shops."

Filipe added, "Also faster than having to depressurize and repressurize in between every guest."

Harry said, "You should do both. Increase foot traffic when we're docked for our courtyard businesses."

Dr. Helix added, "I hear they have excellent disinfection features."

Frank added, "And security sensors."

Captain Jake said, "I'm sold. Write up the request forms for me to sign and make the installment appointment."

Davinie asked with a disapproving tone, "What's our mission on Chuck Norris? I didn't receive anything from Admiral Noem."

Captain Jake answered, "We're following up on heaven's bliss on behalf of Beta Mining. As I understand it, godlings are geniuses who happen to be the experts on all cutting-edge technology."

Dr. Helix said, "That's an excellent idea, Captain."

Stacy asked, "Do they have animals there?"

Harry answered, "Nope."

Stacy looked disappointed.

Calvin got excited and exclaimed, "They have Thread the Needle!"

Frank said, "Godlings are abominations. Are you certain we have to deal with them?"

Stacy scolded Frank. "That's not a nice thing to say."

Dr. Helix said, "The godlings wouldn't be offended. They are genetically engineered with a complete lack of aggression."

Harry said, "The most boring race in Einstein. Ever hear the one about how many godlings it takes to crack a smile?" After a moment of silence, Harry gave the answer. "No one knows how many it takes because it's never happened."

Calvin said, "That was so lame."

Captain Jake said, "I'll be going down to the surface on Serenity to meet these godlings. The rest of you can stay on Equality, which will be docked at their space station, Shell City."

Calvin added, "Playing Thread the Needle."

*****

Equality reached Chuck Norris space three days later. Captain Jake was sitting on the bridge alone, reviewing applications for new crew members, when the Carrie effect drive shut off to abide by local speed limit regulations. To his surprise, Calvin and Tie walked onto the bridge and took their seats.

Captain Jake asked, "What's up, guys?"

Calvin replied, "You're joking, right?"

Captain Jake answered, "No."

Calvin said, "Since you became captain, you've been living in your own little world. How many times have I mentioned Thread the Needle to you?"

Captain Jake replied, "A few. It's something to do with space battles, right?"

Tie said, "Dolly, magnify the main screen to show the captain here what Thread the Needle is."

Dozens of spaceships suddenly filled the screen. They ranged in size from bucketship to cargo ship (cargo ships were twice the size of an eighteen-wheeler). All of them had FP shields shimmering around them.

Captain Jake noticed a jet arm flying toward a large ring in the center of the screen. Just before reaching the ring, the jet arm was blasted with a rail gun shell that sent it hurtling away from the ring. The jet arm's FP shield kept it from taking any damage.

Captain Jake said, "That's insane. What are the rules?"

Tie explained, "There are eight satellites forming a cube marking the boundaries. Ships participate in groups of three. When you fly into the cube, you're assigned a color letting you know who your teammates are. Don't like your team, fly out and try again. First team to five wins earning points toward the purchase of free rail gun shells. Earn points by flying through that ring in the middle, and you have to earn a point to earn prize points."

Captain Jake asked, "What if a rail gun shell hits the planet?"

Tie answered, "The godlings produce the rail gun shells. The ones used for the match have low metal content, so they pack less of a punch. Anything entering the atmosphere will burn up harmlessly."

Calvin added, "The game never stops. It runs twenty-four seven. Can we play?"

Captain Jake replied, "Not with the kids and civilians onboard."

Calvin sighed, "You're no fun anymore."

Captain Jake said, "Of course, we could play while all nonessential personnel are shopping at Shell City. Our shops can't operate anyways while the easy airlocks are being installed."

Tie said, "It's about time we got in some real space combat training."

Captain Jake asked, "Can Equality even fit through that ring?"

Tie replied, "The ring adjusts its size for ships. It also has thrusters to move it back into place should it get hit."

Captain Jake said, "Okay, make the arrangements to play after Serenity returns tomorrow."

The next morning, after Serenity departed for the surface, Equality docked at the space station Shell City that orbited Chuck Norris a thousand miles above the planet's space elevator. Frank warned everyone that the outer rings could be dangerous, so everyone was to where power attire and open carry.

While at Shell City, Samantha invited Tie and Calvin to join her for lunch at a pizzeria she claimed made the best pizza in the outer ring.

The restaurant was small with open seating for no more than ten. There was a big screen TV streaming the Thread the Needle game. The front of the room was plexiglass, giving an overview of the courtyard as they were on the third floor.

Tie stared at the TV screen, watching the game, and said, "I can't wait until we get the chance to play. It will be a true test of how sturdy Equality is."

Samantha said, "I'm just happy that I don't have to sit on someone's lap this time."

Calvin asked, "Why were you sitting on someone's lap? Isn't that dangerous?"

Samantha replied, "We were only in a bucketship. Nowhere else to sit. Plus the danger made it hot."

After they were seated, Calvin looked over to see an older man and presumably his daughter sitting down at a table across the room. The girl looked to be about his age, and she was a cute little thing, so Calvin used his W2 contact lenses recognition program to see if she was on Facebook. She was.

Her name was Star of Shell City. Her profile said she was age twenty-four and single. Calvin scrolled through her media pictures where one picture in particular caught his attention. It was of Star's backside where she was wearing nothing but a string bikini. The caption said, "18 ink."

Calvin asked, "What's 18 ink?"

Samantha answered, "It's an app needed to see certain ink used in tattoos. I have a couple of them, and no, you will never get to see them. App or not."

Calvin immediately rushed to find and download the app. He looked at Star's photo again where he could now read the caption "Buy Beer to Ride." Calvin was getting turned on.

Calvin decided to play it safe and check out the man before making a move. His profile read Ted of Hades, age fifty-three and single. Kids' section was left blank. Owner/operator of the cargo ship SS Exterminator.

Calvin decided to go for it and sent Star a hookup request.

After they placed their order, Tie asked Samantha, "Did you like traveling with the pirates?"

Samantha replied, "Getting drunk every night with people that had the same mentality as me was nice."

Tie asked, "What mentality is that?"

Samantha answered, "Getting fucked up and watching the world burn."

Tie looked at Samantha's innocent-looking face then said, "I seriously doubt you want the world to burn. You wouldn't be with us if you did."

Samantha explained, "I didn't get much of a choice about joining you guys. It was join you, or Alpha Mining was going to send me back to the pirates. The pirates were okay, but I have this rule about never sleeping with the same person twice. They didn't have anyone left for me to screw, so here I am."

While Tie looked upset over this answer, Calvin stated, "You haven't slept with me yet."

Samantha replied, "And I never will. Even we sluts have standards."

Calvin looked over at Star, who was just getting up, and whispered, "Hopefully not all sluts."

Samantha suddenly yelled, "Clair!" Then she began waving at the front window.

Clair was right outside, holding a new plushy barbie doll, when she saw Samantha waving at her. Clair immediately lit up, running into the pizzeria with her new plushy barbie doll outstretched to show Samantha. Clair shouted, "Look at what?" Clair wasn't looking at where she was going and ran right into Ted and Star, who were leaving.

Ted had dark, cracked, and wrinkled skin with long stringy black hair. His body was aged beyond it's time due to a lifelong abuse of drugs and alcohol. Ted's left arm was a prosthetic black metal arm. The knuckles were painted red to look like blood. Blood that appeared to shift as his hand moved as if it were real fresh blood.

Ted looked down at Clair while talking to Star. "Hey, babe. Ever had plushy steak cooked on a sawsword?" Ted paused to lick his lips toward Clair then continued, "It melts in your mouth."

Star replied, "No, I haven't, babe. Would you cook some up for me?" Star proceeded to squeeze what little she had for breasts up against Ted's flesh arm and said, "I'll reward you if you do."

Ted placed his hand on his sawsword's hilt, which made Clair scream, "Haaa!"

Irene was still outside the pizzeria, only now reaching the window outside. When she heard Clair scream, she let go of the bags she was carrying (letting them float off) and rushed inside. Irene shouted, "What's going on here?" Clair ran to her mother, wrapping her arms around Irene's legs.

Ted looked at Irene and replied, "Just messing with your pet."

Tie was already on his feet, about to intervene when Irene burst in. Tie stated in a firm tone, "She's no pet."

Star turned and began staring at Calvin. Star said, "Hey! Ain't you one of those ancient people?"

Calvin was feeling embarrassed and hoping Star hadn't looked at his hookup request yet. Calvin replied, "Never thought of it like that, but yeah, that's me."

Ted said, "That means you're one of them EPF fools here to tell us outer ringers how to live." Ted spit in Calvin's face.

Tie pushed Ted back.

Samantha shouted, “I’m an outer ringer and part of the EPF! They have no agenda!”

Star squealed, “Kick their ass, babe!”

It looked like Ted was about to start swinging his metal arm when a space station police patrol came into Ted’s view. Ted said, “If you inner ringers have any balls, you’ll meet me in the Thread the Needle cube. Name’s Ted. My ship’s the Exterminator.”

Samantha screamed, “I’m not an inner ringer, and we were going to play anyway!”

Ted ignored Samantha, grabbed Star, and said, “Let’s go, babe. You can suck me off for luck.” They left the pizzeria.

*****

Jesus took a course down to planet Chuck Norris parallel to the space elevator since the city of Texas was at the base of the space elevator.

Captain Jake was in the cockpit with Jesus and asked, “How do you think they were able to build a space elevator? Earth couldn’t even build one.”

Jesus replied, “I heard that’s what they were programmed to do when they got dropped off—build an elevator then start sending up ore. I just don’t get why they stopped short.”

Captain Jake replied, “That’s easy. Wasn’t safe to go any higher. They already started playing that Thread the Needle game. Didn’t want all that hard work undone by a stray rail gun shell. You going to be okay hanging out at the repair shop while the easy airlocks are installed?”

Jesus laughed and said, “You mean at the repair shop literally named the repair shop. You know these he/shes don’t even have bars. I don’t think I’ll be missing out on much staying on board.”

Captain Jake said, “Emily, Zac, and July will be staying behind to keep you company.”

Jesus said, “Why July? Take her and leave me June.”

Captain Jake asked, “Why? Can you even tell the difference?”

Jesus replied, "Yes. The difference is July has a boyfriend back on Romeo while June is single."

Captain Jake chuckled then replied, "Sorry, Jesus. June has seniority."

Jesus replied, "How does she have…oh shit. I always forget they're not actually identical twins."

As they approached the city, they could see large cacti surrounding the city in place of buildings. Jesus said, "You have got to be shitting me."

Serenity landed next to the repair shop, which was constructed out of a large hollowed-out cactus. Captain Jake, Stacy, June, and Dr. Helix stepped outside of the airlock. All but Stacy were wearing power suits. Stacy wore her power armor, but the FP shield was deactivated as part of standard protocol set after Jake's education on power attire by April.

They were met on the ground by a godling. The godling was hairless, standing five feet tall with purple skin and wearing a green onesie. The godling appeared to be too busy typing on their W2 to be bothered to say anything.

June said, "I'm going to do a perimeter sweep real quick." June began to walk around.

Captain Jake had to have his visor down because the atmosphere wasn't breathable for humans. Captain Jake loudly said, "Hello, I am Captain Jake."

The godling spoke while still active on their W2. "I know. My name is 607913. You may call me Thirteen for short.

Captain Jake said, "Pleasure to meet you, Thirteen. We are here—"

Thirteen cut Captain Jake off, never looking up from his W2. "I read your request. Follow me please." Thirteen took off in a sprint, still typing on his W2.

Captain Jake, Stacy, and Dr. Helix looked at each other in confusion then quickly began to give chase to Thirteen.

June returned moments later to find everyone gone. June said to herself, "Where the hell are they?" June opened up her W2 to activate GPS tracking then exclaimed, "Son of a bitch!" June began to give chase.

With the aid of the power attire, Captain Jake, Stacy, and Dr. Helix were able to slowly catch up to Thirteen. As they ran, Captain Jake looked about to see that the city had no visible vehicles, only the occasional metal wagons with pull arms. There were other godlings about, all of whom were on their W2s.

June finally caught up with Captain Jake and the others, running at a speed of 42 mph. June wasted no time in identifying which power suit was Captain Jake, then she tackled him.

The two rolled uncontrollably, forcing several godling bystanders to jump out of the way (still never taking their eyes off their W2s). Finally, a giant cactus building stopped their tumbling.

June was back on her feet in an instant, then she pounced on Captain Jake, who was still in a state of bewilderment. June began to yell, "Don't ever leave without your security detail!"

Captain Jake immediately said, "Sorry, June. Wasn't even thinking about it."

June replied, "Do it again and I'll cut off both your legs. Then I'll give your legs to Dr. Helix over there to reattach backward to always remind you."

Captain Jake pondered for a moment whether or not this was even possible then decided he didn't want to find out. Captain Jake said, "I promise, June."

Stacy shouted, "Hey, lovebirds! Thirteen's getting away."

Forty-five minutes later, Thirteen finally stopped running. Thirteen was standing next to an endless field of blue cactus fruit growing only five feet tall. On one side of the field was a mountain range, and on the other side were dozens of tall green cactus buildings. Coming out of these buildings were godlings pushing carts full of the blue cactus fruit.

Thirteen, still typing on his W2 and not even breathing hard after the run, said, "This is where we grow our food supply. Stacy may explore if she wishes while we speak."

Stacy was still trying to catch her breath. Once she could, she asked, "Haven't you guys heard of vehicles?"

Thirteen replied, "I am not a guy. We have industrial vehicles where needed. Good cardio translates to good health and optimal brain function."

Stacy said, "I am going to look around. Have fun, Jake."

June said to Captain Jake, "I'll go with her and do a perimeter sweep. You know what happens if you try to leave without me."

Thirteen, never looking up, said, "Your theory that heaven's bliss is a smart implant is intriguing. Your coming here to discover if we are making it shows a lack of intelligence on your part."

Captain Jake said, "I never said you were making it."

Thirteen replied, "The thought occurred to you."

Captain Jake said, "I wasn't ruling anything out."

Thirteen said, "I brought you here, Captain, to see this." Thirteen finally looked up and pointed at the fields of blue cacti then returned to his W2 and said, "Cactus is all that can grow here. We have no research facilities. No building sealed with your oxygen to experiment with. Only computers that run simulations. I've been working on 102 different experiments since we started talking today regarding your inquiries."

Captain Jake asked, "What have you found?"

Thirteen answered, "A smart implant is possible depending on the drug used. A drug that can disappear completely and have the effects you describe doesn't exist. Booster drugs mimicking the effects you speak of exist. None of these drugs alter the brain as the MRIs we've been sent suggest."

Dr. Helix asked, "Have you found a cure for Kevin?"

Thirteen replied, "Still running simulations. I have sent you the most promising gene therapy treatment so far. It will only return an additional 10 percent of Kevin's cognitive functions."

Captain Jake asked, "Who is capable of making heaven's bliss?"

Thirteen replied, "I already told you, the drug doesn't currently exist. It also cannot be manufactured with known ingredients of Earth or Einstein. If you want to know more about heaven's bliss, then you have to supply us with the missing data."

Captain Jake replied, "What missing data?"

Dr. Helix answered, "Thirteen is saying heaven's bliss is being made with alien ingredients."

Thirteen said, "Not necessarily alien. Chronos could easily have undiscovered vegetation or perhaps a venom of some sort. SS Exploration left with a complete set of samples from Chronos. Perhaps they have something they forgot to log in. Human error is common among your race."

Captain Jake said, "SS Expedition was Samantha's home. It left this star system years ago. Chronos is off-limits, isn't it?"

Thirteen replied, "Are you saying your race would never steal?"

Dr. Helix said, "It's worth looking into, Captain."

Stacy returned and said, "Nothing much to see here. You guys finished yet?"

Thirteen replied, "We are finished. The easy airlocks will have been installed on our ship by now and my things loaded on to it."

Stacy repeated, "Our ship? Your things?"

Thirteen replied, "I was designated to travel with you as your head science officer a year ago."

Stacy retorted, "We weren't even here a year ago."

Thirteen stated, "Our simulations said you would be here."

Stacy mockingly said, "Your simulations predict everything?"

Thirteen replied, "Not everything. We foresaw Admiral Noem would remain on board until after the new crew was assembled. Captain Jake is far less predictable when determining future outcomes."

Stacy laughed and said, "You hear that, Jake? You're unpredictable."

Captain Jake replied, "I don't think he meant that as a complement." After a moment of hesitation, Captain Jake said, "We should get back with our new crew member."

Stacy exclaimed, "Seriously! You're letting him join the crew?"

Captain Jake said, "Melting pot mandate."

Dr. Helix said, "Thirteen has come up with a new treatment to help Kevin."

Captain Jake asked Thirteen, "Do you need a suit or something?"

Thirteen replied, "It's uncomfortable, but I can breathe your air."

Jake was about to start running back when he suddenly remembered June wasn't with them. A bead of sweat was forming on Jake's brow as he called June to let her know they were heading back.

*****

In Shell City, the passengers and crew (with the exception of Calvin) of Equality gathered in the waiting area. Although not everyone was going to be able to board until after the Thread the Needle match. Everyone wanted to be together to watch.

Irene approached Samantha and Tie then said, "Thank you for your help back there."

Samantha replied, "That guy pissed me off."

Tie said, "That guy is already playing Thread the Needle and crushing it. He already has two wins and is only a point away from a third."

Irene said, "Didn't Captain Jake give you permission to play? I don't like the thought of that man winning after what he did to Clair."

Tie replied, "Captain said we could play after he got back. He's still on the surface."

Samantha said, "This should count as extenuating circumstances. Let's just go shoot the shit out of that asshole."

Tie replied, "Davinie is in charge. You need her permission."

Samantha charged, with Tie following behind, toward Davinie, who was sitting on the other side of the room with Clair sitting on lap. As she approached, she could see that Clair was resting her head on Davinie's breast with tears rolling down her face.

Samantha pushed Tie in front of her to ask permission, but Davinie spoke first in a loud whisper. "What are you still doing here? This poor girl is in tears while that creep is out there having fun. Go kick his butt."

Tie lipped a silent "Thank you" to Davinie before the two turned around to head toward Equality.

Samantha said, "Let's go kick Ted's ass."

Tie said, "We need a plan."

Samantha replied, "I fly. You shoot Ted with the rail gun repeatedly. Plan made."

Tie stopped Samantha and said, "Equality isn't a bucketship. We need engineers with us, or we'll be done after one hit. Emily would do it, but she's on Serenity. I'll ask Filipe. I don't think Ron will do it."

Samantha replied, "Let me ask Ron. He'll help."

Tie replied, "Okay. We could still use another set of eyes on the bridge. I haven't been able to reach Calvin."

Samantha said, "What the hell! He was the one person more gung ho than you about playing." After a pause, Samantha said, "Screw it. New plan is I fly, you shoot, and the engineers keep the ship together."

"You need someone keeping track of the score and other players" came April's voice from behind them.

Frank was standing next to April and added, "You also need someone to strategize if you want to accomplish more than just occasionally bumping into Ted."

Tie cheered, "Let's do this!"

*****

Jesus was in the cockpit of Serenity and piloting it back to Shell City so Captain Jake and his crew could board Equality in order to play Thread the Needle. Captain Jake, in the meantime, was in the passenger cabin talking with Dr. Helix and Stacy.

Jesus called back to Captain Jake, "Captain, you might want to get up here."

Captain Jake entered the cockpit and asked, "What is it?"

Jesus answered, "Equality's already playing."

Captain Jake stated, "They were supposed to wait for us. Dolly, open a channel to Equality's bridge."

Dolly replied, "You got it, sweety pie."

Jesus laughed and said, "Stop asking Calvin to fix it. It's like you're begging him to make it worse."

An image popped up on the Serenity screen of Frank sitting in Equality's captain's chair. Tie and Samantha could also be seen in their seats while April was sitting at Calvin's station.

Captain Jake asked, "Why have you started without me, and where is Calvin?"

Frank replied, "Good to see you, Captain. There was an incident on Shell City that required action. Afraid waiting for you wasn't an option."

June poked her head into the cockpit of Serenity and asked with a mocking tone, "Did your precious Juliet pride get bruised?"

April answered, "It involved Clair."

June's tone turned serious as she asked, "Who we gotta kill?"

Captain Jake said, "Simmer down now. We don't have the facts yet."

April ignored Captain Jake and answered, "Cargo ship named Exterminator. Part of the red team."

Jesus asked, "Is Clair all right?"

Samantha answered, "Ted threatened to cook her for dinner. Clair cried."

June said, "We kill him now. Decide where to incinerate the body later."

Frank said, "Ted was on a winning streak at Thread the Needle. We entered to put a stop to that, but Ted has apparently been busy trash-talking the EPF to anyone who will listen. He's saying we're here to enslave them."

Captain Jake replied, "That's nonsense."

Frank said, "I know, Captain, but everyone here seems to be buying it. We can't maintain a full team or go—" Equality was suddenly struck with a rail gun shell that sent it flying uncontrollably for twenty seconds.

Filipe's voice came over the comm, shouting, "Emergency thruster canisters are almost all empty! A couple more hits, and we won't be stopping!"

May's and July's voices came over the comm and said, "Refiling as fast as we can."

Frank said, "We could really use Serenity's help, sir. We're the orange team."

Captain Jake replied, "We're on our way. Dolly, switch to audio link only. We don't need to be blocking their view."

Dolly replied, "Right away, Captain Sweety Pie." The screen went dark.

Captain Jake turned to June and said, "Can you let everyone in the passenger cabin know what's going on? Also, have Zac call his wife to get the full story on what happened. I'll head to the engine room to help Emily prep extra emergency thruster canisters."

June replied, "Right away, Captain Sweety Pie."

Captain Jake whispered to himself, "Where is Calvin?" as he headed to the engine room.

*****

A short time later, April said, "Cargo ship just left our team. It's just us and the mothership Drill er Deep."

In the lower corner of the bridge's main screen was an image of the Drill er Deep bridge focused on its captain, Mickey. Captain Mickey was a short white-haired older man. He was bald on top, but a long white beard he had banded into spikes on the sides and one long one at the bottom.

Mickey said, "If you're still low on canisters, we can meet in the corner. I have a couple extra I can send your way."

Frank said, "That would be much appreciated."

Samantha said, "I normally like getting pounded, but this is getting ridiculous. How about a plan where we don't get shot, Mr. Strategist?"

Mickey burst into laughter then said, "I like this girl. Ever been to Front Door Back Door?"

Samantha replied, "Been there. I have a standing job offer from them."

Mickey replied, "You ever start working there, you have to send me your link."

Samantha said, "Why wait? Sending it now. Hope your heart can take it."

Micky grinned and said, "In that case, you have a standing job offer from Drill er Deep as well."

Samantha got an evil look on her face then asked, "Just how deep do you drill?"

Mickey got all excited and shouted, "We drill balls!"

Frank shouted over at Mickey, "We're ready to receive those canisters now!"

Mickey got a sad look on his face then said, "Yes, give me a second."

April said, "Pink team scored their fifth point. Points are resetting and…shit! Ted just scored a point."

Tie said, "Was able to collect that last shell that struck us. It's loaded and ready to fire."

Mickey added, "I have one shell as well."

April asked, "What's the plan, Frank?"

Frank sneered an evil grin then said, "With Mickey's help, we make certain the red team wins this round."

*****

Jesus spoke over the comms. "You sure about this plan, Captain? Our plasma rockets aren't allowed. To get enough force to trigger the safety shutoff on the Exterminator's main ion engine without them, you will need to manually release our rear emergency thruster cannons at just the right moment."

Captain Jake responded, "Not to worry. I got a hold of Calvin. He wrote us a program to let us know when to hit the release on the thrusters."

June added, "Captain's got the right set, and I have the left set."

Jesus asked, "Where was Calvin?"

Captain Jake ended up having to emergency open a link to Calvin's W2 to reach him. What Captain Jake ended up seeing wasn't something he wanted to be reminded of. Captain Jake answered, "Calvin met a girl. He's still in Shell City."

Jesus said, "Entering the cube now." After a moment of silence, Jesus said, "We're part of the green team. Want me to exit and try again?"

Captain Jake answered, "No. Our team color doesn't matter with what we have planned."

*****

Ted was on the bridge of his cargo ship, the Exterminator. Ted had customized the Exterminator over the years, adding a rail gun and building emergency thruster canister holders. He also added a quick transference system, so he only needed two crew members to compete.

Ted was having the best Thread the Needle run of his life. He already earned enough points to buy five rail gun shells. Selling those to the right buyer would triple his profits for this run. The reason he was doing so well was that he got the other teams riled up against Equality. The other teams were targeting them and leaving Ted alone to score easy points.

Ted was making his run for the red team's fourth point when one of his teammates said over the comm, "Hey, Ted! I still need a point to earn reward points."

Ted replied, "There's still going to be one left after this one. There's a blue team ship trying to intercept me. Block 'em, would you?"

The player responded, "Fine, but you better let me have the last point."

Ted replied, "Sure will, mate." Ted didn't care if his teammate scored or not as long as they won the round. Of course, Ted was going to try to score himself first anyway.

Ted's third teammate yelled, "Watch out, Ted! Drill er Deep has you locked in its sights."

Ted cursed. "Mickey, you perverted old shit! You're supposed to be retiring from this game." Ted knew he was going to get shot just before scoring his fourth point. To Ted's surprise, he made it through the ring to score. Just as Ted began to rejoice, he was struck with a rail gun shell.

Once the emergency thrusters were able to slow the ship. Ted laughed and said, "Senile old bugger fired too late."

Ted's teammate said, "Ted, the Equality's preparing to fire from the same direction."

Ted shouted, "I need main engines back online!"

Ted's engineer said, "They're up."

Ted quickly turned the Exterminator to face the incoming shell. With his emergency canisters just set off on one side of his ship, another hit from that direction could send him out of the cube, forfeiting his points for the round (should they win). Ted got the Exterminator turned just in time. The shell struck, knocking out the main engine again (this kept the ship from trying to fly in multiple directions as the emergency thrusters kicked in to counter the impact). The force of the impact activated emergency release valves on thrusters pointed in the opposite direction of the impact.

Ted said, "Sly devils, but you can't beat me. Not today." Ted raised his voice and said, "Get that main engine back online."

His engineer replied, "I need a second. Engine doesn't like it when it gets kicked back off that quickly."

Outside of Ted's bridge window, he could now see Serenity barreling toward him. Ted shouted, "I need those engines now!"

The engineer said, "They're back."

Serenity struck the Exterminator, pushing it toward the out-of-bounds line. Ted attempted to push back, but the controls wouldn't respond. Ted screamed, "Where are my engines?"

The engineer responded, "That hit knocked them back offline."

Ted said, "That's impossible. A ship can't hit us hard enough to do that."

The engineer took a moment then replied, "They could if they also released their emergency canisters at the back of their ship for an extra kick."

As Ted went out-of-bounds, he looked across into Serenity's cockpit to see Jesus, Zac, and Stacy giving him the finger.

While the Exterminator was out-of-bounds, Drill er Deep blocked for Ted's red teammate who had yet to score. With this red player's score, the round was over, and Ted, being out of bounds, meant he won nothing.

At learning this, Ted said to himself, "Those cheating motherfuckers." Then in a louder tone, Ted said, "Jacky boy! Break out the cocaine. We need to celebrate."

Destroy and Kill

After the red team scored the winning point, Captain Jake said over the comms, “Great job, everyone.”

Captain Mickey joined in on the celebration and said, “That’s one hell of a way to play my last Thread the Needle match. Thank you lot for giving this old codger a bit of excitement. I’m getting out of here now before they start firing the spider cannons at us. Samantha, hope to catch up with you at Front Door Back Door.”

Samantha asked, “Do you want me to meet me in the front door or the back door?”

Captain Mickey grabbed his chest then said, “You got this old man’s blood a pumping.” Mickey stroked his beard, and the link ended.

Captain Jake realized the other ships stopped playing and asked, “What’s going on?”

Jesus asked over the comms, “What did Mickey mean by spider cannons?”

Thirteen answered over the comms, “You were clearly cheating. The godling referees are currently reviewing the footage of the match to confirm who was and was not involved before issuing the penalty. In this instance, the penalty will be loss of FP. You either willingly release our ship’s FP fields, or every ship here gets to fire their spider cannons at them.”

Captain Jake asked, "Did you know about this when you came up with the plan, Frank?"

Frank replied over the comm, "No, Captain. In King of the Hill, this sort of thing would have been legal."

Jesus exclaimed over the comm, "This isn't King of the Hill!"

April repeated Frank's words over the comms. "If it was King of the Hill, this would have been legal. Frank couldn't have known."

Samantha smugly stated over the comms, "I knew. That's why I changed course as soon as the match was over. We're on our way to pick up the crew from Shell City. They can only shoot at us if we're still in this sector of space."

April could be heard over the comms, yelling, "Psychotic slut! You should have said something!"

Captain Jake returned to the cockpit in time to hear Jesus say, "I'm following Samantha's lead."

Captain Jake said, "We don't have enough time to run."

Tie said, "Most ships don't have spider cannons."

Captain Jake asked, "Thirteen, you knew the rules. Why didn't you say anything?"

Thirteen replied, "You didn't ask."

Stacy exclaimed, "That makes it all right to get us killed?"

Thirteen replied, never changing his tone or looking up from his W2, "Relinquishing FP is not death. You have FP reserves to redeploy. Not enough for normal Carrie effect drive speed, but still enough not to have to worry about it."

Captain Jake said, "That's what we'll do, people. We screwed up. We'll pay the price."

Jesus and the rest of the crew gave a sigh of relief. Jesus said, "Well, at least they aren't trying to kill us."

The main screens of Serenity and Equality suddenly lit up with a message written in red letters that read, "Your ship and its crew have been accused of fixing and profiting from a Thread the Needle competition. You have one hour to dispute the allegations. After time has expired, there will be a destroy and kill issue ordered for your ship and its crew. All Thread the Needle matches will be suspended until this matter is resolved, or all parties are out of the Chuck Norris sector of space."

The main screen of Serenity returned to show the bridge of Equality as Captain Jake asked, "Thirteen, what is this? And how do we stop it?"

Thirteen replied, "A member of your crew must have placed a large enough wager on the match to get flagged."

Tie said, "Ships are charging spider cannons."

Captain Jake said, "I thought we had an hour?"

Thirteen stated, "That's for the destroy and kill order. The cheating infraction gets settled now."

Captain Jake said, "Dolly, captain's override. Shot off magnetic lock to release FP from Serenity and Equality."

Dolly replied, "Right away, Captain Sweety Pie."

The view out the bridge windows was typically filtered to prevent the FP shield from blocking the view. With the magnetic lock off, so was the image filter. For only the briefest second, the FP could be seen as Serenity flew through them.

Thirteen said, "We can't redeploy FP until we leave Chuck Norris space. You need to leave the crew behind on Shell City and reconnect with Equality. After that, you can use the plasma rockets to escape in time."

Zac said, "My family's on the station."

Thirteen said, "Equality and its mission are more important."

Zac got out of his seat, looking to take a swing at Thirteen who was still active on his W2.

Captain Jake shouted, "Calm down! Thirteen, are his family and the rest of the crew safer in Shell City than with us? Until we get this misunderstanding cleared up."

Thirteen answered, "Depends if the person placing the wager was on one of our ships or Shell City."

Captain Jake said, "Dolly, call Davinie and put her on speaker."

Dolly replied, "Anything for my Captain Sweety Pie."

Davinie answered, "What the hell did you fools do?"

Captain Jake replied, "You know what's going on then?"

Davinie said, "We all got alerts on W2s. Even Clair. She started to cry all over again."

Captain Jake asked, "Is there anything we can do?"

Davinie answered, "I already asked everyone here. No one placed a bet on the red team. Some people placed a bet on Equality, and they're pissed."

Captain Jake said, "No one out here bet on red either. We clear that up and the death sentence gets called off, right?"

Davinie replied, "Yes, but we still get banned from the Chuck Norris sector of space. Admiral Noem's going to be pissed at you."

Tie interjected, "You're the one who gave us permission to play."

Davinie retorted, "I gave you permission to kick Ted's butt, not rig a game people across Einstein bet on."

Captain Jake said, "It doesn't matter now. We just need to get in contact with the officials and let them know there's been a mistake."

Captain Jake could suddenly hear Calvin shouting in the background of Davinie's call, "You guys will never believe how much FP I made today. I'm rich!"

Davinie rushed over to Calvin, shouting, "You stupid son of a—"

Calvin replied, "What?"

Davinie asked, "Don't you know what's going on? Didn't you receive an alert on your W2?"

Calvin responded, "I thought it was an amber alert and shut it off. Why? What's going on?"

Captain Jake spoke to Calvin through Davinie's W2. "Do you know anything about a member of our crew betting on the red team? Ted's team. To win."

Calvin answered, "I might. See, there was this girl I met, and she said she got turned on by betting. She said she liked the red team, so I placed a wager. What's the big deal?"

Davinie replied, "The big deal is there's a death warrant on us for rigging and profiting from a Thread the Needle match."

Calvin exclaimed, "Jake! I didn't know you were rigging the match when you asked me to write that program. I thought it was to help you win."

Tie asked, "This girl…it didn't happen to be that girl who was with Ted earlier today?"

Calvin's face turned red as he answered, "Maybe."

Davinie threw her arms up in the air, exasperated. "We just got played by a space rat!"

Captain Jake said, "We can't fight it then. We are on our way back to pick you and the crew up, Davinie."

Thirteen said, "They will not let you dock. I repeat, you need to leave them behind. The flagship of the EPF is more important than a few individuals."

Zac shouted, "We are not leaving my family to die!"

Thirteen replied, "There is a chance that they die regardless."

Frank said, "We pick up the crew and we leave. Anyone trying to enforce the destroy and kill order gets blown to pieces."

Tie said, "I don't see anyone here with both plasma rockets and spider cannons. We can use our plasma rockets to get enough distance from everyone to deploy our FP reserves. After that, we can use our Carrie effect drive to clear Einstein space."

Captain Jake said, "They already have our FP. I doubt anyone is mad enough to want to destroy a ship filled with civilians and children that's leaving the area. Davinie, you and anyone wanting to come with us will have to jump out an airlock so we can pick you up."

Davinie replied, "I'm too old for this shit. Fine. I'll pass the word around."

Jesus said, "Course set. I'll be right back, Captain." Jesus left the cockpit and entered the passenger cabin where he sat down next to Thirteen. Jesus whispered, "You said if we pick up the crew from Shell City, we could all die. Out of curiosity, what's the odds on that happening?"

Thirteen replied in his normal tone, still staring down at his W2, and answered, "In a million simulations, it happened once."

Jesus was smiling when he replied, "One in a million. That's why you had me scared. You godlings are more afraid to die than I am."

Thirteen replied, "My life is already forfeit. Equality's mission is all that matters. It's not worth taking any risk for failure."

*****

After giving Ted his blowjob, Star checked her W2 and began laughing.

Ted asked, "What's so funny, babe?"

Star showed Ted her W2 and replied, "That ancient guy from earlier sent me a hookup request."

Ted laughed and said, "Make sure you don't brush your teeth before you meet up. Let him know what a real man tastes like."

Star asked, "Think I should? He's sorta famous, but he looks kinda sickly."

Ted thought for a moment then replied, "Yeah, say you have to meet up right away or not at all. Then keep him busy so he can't play Thread the Needle against me."

Star asked, "How, babe?"

Ted replied, "Handcuff him to a bedpost if you have to. Just keep him from playing in Thread the Needle. If they have to use a second-string player, then it could help me win."

Star said, "Okay, babe. If you want me to."

Ted said, "One more thing, babe. Get him to place a let it ride bet on me while I play."

Star asked, "How do I do that, babe?"

Ted replied, "Tell him gambling is a turn-on for you. Get him to bet as much as you can, babe."

Star replied, "Sure, babe, but why? You are going to win, so why do you want him to make money?"

Ted replied, "If I win while he's screwing my babe, he may think he's the one who won. If his shipmates find out that's why he wasn't playing, they may even consider that a win for them. However, if ancient boy turns a profit by betting against his team." Ted laughed and said, "They're going to fucking hate him."

Star asked, "How will they find out he bet against them, babe?"

Ted replied, "Their ship Equality is military grade. That means any unusual bets by their crew members automatically get flagged. A notification will get sent to the ship after the match."

*****

After Equality left Chuck Norris space unassailed, they set course for Chronos along the third ring. Before Captain Jake could send Admiral Noem a report on what transpired, he received an encoded message from Admiral Noem.

The video showed Admiral Noem sitting behind her desk as she said, "Woke up today to good news. The new volunteer patrol ship Eagle One made its first patrol last night. They managed to scare off some pirates who were about to collect their reward after disabling a cargo ship's Carrie effect drive. That's great PR. Then tonight, I turned on my news feed to find out that the EPF flagship Equality participated in a game of Thread the Needle. A game, for whatever reason, you rigged so another team could win. This action caused a destroy and kill order to be placed on you and Equality." Admiral Noem softened her tone as she continued, "I heard you made it out safe without any casualties. That's what matters most, Jake. I also saw the footage of you dumping your FP. For the moment, Chuck Norris is lost to the EPF, but there are three major colonies on the outer rings. You can't be seen running away, Jake. I'm sorry. I know it would be safer to return to the inner rings for a resupply of FP, but you need to stay there for now. Hades is closest to purchase more FP. Have Harry work on a PR campaign. I'm sure you had your reasons for doing what you did, and I can't wait to read that report. Stay safe, Jake."

Harry started his PR campaign, which included interviewing Clair over what happened that day at the pizzeria. Eventually, Captain Jake had to give a public apology for his ignorance of the rules of Thread the Needle and letting emotions get in the way of reason. Details of Calvin sleeping with Ted's girlfriend were left out of the news casts.

The journey to Hades would have normally taken a week at normal FP levels. It was taking Equality ten days at their reduced levels.

On the seventh day of the journey, Captain Jake was sitting alone on the bridge, streaming news feeds from Hades City. Captain Jake came across a news story that at first shocked him but then gave him hope. He immediately sent a coded message to Admiral Noem. Once she responded, Captain Jake called for an officers' meeting so they could all see their next mission.

*****

Ted's metal arm was a byproduct of the criminal justice system of Hades City. All crimes there were dealt with in the livestreaming battle arena. All criminals battled in giant mechanized battle suits, needing to accumulate a certain amount of damage dealt against their opponents to earn their freedom. Proceeds from the match went to pay the victims for damages received, and if a contestant does well enough, they, too, receive a portion of the profits.

Although considered safe, accidents in the battle arena were a common occurrence. Ted's crime was not paying child support (Ted didn't see why he had to pay for children he never met). Ted did well enough in his match to pay for his new upgraded arm as well as make a down payment on his ship, the SS Exterminator.

Ted took great joy in the capabilities of his new left metal arm. Ted would even carry around rocks with him when he went to the bar. This was so he could crush them in his hand to impress whatever woman he was trying to get with that night. To keep from accidentally crushing someone's hand or accidentally destroying a device like his W2, Ted had a countdown limiter placed on his metal arm.

To Ted, this countdown limiter was an aphrodisiac. When one of his girlfriends (Ted had one on several different planets and space stations) got out of line, Ted would grab them by the arm with his metal prosthetic and begin to squeeze. As they screamed out in pain, Ted would start his countdown from five. His girlfriends—knowing that when Ted reached one, their bones would be crushed—would quickly begin to plead and apologize for whatever infraction they might have committed. Ted would feel such a rush of power from this that it was almost always followed up with sex (regardless of the tears streaming down his girlfriends' face).

Ted considered it a personal victory to get a destroy and kill order placed on Equality. He and his crew celebrated the whole four-day trip (Ted didn't believe in speed limits) back to Hades. This celebration consisted of alcohol and several different illegal recreational drugs. Little to no sleep was had by Ted the entire journey home. Once Ted returned to Hades City, he was feeling the need to get laid. Ted's girlfriend in Hades City was Theresa.

Theresa was a blond twice the size of Star. Ted considered her a far better lay, but not nearly as obedient as Star. Ted lost count of how many times he had to grab hold of Theresa's arm and start a countdown to remind her who he was. Ted realized this was probably also the reason he found her to be the better lay.

Ted didn't call that evening before arriving at Theresa's. The last of Ted's cocaine was keeping him wide awake as he popped a Viagra before entering her home. Ted also brought along a couple of ecstasy pills to ensure Theresa would be prepared to celebrate with him all night long.

As Ted approached, the front door recognized him and opened automatically. Once the door opened, Ted could hear sounds from within. Once inside, Ted followed these sounds to the kitchen.

Ted now recognized the noises he heard as sounds of passion as he slowly crept toward the kitchen. Ted stood in the kitchen archway, watching Theresa being bent over the kitchen table. Theresa screamed, "Pull my hair!"

The man, with his back to Ted plowing into Theresa, grabbed hold of Theresa's long blond hair with his left hand while slapping Theresa's ass with his right hand and asked, "You like that, my whore?"

Theresa screamed in delight, "I love being your whore!"

Ted now recognized this man as his supposed friend, Scotty. Anger was now building up inside of Ted. Not because Theresa was cheating on him. Ted didn't care who else she screwed. No. Ted was angry because Theresa said she was somebody's whore. Ted decided he was going to remind Theresa that she was Ted's whore.

Ted marched up to Scotty, grabbing him by the back of the neck with his metal hand. Ted slowly pulled Scotty backward.

Theresa said, "Ow! My hair. Not so hard, babe."

Ted shouted, "Five!"

Theresa flipped over, turning white as a ghost as she saw Ted. It was a look that always turned Ted on. Scotty tilted his head slightly backward to see Ted. A look of terror was in his eye. Ted found this feeling of power exhilarating as he said, "Four."

Scotty muttered something about it hurting while Theresa was shaking her head no. Ted began to have flashbacks of all the times Theresa would make that face before Ted would shove his dick in her mouth to shut her up. Ted could feel the Viagra kicking in as he gently said, "Three."

Scotty tried to squirm free, but Ted's robotic grip held firm. Theresa began to plead with Ted to stop, but this heightened Ted's feeling of superiority. Ted didn't even realize he was still holding on to Scotty as he softly said, "Two."

Theresa began to cry as she pleaded with Ted to let Scotty go. She knew by the sight of Ted's bloodshot eyes that Ted wasn't in his right mind.

Watching tears run down Theresa's face onto her exposed breasts was the final aphrodisiac. Ted could feel himself cumming as he whispered, "One."

Hades City

Captain Jake held an officers' meeting and played Admiral Noem's video. Admiral Noem was sitting behind her desk and said, "I'm sorry you can't go to Chronos, Jake. I am looking into it on my end, and I'm sending more jet arm drones to their moon base to increase patrols for now. In the meantime, I have a new mission for you. I contacted the Hades City government as you suggested, and they are open to the possibility of commuting Ted's sentence to life on Titan. When you get to Hades City, Davinie will need to meet them in person to iron out the details. Harry has done good work to salvage our reputation. Ted has done even more with his actions, as wrong as they were. I'm sure I don't need to tell you to be on your best behavior this time. And don't do anything without checking with Davinie first. She's there to keep you out of trouble in this new world, Jake. Listen to her, and stay safe."

Stacy asked, "Who the fuck did Ted kill?"

Captain Jake answered, "His girlfriend's lover."

Everyone turned to look at Calvin.

Captain Jake clarified, "Different girlfriend, and different lover."

Stacy asked Calvin, "Have you been tested yet?"

Dr. Helix answered, "No. He hasn't."

Calvin replied, "I have home testing kits."

Davinie began reading Ted's file. "According to this, Ted killed Scotty of Omega Mining. Scotty was doing Theresa of Hades City in her home at the time. Toxicology report has Ted's blood alcohol level at triple the legal limit. Not to mention he was suffering from sleep deprivation and half a dozen recreational drugs including cocaine, acid, pot, and Viagra. In the inner rings, this would be clear-cut temporary insanity. Ted would get sentenced to a nanite injection that nullified all recreational drugs and alcohol. It's nothing that warrants the death sentence, regardless of how big of an ass Ted is."

Stacy replied, "He's the reason we got a destroy and kill order issued on us at Chuck Norris."

Frank stated, "It was my actions that caused that."

Stacy said, "He started it."

Frank asked, "Why are we helping him?"

Harry answered, "It's good PR to help our enemy. Shows we have a heart."

Stacy asked Captain Jake, "Does Hades City have animals? You promised me animals."

Harry answered for Captain Jake, "Yes, they do."

Stacy let out a squeal of joy.

Captain Jake said, "We can't risk another incident on the outer ring. There might be people here who lost FP because of us and want payback."

Frank said, "I can send some security personnel down as escorts."

Stacy repeated, "You promised, Jake."

Captain Jake said, "Fine. You can go down as long as you stay with Davinie and her security team."

Filipe said, "Can I go as well? I want to pick up some drones that they only sell here. Very advanced."

Captain Jake replied, "As long as you stay together."

Frank said, "We have three entrepreneurs wanting to leave Equality while we're here. Are they allowed?"

Captain Jake replied, "This isn't a prison. They can uber a ride off Equality anytime they want. Although I am sad to see them go."

Frank replied, "I don't believe it's permanent, Captain. Also, although several applicants have withdrawn their applications to join Equality, there are plenty to comb through. I'm having trouble finding candidates who can pass their background checks."

Davinie said, "It's there stupid justice system. Commit a crime to earn a chance at fame and fortune."

Tie said, "Not all crime. Murder someone like Ted did, and it's instant death sentence."

Captain Jake said, "We are here to show acceptance, not judgment. Our mandate is to become a melting pot with citizens from every sector of space. Frank, you will need to be laxer in your background checks to accommodate. You have permission to conduct truth serum interviews. Let candidates know of the change before they make the trip here."

*****

Equality approached the glass dome city on the moon orbiting Hades. Hades was a volcanic planet too hot to colonize, but the view of the planet brought many to colonize the glass dome known as Hades City.

Equality stopped to take a stationary orbit above the moon so its courtyard shops could open for business. As Captain Jake sat alone on the bridge, he looked out to see two gigantic robots. Captain Jake opened up the ship's comms and said, "There are two giant robots duking it out on the moon's surface if anyone wants to watch."

One of the robots was painted blue, and the other red. Both appeared to be sliding rather than walking as they moved to throw jabs at each other like the kid's game Rock 'em Sock 'em robots. Finally, the blue robot struck the red robot, launching its head high up into the air just like the toy version. Unlike the toy version, a black dot seemed to get ejected out the top.

Captain Jake said, "Dolly, zoom in on whatever that dot is."

Dolly replied with a sexy voice, "Anything for you, Captain." The screen changed to show a man wearing a jetpack being flung into the air.

Stacy's voice came over the comms, screaming, "We are playing, Jake!"

Captain Jake replied, “Go this trip without getting into any trouble, and we can play before we leave.”

Stacy stated, “Prepare to fly, beeauch!”

*****

Serenity landed next to the glass dome that held Hades City. The base of the dome was surrounded with easy airlock ports that allowed Serenity to try out its own newly installed easy airlock.

The away group for this mission was supposed to consist of Davinie, Stacy, and Filipe with June and July going as the security detail (power attire was banned, so the sisters only brought drill darts with them). May, Emily, Zac, and Jesus were to stay aboard Serenity on guard duty. Stacy decided Jesus and Emily needed to join her to help pick out animals on the ride down. Davinie said she had no objections as long as the group stayed together.

Once inside, the glass dome Hades City looked like a typical city. The roads were paved with electric cars bustling about. There was even a yellow electric hummer with the word *Taxi* painted in black along the side waiting for them.

The taxi driver was a large older woman with a scarred cheek and two metal arms. “Where to?” she asked in a deep and almost artificial voice.

Davinie answered, “I need to get to the municipal building.”

As the taxi drove, they looked out the window to see the city. The major divergence between this city and the cities from back on Earth appeared to be that every other person they saw seemed to have a mechanical prosthetic of some sort.

Stacy asked, “What’s up with all the metal prosthetics?”

Davinie answered, “Barbaric justice system.”

Stacy said, “I remember you saying something about that, but why metal instead of organic?”

The taxi driver remarked on their conversation in her artificial voice. “There’s nothing wrong with our justice systems. You softies just can’t understand what it is to be strong.”

June replied, “Careful who you call a softie.”

Davinie snapped at June, "No incidents this trip."

June reluctantly apologized. "Sorry for my tone, ma'am."

The taxi driver scoffed, "Soft."

They reached the heart of the city where the municipal building was located and exited the cab, wanting to walk around from there.

Davinie told the group, "This will probably take all day. I'll call you when I'm finished. Don't get into any trouble."

The group promised they wouldn't, and Davinie went inside.

As they walked, Filipe asked, "Where to first? Drone shop or pet store?"

While the group pondered this question, Stacy caught sight of a bar. Stacy stopped and stared at the bar as she asked, "Wonder what kind of drinks they have in Hades?"

Filipe replied, "I came to buy drones."

Emily said, "I think hydration could aid us in our search for drones."

Stacy grabbed Filipe's arm, batted her eyes, then said, "Just one. Please?"

Jesus said, "I could have one."

Emily replied, "No, you can't. You're designated driver."

Jesus replied, "The hell I am. That's Dolly's job."

July said, "I wonder if they have anything fruity?"

June stated, "We're on duty."

July copied Stacy's action, grabbing June's arm and batting her eyes as she asked, "Just one. *Please*?"

June replied, "Only if Filipe agrees."

July instantly let go of June's arm and grabbed ahold of Filipe's other arm.

Filipe looked from July to Stacy as both were holding an arm and batting their eyes at him. Filipe had no choice but to say, "Just one."

They entered the bar named Red Oasis to find it mostly empty. Only a couple of patrons were sitting down to lunch. At the foot of the bar was a Doberman pinscher with a metal dome covering its head. The dog was licking out of a saucer as it lay on the floor.

Stacy immediately lit up at the sight of the dog running up to pet him. The moment Stacy's hand touched the back of the dog, she heard a strong male voice say, "Who…the…hell…wants…to… lose…a…hand?"

Stacy jumped back, startled. As the dog turned to look at Stacy, she could see that the dog was wearing a pair of sunglasses. The sunglasses appeared to have lines of writing that were changing. Stacy inched back closer, noticing the dog's front legs were replaced with metal prosthetics. The prosthetic limbs had small hands with three fingers and a thumb instead of paws.

The dog said, "Oh!" It looked Stacy up and down then said, "You're…cute. You…may…pet…me…all…you…like."

Stacy's eyes went wide, then she exclaimed, "A talking dog! You got to be fucking me!"

The dog replied, "Name's…Rex. You're…not…my…species… but…buy…me…a…few…rounds…and…we…will…see what… happens."

Filipe said, "Guess they didn't have talking animals in your time. Those shades he's wearing have keyboards that track his eye movement. He blinks whenever he wants to click on something. That metal cap on his head is the processor and has speakers."

July added, "They're pretty common on Juliet."

Stacy exclaimed, "They're that smart!"

June scoffed. "The ability to talk doesn't make them smart."

Rex raised a prosthetic front leg, extending his mechanical middle finger at June, and said, "That…smart…enough…for…you?"

June said to the bartender, "Mutt's next round is on me."

July bent down, gave Rex a hug, and said, "Does that mean we can keep him?"

Rex replied, "I'm…no…pet…crazy…lady." After July let go, Rex looked up to see her face then said, "Wait." Rex turned to look at June then said, "Twins."

July, in her always overly cheery voice, said, "Quadruplets, actually. Our sisters are back on our ships. Want to reconsider being our pet now?"

Rex replied, "I'm…no…pet." Then after a short pause, he said, "But…I…am…looking…for…work. Ships…you…say?"

Stacy answered, "Yep. And I'm here to do some hiring for agriculture. You any good at farming?"

Rex replied, "If…you're…asking…a…dog…if…he…can…dig…a…hole…to…bury…something…the…answer…is…yes."

July yelled, "Hey! He's clearly the coolest guard dog ever! Rex should join security."

Rex replied, "I…don't…shy…from…a…fight…but…I'm…no…guard…dog."

Stacy gleefully stated, "That settles it. Agriculture for Rex."

June said to July, "Don't pout. He's going to be in the courtyard for you to visit every day."

Rex said, "I…haven't…agreed…yet." Rex took a few licks of beer from his bowl then asked, "What's…the…pay? And…is…there…booze…on…your…ships?"

Jesus said, "Starting pay, I believe, is two times the minimum wage on Middleman."

Rex's ears perked up at hearing this.

Filipe said, "I'm officially in Hades City to pick up some drones. Unofficially, I'm here to pick up some parts I need to complete a still that I've been working on in engineering."

Emily interjected, "More like a still that I've been working on."

Filipe retorted, "I started it."

Rex asked, "Engineering…hiring?"

Stacy slapped Rex in the side of the neck then said, "They're not hiring. I am, you ungrateful mutt. Who do you think they're going to be getting the hoops from to run their still?"

Rex yelped then said, "Fine…agriculture…it…is."

June pulled July to the side then whispered, "Think you and Rex can handle things here? There's something I want to check out without Mother April knowing."

July said, "Yeah, sure, but I want details later."

June smiled then said, "You got it. Thanks, sis."

*****

Serenity merged with Equality late that evening. Captain Jake heard slurring in Jesus's voice when he called to get permission to dock. This didn't surprise Captain Jake since Stacy was there. Captain Jake imagined the whole away crew ended up at a bar, so Captain Jake waited in the courtyard by the entrance for Serenity. Captain Jake wanted to watch them do the walk of shame as they tried to hide their drinking binge from him.

First to come up on the lift were May and Filipe with crates of supplies. May nodded to Captain Jake then rushed off. Jake heard May get on her W2 and ask, "April, where are you?"

Filipe was avoiding eye contact with Captain Jake. Filipe immediately started to clear the cargo from the lift so it could go back down to raise the others. Captain Jake moved in to help Filipe clear the lift. Captain Jake instantly smelled the medical grade menthol doctors gave to alcoholic patients to remove the stench of alcohol as they worked.

Captain Jake said, "May was moving pretty fast. She must not have joined you guys at the bar."

Filipe paused for a second then continued to move crates then said, "No, she wasn't. I'm sorry, Captain."

Captain Jake said, "I know how Stacy is. If I was there, I would have gotten dragged to the bar with you."

The lift lowered back into Serenity as Filipe walked off silently, taking a crate with him. The lift then returned, this time carrying Stacy, Emily, Zac, Jesus, and a half metal Doberman pinscher wearing sunglasses.

Captain Jake said, "Guess you found your animal."

Rex responded, "I'm…no…one's…pet."

Captain Jake was taken aback as he replied, "I didn't say you were a pet." Captain Jake noticed the strong stench of alcohol coming from the dog.

Everyone was refusing to make eye contact with Captain Jake. Stacy said, "We're even now, Jake. Come on, guys. Let's take these crates to engineering for Filipe."

The lift lowered and returned carrying Davinie and July.

July had a look of terror in her eyes as she frantically looked about. July asked, "Is April here?"

Captain Jake responded, "Ahh. No. Where's June?"

Davinie answered, "There was an incident at an establishment called Front Door Back Door."

Captain Jake shook his head no then said, "That's impossible. Samantha was with us."

Davinie replied, "No, Captain, it was—"

"July!" echoed throughout the courtyard as April sprinted toward them with a look of rage on her face.

July grabbed Captain Jake, hiding behind him as a shield. July pleaded, "Please don't let her kill me."

April stopped in front of them, clutching a drill dart in her hand. April yelled, "Tell me why you let June leave her post before I jam this drill dart down your throat!"

July squeezed Captain Jake as if holding on for dear life and pleaded again, "Don't let her kill me."

Captain Jake replied, "She can't kill you with a tranq dart."

July replied, "That drill dart isn't a tranquilizer."

Captain Jake asked, "What's going on?"

Davinie held her head slightly lowered as she answered, "June has been arrested in Hades City. Charged with rape."

Captain Jake reiterated, "June was raped?"

July, in a slightly proud voice, stated, "Nope, my sister was the one doing the raping."

April inched forward, causing July to sulk back behind Captain Jake.

Captain Jake asked July, "Did you and the others witness this?"

July got an awkward smile on her face then replied, "Well, see—"

Davinie explained, "After I left the group to enter the municipal building, they decided to stop at the Red Oasis bar right across the street. They stayed there all day getting drunk, except for June, who ducked out."

July said, "They said we were only going to stop for one."

Captain Jake asked, "What about the supplies you just brought aboard? And the android dog? You had to have left the bar at some point."

Davinie explained, "They met the booze hound Rex at the bar. Rex talked them into ordering everything online so they could keep drinking at the bar."

July said, "If you think about it, we were actually being very efficient."

Davinie said, "We have to wait until morning before we can see June. That's when we'll get June's side of the story."

Captain Jake said, "I can't believe June raped anyone. Shouldn't her W2 contact lens feed have exonerated her?"

April got a frustrated look on her face then holstered her drill dart before stomping off.

Davinie, in a gentle tone, said, "June's W2 feed is how they know she's guilty."

*****

The next morning, April, Davinie, and Captain Jake were escorted to an interview room in the Hades City jail. Inside the interview room was June handcuffed to a desk.

April angrily asked, "What the hell was going through that brain of yours?"

June looked at Captain Jake and asked, "Why'd you have to bring her?"

April replied, "I'm still your legal mother, or did you forget?"

June looked at Davinie then said, "You're a lawyer. Is there a way to get unadopted?"

April began to explode. "After all I did!"

Davinie interjected, "Calm down or get out!"

April shut her mouth, pulled out a chair, and then slammed it down before sitting down. Davinie and Captain Jake sat down in a calmer fashion. Davinie then asked, "Are they treating you all right, sweety?"

June nodded then said, "Yeah."

Davinie asked, "Can you walk us through what happened?"

June focused her gaze on Davinie as she spoke. "I've heard a lot of stories about this place called Front Door Back Door. I was just curious to see."

Davinie said, "That place is infamous, girl. I've heard plenty of stories myself."

June said, "All true and more."

Davinie said, "From the beginning. Don't leave out any details."

June began to tell her story. "I walked in to find two doors to choose from. Door on the left was labeled front, and the door on the right was labeled with a picture of a butt. I don't do butt stuff, so I went through the front door. That took me down a corridor leading to two more doors. One had an image of dancing men and the other an image of dancing women. I went for the dancing men. I ordered a drink as I checked out the merchandise. They were all fit, but there was this one guy. I'm talking surgically altered, ribbed for my pleasure."

April whispered, "Slut."

Davinie said to April, "Last warning. Next time, you leave the room." Davinie then said to June, "Please continue."

June said, "After I paid the upfront price, he led me to a room. The room looked cheap and kinda tacky, but I only paid for an hour. They guarantee the hour or your money back. I was determined to put that to the test. Soon as we got in there, I threw him down on the bed. I won't let a man ride me anyways, but I got on top. I gave him every move I had. It was a personal best for me."

Davinie noticed Captain Jake looking uncomfortable at the topic and said, "Can we get to the part where this turns into rape?"

April asked, "How can you rape a prostitute who's already accepted payment?"

Davinie answered, "No means no regardless. June, please continue."

June continued, "So we were going at it, and the hour was about up. I wanted to get him to finish before the hour was up to get my money back, so I cranked up my grind to eleven. This guy was getting close. I could see it. Then suddenly, he says stop, but he was smiling when he said it. I figured he just didn't want me to have to give me back my money, so I went harder, driving him home. The guy came hard. That's when the bouncers busted in, claiming their employee was being raped."

Davinie said, "I've heard of this before. It's a shakedown tactic. They get you on tape refusing to stop then threaten to call the cops. Unless you turn over half of your current checking account balance to them."

April asked, "How can it be rape if he's smiling when he says stop and gets off?"

Davinie answered, "The law is clear. No means no and stop means stop. It doesn't matter how you say it or how much someone comes."

April said, "Fine. Then my stupid slut of a daughter pays. If she doesn't have enough, I'll pay the rest. Let's get it done and get out of here."

Captain Jake asked, "If it was a shakedown, why are we here? You said the victim gets shook down before the cops are called."

Davinie replied, "That's not always the way it happens. In cases where the victim is famous, they make more money by letting the victim fight in the battle arena. The more famous the victim, the more people purchase the pay per view. The bigger the victim's cut from the match. June is a famous quadruplet sister."

April slammed her fists on the table.

June said, "It's fine, April. I'll kick so much ass that I'll walk away rich myself."

April replied, "You don't get it, you stupid slut. This stays on your record. Admiral Noem will have no choice but to kick you out of the EPF. After all the trouble I went through to bring us together. After all the effort you, May, and July did to get into the Romeo Security forces. Now after this, we'll be broken up."

Captain Jake replied, "No one's kicked out yet. We can have Harry work on a PR campaign to set the record straight. Expose the corruption that Hades City's justice system has created."

Davinie stated, “I’m on track to get Ted’s sentence commuted. Start a PR campaign against Hades City justice system, and our mission is over.”

Captain Jake stated, “Our crew comes first.”

Davinie added, “June’s battle arena trial has already been set for two days from now.”

Captain Jake remarked, “So soon?”

Davinie explained, “Video evidence of the crime gets it fast-tracked. We could get it delayed a day if we ask for a truth serum appeal. But after what June had to say, I don’t see that helping. Admiral Noem also has another mission for Equality once Ted is in our custody.”

June said, “Don’t throw away everything that the EPF has been working for. I’m a fighter, Captain. Let me fight.”

Captain Jake replied, “Okay. In two days, you fight, but you’re returning with us when we leave.”

Davinie said, “I can have things finalized with Ted by then, but June has to do at least 40 percent of the total damage in her match to earn her release. If she doesn’t, there’s no telling when the next match could be.”

April stated, “That won’t be a problem.”

*****

Ted sat in his cell, staring at the bars. A guard wearing an exoskeleton suit arrived pushing a food cart. The guard asked, “Ready for your last meal, Ted?”

Ted licked his lips and replied, “It’s the only thing I’ve been thinking about since I got here.”

Sitting on the cart was a sheathed sawsword along with a twenty-ounce steak. The guard drew the blue chained sawsword from its sheath then said, “I never understood why so many of you choose this as your last meal.”

The guard placed the sawsword on top of the sheath and then fired his spider pistol at the sawsword. The sawsword began to glow red. The sound of sizzling meat filled the room once the guard placed the steak on the sawsword.

Ted explained, "Before I ran cargo, I was a miner. Every asteroid needed dozens of survey samples done before you could say with any certainty that it was good or worthless. You could end up spending weeks out there just surveying. Bucketships don't have shit for amenities. But what they did have was a culture grower and bio printer. After a long day, there was nothing better than warming up your bucketship with a spider pistol shot as you cooked your dinner."

The guard asked, "Want any seasoning?"

Ted replied, "No need. Cooking with the sawsword gives the meat a special something you can't get any other way."

The guard fired his spider pistol at the sawsword a second time. Ted could now smell the meat cooking, and it made his mouth water with anticipation. The guard asked, "How do you like it?"

Ted replied, "Medium with a little blood left in it."

The guard's W2 beeped. The guard answered the call then nodded as he listened. The guard said, "Understood." He then slid the steak off the sawsword onto a plate. He then shook grease off his sawsword before returning it to its sheath on top of the cart. The guard then began to spin the cart around to leave.

Ted asked, "Where the hell are you going with my steak?"

The guard paused to pick up the steak with his exoskeleton hand. He then blew on it a couple times before saying, "You just got a stay of execution. Seems some ship from that new EPF is here to get you sent to Titan."

Ted said, "Seriously? I heard they had a mothership patrolling the inner rings. I didn't know they had one out here already." The guard took a big bite out of the steak. Ted asked, "How's my dinner taste?"

The guard replied while chewing, "You're right. The sawsword does give it a special something. It's not a mothership. It's the flagship Equality. I hear you've already met."

Ted smiled and said, "The ones I got a destroy and kill order placed on are here to save me." Ted began to laugh uncontrollably.

The guard walked away and said, "Laugh while you can. It's a long way to Titan if you make it. Oh, and don't worry. I'll come back with some oatmeal for your dinner."

Battle Arena

June only had two days of training as she stood wearing her ten-foot-tall battle suit. The left arm of her suit was a high-pressure cannon that fired cannonballs which could be found throughout the arena. The right arm of the suit from the elbow on was a giant sawsword with a pink diamond chain.

All battle suits were painted to represent their user. Harry suggested that they have June's battle suit painted with the letters *EPF*. Harry said that if June does well, it would actually help the EPF gain popularity in the outer rings. Captain Jake agreed, wanting to show June that they supported her (although leaving this detail out of his report to Admiral Noem).

June now stood staring at a concrete wall, waiting for the match to begin.

*****

April, Davinie, and Captain Jake were standing in a sports booth above the battle arena. The rest of the crew remained aboard the ships, watching the match as a group.

Finally, the announcer came on the screen. One look and you could tell that he was a past contestant. Both his arms were mechanical prosthetics with several small scars on his face. He had long blond hair and was wearing sunglasses that he immediately ripped off his face.

The announcer stared intensely into the camera and said, "Slice and Dice Pete here to bring you another exciting, heart pounding Hades City brand of justice battle arena three-way matchup!" There was a sound reel in the background that started to play sounds of a crowd cheering.

Samantha said, "I have wanted to do that man since I watched his first match."

Stacy asked, "Can you name a man you haven't wanted to do?"

Samantha noticed May standing close by, looking at her, and answered, "I don't only do men."

May quickly looked away as her face turned red.

Slice and Dice Pete (Slice for short) continued, "First up is Pickax Max. Convicted for a third time of claim jumping. If you recall, Pickax Max here lost his leg in his first match, but since then, he's been an unstoppable menace." Clips began to run in the background of Pickax Max's previous matches.

Pickax Max's battle suit was painted with an illustration of a man burying his pickax into a skull. Slice said, "This slayer of bots would be my pick to win if not for our criminal scum bucket."

A clip of a battle suit with a black belt painted on it as well as ninja stars where a person's nipples would be started to play. The clip showed the ninja painted suit cutting off the legs of another battle suit.

Rex said, "June's...screwed."

Stacy replied, "You never got to see June fight."

Rex said, "No...but...I've...seen...him...fight. June's... screwed."

Slice continued, "Jerrad the Drunk." A soundtrack of boos played in the background. Slice continued, "Yes, he's back. Convicted of yet another case of spousal abuse. Reminder, repeat offenders can't earn a profit from the battle arena matches regardless of how well they do. The victims of domestic violence also don't receive any profit shares from their match. Instead, their proceeds go directly to battered women shelters. If the victim decides to leave the dirtbag, she will have relocation funds waiting for her. This goes for all victims of spousal abuse. That said, I hope somebody wrecks Jarred. In Jerrad's last match, he left unscathed with a record setting 82 percent damage dealt." A soundtrack played boos in the background.

Emily was sitting in the courtyard aboard Equality with her husband, Randolf, and son, Johnny, watching the match with the crowd. Emily said, "June better wreck that asshole."

Randolf said, "I've seen June train. That Jerrad's in for a reckoning of a lifetime."

Johnny asked, "Can I go compete in the battle arena sometime?"

Emily and Randolf replied simultaneously, "No!"

The picture changed to show a battle suit with EPF written on it. The crowd stood up and cheered.

Slice said, "Last up is someone we've all heard about. She's one of the famous cloned quadruplet sisters from Juliet. Now a member of the Einstein Protection Force serving aboard SS Equality. A ship that just recently had a destroy and kill order placed on it by the Chuck Norris system for rigging a Thread the Needle match." The soundtrack played a round of boos in the background.

Slice continued, "This quadruplet sister, June, has been convicted of..." Slice stared at the teleprompter for a minute. Slice shook his head then pulled out a pair of reading glasses to read the teleprompter better. Finally, Slice said, "This can't be right." Slice then held his hand over his ear, nodding as if someone was talking to him.

Slice announced, "It's true, folks. June the quadruple terror has been convicted of rape against one Melvin of Hades City. This guy clearly doesn't like sex, folks. June, I'm sending you my contact link. Next time you feel the urge to commit this heinous crime, I'll be your victim."

Harry pumped his fist then said, "Couldn't have written that better myself."

A buzzer sounded, and the giant doors to the battle arena opened.

June wasted no time. She already knew the layout was a barren cavern with random twelve-foot-tall walls scattered about. The walls got shifted in between every match.

The battle arena was one square mile with each player having a radar to tell them where the other players were. It did not, however, tell them which player was which. Each player also had a vanish button that would remove the player from radar for a limited time. To help cancel this effect, each player was also given one phone a friend that could be used to speak with their family and friends watching from the sports booth above the arena.

June placed the tip of her cannon arm over a cannonball lying near the entrance. June then pressed the switch labeled Load to suck up the cannonball. June then pressed the button labeled Phone a Friend and asked, "Where?"

April replied, "Ten o'clock." June hung up.

June hit her vanish button before she moved quickly toward her ten o'clock. The plan was to eliminate the weakest player first in order to focus on the tougher opponent. After running for a few minutes, June rounded a wall section to see Pickax Max a hundred feet in front of her, pointing his cannon at her. June also noticed an extra shell setting in front of him. June never slowed her pace as she charged Pickax Max.

Pickax Max fired his cannon arm at June.

June did a spin move to avoid the cannonball while losing little momentum as she pressed on.

Pickax Max lowered his cannon arm to load the cannonball lying in front of him. June quickly fired her cannonball at that one. The cannonball at Max's feet was sent flying back at him, glancing off his right leg. Max instinctively looked down at his mechanical leg to check for damage. That was Max's first and last mistake.

June took advantage of Max's distraction by planting her cannon arm in the ground to use it to pole-vault into the air. June then brought her pink chained sawsword arm crashing down over Pickax Max's head. The sawsword grinded through Pickax Max's battle suit like a hot knife through butter. The sawsword stopped inches above Max's organic head as safety protocols kicked in to prevent his death (although several pieces of metal came crashing in on Max, causing several minor cuts).

It took June a moment to yank her sawsword arm free. The nearest cannonball she saw was in the direction Jerrad the Drunk was coming (according to radar). Suddenly, June's radar went blank, although she could hear Jerrad the Drunk still approaching.

June made a dash for the cannonball, hoping to get it loaded before Jerrad the Drunk arrived. June reached the cannonball and hit the load switch, but nothing happened. June looked at her battle suit's status to see it was registering 10 percent damage taken. June then looked down at the barrel of her cannon arm to see a crack had formed. June said to herself, "Piece of shit must have cracked from the somersault. Without a vacuum seal, I can't load a cannonball."

Jerrad the Drunk rounded a corner, catching June off guard. He swung his blue chained sawsword at June the Quadruple Terror. June was barely able to sidestep and evade. June then half-heartedly raised her cannon arm at Jerrad the Drunk, who quickly sliced off the barrel's tip.

June looked at the tip of her cannon arm, which was now missing the cracked section while now having a tip she could use for a thrusting attack. June said, "Thank you" to herself as communications between players were banned.

Jerrad the Drunk again caught June off guard by leaping backward in the air while firing his cannon arm at June. The cannonball struck June the Quadruple Terror in the top right chest plate and shoulder area.

The impact pushed the metal of June's safety cage in on her right arm. June could no longer feel her right arm. This meant she could no longer use her sawsword arm, and her cannon arm could no longer shoot.

June wanted to charge Jerrad the Drunk while he was down, but the distance was too great. Jerrad would be up and slicing her in half before she could get a blow in. June knew she needed to get a blow in. Damaging her own suit while taking out Pickax Max would take away from her damage percentage. June knew she had to reach 40 percent of total damage dealt or risk getting left behind by Equality.

June moved quickly to get on the backside of the large brick wall Jerrad the Drunk used to conceal his approach. June then stood there, watching and waiting for Jerrad the Drunk to approach.

Jerrad the Drunk, seeing how damaged June the Quadruple Threat's battle suit was, didn't hesitate to go after her. Once he was close enough, June the Quadruple Threat jumped into the air, kicking at the top half of the brick wall.

Pieces of brick went flying at Jerrad the Drunk, causing a distraction that June the Quadruple Threat used to lunge at Jerrad the Drunk with her improvised bayonet cannon arm.

Jerrad the Drunk tilted to avoid, but he wasn't fast enough as June the Quadruple Threat lodged her makeshift bayonet into Jerrad the Drunk's cannon arm's shoulder.

Jerrad the Drunk wasted on time cutting off the bottom section of June's left mechanical leg, barely missing her real foot. June the Quadruple Threat then fell backward, her bayonet pulling free from Jerrad the Drunk's shoulder.

Jerrad the Drunk took his time after that, slowly dismantling June the Quadruple Threat until her battle suit reached 100 percent damage.

*****

April, Davinie, and Captain Jake were only able to watch from the battle arena sports box as Jerrad the Drunk chopped up June's battle armor into little pieces.

April said, "I'm going to kill that Jerrad."

Davinie said, "No, you not. We don't need to replay this scenario."

Captain Jake asked, "Do you think she hit the 40 percent mark?"

April replied, "Of course she did. She took out one player, and Jerrad took out one player."

Davinie said, "Each suit is only worth up to 30 percent."

April exclaimed, "With three suits, that's only 90 percent! That makes no sense!"

Davinie explained, "The other 10 percent is for the judges' discretion. They give out these percentage points based on performance or sympathy if a player gets injured."

April replied, "So they can hate June and give her none because they don't like her."

Davinie replied softly, "It's possible."

April made a call on her W2 and asked in a soft tone, "Frank, did she make 4 percent?" April nodded then said, "Thank you, Frank." April hung up then threw her W2 at the window overlooking the battle arena. The W2 hit the plexiglass then bounced back toward Captain Jake, who had to quickly move to avoid it.

Captain Jake said, "Hey."

April said, "I'm sorry, Captain. I didn't mean to."

Captain Jake replied, "I know. What did Frank say?"

April replied, "June damaged her battle suit when she took out Pickax Max. She needs judge's points to reach 40 percent."

Davinie said, "June fought like hell. The judges are sure to award her points."

Captain Jake replied, "That attack was vicious. If Pickax Max got injured, he gets sympathy points."

Davinie asked, "Who's side are you on, Captain?"

Captain Jake received a text message form Thirteen that read, "This match set new records for viewership. Unless injured, June will have to stay and fight again. Equality needs to leave for the next mission."

April said, "It's fine, Davinie. If June has to stay to fight again, I will too. Sorry, Captain, but June needs me."

Davinie added, "I've never left a client. I'll be staying, too, Captain, if it comes to it."

Captain Jake said, "We will all stay if it comes to it."

April replied, "You will not, Captain. Me and my sisters joined the EPF because we believed in what you were trying to do. Staying parked here doesn't accomplish that. Another cargo ship just got hit yesterday. Captain Spike needs to be stopped. Heaven's bliss needs to be stopped. None of that is getting done while Equality is parked here."

Suddenly, there was a beeping in the room, and the window overlooking the battle arena changed to display a message that read, "Your convict was injured. Please head to the emergency room for more details."

Captain Jake smiled and said, "Looks like we shouldn't have to worry about that now. Thankfully, June was injured."

*****

It wasn't until the next morning that they were allowed to see June. They were told that June suffered serious injuries to her right arm that required emergency surgery. The three stayed the night in the hospital waiting room until they were allowed to see June.

When a nurse finally took them to see June the next morning, April was frantic to get into the room. April burst into the room to see a patient in a bed with a doctor standing there, blocking her view.

The doctor was talking to the patient. "Just keep squeezing the ball. It will help your nerve endings fuse to the new arm."

April shoved the doctor to the side then shouted, "What the hell is this?"

Davinie and Captain Jake approached to see June's right arm (all the way to the shoulder) had been replaced with a new pink camo-colored metal arm.

June, with a big smile on her face, said, "Isn't this the coolest arm ever?"

April exclaimed, "You're dangerous enough with a normal arm!" April shook her head no and said, "When we get back, Dr. Helix is going to grow you a new arm."

June replied, "Like hell he will!" June then looked at Davinie and Jake then said, "You guys don't look so hot. Did you not sleep last night?"

Davinie walked over and kissed June on the forehead then said, "We just wanted to make sure you were all right, baby girl."

June said, "Yeah, I'm fine. Sorry about worrying you guys. They haven't given me back my W2 yet."

April asked, "Are you sorry for making me worry?"

June replied, "Depends. Are you going to stop hassling me about my arm?"

April answered, "Fine."

June replied, "Then I'm sorry, *Mom*!"

April said, "I don't care that you're in a hospital bed. I will still kick your ass."

Davinie asked, "Did you hear about how you did?"

June answered, "Yep, . 43 percent. That extra 3 percent was enough to pay for this arm. It's top-of-the-line with crazy torque strength."

April freaked out. "You better have limiters on that thing. Did you forget the whole reason why we came to Hades City? Ted accidentally killed someone with his artificial hand."

June replied, "Relax, Mom. Ted was stoned out of his mind. I know what I'm doing."

April shouted, "Stop calling me Mom!" She swung at June with an open hand.

June instinctively caught April's arm with her new mechanical hand. April screamed out in pain.

June let go and said, "Sorry, I didn't mean to."

The doctor ran over and said, "Let me look at that." April's arm was already starting to change colors and swell. The doctor said, "Let's get you to x-ray."

April pulled away, screaming, "Hell no! My doctor will look at it. Can June go?"

The doctor replied, "Well, yes, but…"

April was now forcing tears back as she said, "Let's go" in a stern tone.

June jumped out of the bed, grabbing her clothes. June said, "I will have Filipe install limiters as soon as we get back."

April spoke through clenched teeth, "When my arm's healed, I'm cutting that fucking thing off!"

*****

Serenity merged with Equality. During the trip, Captain Jake sprayed topical painkillers on April's arm. Although April said it helped, Captain Jake could see April was still fighting back tears.

The lift raised them up into Equality where a crowd had gathered. The crowd was cheering for the conquering hero June when they saw June with April, who was holding her arm in pain. The crowd quickly went silent.

June waved to Dr. Helix, who was standing in the crowd to come join them. Frank, however, moved faster, racing to April's side.

June said to Dr. Helix, "Her arm's broke."

Dr. Helix took one look at April's arm and said, "That's not broke. It's crushed."

As the lift disappeared into the next floor, Calvin asked Tie, "Frank was seeing April, right?"

Tie answered, "Pretty sure."

Calvin said, "That means April's hurt. I thought June was the one who fought in the battle arena?"

The lift went back down then returned to Equality with Davinie and Captain Jake.

Stacy walked up to Captain Jake and asked, "What happened to April?"

Captain Jake answered, "There was an accident. Dr. Helix will fix her up. We need to start preparing for our next mission."

Stacy said, "Hell no, we don't."

Captain Jake asked, "What?"

Stacy stated, "You promised we'd play Rock 'em Sock 'em before we left."

Captain Jake was feeling exhausted from staying up all night as he said, "I said if you stayed out of trouble."

Stacy replied, "I didn't get into any trouble. June was the one who raped a guy, not me. Besides that, you haven't been having any fun lately, Jake. You need some fun."

Captain Jake said, "Okay. We have to go back anyways to pick up Ted. We can go tonight *after* I sleep."

*****

The last trip for Serenity to Hades City was to the spacer's market located a mile from the glass dome. It was a place for vendors to quickly stop and set up shop without the permits required to conduct business within Hades City.

There were also attractions for all ages. These included renting moon buggies, shooting ranges, drone races, and the giant Rock 'em Sock 'em robots. Captain Jake gave an open invite to all off duty crew members who might want to join the trip to the spacer's market.

Captain Jake entered Serenity, surprised to see just how full it was. Even more surprising to Captain Jake was seeing April and June aboard. Captain Jake walked over to them and said, "Neither of you needed to come along on this trip. You have both been through enough for one day."

June replied, "I've had enough time off. Besides, I'm volunteering to go with Davinie to pick up Ted. July volunteered to stay aboard Equality while May is serving guard duty here on Serenity, freeing up April to have a date night."

April said, "My sisters are being nice to me, and all it took was getting my arm crushed." April moved her arm around freely and said, "For me, it's actually been three days since the incident. Dr. Helix put me in the time dilation pod to get me healed up right away."

Frank casually put his arms around April's waist then said, "I'll be here this time to keep them out of trouble."

April looked up at Frank with an adoring look on her face then said, "I dare anyone to mess with us."

July snuck up on them and shouted, "Barforama! I preferred when you two were sneaking around, acting like we didn't know you guys were bumping uglies."

April asked, "What are you doing here? May was supposed to be working guard duty aboard Serenity."

July answered, "May wanted to switch. I think she's just trying to get close to Saman…ouch!"

Although July was wearing her power suit, the power suit had pain sensors to make them more comfortable to wear for extended periods. This feature allowed July to feel it when June subtly stabbed July in the back with her finger.

July whirled around to look at June then asked, "What was that for?"

June nodded back toward April and muttered, "Idiot."

July turned back around slowly to see a look of rage building on April's face. July whispered, "Oh shit!"

June said, "May just has a crush. Nothing is actually going on."

April said, "May is not going to touch that nasty."

Frank squeezed April's waist closer to him then said, "This is our day."

April took a deep breath then said, "Yes, it is, my love."

June took her seat then said, "I'm not calling Frank Dad."

July sat down next to June then said, "Did I tell you I got to see Samantha naked once? Her breasts are amazing."

April was about to say something, so Frank nudged April toward her seat then repeated, "Our day."

*****

The moment the Serenity crew began to exit the easy airlock, they were taken back by the noise. Loud sounds of metal striking metal echoed in their helmets as the Rock 'em Sock 'em robots battled.

Captain Jake asked, "How are we hearing this?"

Rex answered, "Not...breathable...but...there's...an...artificial...atmosphere...that...carries...sound...and...smells...if...you...have...sensors...like...me."

Stacy said, "This is awesome."

Davinie said, "June and I will go pick up Ted. Try not to get into another incident while I'm gone." Davinie turned to June and asked, "You ready?"

June was about to say yes when a young girl in a miner's space suit walked up to her and asked, "Are you June the Quadruple Threat?"

June smiled at the little girl and answered, "That's me." June was quickly swarmed by new fans wanting a selfie.

April got annoyed at seeing this and muttered, "She didn't even win."

Frank said, "Let's go to the shooting range. Hitting some exploding targets will help you relax."

Stacy grabbed Captain Jake by the arm then said, "Let's go. After we sign up for Rock 'em Sock 'em, Rex's going to show us where to get the best beer cartridges."

Davinie shouted after them, "Don't you dare get drunk!"

After Stacy and Captain Jake got signed up for Rock' em Sock' em, Rex did indeed show them to a beer cartridge dealer. There, Captain Jake only got one Bud Light cartridge while Stacy ordered three.

Rex said, "Light…weights." Then he proceeded to order three beer cartridges, two whiskey shot cartridges, and a shot cartridge of something called Around Einstein in Thirty Days.

Time passed, and they headed back to the giant robots for their match.

Stacy strapped on a jetpack they supplied then asked Rex, "Want to join me in the cockpit? Help me kick Jake's ass."

Rex shook his head no then said, "My…paws…stay…on…the…ground."

Stacy refuted, "You ride with us on a spaceship."

Rex replied, "Where…my…paws…stay…on…the…ground."

Stacy said, "Suit yourself." She initiated her jetpack to fly to the cockpit of her red robot.

Captain Jake also flew to his cockpit. As he flew, he noticed metal bars wielded to the robots arms at the joints. He recalled Harry telling him that the robots were once used to help construct the glass dome. After it was finished, the robots were modified to work like the kids' game Rock 'em Sock 'em. The ground underneath was replaced with giant magnets so the robots could also move about like the game bots would. The robots themselves stood fifty feet tall.

While Stacy and Captain Jake got strapped in, Rex felt the need to evacuate some of the alcohol getting built up in his suit. Rex decided the best place to do this was on Stacy's red robot's leg. For luck.

Rex stood there a minute, letting loose, when his suit's smell sensors started to pick up something strange. Rex immediately called Stacy then said, "Get…out…bomb."

Stacy casually responded, "I think you've had enough, Rex."

Rex cranked up his volume then shouted, "BOMB!"

Stacy added Captain Jake to the call then said, "Rex says there's a bomb."

Captain Jake asked, "Where?"

Rex answered, "IN…STACY'S…ROBOT!"

Captain Jake recoiled from the decibel levels of Rex's voice then said, "Turn down the volume, Rex." Captain Jake then tried to raise the safety bar he just lowered, but it wouldn't budge. Captain Jake said, "I can't get out to look. Rex doesn't have W2 contact lenses for me to link to."

Stacy said, "Rex didn't see it. He said he smelled it."

Captain Jake said, "Of course he did. Dolly, can you link to Rex's suit and check his smell sensors? He says he smells explosives, but he's also drunk."

Dolly replied, "C-4 explosive detected, hot stuff."

Captain Jake asked, "Stacy, can you get out?"

Stacy replied, "No, I'm locked in."

Captain Jake said, "Red alert."

Moments later, Davinie's voice came over the comms. "You better not have just ordered a red alert just so we could watch you two play a child's game. You about gave me a heart attack."

Rex repeated, "Bomb."

Tie asked, "What kind of bomb?"

June asked, "Where?" at the same time.

Captain Jake answered, "C-4. It's on Stacy's red robot for sure. We need to get her out, but we're both locked in. I can't even break out with my power suit at full strength."

Davinie asked with a sarcastic tone, "Did the pooch get in the hooch again?" Captain Jake could hear a drilling noise in the background of the comms.

Captain Jake answered, "Yes, but I had Dolly confirm it."

Calvin's voice came over the comm. "You probably have to start the robots up then forfeit the match before they let you out."

Captain Jake asked, "What if that sets off the explosives?"

Stacy announced, "I started mine."

Captain Jake could now hear small explosions like popcorn popping. Captain Jake looked over at Stacy's red robot to see all the limiter bars being blown off.

Filipe's voice came over the comms. "Look down at the safety bar for me, Captain." Captain Jake did as he was asked, then Filipe said, "Bars have been reinforced with titanium X. You're not going to budge it by strength."

Frank's voice came over the comm. "Use you sawsword to cut your way out."

Captain Jake replied, "Not enough room to draw it."

July's voice came over the comms and said, "Just use drill darts on the bar."

Captain Jake asked, "What good is a tranq dart?"

July replied, "Don't use one of those, silly. Use an acid one."

April shouted, "You gave him acid drill darts? I never told you to do that!"

July replied in a timid voice, "You didn't tell me not to. May packed them."

May's voice came over the comm. "I load all the belts the same. You were supposed to swap them out."

April scolded July, "We never showed him how to use acid darts. What if he tried to knock somebody out and grabbed the wrong one?"

July replied, "I didn't know that he didn't know about acid drill darts."

April angrily said, "You were there when we showed him how to use the drill darts."

Captain Jake's blue robot started to move, kneeling down in front of Stacy's red robot. Captain Jake said, "Just tell me which one is the acid."

May said, "The three on the far ends of either side are acid. They will be marked with a skull and crossbones engraved on the side."

Captain Jake pulled out one of these drill darts and checked the sides. Sure enough, he found the skull and crossbones.

Frank said, "Use two at once. Place each one on the bar coming down over your shoulders. The drill won't go very deep before it starts releasing acid. You want to be quick so as not to get any on your power suit. The acid will eat right through that as well."

Stacy asked, "What about me? My robot's arm is raising above Jake's head."

Captain Jake used his drill darts and replied, "I'm coming to get you out, Stacy." Captain Jake could now hear the crackling sound of lightning as his cockpit's display screen read, "Sorry, Jake."

*****

April aimed the rail rifle at a TV with two arms and three legs. The screen had a smiley face being displayed on the screen. April pulled the trigger then heard the satisfying sound of magnets charging. April held her target in her sights as it moved back and forth along a track. The rail rifle fired three seconds after April pulled the trigger. The bullet struck the TV in the smiley face's left eye. The front of the TV exploded as the TV flopped backward.

Frank said, "Nice shot. That makes you the winner."

April looked up at Frank and said, "You let me win."

Frank replied with a small smile on his face, "Never."

April set her rail rifle on the ground next to its battery pack. She took hold of Frank's hand while leaning her head against Frank's shoulder then said, "I needed this. Thank you."

Frank took a moment to respond. Never had he imagined this sort of thing would make him happy. Frank said, "Shall we rent a moon buggy next?"

April squeezed Frank's hand then said, "I think Tie and Jesus are already over there. Let's challenge them to a race."

Frank said, "Okay, let's call them."

April sighed then asked, "Mind if we take the long away around to get there? Getting sick of people asking if I'm June the Quadruple Threat."

Frank was about to answer when the red alert sounded. April and Frank opened the link to see and hear through Captain Jake's feed. The image they saw was a view from Captain Jake's cockpit looking at Stacy's red robot. They immediately started to sprint toward the Rock 'em Sock 'em robots.

As April and Frank approached from the backside of the red robot, they could see that the red robot was slowly raising its right arm high up into the air.

April asked, "Will that actually hurt Jake?"

Frank replied, "Jake doesn't have an FP shield. His visor will break."

April said, "Right leg." She then began to pull and throw six drill darts that connected with the right leg of the giant red robot.

While April was doing that, Frank had not only drawn his own spider pistol but also reached over and drew April's spider pistol. From a distance of forty feet, Frank fired both spider pistols at the red robot's right leg.

The red robot's right arm reached its peak height. Between the acid and the overheated metal in the robot's right leg, the giant robot buckled under the weight.

April and Frank then moved to catch the giant robot.

*****

June was in the process of escorting Davinie and Ted back to Serenity when they got the red alert. June assessed the situation then stabbed Ted in the chest with a drill dart.

Ted looked down at the drill dart and could hear the drill bit drilling through his bright yellow space suit. Ted's shackles prevented him from removing the drill dart, and his prison space suit had a silence feature activated. Ted said to himself, "What the fuck, you crazy…" Ted fell asleep.

June caught Ted as he fell then placed Ted in Davinie's arms. June said, "Take him to Serenity. Make sure that drill dart doesn't get removed until you're inside, or he dies."

Davinie exclaimed, "I'm old! I can't carry this guy."

June replied as she began to run off, "Your power suit will do all the work."

Davinie moved her arms up and down slightly then said to herself, "Light as a feather."

June got to the Rock 'em Sock 'em robots, approaching from behind the blue robot that was kneeling down in front of the red robot. June heard a crack of lightning then saw the red robot begin to buckle and twist as it collapsed.

June charged full speed at the red robot, climbing the kneeling blue robot along her path. June leaped off the shoulder of the blue robot's shoulder to ram her shoulder into the red robot's chest. This changed the twisting red robot's descent to a straight back fall to April and Frank, who caught the giant red robot at a forty-degree angle.

After June struck the chest of the red robot, she landed back on the blue robot. Captain Jake was still waiting for the acid to eat away at the metal enough to remove the safety bar. June walked over and used her pink camo arm to snap off the safety bar then threw it to the side.

Captain Jake wondered for a second if June actually had Filipe install limiters on her arm, but she didn't have to think about that now. Captain Jake stood up then said, "Thank you."

Stacy shouted, "What the fuck's going on out there?"

Captain Jake replied, "We're on our way." Captain Jake then startled June by grabbing her by the waist and said, "Hold on tight."

Captain Jake activated his jetpack that struggled under the weight. They slowly crossed over to Stacy. Captain Jake could now see April was on Frank's shoulders, holding up the red robot by its right butt cheek. Rex was also helping by clearing the area of civilians and vending stands so the robot could be set down safely.

Once Jake reached Stacy's cockpit, June used her sawsword to slice through the safety bar, releasing Stacy. Stacy then used her jetpack to fly away as the red robot was set down gently.

Once on the ground, June asked Captain Jake, "What the hell was that?"

Captain Jake replied, "An attempt to turn my execution into one hell of a show."

CHAPTER 12

Timmy

After giving their statements and copies of their W2 visual and audio feeds to the local authorities, the away crew returned to Equality with the prisoner Ted. Captain Jake immediately called for an officers' meeting.

The moment everyone gathered around the conference table, Captain Jake asked, "What do we know?"

Calvin brought up images of static on the conference table TV screen then said, "This is security footage from the spacer's market three days after we arrived."

Davinie asked, "What the hell happened to it?"

Calvin answered, "Corrupted."

Harry brought up multiple images of the spacer's market and said, "I found people Facebook feeds for that corrupted time frame. You can clearly see a dozen men in space suits labeled *Maintenance* working on the Rock 'em Sock 'em robots. All their visors are tinted, so we can't ID anyone with facial recognition software. There was no scheduled maintenance."

Filipe zoomed in and out on several suits then said, "There's no serial numbers on any of these suits."

Captain Jake said, "The display screen on my robot displayed *Sorry, Jake* just before the red robot was supposed to crush me."

Frank said, "From now on, you should wear the power armor the Juliet government gave you. You don't have to walk around with the FP shield activated, but you'll have it in case of emergency."

Captain Jake replied, "If I had been wearing it, I'd probably be dead. They had time to set explosives. They could have just blown me up, but they wanted to make a show of it."

Calvin said, "Couldn't have been remote controlled. If it had, they would have sped up the process when April and Frank showed up or when the captain started dropping acid on the safety bar. There must have been facial recognition software that kicked in when Stacy started up her robot."

Stacy asked, "How was I supposed to know the pirates rigged it?"

Dr. Helix asked, "Are we sure it was pirates?"

Calvin agreed. "It's too organized. This feels like covert government shit to me."

Davinie said, "First things first. What I want to know is how they knew Captain Jake was going to be in the Rock 'em Sock 'em robot in the first place."

"Spy!" came Rex's voice from behind Captain Jake, startling him.

Frank, in a stern tone, said, "Officers' meeting."

Rex ignored Frank as he went around, sniffing everyone.

Davinie asked, "What do you think you're drunk ass is doing?"

Rex answered, "Sniffing…for…explosives. The…guilty…party…will…have…residue."

As Rex sniffed at Stacy, she swatted him in the neck and said, "I was in the robot, dumbass."

Captain Jake said, "The explosives were planted by people dressed in maintenance gear days ago, Rex. If we have a spy, they wouldn't have handled the explosives."

Harry, in a quiet tone, said, "I don't think we have a spy." Everyone looked at Harry, who had a guilty look on his face as he spoke. "In one of my news feeds, I replayed Captain Jake and Stacy's conversation about playing a round of Rock 'em Sock 'em before we left."

Frank exclaimed, "Shit! He did."

Harry said, "I was trying to show the people of Hades City how excited we were to be here."

Captain Jake said, "It's fine, Harry. You have been doing a great job with PR. We advertise every time we enter a new sector of space so our shops can do business. We aren't hiding."

Calvin asked, "Who has assassination teams in Einstein?"

Frank answered, "No one. There are plenty of corporations with their own security forces, but intentional killing is rare."

Davinie said, "I don't see a motive to kill Captain Jake. He just got here, so he doesn't have enemies. Except the pirates."

Filipe asked, "What about the Thread the Needle match?"

Captain Jake said, "We paid the other players when we dropped out FP shields. There's no actual bounty on me that I know of."

Stacy said, "They said *Sorry, Jake* before trying to kill you. What kind of an assassin does that?"

Captain Jake looked to Thirteen, who was on his W2, and asked, "Thirteen, what do you think?"

Thirteen replied, "We should be heading to Omega Mining. We are already behind schedule."

Stacy said, "He's asking about the attempt to kill him."

Thirteen replied, "There is not enough information to form a hypothesis at this time. They tried once, they will try again. We may learn more from the next attempt. Now can we get going to Omega Mining?"

Stacy exclaimed, "You cold-hearted son of a bitch!"

Captain Jake said, "It's fine, Stacy." Captain Jake then called Samantha and said, "Start a course to Omega Mining."

*****

Omega Mining was located on the outer ring at the opposite side of Einstein. Two days into their journey, Equality received a distress signal.

Captain Jake entered the bridge to find everyone already at their stations. Captain Jake asked, "What's the situation?"

Calvin answered, "Distress signal is from a mobile space home floating out in deep space by the magnetic void. There's no message with the signal."

Harry added "Not answering my calls either."

Captain Jake looked confused as he asked, "How are we receiving a distress signal from deep space? Shouldn't we be approaching the fourth ring by now?"

Samantha turned to Captain Jake and asked, "Why would we be in the middle of Einstein?"

Captain Jake still had the confused look on his face when he replied, "Because we are headed to Omega Mining, which I thought was on the opposite side of Einstein."

Samantha explained, "It is, but if you go straight across, then you have to obey speed limits. Going around may be more distance, but we can travel faster. I thought we were in a hurry."

Captain Jake muttered, "That explains why it's taking so long to hear from Admiral Noem."

Tie said, "If it's a trap, I'm ready to take on some pirates."

All four quad sisters' voices came over the comm and said, "So are we, Captain."

Davinie's voice came over the comm. "We don't know it's a trap. Someone might need help."

Harry said, "The home is registered to Joy and Megan of Nowhere. Occupation, antique restoration. Both women are in their sixties with one adopted child, an eight-year-old named Timmy of Nowhere."

Harry put their ID pictures up on the main screen. Both women looked to be in their early forties. They were also both short with some extra weight on them. While one woman had darker skin and dreadlocks, the other woman was bald, and both ladies had smiles radiating warmth. The boy, Timmy, was a scrawny thing with black as night skin and a blond mohawk.

Captain Jake said, "Cancel the Carrie effect drive then set course to that mobile space home."

Thirteen's voice came over the comms. "If they are not answering, then they are most likely dead, or it's a trap. Either way, we should forward the distress signal to Hades City and continue to Omega Mining."

Captain Jake replied, "Your concern for human life is noted, Thirteen. We are still going to go check it out."

Equality arrived at the sight of the mobile space home an hour later. The home looked like a gray double-wide with all the windows tinted. After the drones searched the outside of the home and finding nothing wrong, Serenity connected its easy airlock to the home, which also gave Serenity and Equality access to the home's internal sensors.

April, June, and Zac waited in the Serenity's main airlock with half a dozen drones for the clearance to go aboard the home.

Dr. Helix said over the comms, "Life support seems to be working fine, but the temperature is turned down to thirty-two degrees."

Captain Jake said, "Open the doors. Send the drones in first. They have much better sensors to let us know what's going on."

The doors for the main airlock to the easy airlock opened. The easy airlock was extended ten feet to the home's front door with small white lights illuminating the passageway. The drones flew straight across then had to wait a moment for the front door of the mobile home to open. Once the door opened, the drones flew inside to survey the area with all officers and security personnel watching the intensely.

The inside of the home had wood paneling on the walls to make it look like a log cabin. There was still the occasional vine on the wall to assist with oxygen circulation. The grass on the floor was pitch-black shortgrass.

Samantha said, "That grass is so cool. Is it painted or bioengineered?"

Stacy replied, "Never heard of black grass, but I'm not all caught up yet on the five hundred years' worth of advancements I missed out on."

Frank said, "The drones aren't picking up any explosive residue so far."

Dr. Helix stated, "The drones are picking up an unknown toxin."

Filipe said, "Found the family in the master bedroom. Take the hall on the right to the last door."

Dr. Helix said, "I'm picking up very faint life signs."

Frank said, "You're clear to enter, but keep your visors down." April, June, and Zac had already entered the home and were making their way down the hall.

The drone hovered over the three, who were zipped up together in a bed. All three were wearing space helmets with their onesies. The little boy was sandwiched between his mothers.

Dr. Helix said, "Megan is deceased from respiratory distress and the complete shutting down of her adrenal glands. She's been gone five hours. Joy has been deceased for twelve hours with the same cause of death. The boy is still breathing."

April was the first in the room. She moved quickly to unzip the sleeping bag so June could remove Timothy from the bed. Zac paused to pull an oxygen tank out of his emergency medical bag.

As June pulled Timothy from the bed, a hyper spray gun began to float away into the bedroom.

Dr. Helix asked, "Can the drone collect and scan that hyper spray gun? I need to know what's in it."

Filipe replied, "Not a problem, Doctor." Filipe moved the drone to collect it.

Zac said, "If this is environmental poisoning, I need a bubble to transport Timothy aboard Equality."

Emily said, "I'll place one in the airlock."

June said, "I'll go get it."

Captain Jake asked, "Any idea what could cause this?"

Dr. Helix replied, "Getting the readings from the hyper spray gun now. What the hell."

Captain Jake replied, "In medical terms, Doc."

Dr. Helix said, "Yes, sorry. The hyper spray gun was filled with DMT and Clorox."

Captain Jake asked, "Isn't DMT a drug that makes the brain think the body's dead?"

Dr. Helix replied, "Yes, it is, Captain."

Calvin said, "Clorox is used to kill viruses, right? So that's what this is. Some sort of virus."

Dr. Helix replied, "Viruses generally hate heat, not cold. I think they were trying to slow the spread of something until help could arrive. One of these moms is a hero."

Stacy asked, "Filipe, can you zoom in on some of that black grass?"

Filipe replied, "Sure. Check out drone three."

Stacy said, "Fuck me. That's black mold on the grass."

Dr. Helix replied, "That fits the symptoms, but I've never seen a strain that attacks grass. It has to be bioengineered."

Captain Jake asked, "Can it be treated?"

Thirteen said, "I have analyzed the mold and sent the treatment regimen to Dr. Helix's inbox. The boy." Thirteen suddenly went silent.

Captain Jake said, "Thanks, Thirteen. What about the boy?"

Thirteen wouldn't respond.

*****

Timothy opened his eyes to see a young girl with white fur standing next to him. Timothy asked, "Did I get sent to cat heaven?"

The girl shook her head no then said, "You're in regular heaven. Angels just have beautiful fur." The girl extended her right arm to Timothy then said, "It's really soft, if you want to touch it."

Timothy pet her arm then said, "I like heaven."

The girl giggled then said, "You're not really in heaven, but I am an angel. At least that's what my dad tells me. I'm Clair."

Timothy responded, "I'm Timmy."

Clair said, "I know. We were both eight, but doctor Helix says you're nine now. Says he had to age you a whole year to make you better."

Timothy quickly looked at his arms then said in disappointment, "I'm still too small." He then looked about the room, his eyes settling on the time dilation pod.

Now Clair was the one to look disappointed as she said, "You already know what that is, don't you? I wanted to be the one to tell you."

Timothy said, "Sorry. I asked my parents for one last Christmas. I got tired of being treated like a kid."

Clair exclaimed, "Me too! Like telling me when to go to bed and telling me I can't have candy before dinner, and they make me eat eggplant."

Timothy asked, "Where are my moms?"

Clair lowered her head and softly said, "I'm sorry. My mommy said they didn't get there soon enough to save them."

Timmy's eyes started to water up, but then he wiped away his tears with a resolute look coming over his face. Timothy asked in a serious tone, "Can you help me with the time dilation pod? I have to get big."

Clair replied, "Sure. What do you need me to do?"

Timothy unzipped his sleeping bag, finding all his limbs were stiff and difficult to move. Timothy asked, "Can you help me break my onesie's magnetic lock to the bed so I can float? I'm really weak right now."

Clair replied, "Sure." As she helped Timmy free himself, Clair asked "Can I get big too? If we're both big, we can get married and go to bed whenever we want."

Timothy was finally free of the bed, holding Claire's hand as he floated in the air. Timothy answered, "Yeah. It'd be cool to marry an angel."

A stern male voice shouted at them, "Put him back in bed right now, young lady!"

A man covered in orange fur entered the room. Clair said, "But, Dr. Helix, I'm helping."

Dr. Helix repeated, "Back in bed right now." Dr. Helix marched over and took hold of Timothy. As Dr. Helix set Timothy back in bed, he asked, "What do you think you were doing?"

Clair answered, "We need to use the time thingy to get big so we can get married."

Dr. Helix couldn't help but burst out laughing as he zipped up Timothy's sleeping bag.

The medical bay door opened, and a blonde woman walked in and asked, "What's so funny?"

Clair stated, "It's not funny. This is Timmy, and we're going to get big and get married." Clair then turned to Timothy and said, "This my mom, Irene, but you can call her mom since you're going to be my husband and all."

Irene walked over and said, "You're not even old enough to date, let alone get married."

Clair repeated, "That's why we need the time thingy."

Dr. Helix said, "That's a complicated machine. You wouldn't even know how to turn it on."

Clair confidently stated, "Timmy knows how to use it. He asked for one for Christmas." Clair then stuck her tongue out at Dr. Helix.

Dr. Helix retorted, "Asking for something doesn't mean you know how to use it."

Clair stomped her foot and then said, "He does too. Timmy, tell him."

Timothy looked at Dr. Helix dead in the eye and said, "Can you please give Clair and I a moment alone? You say I don't know how to use the time dilation pod, so there's no harm."

Both Dr. Helix and Irene were taken aback by Timothy's chilling demeanor. Irene asked, "Why do you want to age, Timothy?"

Clair interrupted, "His name is Timmy."

Irene corrected herself. "Why do you want to age, Timmy?"

Timothy answered, "Because adults don't listen to kids. I tried to warn my moms, but they wouldn't believe me."

Dr. Helix asked, "Are you talking about the black mold? We know about it. Your moms had to have known too. They took extraordinary measures to save your life."

Timothy began to cry as he spoke, "No, they didn't. They wouldn't listen, so I tried to make them listen. They died because of me, but I can still save everyone else. We have to warn them about the mold."

Irene leaned in, wiping away some of Timothy's tears as she said, "Shhh, it's not your fault. And a warning about the mold was already sent out. You don't need to do anything but recover."

Timothy violently slapped Irene's arm away and angrily stated, "Adults never listen! The black mold only appears as three black dots at the base of the grass. I noticed it after my moms were visited by this kid calling himself Captain Spike."

Dr. Helix stood there with a blank expression on his face. In his mind, he was seeing that look of anger on Timothy's face on an older version of Timothy. That version was screaming into a camera, "I'm going to Russell Arthur all your asses!"

Irene said, "Captain Spike the pirate?"

Timothy shrugged his shoulders and said, "I don't know."

Irene said, "Continue, Timmy."

Timmy said, "I tried to warn my moms about it, but they wouldn't listen. So I mixed together some of the chemicals they use for artificial aging replacement parts in their restoration business." Tears began to stream down Timothy's face as he continued, "The mixture was an accelerant. I was only going to use it on a few blades of grass, but my mom walked in, startling me, and I knocked the vial over on the floor." Timothy had to wipe tears away and suck some snot back before he could continue. "She made me go to bed, but I already had my space helmet on. I swear I didn't think it would spread so fast. By morning, I couldn't wake my moms up."

Dr. Helix said, "You're saying you're the one who mixed together the hyper spray of DMT and Clorox? And lowered the temperature."

Timothy added, "And activated the emergency beacon. But I didn't save them." Timothy burst out sobbing.

Irene sat down next to Timothy and lifted him out of the bed to hold him. Then she whispered, "You did an incredible job. Your moms would be so proud of you. How did you know to do all that?"

Dr. Helix said, "Dolly, we need security in the medical bay."

*****

One hour after Dr. Helix's conversation with Timothy, there was an emergency officers' meeting. Everyone in attendance had watched their conversation and were trying to process it.

Frank was the first to speak. "I can have a cell prepared for the boy."

Stacy screamed, "For what?"

Calvin answered, "Murdering his parents. That is illegal here, isn't it?"

Davinie stated, "He's too young to be charged with murder."

Calvin replied, "Let's age him. That's what he said he wanted anyways."

Stacy replied, "You can't actually believe his story? An eight-year-old who mixes up a magic potion to weaponize mold."

Thirteen stated, "Science backs up the clone's story."

Captain Jake asked, "What's being a clone have to do with anything? Are you saying he was genetically altered?"

Dr. Helix said, "He wasn't. It's who he is a clone of that's the issue. Maybe."

Davinie stated, "Dr. Helix, you of all people know a clone has nothing to do with their original. They are their own person with their own identity. Just look at the quadruplet sisters if you need an example."

Captain Jake said, "I know Clair's is an altered clone who was flagged as possible special needs due to her original. I also know you adore her, so what's the issue this time?"

Dr. Helix replied, "I may just be overreacting, Captain. The boy did go through extreme lengths to save his mothers."

Calvin said, "After he poisoned them."

Dr. Helix said, "The mold before Timmy weaponized it was still dangerous. The effects come on slower, but it would still cause stunted growth, weakening bones, and pneumonia. It just would have occurred over a longer period."

Calvin added, "And time to be discovered without anyone dying."

Harry said, "We heard nothing back after the warning of black mold the first time. After I changed it to three black dots, we're getting responses. EPF is finally getting some good PR in the outer rings."

Suddenly, Frank looked up from his W2 and shouted, "Timothy's a clone of Russell Arthur!"

Thirteen stated, "It took nearly a day for the head of security to figure that out. We should be looking to upgrade the position."

Frank looked at Thirteen and said, "You knew?"

Stacy said, "It doesn't matter who he's a clone of. He's still a child."

Frank said to Captain Jake, "He's already murdered his mothers. At least let me put him in a cell."

Davinie stated, "Legally, all that can be done is to send the boy to a juvenile detention center for rehabilitation."

Frank stated, "There was an original Russell Arthur and one known clone of Russell Arthur. We all know how both instances played out."

Davinie stated, "You're dating a clone of President Taylor. I don't see April winning any popularity contests."

Captain Jake asked, "Is the boy still in the medical bay?"

Frank answered, "With July keeping watch, Captain."

Stacy said, "You can't, Jake."

Captain Jake replied, "I'm an orphan myself, Stacy. Timmy won't be locked up, but he will need to be watched. I think I know just the candidate."

*****

Captain Jake and Rex entered the medical bay to find Irene at Timothy's side, helping him to walk about the room. July, in the meantime, was in the corner, playing games on her W2.

Captain Jake asked, "How's the patient?"

Irene answered with her always pleasant tone, "He's a true champion."

Timothy casually said, "Hi, Jake." Then he looked at Rex and asked, "Is that a neuro scanner cap with a keyboard?"

Rex replied, "No…neuro…scanner."

Timothy looked disappointed and stated, "That's why your speech is so slow."

Rex gave a low growl then said, "I...don't...like...this...kid."

Captain Jake asked Irene, "Mind if I walk with Timothy for a minute? I'd like me, him, and Rex to have a minute."

Timothy said, "Call me Timmy, please."

Irene replied, "Sure thing, Captain."

Timothy looked up at Captain Jake as he took his arm and repeated, "Captain? What happened to Captain Noem?"

Captain Jake replied, "She's an admiral now. How do you know who I am?"

Timothy replied, "My moms had me watch your time capsule footage when Minnow arrived in Einstein. It was part of my history lessons."

Captain Jake looked over at July, who was now petting Rex, and asked, "Mind leaving us for a minute as well?"

July replied, "As long as you don't give him any tips on how to play Uno. Me, him, Irene, and Clair have a match set up after his rehab session."

Timothy replied, "I already know how to play. You won't beat me."

July said, "We'll see, kid." July and Irene left the room.

Timothy stopped walking to take a closer look at Rex's CPU cap then said, "I think I can add neuro scanners. This cap should have the necessary RAM. May I take a look at the inside of the cap?"

Rex looked up at Captain Jake, who said to Rex, "Dr. Helix says he's a genius."

Rex said, "Fine."

Timothy pulled Rex's cap-shaped CPU off Rex's head then made a funny face and asked, "When was the last time you washed this? It stinks!"

Rex let out a low growl.

Captain Jake waved his hand in front of his nose then said, "He's right. It stinks."

Timothy asked Captain Jake, "Can you help me walk to the back? I need to add some neuro adaptors to this."

Captain Jake helped Timothy to the back while he asked, "I heard you got to spend some time in the time dilation pod. Do you feel older now?"

Timothy replied, "Not really. Dr. Helix only aged me a couple of months to get the black mold out of my system. Clair thought Dr. Helix aged me a year because my birthday is next month. I'm physically nine now, but it doesn't really feel like it. Clair is going to be my wife someday, and my moms always told me never to correct your wife unless you have to. Happy wife, happy life, they always said."

Captain Jake smiled and said, "That's good advice."

Timothy looked through drawers as he asked, "Are you here because I killed my moms?"

Captain Jake replied, "Your moms' death isn't only on you. We got delayed at our last stop. If we had left when we were supposed to, we would have been in time to save you and your moms."

Timothy turned to Rex while pointing at a table then said, "I need you to get up on that table."

Rex jumped up on the table while Captain Jake asked Timothy, "You know that's a surgical table, right?"

Timothy replied, "I need to scan his brain for this to work." Timothy handed Rex's cap to Captain Jake and asked, "Can you plug this in to that computer?" Timothy pointed at a nearby computer terminal then asked, "And then help me up into the chair. I need to update the software."

Captain Jake did as Timothy asked while he said, "We did send out the warning about the mold. The three black dots at the base of the blades of grass. We already heard back from smaller ships like yours that they found some. You helped a lot of people."

Timothy spoke with a bitter tone. "But I couldn't save my moms." Timothy then yelled, "Rex! Sit still so I can scan you."

Captain Jake said, "You tried. That means something." After a moment of silence, Captain Jake asked, "You're going to have to stay with us for a while. Hope that's all right?"

Timothy yelled, "Rex! I said don't move. I'm going to strap you down so you can't fidget." After a few keystrokes, white straps auto raised from the left side over to the right side. The surgical straps then tightened down, restricting Rex from moving in any way.

Captain Jake said, "You might want to be nice to Rex. While you're on board, he's going to be escorting you. Just to make sure you don't get into anything you shouldn't."

Timothy replied, "Rex will like me just fine after I improve his speech. Can you go over to my bed? There should be a USB connector cable I need."

Captain Jake looked around for a minute, not seeing anything, then said, "I'm not seeing it. Are you sure it's over here?"

Timothy replied, "Check under the pillow. If not there, check around the floor. I might have accidentally knocked it off the bed."

Captain Jake took a long couple of minutes to look around before giving up. He turned back toward Timothy and said, "I can't find it. There's an electronics store in the courtyard." Captain Jake's jaw dropped as he saw a sound barrier around Rex's surgical table.

Captain Jake quickly crossed the room where he now saw Rex's skull was now shaved. There was a robotic arm inserting long needles into Rex's skull. Captain Jake exclaimed, "What are you doing?"

Timothy casually replied, "I told you I was going to add neural sensors."

Captain Jake exclaimed, "To the cap! Not to Rex!"

Timothy replied, "I did add neural sensors to the cap, but that doesn't do any good without the actual neural connections."

Captain Jake asked, "Weren't there safeguards locking you out of the system?"

Timothy proudly said, "Yep. Good ones too." The sound barrier lowered, and Timothy handed Captain Jake Rex's cap then asked, "Mind putting this back on Rex? Just line up the pins with the receivers."

Captain Jake carefully placed the cap back on Rex's head, whispering, "Don't be brain damaged."

The moment the cap latched into place, Rex yelled, "I'm going to rip that kid's throat out!"

Captain Jake asked, "Rex? You all right?"

Rex shouted, "Get me out of these restraints so I can rip his throat out!"

Timothy replied, "Not until you say thank you. My moms said manners are important."

Rex shouted, "Thank you for what?"

Timothy replied, "For fixing your voice."

Rex exclaimed, "You didn't. Wait, I'm talking without typing. Holy shit!"

Timothy said, "Language. I'm waiting."

Rex reluctantly said, "Thank you." Then the restraints loosened and retracted.

Michael the Magician

After leaving a warning beacon for toxic materials on Timothy's home, Equality continued on its course to Omega Mining. Two days before their scheduled arrival at Omega Mining, Captain Jake received an encoded message from Admiral Noem. After watching it, Captain Jake canceled the Carrie effect drive and ordered an emergency officers' meeting at the conference table.

Once everyone arrived, Captain Jake began the meeting by saying, "There's been a change in plans. We will need to go dark in a couple of hours and stay dark for at least a month. Harry, I need you to let the residents know. Tell them I'm sorry for the inconvenience, and I'll let them know what's going on after we go dark."

Frank asked. "What's going on?"

Captain Jake answered, "New orders from Admiral Noem. We will be traveling to a secret research space station called the RO. It's located at the edge of the magnetic void a day's travel from us. Equality and Eagle Two will be receiving hull upgrades before assisting in a weapons test. Eagle Two will only have a skeleton crew. To keep this new weapon from falling into the pirates hands, secrecy is key."

Calvin asked, "What type of weapon?"

Captain Jake replied, "A missile of some sort. Serenity will be fitted with the missile while we and Eagle Two patrol. I'm not sure Admiral Noem even knows what the missile actually does. It's next gen weapons research that was started months before we got here. Extremely hush-hush."

Frank said, "I understand that Dr. Helix will be releasing Timothy from the medical bay tomorrow."

Dr. Helix stated, "I will. Timmy's moving around much better now."

Frank said, "I would like to request that Timothy be placed in a cell upon release."

Stacy exclaimed, "He's a kid!"

Davinie said, "We already decided to rule the incident with Timmy and his moms an accident."

Frank replied, "What about Rex? The kid performed brain surgery on him."

Dr. Helix said, "Rex is fine. Better than fine, actually."

Captain Jake said, "Rex will be keeping an eye on Timmy to ensure he stays out of trouble."

Thirteen stated, "The clone should be locked up. He performed brain surgery while you were watching him, Captain. What do you imagine he could accomplish with a dog watching him at a top-secret research facility?"

Captain Jake replied, "Timmy will not be allowed aboard the RO Space Station. Timmy is a child who should get to be a child as much as is possible considering his circumstances. I don't want to hear anything more about locking him up."

*****

Equality was en route the next day as Captain Jake sat eating lunch at a new Chinese restaurant in the courtyard.

Calvin approached and sat down next to Captain Jake then said, "We must be getting close. There are some relay satellites ahead of us set to jam instead of relay."

Captain Jake said, "We better slow down then. The RO Space Station has a private security force that deployed spacemines. Don't need to go losing all our FP again."

Dolly spoke through Captain Jake's W2, "Incoming call from an Eagle Two jet arm, Captain Hot Pants."

Captain Jake looked at Calvin and said, "Enough."

Calvin said, "Dolly, I'm a leaf on the wind."

Captain Jake smiled and said, "That's a good cancelation phrase."

Calvin replied, "Just for you, Jake."

Captain Jake said, "Dolly, open up a link for the officers and security then answer the call."

An image of a handsome man's face with a brown mullet appeared in the corner of Captain Jake's W2 contact lens. The man said, "Hello, I'm Michael. I hear you guys want to test-fire a rocket."

Captain Jake replied, "That would be us."

Michael said, "You guys are late. Eagle Two finished its upgrades yesterday. There's a group of engineers waiting on you."

Captain Jake said, "Sorry about that. Issues came up along the way. What exactly are they doing to our hull?"

Michael answered, "As I understand it from Dr. Stevens, they are adding a layer under the FP magnets to strengthen the hull from scattershot pellets that get past a weak FP shield. There's also a thin layer of lead for solar radiation, he said."

Captain Jake asked, "This test isn't going to deal with radioactive scattershot, is it?"

Michael replied, "I have no idea, Captain. I'm just a volunteer here to lead you the rest of the way. There are some spacemines about that have been moved to clear you a path. After your past, I have to move them back."

Captain Jake said, "Appreciate that."

Michael said, "One more thing, Captain."

Captain Jake asked, "What's that?"

Michael said, "It's my understanding you have a small town aboard your ship."

Captain Jake replied, "Less than fifty residents and crew so far. We wanted to limit bringing full families aboard right away. Shops will be open if you want to stop by and shop."

Michael smiled then said, "I'll be sure to do that, Captain. The reason I ask is that I happen to be a magician when not volunteering for the EPF. Michael the Magician is my stage name. I was wondering if I might be allowed to put on a show in your courtyard?"

Captain Jake answered, "Some live entertainment sounds great. Harry, are you on the link?"

Harry's voice entered the conversation. "I'm here, Captain. A live show for our residents would be a good idea. They didn't take too kindly to having to cancel appointments at Omega Mining."

Captain Jake said, "I'll let you two hammer out the details. I'm looking forward to watching your show, Michael."

*****

Timothy and Rex entered the courtyard aboard Equality. It was Timothy's first day out of the medical bay, and he was excited to get to roam about. Timothy went to an apple tree first and picked an apple. He then noticed Clair sitting at a picnic table with Johnny and his father, Randolf. All three had their laptops out.

Timothy said to Rex, "I'm going to go see Clair."

Rex replied, "I'm going to go see Stacy. Don't leave the courtyard without me."

Timothy began a slow run toward Clair, yelling back, "Okay!"

At the sound of Timothy's voice, Clair turned around. Her eyes lit up at the sight of Timothy, and she shouted, "Timmy!"

Timothy reached the picnic table and said, "Hi, Clair."

Clair said, "Johnny and Mr. Randolf, this is Timmy. He's my future husband. Future husband, this is Johnny and his dad, Mr. Randolf."

Timothy shook their hands and said, "Pleased to meet you."

Mr. Randolf said, "We were just having a school session. We have an extra laptop for you when you're ready."

Timothy said excitedly, "I'm ready now. Do you have it with you?"

Mr. Randolf smiled and said, "Sure do." He then reached into a backpack sitting by his side and pulled out a laptop that he handed to Timothy and said, "I found your profile and loaded it already. I'm impressed. It says you're at the seventh-grade learning level."

Timothy sat down next to Clair with a disappointed look on his face then said, "That's the profile you loaded? That was the one I just had so my moms could help me with my homework. They liked to do that, so I let them. Even though they gave me the wrong answers a lot. My real profile is Omegadragon64. I'm just about to finish getting my master's in quantum mechanics."

Clair proudly said, "My future husband is very smart."

Johnny stated, "He's a liar."

Mr. Randolf, in a lowered tone, said, "Johnny."

Johnny replied, "You know he is, Dad. He has to be." Johnny pushed his laptop in front of Timothy then said, "If you're so smart, prove it. Finish my calculus homework."

Timothy stared at the laptop. He hesitated as Clair screamed, "He is not lying! He's not going to help you cheat. Do your own homework, Johnny."

Mr. Randolf, in a soft tone, said, "Calm down, everyone."

Timothy said, "The answer is y squared over pie, but you have to prove it yourself. Like Clair said, I'm not doing your work for you."

Johnny said, "That can't be the right answer. You didn't even use a calculator. Dad, he's lying again."

Mr. Randolph asked, "Dolly, was that the right answer to the problem?"

Dolly replied, "Yes, it was."

Clair stated, "I told you so!" Clair stuck her tongue out at Johnny.

The four of them, along with everyone else in the courtyard, were suddenly startled by a loud bang and a poof of smoke appearing from a side entrance to the courtyard. Once the smoke cleared, there appeared a man with a mullet. He was wearing a black tux with a black cape that had a red inner lining. The man began to levitate over to Mr. Randolf and the kids.

Once the man reached the table, Timothy exclaimed, "Wow! You have repluser shoes that make you float. You must have really good balance, but how did you propel and stop yourself?"

The man announced, "I'm Michael the Magician. It's magic." Michael then pulled out a deck of cards from thin air and said, "Pick a card. Any card."

Timothy ignored Michael as he walked around him, searching for clues as to how he propelled himself over to them.

Clair gleefully said, "I'll pick a card."

Michael held out the deck of cards to Clair then said, "Draw a card, but don't show me."

Clair nodded in understanding then drew a card. Michael threw his hands up in the air, making the rest of the deck disappear.

A small crowd had started to grow around them, and everyone except Timothy gasped in amazement at the disappearing deck.

Michael then pulled up his right sleeve, exposing a tattoo of the ace of diamonds, and asked, "Is this your card?"

Clair proudly held up the ace of diamonds, giggling with excitement as she announced, "Yes, it is!"

Johnny took the card to check if it was marked. After not finding anything, he asked Michael, "Is that a real tattoo?"

Michael the Magician replied, "It is." Michael the Magician then spoke very loudly for the small crowd to hear. "I will be hosting an illusion show in the courtyard tonight." Pamphlets started to drop out of the air, and Michael the Magician said, "Please let your friends and families know."

Timothy looked up in the air where he saw nothing and said, "Oh. That's how you did it. Is it preprogrammed or—"

Michael began to laugh loudly to cut Timothy off. Michael grabbed Timothy and dragged him to the side, where he began to whisper, "Please, kid, don't tell anyone about the you-know-what. It will ruin the illusion for everyone else."

Timothy asked, "Aren't cloaked drones illegal?"

Michael said, "Shhh. Not so loud, kid. I'm a volunteer with the EPF. That drone is technically government property."

Timothy asked, "Is that why a magician would join the EPF? To get your hands on cool tech. Do you have more tech? I want to see it."

Michael said, "Sure, kid. If you promise not to tell anyone about how I do any of my tricks."

The small crowd had started to disperse, taking away fliers as Timothy shook Michael's hand and said, "Deal." Timothy turned back to Clair and the others then said, "I'll be back. Michael the Magician is going to show me his cool magic tech."

Clair said, "I want to know how he knew what card I had."

Timothy rushed back to Clair, pulling her to the side then whispering in her ear, "All the cards were the ace of diamonds, but don't tell anyone, okay?"

Clair looked angry at hearing this as she now glared at Michael then said, "I won't."

Timothy returned to Michael's side, where Michael said, "You just promised not to tell anyone."

Timothy replied, "That's Clair. She's going to be my wife. We don't keep secrets from one another. Don't worry, anything I tell her is covered by husband-wife confidentiality."

Michael shook his head in disbelief at what he just got himself into. Unfortunately for Michael, cloaked drones were highly illegal regardless of who you work for. Should anyone find out about the drone, Michael would be in serious trouble.

"What's the commotion over there? What's with all this trash littering my courtyard?" came a woman's voice, shouting.

Johnny picked up a flier and ran it over to her and said, "Stacy, this is Michael the Magician. He's putting on a show in the courtyard tonight." As Stacy read the flier, Johnny stared at Stacy's ample breasts.

Stacy looked up from the flier to catch Johnny staring at her breasts (although he quickly turned his gaze). Stacy took it as a compliment that she still had it, but she tried to hide her smile. Stacy walked toward Michael the Magician and said, "Well, Mr. Michael the Magician, you better be cleaning up this mess, and best not even think about leaving a mess after tonight's show."

Michael rushed up to meet Stacy, taking her hand and kissing it as he bowed to her and asked, "Will the fair maiden be watching my performance?"

Stacy giggled then said, "Hold your roll, Rico Suave. I'd have to be pretty stoned to watch a magic show."

Michael spun Stacy so that their backs were turned to the others and made a joint appear in his hand. Michael asked, "How about now?"

Stacy took the joint then said, "Okay, Magic Mike. I'll check out what you got."

Timothy walked over to them and asked, "Can we go see your magic tech now?"

Rex also joined the group at this time and asked, "You weren't going to leave without me, were you?"

Michael looked down at Rex in amazement and said, "That's the best animal speech I've ever heard. How do the neural sensors work so quickly?"

Timothy proudly stated, "This is my bodyguard, Rex. I inserted neuro sensors directly into his brain to speed up the process."

Michael asked, "Did you perform brain surgery on Rex?"

Rex stated, "He tricked me."

Timothy nonchalantly said, "The machines did all the work. I just pushed the right buttons."

Stacy walked over to Timothy, grabbing his arm. Stacy then dropped to one knee and bent Timothy over it. Stacy raised her hand and brought it down with thunderous might onto Timothy's butt.

As Timothy cried out in pain, Stacy angrily said, "I don't care that you're an orphan!"

Mr. Randolf stepped forward to stop Stacy, but Stacy shot Mr. Randolf a murderous glance that stopped him in his tracks.

Stacy raised her hand again and shouted, "NEVER!" Stacy brought her hand down even harder this time. Stacy raised her hand again and shouted, "EVER!" Again, Stacy dropped the hammer as tears began to well up in Timothy's eyes. Stacy said, "Do brain surgery on anyone without their permission!" Stacy hauled back and smacked Timothy's butt one final time before standing him back up.

Timothy's screams of pain subsided. Knowing Clair was watching, Timothy tried to stand up straight and show bravery.

Stacy now kneeled down to look Timothy straight in the eye and said, "That was also for what happened to your moms. Don't ever do dangerous experiments without adult supervision. Do you hear me?"

Timothy nodded yes as he choked back the tears.

Stacy said, "That's also so you never forget. We don't hurt people to help them. Do you understand, or do I need to put you back over my knee?"

Timothy shook his head no as he said, "I understand."

Stacy stood back up then asked, "Have you had breakfast?"

Timothy softly answered, "I had an apple."

Stacy said, "There's some bananas in the hydroponics bay if you want. There's also some cookies on the table. Only take one cookie. Rex can show you the way."

Rex said, "Let's go, kid. Watching that made my butt hurt."

Timothy began walking next to Rex and said, "My moms never spanked me."

Rex replied, "Considering what happened to them, maybe they should have."

Clair asked Mr. Randolf, "Can I go too?"

Mr. Randolf replied, "If it's okay with Stacy."

Stacy said, "Sure, you can have a cookie."

Clair said, "Thank you, but I just want to see Timmy." Clair rushed to catch up with Timothy.

Johnny followed suit and said, "I want a cookie."

Mr. Randolf asked, "What kind of cookies?"

Stacy replied, "Chocolate chip with walnuts."

Mr. Randolf's eyes lit up as he asked, "May I?"

Stacy answered, "Of course."

With everyone gone, Michael asked, "What happened to that boy's moms?"

Stacy asked, "Did you hear about that black mold being found in mobile homes across Einstein?"

Michael answered, "Yeah. We shut off a signal jammer every couple of days to get news updates. You guys are heroes for discovering it."

Stacy replied in a soft tone, "Wasn't us. It was that kid."

Michael replied, "Really?"

Stacy said, "Yeah. His moms wouldn't believe him though. Kid pulled some mad scientist shit to make them listen, but it went wrong. They died, and the kid nearly died as well."

Michael asked, "What exactly is that kid?"

Stacy replied, "According to Dr. Helix, the smartest boy ever born. Timmy's still a kid who needs to be taught right from wrong."

*****

Michael, Rex, and Timothy entered the Eagle Two mothership. The hall was circular shaped and narrow. The walls themselves were completely covered in vines, but the floor was metal with no grass covering it. The doors along the outer walls were labeled jet arm 1, jet arm 2, and so on. There were also intersecting straight corridors that led to a small habitat in the center of the ship.

After giving a short tour, Michael led them to one of the rooms along the first ring corridor. He opened the door then said, "This is where Captain Marshall lets me keep all my magic equipment."

Timothy was full of excitement as he looked about the small room lined with shelves. Timothy asked, "Is this a crystal ball with a holographic projector in the center? Do you use it to make people think you encased an object you took from them?" Timothy quickly looked at a different shelf and asked, "Is this a portable 3D printer with clear resin? I bet you use this to actually encase objects you take from people."

Rex was sniffing about and asked, "Is there anything dangerous in here?"

Michael answered, "Not really."

Timothy noticed a large drone suddenly appear in the corner of the room. Timothy approached it and asked, "Is this the—"

Michael hastily cut Timothy off and said, "That is a drone, young sir. Nothing special about it."

Timothy gave Michael a confused look.

Michael quickly nodded toward Rex, who was still sniffing about.

Timothy gave a nod of understanding then went to work typing on his W2. A minute later, Timothy said, "We can talk now. As long as we speak in a normal even tone, Rex can't hear us."

Michael asked, "What are you talking about?"

Timothy explained, "When I upgraded Rex's cap for the neuro sensors, I connected it by Bluetooth to my W2. Had to update the software for it to work. Since then, I've written a few programs. The one I'm using now won't let his brain register decibels between fifty-five to sixty-five so we can talk. Does the drone also have a sound dampening feature? Is that why I didn't hear it enter?"

Michael looked down at Rex then asked, "Is that true?"

Rex looked up at Michael staring down at him then asked, "What? You never saw a dog sniff before?"

Michael replied, "No. I mean yes."

Rex tilted his head as if to suggest something was confusing him.

Timothy shouted, "Talking dogs should be above that!"

Rex replied, "I sniff what I want. Why are you shouting?"

Timothy whispered, "No reason."

Rex muttered, "I hate kids." Then he returned to sniffing about.

Michael stood there speechless to what he was witnessing.

Timothy repeated, "Does the drone have sound masking?"

Michael returned to his senses and answered, "Yes. Along with miniaturized 360-degree cameras on all sides that record and project to camouflage. Have you considered becoming a magician?"

Timothy replied, "I like cool technology. Magicians have a lot of cool technology. Why are you really with the EPF? I read the laws on the way over here, and I know cloaked drones are illegal, even if you're part of law enforcement."

Michael smiled and replied, "Can't pull anything over on you, kid. You going to turn me in?"

Timothy picked up a canister and read the label. "What's solar writing?" Timothy asked.

Michael replied, "I'll tell you if you promise not to turn me in."

Timothy answered, "Me and my moms lived in a mobile space station out by the magnetic void. When I asked my moms why we lived so far away from everyone, they told me, 'There's a difference between doing something illegal and doing something wrong.' They said the way they had me was considered illegal, but it wasn't wrong. You use your drone to make people happy. It's illegal, but it's not wrong."

Michael said, "Your moms sound like amazing people. Solar writing is my ultimate magic trick. Every great magician needs one."

Timothy asked, "What is it?"

Michael answered, "It's a gas with metal particles in it that has a flash point of three thousand degrees. Once ignited, the gas should chemically react to shine as bright as a mini sun for a few seconds. I can write a message out here in deep space that could be seen all the way to Romeo and Juliet."

Timothy said, "That's why you joined the EPF. You need a spider cannon to ignite it."

Michael replied, "You really are a genus. I volunteered for this trip to deep space to test my formula. Only I found out after we got here that it's a secret space station that needs to stay secret."

Timothy replied, "You can test it the day they test-fire the missile. They have to leave the area after that anyways."

Michael asked, "Why's that?"

Timothy replied, "Because there will be radiation after the test, so the area has to be cordoned off. That means registering the area with all sectors of space so flight paths aren't scheduled to fly through it. They have to leave. Can I see your formula for solar writing?"

Michael replied, "Sorry, kid. Magician's secret." Michael thought, *If it doesn't work, the kid's a genius. He could perfect it.*

Timothy asked, "What if you made me your assistant?"

Michael thought for a second. *Considering what Timmy did do with Rex, the kid could take my act to a whole 'nother level.* Michael shook his head no then said, "Sorry, kid. Child labor laws won't allow it."

Timothy replied, "There's a time dilation pod in the medical bay aboard Equality. If you help me use it, I could be old enough in an hour."

Michael replied, "Don't you dare. Stay a kid as long as possible."

Timothy replied, "I hate being a kid."

Michael said, "It may seem like it sucks now, but once you get old, you'll look back and wish you were young again. Trust me." Stacy's word suddenly echoed in Michael's head: *Still a kid who needs to be taught right from wrong.*

Timothy reluctantly said, "Fine."

Michael said, "You know there's another way that you could be my assistant."

Timothy got excited and asked, "How?"

Michael answered, "I could adopt you. No law saying a son couldn't help out his father."

Timothy exclaimed, "Seriously!"

Rex perked up and asked, "Seriously what? Why have you been so quiet, Timmy?"

Timothy ran over to give Michael a hug.

Rex asked, "What's going on?"

*****

The night of Michael the Magician's Illusion Extravaganza (as he called it) went off without a hitch. Almost all the people in the sector were there to watch. Stacy was so impressed with the show that she visited with Michael in person afterward to congratulate him.

Over the next month, Timothy followed Michael around with a deck of cards. He was constantly practicing sleight of hand tricks that Michael had shown him. Timothy had never excelled at hand-eye coordination, but Timothy had also never had a father figure before. Timothy was determined to make Michael proud of him.

Michael spent most of his free time that month helping Stacy in the hydroponics bay. Their budding romance was blossoming quickly. This, in turn, meant Timothy spent more time with Stacy, growing their own bond.

It wasn't all sunshine and rainbows for Timothy. Most nights, Timothy would suffer from night terrors. In his nightmare, Timothy would be standing on the edge of a cliff, watching his mothers fall to their deaths. Timothy would reach out to catch them, only to fall off the cliff himself. Timothy would then wake up still feeling as if he were falling, and he would be covered in sweat.

Only Rex knew about Timothy's night terrors. Rex took to sleeping at the foot of Timothy's bed so Timothy wouldn't have to go through it alone.

Still, Stacy, Michael, Timothy, and Rex found a new type of happiness that month.

Weapons Test

During the one-month stay aboard RO Space Station, Captain Jake found everyone aboard the research station to be very pleasant yet secretive. Even up to the day of the weapons test, Captain Jake didn't know exactly what it was that they were testing. This was one of the topics of conversation that took place at the officers' meeting while Equality traveled to the weapons test site.

Captain Jake asked Calvin, "Are all requested security measures in place?"

Calvin answered, "Yes, sir. There will be a blackout of all communication devices aboard Equality during the weapons test. The only comm lines open will be between us on the bridge, Captain Marshall on Eagle Two, Dr. Stevens in his observation ship, and then Jesus on Serenity."

Frank added, "Don't forget about all the jet arms patrolling. Wouldn't do much good for them to spot trouble and not be able to warn us about it."

Calvin said, "Yes, them too."

Frank looked at Captain Jake and said, "As head of security, I should be a part of this link, and security personnel should be aboard Serenity for the test firing."

Captain Jake replied, "I agree with you, Frank. Unfortunately, it's not up to me. I wish I knew what all the secrecy was about."

Stacy stated, "It's your ship, Jake. Make Dr. Stevens tell you."

Davinie explained, "We tried asking Dr. Stevens. Once he realized it wasn't a joke, he showed us his NDA [non-disclosure agreement]. It's the strictest document I have ever read. Dr. Stevens literally can't talk to anyone about the project except with the other scientists on the project. Even then, they are forced to talk in code. Anyone caught breaking the rules before the weapons test successful forfeits millions in FP bonuses."

Calvin said, "So if the weapons test is successful, we get to know what it is. If it fails, do we have to stick around and wait for another test?"

Harry said, "They are more than confident that the test will go off without a hitch. Scientists back at RO are packing their things as we speak."

Frank said, "I will at least be the guard Dr. Stevens requested be placed outside Equality's bridge, should anything happen."

Captain Jake asked, "Thirteen, any ideas on what they are testing?"

Thirteen, while typing on his W2, replied, "I cannot say."

"Thirteen's as useless as ever" came Rex's voice from behind Jake, startling him.

Frank angrily said, "Rex! How many times do I have to tell you that you can't be here during officers' meetings?"

Stacy said, "Sorry, Rex, but you really shouldn't be in here this time. Where's Timmy?"

Rex answered, "He's locked himself in his room. Says he has to help Michael prep for some magic trick."

Davinie said, "Speaking of Michael, adoption papers came in for that man of yours, Stacy. Once this mission is over, he can sign the papers, and Timmy will legally be his son."

Dr. Helix stated, "That's wonderful. Just watching those two together, you'd never know they just met a month ago."

Frank scoffed. "Great idea! Let's train the greatest terrorist in history how to deceive people. Like he wasn't—"

Stacy cut Frank off, shouting, "Timmy is not Russell Arthur!"

Captain Jake said, "We have been over this, Frank. Enough."

Frank reluctantly said, "Yes, Captain."

Stacy, in a much quieter tone, said, "And Michael is not my man. We have only known each other a few weeks."

Captain Jake said, "Still, Stacy, we all know how close you, Michael, Timmy, and even Rex there have gotten. If you wanted to transfer to Eagle Two or, better yet, Michael transfer here, consider it done."

Stacy blushed then said, "Thank you, Jake. Like I said, it's only been a couple of weeks, but I will let Michael know what you said."

Rex stated, "No one cares if the boy leaves."

Davinie shouted, "Shut up, mutt! I already saw your transfer request to Eagle Two."

The officers all began to giggle.

Rex said, "That has nothing to do with Timmy. I'm just sick of all of you." Rex then walked over to Stacy and attempted to whisper, "Let me know if Michael does decide to transfer here." Most of the room still heard Rex, and another round of giggles took place as Rex left the conference table area.

Davinie said, "One bit of possible interference with this Michael situation is that Admiral Noem has a request for Eagle Two. They don't have to do it because they didn't originally sign up for such a long mission away."

Captain Jake asked, "What's the mission?"

Davinie answered, "The godlings have agreed to listen to arguments for lifting our exile from their sector of space. If Captain Marshall agrees, I would travel with them to Chuck Norris to make the argument."

Calvin said, "Shouldn't we all go?"

Davinie replied, "Put your pecker away. We aren't letting you anywhere near that girl Star again. Equality can't enter that sector of space anyways while that destroy and kill order is in place. I can go because I wasn't aboard either ship during that nonsense."

Calvin replied, "What? I was just asking."

*****

Timothy opened the door to his living quarters to allow Clair and Johnny in.

Johnny said, "We're here. Now can you tell us why?"

Clair asked, "Why isn't my W2 working?"

Timothy answered Clair first. "It's not working because they're doing a weapons test today. You can watch the test if you want, but we have to watch Michael's ultimate magic trick first."

Johnny said, "We can't watch that. All the blast doors are closed."

Timothy responded, "I know I can trust Clair. Johnny, I need you to swear you won't tell anyone about what I'm about to show you."

Johnny was fourteen and towered over Timothy. Yet Timothy was the one who started torturing Johnny in his schoolwork this past month. Johnny said, "I promise."

Timothy proceeded to turn on a projection screen that displayed an image of a jet arm flying in deep space.

Johnny exclaimed, "You hacked the security feed! You're in so much trouble."

Timothy replied, "I didn't hack the security feed. I mean, I did have to hack the security systems to piggyback in this signal, but this isn't security footage. This is from Michael's drone. He's going to do his new magic trick, and I'm going to help record it."

Johnny said, "Isn't that kinda stupid? I mean, my mom says this weapons test is going to be spectacular. Won't that make Michael's magic trick seem lame?"

Timothy replied, "Nope. Their test is going to be with radiation that you can't even see. They're basically just going to turn a thirty-mile diameter of space into a giant microwave, but nothing will be in it to watch cook. Just a bunch of sensors analyzing data. Boring."

Clair asked, "Isn't that dangerous? My mom tells me never to stand next to the microwave while it's running."

Timothy replied, "It's fine. We will be far away. Michael is scheduled to patrol the far end of the test site. He's not going as deep as I want him to go because he's afraid if he gets too close to the magnetic void, it'll interfere with his magic trick. I could have told him if it would or not, but he wouldn't let me look at his formula. But as long as Michael does a loop to finish his trick, he'll be fine."

Johnny replied, "I have no idea what you're talking about, but I think it's started."

Michael's jet arm was now flying erratically with white smoke being released behind it.

Timothy exclaimed, "This is it!"

Clair yelled, "That's an *M*! He's drawing an *M*!"

Timothy said, "He's going to write his name—Michael the Magician."

Johnny asked, "It's kinda cool. I've never seen space writing before, but it's not something I'd call an ultimate magic trick."

Timothy replied, "He's not finished yet."

A few minutes later, Clair said, "The *M* is starting to fade."

Timothy said, "Michael sees it. He's speeding up to finish the *N*. After that, he just has to do a loop."

Johnny asked, "What's he going to do after he finishes writing it?"

Timothy answered, "He's going to shoot it with his spider cannon." Timothy jumped up from his seat and shouted, "No!"

Clair asked, "What's wrong?"

Timothy started to run out of the room as he answered, "He's not doing a loop! He's going to fly right into the microwave. I have to get the captain to warn him!"

Timothy's quarters were located on the third floor. It was a straight shot from Timothy's doorway to the bridge on the far side of the ship. Timothy ran as fast as his little legs would carry him. Timothy knew he had less than a minute to save Michael's life.

Timothy could see Frank standing in front of the bridge door. Timothy yelled as he ran, "Open the door!"

Frank shouted back, "Slow down!"

Timothy attempted to run past Frank, hoping the door to the bridge would open automatically, but Frank easily snatched Timothy up.

Timothy immediately began to thrash about, shouting, "Let me in! I need the captain to save Michael from the radiation!"

Frank smiled and replied, "You of all people aren't getting in there. Dangerous weapons are being tested, and I won't let you get near the controls."

Timothy screamed, "Captain! I need to save Michael! *Captain*!"

Timothy continued to scream as Frank said, "Scream all you want, kid. The rooms are soundproof. You're not getting in."

*****

Captain Jake sat on the bridge with Samantha, Calvin, and Tie at their stations. Displayed on the main screen was a split image with Jesus on the right, piloting Serenity. On the left was Dr. Stevens.

Dr. Stevens was a short man with short dark hair. He chose to wear glasses that he always had to push back up into place. His ship was a modified cargo vessel filled with equipment to collect data from the weapons test. The target for the test was a metallic orb filled with sensors.

Captain Jake spoke with Captain Marshall over an open verbal link and said, "Captain Marshall, is the target area clear?"

Captain Marshall replied, "Yes, sir. Long-range scans are also clear. We are alone."

Captain Jake said, "Jesus, are you in position?"

Jesus replied, "Forty miles from target. Blast shields are down. I'm ready when you are, Captain."

Captain Jake asked, "You ready, Dr. Stevens?"

Dr. Stevens replied, "We are, Captain."

Captain Jake said, "Jesus, you have permission to fire."

Jesus said, "Missile away."

Calvin said, "Captain, white exhaust just started coming out of Michaels jet arm."

Captain Jake said, "Michael, you all right out there?"

Michael replied, "Everything fine out here, Captain. You just watch your weapons test."

Tie said, "Thirty seconds to impact."

Calvin said, "That's an *M*. Michael's sky writing in space."

Captain Marshall said, "This is no time for one of your magic tricks, Michael."

Michael replied, "This is the last chance I'll get. Can't waste it."

Tie said, "Missile is firing reverse thrusters. It looks like it's parking right next to the target."

Calvin asked, "Is that what it's supposed to do? Are we here to test driver assist parking?"

Captain Jake replied, "Maybe it's a dud after all?"

Samantha remarked, "Like every man who boasts about being good in the sack. They talk a good game, but ten seconds after you get their onesie off, they're done."

Calvin was about to make his own remark when something on his computer terminal caught his eye. After taking a second to review it, Calvin exclaimed, "Holy shit, it's a nuke!"

Captain Jake asked, "What's a nuke?"

Tie answered, "The missile was."

Samantha said, "Aren't nukes supposed to make a mushroom cloud? I don't see a mushroom cloud. Speaking of shrooms, does Stacy grow any?"

Tie ignored Samantha's shroom comment but answered her nuke question. "There's no atmosphere in space to make a mushroom cloud. It's just pure radiation, ten times stronger than what it would be in an atmosphere. It's never been done in Einstein before. I don't think it's legal too."

Captain Jake asked, "Dr. Stevens, did we just test-fire a nuclear weapon?"

Dr. Stevens pushed his glasses back up on his face then replied, "You know I can't answer that."

Michael shouted over the comms, "Be witness to the greatest illusion ever performed!"

Captain Marshall said, "Michael, you don't have authorization to fire your spider cannon."

Captain Jake said, "Dolly, can you magnify and put on the screen what Michael's doing?"

The main screen changed to show *Ichael the Magician* written in white smoke with Michael flying toward them.

Michael said, "Damn! It didn't."

Captain Jake shouted, "Michael! You're heading toward the cordoned off area."

Calvin replied, "He's already in it, Captain."

Captain Jake shouted, "Get out of there, Michael! You can't see it, but that area's filled with deadly radiation." After a moment of silence, Captain Jake said, "Dolly, put Michael's cockpit feed on the main screen."

The main screen changed to show an image of an orange power suit with the letters EPF written across the chest (standard suit for EPF volunteers). The tinted visor was down with an image of a wizard holding a magic wand being displayed on it.

Captain Marshall ordered, "Michael, talk to me right now."

Captain Jake said, "Calvin, cancel the band on communications. Get Dr. Helix on the comms."

Dr. Stevens exclaimed, "You can't do that! I'm not losing my bonus because you broke the contract."

Captain Jake repeated, "Now, Calvin."

Calvin replied, "Communications back online."

Dr. Stevens asked, "Why? There's nothing left of your man except melted, boiling organs. You can't go to him or bring his body back. It's too radioactive."

Captain Jake looked at Dr. Stevens's image in the corner of the main screen. He was trying to hold his temper. Captain Jake said, "Dolly, end link." The main display screen went blank. Captain Jake then said, "Dolly, call an emergency officers' meeting right now."

Captain Jake moved to leave the bridge, but he stopped in his tracks the moment the bridge doors opened and a child's frantic screams of "CAPTAIN! CAPTAIN!" filled the room.

Frank sensed the bridge doors open and turned, still holding the thrashing Timothy under his arm. Timothy's eyes were so full of tears he didn't even see the bridge door open. He just continued to scream.

Captain Jake stood frozen, muttering, "How did he know?"

Samantha pushed Captain Jake to the side to take Timothy from Frank's arm.

Timothy stopped screaming as he wrapped his arms around Samantha and asked, "I let Michael die, didn't I?"

Calvin asked Frank, "How long was he out there?"

Frank answered, "Five to ten minutes. He wouldn't calm down."

Samantha glared at Frank while holding and rubbing Timothy's back then asked in an angry whisper, "Why the fuck didn't you let him in?"

Frank looked about the room at all the long faces then asked, with the soft tone of someone who already knew the answer, "What happened?" After a long moment of silence, Frank whispered, "I was just doing my job."

Samantha sneered, "What a good soldier you are."

Captain Jake regained his composure then said, "Officers' meeting now. Samantha, could you please bring Timmy?"

While the officers gathered inside the sound barrier of the conference table, the rest of the crew gathered outside, awaiting the news of their return to Einstein.

Stacy was already at the conference table when she saw Captain Jake with Samantha, carrying Timothy, approach. Stacy immediately rushed to them and asked, "What happened?"

Timothy, in a hoarse voice, replied, "I'm sorry. I let him die."

Captain Jake said softly, "It wasn't your fault, Timmy."

Stacy asked, "What's going on, Jake? Who died?"

Captain Jake placed his hand on Stacy's shoulder and said, "Let's talk in hydroponics."

Stacy pulled back and shouted, "No! Tell me now!"

Captain Jake softly said, "There was an incident. We—"

Stacy slapped Captain Jake as hard as she could as tears started to form in her eyes. Stacy strongly said, "No!" After a long pause, Stacy took Timothy from Samantha then said, "Let's get you some water." Stacy then walked, carrying Timothy toward the hydroponics bay.

Captain Jake attempted to follow them, but Stacy paused and angrily said, "Stay here, Jake."

Rex now approached and asked, "What's going on?"

Stacy said, "Come with us, Rex." Then the three walked into the hydroponics bay.

Equality remained near the test firing site for the evening, setting up warning beacons around the area. Dr. Stevens and his scientists finished gathering their data. All officers aboard Equality were fully informed of what transpired and given the evening to process it with an officers' meeting scheduled the next morning.

*****

Captain Jake woke up early and stopped by Timothy's room to have a chat with him, but his room was empty. Captain Jake then moved his search to the second floor where Stacy's quarters were located.

Stacy opened the door and pleasantly said, "Good morning, Jake."

Captain Jake replied, "Good morning, Stacy. How are you holding up?"

Stacy replied, "I'm better now. What do you need, Jake?"

Captain Jake replied, "I need to speak with Timothy about what happened."

Stacy stepped into the hall then snapped her fingers, causing the door to close behind her. Stacy asked, "Why Jake?"

Captain Jake replied, "Because he knew Michael was going to die before I knew anything was wrong. I have to know how and if he knows anything else."

Stacy stated, "You're not locking him up, Jake."

Captain Jake said, "I won't. This stays between us."

Stacy snapped her fingers again to open the door.

Captain Jake entered the room and was immediately met by Rex, who let out a low growl then asked, "Why didn't you let him onto the bridge?"

Captain Jake answered, "I didn't know he was there, or I would have."

Timothy was sitting on a couch in the next room, watching cartoons. Timothy said, "It's okay, Rex. Frank was the one who wouldn't let me enter the bridge."

Captain Jake walked over and sat down next to Timothy on the couch. Captain Jake said, "Frank feels horrible about what happened. We all do. How are you holding up?"

Timothy replied, "Stacy let me and Rex sleep with her last night."

Captain Jake said, "Stacy's an amazing woman. You know she's the reason I came here to Einstein."

Timothy asked, "Why is that?"

Captain Jake blushed briefly at how much of a crush he had on Stacy back then. Captain Jake answered, "She and I were friends. Stacy was the first real friend I ever had. When she decided she wanted to come here, I decided I wanted to come with her."

Timothy said, "Yeah, I can see that."

Captain Jake asked, "Timmy, how did you know Michael was in danger? Did you hack into the security feeds?"

Timothy suddenly lit up and exclaimed, "The solar writing! I forgot all about it. Did it work?"

Captain Jake asked, "What's solar writing? Was that what he called the smoke coming out of his jet arm?"

Timothy got a look of disappointment on his face then said, "Must not have. May I see the sensor readings of it so I can find out what went wrong?"

Captain Jake said, "Afraid not. The sensors also recorded weapons test data that's classified."

Timothy started to type on his W2 as he said, "I don't need the radioactive data." The TV, which was playing cartoons, now displayed a video of Michael's jet arm space writing. Timothy spoke as they watched. "See how the *M* is starting to disappear. That's when Michael kinda panicked and sped up, which would have been fine, but you see there? I told him a dozen times, 'After you finished writing, you need to do a loop to get back to the writing.'"

Captain Jake asked, "Why does he have to get back to the writing?"

Timothy answered, “Because the EPF is cheap and didn’t pay extra to have rotational self-targeting spider cannons installed on the jet arms. They only shoot at what Michael is flying at.”

The screen now showed Michael approaching the letter L of smoke and firing his spider cannon. A pink flash of lightning shot forth from the spider cannon, but the lightning never reached the smoke.

Captain Jake asked, “What was supposed to happen?”

Timothy explained, “The lightning was supposed to strike metal particles in the smoke, creating a chemical reaction that would make the smoke turn bright as the sun. The words *Michael the Magician* were going to be seen throughout Einstein.”

Captain Jake said, “Looks like he was in range when he fired. Must not have been enough metal in the smoke for the lightning to target it. If there was, the lightning would have been red instead of pink.”

Timothy said, “I asked Michael to let me review his chemical composition, but he said it was his secret.”

Captain Jake asked, “How did you know the weapons test was radioactive? I didn’t even know about that.”

Timothy replied, “Really? How did you not know they were testing a nuclear weapon?”

Captain Jake answered, “They couldn’t tell us. They signed an NDA.”

Timothy replied, “So what? Their name is the RO Research Station. That literally tells you what they’re researching right there.”

Captain Jake was suddenly feeling like an idiot for never asking what RO stood for. Captain Jake now asked, “What does RO stand for?”

Timothy replied, “Robert Oppenheimer, the creator of the atomic bomb.”

Captain Jake said, “Not even Thirteen caught on to that.”

Timothy replied, “I doubt that.”

Captain Jake wondered for a second if Thirteen really had known what they were testing but then said, “You do know it was wrong to hack into Equality’s security feed.”

Timothy replied, "This video isn't from a security feed."

Captain Jake asked, "Where's it from then?"

Timothy replied, "I'll tell you on one condition."

Captain Jake smiled and said, "A condition, really?"

Timothy said, "No, make that two conditions. Wait, three conditions. Yes, three conditions."

Captain Jake tried not to laugh as he asked, "And what are these conditions?"

Timothy replied, "The first condition is that I want all of Michael's research data and magic equipment."

Captain Jake said, "I don't know if that's possible. Michael might have had family."

Stacy said, "Michael's parents aren't into magic. They won't object."

Captain Jake said, "All right. As long as there's nothing dangerous. What's the second condition?"

Timothy answered, "A direct line to you so I don't have to let anyone else die."

Captain Jake was taken aback by this request. After a moment of pondering, Captain Jake responded, "How about I do one better?"

Timothy asked, "What do you mean?"

Captain Jake said, "I hear you just finished college."

Timothy nodded yes then said, "There are still some master's degrees I'm thinking about getting though."

Captain Jake asked, "Well, do you know what my first job aboard this ship was?"

Timothy answered, "Floater. You had to learn every department to help out wherever needed."

Captain Jake said, "That's right, and my position was never filled after I got promoted."

Timothy lit up then said, "Really! I can have your old job?"

Rex moaned, "You're going to put him to work? Isn't that illegal?"

Captain Jake said, "His title will be junior apprentice floater. I'm sure Davinie can make a legal argument for a college graduate to be able to work."

Timothy looked up at Stacy and said, "Did you hear that, Stacy? I'm going to have a job. I'm going to get to work with you just like you used to work with Captain Jake."

Stacy smiled then said, "Yes, you will. I'm going to make you work harder than Jake ever did."

Timothy exclaimed, "That's not fair!"

Captain Jake smiled then asked, "What's the third condition?"

Timothy lowered his head then said, "The third kinda goes with the first." Timothy raised his head and his hand then said, "We need to shake on it first. That's how Michael said men give their word. No takebacks."

Captain Jake shook Timothy's hand and said, "Okay. Now what's this third thing that goes with the first?"

Timothy replied, "I need you to go get me Michael's secret cloaked drone that's out in space. Its camera feed is what we were watching before. Remember, no takebacks."

*****

Shortly after Captain Jake's conversation with Timothy, the officers gathered around the conference table for their emergency morning meeting.

Captain Jake asked Filipe, "Are all the warning beacons deployed?"

Filipe replied, "Jesus and Eagle Two are still deploying. They should be done within the hour."

Stacy asked, "What are we doing about the RO Space Station?"

Davinie said, "Legally, they did nothing wrong."

Frank said, "Isn't making a nuclear weapon illegal?"

Davinie answered, "No. It actually isn't. Not making one has just been common sense until now."

Calvin said, "I started tracing the money funding this project. It's not actually the EPF founding this operation."

Davinie asked, "What do you mean it isn't the EPF?"

Calvin answered, "The fund is under the EPF name, but no EPF funding has ever gone into the account. Before it was an EPF fund, it was labeled under the Middleman defense fund. Again, no Middleman defense funds were placed into the account."

Captain Jake asked, "Where's the money coming from?"

Calvin replied, "Shell companies. Untraceable. This account is only used for two things. The RO Research Station and Icarus Innovations on planet Icarus. The current balance in the account is zero."

Stacy asked, "Are the people funding this the ones who tried to kill Jake in Hades City?"

Thirteen said, "The same people are most likely responsible for that, as well as working with the pirates to disperse that black mold."

Calvin asked, "Does that mean that the pirates were raiding ships so they could fund building nuclear weapons?"

Captain Jake said, "If that was the case, then the pirates would be the ones out here, not us."

Frank said, "We should destroy the space station."

Dr. Helix objected, "You can't kill those people."

Frank said, "Of course not. We can evacuate the station first. People were already packing to leave."

Captain Jake said, "It is EPF property. I certainly don't want any more nuclear weapons built. Dolly, call Dr. Stevens and put the call on the conference table screen." An image of Dr. Stevens pushing up his glasses appeared on the conference table screen.

Dr. Stevens said, "I'm busy analyzing the data. Make this quick."

Captain Jake replied, "You're fired. Is that quick enough for you?"

Dr. Stevens exclaimed, "What! Why? It's not my fault your man broke protocol."

Captain Jake said, "I don't know who hired you, but there's no way the EPF will be using nuclear weapons. We will not allow anyone else to put this deadly technology back in play."

Dr. Stevens was outraged as he said, "I did exactly what your people hired me to do! Captain Spike made it very clear—"

Captain Jake cut Dr. Stevens off, "Did you say Captain Spike?"

Calvin said, "I told you."

Dr. Stevens screamed, "This is entrapment! You made me say his name just so you could invoke my NDA!"

Davinie said, "I'm an attorney, Dr. Stevens. I'm telling you right now the NDA you signed with the wanted pirate Captain Spike isn't valid."

Dr. Stevens repeated, "Pirate?"

Captain Jake said, "Dolly, show Dr. Stevens a picture of Captain Spike." An image appeared in the corner of the screen of a one-eyed pirate in his forties.

Dr. Stevens said, "That's not him. This man was on 15 for Life."

Captain Jake said, "We don't have pictures of Captain Spike since he started taking 15 for Life."

Dr. Stevens replied, "What? But only Romeos can take 15 for Life. He can't be a pirate. That would be a death sentence."

Frank said, "If the pirates truly are behind this, it's a trap. They could be back at the space station right now, raiding it."

Captain Jake said, "They don't need to raid it. They think Captain Spike is their employer. Dr. Stevens, how many completed nuclear weapons do you have back on the space station?"

Dr. Stevens replied, "There are no other prototypes or nuclear material. We only received enough for this weapons test."

Davinie asked, "Well, what the hell was the point of this then?"

Captain Jake said, "No idea, but I don't like it. Signal jammers mean we can't call to check on the base. Thirteen, any idea what they're planning?"

Thirteen replied, "I cannot say."

Captain Jake said, "Dolly, put Jesus and Captain Marshall on the screen." Images of both appeared on the conference table screen. Captain Jake said, "I'm taking Equality back to check on the RO Space Station. Keep your eyes open and join us when you're finished. Dolly will be sending you the conversation from this meeting to get you up to speed on what's going on. Dr. Stevens, stay with them."

Dr. Stevens said, "If my people are in danger, I should go with you."

Captain Jake replied, "If there's trouble, you have two ships and seven jet arms here to protect you." Captain Jake then double tapped his left wrist to end the call.

*****

Equality reached the RO Research Space Station, and they were relieved to find nothing had happened. Captain Jake relayed a message of a possible imminent pirate attack that required the evacuation of the space station. People were already packed, and there was a cargo vessel already waiting to take them to Omega Mining, so this wasn't an issue. The only thing concerning the scientists was their bonuses. Captain Jake avoided that question.

While the space station evacuated onto their cargo ship, Serenity and the others safely returned. They were immediately dispatched to help the private security force bring in the spacemines for transport. Captain Jake didn't want to leave anything for the pirates.

It took several hours, but eventually, everyone and every spacemine was ready to leave. Serenity stayed separated from Equality to help carry spacemines and protect the cargo vessel. While towing the spacemines, they would be unable to activate the Carrie effect drive. Only Dr. Stevens's cargo vessel had a Carrie effect drive. The other cargo vessel had no FP shields.

Captain Jake asked, "Is the RO Research Station all clear?"

Calvin answered, "All clear, Captain."

Captain Jake asked, "Do you have any farewells, Dr. Stevens?"

Dr. Stevens appeared in the corner on the main screen. He pushed up his glasses and said, "It's a waste you feel the need to destroy it."

Captain Jake replied, "I don't know what Captain Spike's plan was, but I'll be damned if I'll let him get his hands on this. Tie, is the rail gun ready?"

Tie replied, "Ready to fire and aimed at the station's stormfront battery."

Captain Jake ordered, "Fire."

The rail gun fired, sending a standard shell instantaneously flying into the RO Research Space Station, where it punctured the stormfront battery core. The sudden release of the frozen and electrically charged contents caused the station to explode in a dazzling display of electricity of every color.

Harry said, "The signal blockers are offline. We are back on the web."

Suddenly, Calvin said, "I just registered three more explosions. Jake, the cargo vessels and that security mothership are gone."

Suddenly, the ship began to spin as Samantha turned Equality about to see the other ships, but all they saw was debris with lightning flickering off it like the space station they just blew up.

Captain Jake asked, "Any survivors?"

Calvin replied, "I'm not reading any."

Captain Marshall appeared on screen wearing his orange power suit with EPF written in black letters over the chest. Captain Marshall asked, "What happened?"

Tie said, "I know Dr. Stevens and the mothership had their FP shields up."

Captain Jake said, "Explosives had to have been rigged to their stormfront batteries. Blowing up the station must have set them off."

Calvin said, "Captain Spike set us up. He knew what we'd do."

Tie asked, "Why? What does a bunch of dead scientists get him?"

Harry gasped and said, "Captain! The outer rings know we were testing a nuclear weapon."

Captain Jake asked, "How?"

Calvin answered, "Captain Spike. How many different ways is this guy going to screw us?"

Harry said, "New feeds from the outer rings the past two weeks are full of stories about our nuclear testing."

Captain Jake said, "We checked news feeds daily. How did we not know about these stories?"

Harry answered, "The stories must have been filtered out of the feeds we got."

Tie said, "There's a half dozen ships headed this way. They just dropped Carrie effect drives and are powering up rail guns."

Captain Jake asked, "Captain Spike?"

Calvin answered, "Their markings have them registered as outer ringer ships. Four from Hades City and two from Omega Mining."

Harry said, "They just broadcasted. They are saying we killed all the scientists to cover up the test firing of the nuclear weapon in outer ringer space."

Tie said, "We didn't do that."

Captain Marshall said, "Incoming."

Tie said, "They fired their rail guns."

Samantha said, "They're far enough away. I can still dodge."

Captain Marshall asked, "Are we fighting back?"

Harry said, "They won't answer my calls."

Captain Jake replied, "I have enough innocent blood on my hands today. Red alert. I need all residents to get strapped in."

Samantha said, "It's dangerous to activate the Carrie effect drive while they're firing at us. One rail gun shell hit without it and we're done for."

Captain Jake said, "Captain Marshall, get out of here. You can use us as cover as you activate your Carrie effect drive. Head straight back into the magnetic void and take the long way around. Run through your spacemines on your way out to spread them out."

Captain Marshall said, "I can do that, but without that security mothership to arm them, they're useless."

Captain Jake replied, "I know that. Hopefully, they don't. Jesus, I need you to do the same before we merge."

Jesus replied, "Only because I know we drained the core of these things before we collected them."

Both Captain Marshall and Jesus drove their ships through the stockpile of dozens of mines they were towing. Captain Marshall then used Equality as cover while he safely activated his Carrie effect drive.

Captain Jake said, "Let's find the safest place to merge, Jesus. After that, we can use Serenity's plasma rockets to give us enough distance to safely activate our Carrie effect drive."

Jesus said, “No arguments here, Captain.”

Equality and Serenity began to merge as Equality suddenly shook.

Captain Jake asked, “What was that?”

Tie answered, “Piece of scattershot hit us in a section of the shield that was down while we merged. Hull is intact, and we are merged.”

Captain Jake said, “Samantha—”

Samantha cut Captain Jake off and said, “You don’t have to tell me twice.”

Icarus

An officers' meeting was held the night after fleeing the RO Research Station to discuss their next move.

Calvin asked sarcastically, "Was our mission supposed to be to start a war? Because if it was, I think we succeeded."

Frank said, "The pirates had us set up from the moment we got here."

Captain Jake said, "Captain Spike has had us set up from the moment the SS Minnow showed up in Einstein."

Davinie said, "This isn't a pirate setup. It's much larger than that."

Dr. Helix said, "Forty-four lives lost. For what?"

Stacy ground her teeth as she spoke. "Even if the pirates are just someone else's pawns, they were involved with killing those people. We need to hunt down every person involved."

Captain Jake said, "I'm the one who ordered the death of all those people when I told Tie to fire."

Frank said, "There's no way for you to have known, Captain."

Captain Jake said, "Their blood is on my hands, and I will find out who is behind this. Our next destination is Icarus Innovations. The money that funded RO also funds them. We will go have a talk with them."

Dr. Helix said, "Did you say Icarus? I know it's on the third ring, so it's considered an inner ring planet, but it's inhabited by isolationists. The planet has gravity with no breathable atmosphere or abundance of valuable minerals. They are basically what you would call the Amish of Einstein—a group of people who settled in a worthless planet to be left alone so they could return to a simpler way of life."

Calvin asked, "Why would a group of isolationists have a cool name like Icarus Innovations?"

Harry replied, "It's probably just a shell company."

Caption Jake said, "Being left alone means they could be doing anything without anyone knowing."

Filipe said, "I suggest we stop at Alpha Mining first for repairs. While we were merging with Serenity, we got struck by a piece of scattershot."

Stacy said, "I felt that."

Captain Jake asked, "How much damage did it do?"

Filipe answered, "When we merged, several clamps made of titanium X extended to lock the two ships in place. The scattershot managed to hit one of these clamps, causing a crack."

Captain Jake about jumped out of his seat when a voice from behind him asked, "What's the big deal? We're already connected." Captain Jake looked back to see Rex standing there.

Frank was about to start yelling when Captain Jake started to explain, "Titanium X is extremely strong but becomes extremely brittle once cracked. If it should break, safety protocols kick in, separating the ships."

Filipe added, "Should that happen while the Carrie effect happens, it gets cut off immediately. None of the FP that normally returns to Serenity would be able to return. That FP would most likely float off into space."

Frank asked, "Can't you just 3D print a new part?"

Filipe answered, "No, the material is too hard for that."

Dr. Helix asked, "Shouldn't you have a spare then?"

Filipe answered, "In hindsight, yes. The material took getting hit by a rail gun to crack. I could never have predicted that happening."

Captain Jake asked, "Will Icarus have what we need for repairs?"

Filipe answered, "They should. Titanium X is used to construct pillars. Their settlement is underground."

Harry said, "I can't send a request until we reach orbit. They don't believe in long-range communications."

Calvin said, "Alpha Mining is the same distance from where we are now."

Captain Jake said, "We go to Icarus. If they turn away a damaged ship, then we know they're guilty, and we call Admiral Noem for reinforcements. If they agree to help us, then we can go down and ask questions."

Davinie asked, "If it's a trap?"

Captain Jake asked, "Do they have any planetary defenses?"

Frank answered, "No planetary defenses or armed ships."

Captain Jake said, "Serenity goes down for the part and investigation. In the meantime, our extremely armed Equality watches from above. They won't try anything. Meeting adjourned." As everyone started to stand up, Captain Jake said, "Filipe, can you stay for a moment?"

Everyone left the shimmering barrier of the conference table except Captain Jake, Filipe, and Rex.

Filipe looked down at Rex and asked, "Why are you still here?"

Rex replied, "Because I feel like it."

Captain Jake said, "He's fine. Were you able to retrieve the drone Timmy told us about?"

Filipe answered, "Yes, we have it. Can't believe Michael had a camouflaged drone. That explains how he pulled off a lot of his illusions during his act."

Captain Jake said, "I want Timmy to be able to have the drone."

Rex stated, "Giving that kid a camouflaged drone is the worst idea ever."

Filipe replied, "I'll be removing the illegal tech before giving him the drone."

Rex said, "Still, flying things are unnatural."

Filipe replied, "Don't knock it till you try it. Why don't you let me break the magnetic locks for you so you can try it?" Filipe then took a step toward Rex.

Rex immediately backed up, let out a low growl, then said, "Don't even think about it."

Captain Jake said, "There's another matter I wanted to talk to you about."

Filipe turned his attention back to the captain and said, "Name it."

Captain Jake said, "When Michael died, he was trying to perform what was supposed to be his ultimate magic trick."

Filipe said, "The space writing? I know the *M* faded before he finished. That could be fixed by flying faster, I would think."

Captain Jake said, "There's that, but the real issue, according to Timmy, was how Michael fired his spider cannon at the smoke at the end. It was supposed to turn it into a ball of light that could be seen from Romeo and Juliet."

Filipe replied, "Seriously? That could have blinded us."

Captain Jake said, "That's why Michael did it during the weapons test. We all had our blast shields down."

Filipe said, "Clever."

Captain Jake said, "I want you to have Timmy help you with the formula."

Filipe said, "Sir? He's just a kid."

Rex scoffed. "Kid my ass."

Captain Jake nodded to Rex and said, "You are aware of what that kid can do."

Filipe replied, "I had forgotten. I'll be happy to have his help."

Rex laughed and said, "You think he'll be helping you? That's cute."

*****

Johnny and Timmy were in engineering sitting at a table while cleaning and polishing gears. Johnny said, "I can't believe I had to start working because you got a job."

Timothy replied, "That's not my fault. Besides, don't you like getting to work with your mom?"

Johnny said, "My mom orders me around enough at home. I don't need to go to work so she can do it more."

Timothy asked, "I wish my moms could still order me around. Why does your mom keep checking that screen?" The two looked over to watch Emily staring at a computer terminal.

Johnny answered, "I don't know."

Timothy left Johnny to go see. Timothy asked Emily, "What are you looking at?"

Emily answered, "There's a part we need to keep an eye on. Nothing for you to worry about."

Timothy looked at the screen then asked, "Is that a titanium X clamp sensor? How can titanium X crack?"

Emily smiled at Timothy then said, "I heard you were a bright one."

Timothy replied, "I get that a lot. How long before it breaks?"

Emily answered, "There's no way to know."

Timothy stated, "Yes, there is. It must have happened when the ship shook while we were merging with Serenity. That's really bad luck because only the bottom section has its FP shield down. It had to be a rail gun scattershot that hit it. Only a rail gun produces enough force to damage titanium X, and it had to be scattershot because a standard shell would have ripped right through it. All I need to know when it will break is security camera footage of the scattershot piece that hit us so I can calculate mass, trajectory, and velocity. After that, I need the specs on hardness for this specific clamps composition."

Timothy walked back over to where he was sitting. Emily asked, "Where are you going?"

Timothy took hold of the chair he was sitting in then said, "Dolly, can you release the magnetic seal on this chair for me? Please and thank you." After Dolly removed the seal, Timothy carried the chair back to the terminal then climbed up the chair to reach the terminal.

Emily asked, "You sure you know what you're doing?"

Johnny said, "Just let him do it, Mom. He won't stop bugging you if you don't."

Emily said, "Okay. Dolly will keep you from going anywhere you're not supposed to. If anything starts flashing, come and get me. I'll be doing preventive maintenance on the 3D printers."

Timothy nodded yes as he stared at the screen, making calculations in his head.

Emily left the room as Timothy worked at the terminal for about ten minutes. Once he was finished, he carried the chair back to the table and said, "Dolly, you can reengage the magnetic seal. Thank you."

Johnny asked, "How long before it breaks?" But Timothy didn't answer. He just sat down and stared into space as the wheels in his mind turned.

Emily returned to the room and asked, "Did you learn anything?"

Timmy finally snapped back to reality and, with a smile on his face, said, "It will break when we cancel the Carrie effect drive on our way to Icarus."

Emily repeated, "Icarus. I didn't know that's where we're going. Seems like an odd place to go for repairs. You sure about that?"

Timothy answered, "I had to look at our flight trajectory to determine outside variables that might speed up the crack."

Emily patted Timothy on the head then said, "You really are a bright one." Emily then left the room.

Timothy thought Emily was being patronizing but didn't care. The part breaking when he said it would, would prove him right. Timothy's face returned to a blank expression as he once again entered deep thought.

Johnny stared at Timothy for a minute. Ever since Michael died, Johnny felt guilty for not going with him to the bridge. Johnny thought that if he had, he might have been able to convince Frank to let Timothy talk to the captain and save Michael's life. Johnny was determined to never sit back again if ever that kind of situation occurred. Johnny asked, "What is it, Timmy?"

This time, Timothy answered, "Secret meeting tonight in my room. I need you and Clair's help, or people are going to die."

*****

Equality approached Icarus with everyone at their stations on the bridge. The moment the Carrie effect drive was shut off, red lights began to flash on everyone's consoles.

Calvin stated, "We're losing FP."

Captain Jake replied, "Clamp broke. Keep going, Samantha. Equality can go back for the dropped FP while Serenity goes down to the planet. Assuming we get permission."

Tie said, "Serenity won't have much for FP shields with just its reserves."

Captain Jake said, "We can manually apply Equality's reserves to the hull of Serenity before it goes down."

Harry said, "Request sent. Incoming transmission."

Captain Jake said, "Main screen."

The main screen changed from the approaching view of the brown planet Icarus to an image of a brunette woman. The woman was tall and slender, appearing to be in her late twenties and dressed as a flight attendant from the 1970s. She said, "We have received your request for a titanium X clamp and an audience with the CEO of Icarus Innovations. You may visit our city, but no more than four may enter. One of the four must be Captain Jake. No power attire or weapons are permitted on Icarus." The screen switched back to the view of the approaching planet.

Tie said, "This feels like a trap."

Calvin said, "The assassins are probably waiting for you down there."

Samantha stated, "Of course it's a trap. We're here because the account used to pay RO was also used to fund a company down there. That's how you bait a trap 101."

Captain Jake replied, "They had no way of knowing Calvin would be looking into it. Unless you're saying Calvin's one of them."

Calvin stated, "I only thought to look into it because Samantha kept quoting a movie she just watched."

Samantha giggled then loudly said, "Show me the money!" Then in a normal tone, she said, "You already know I'm a pirate, and I'm telling you it's a trap."

Captain Jake said, "Guess that means none of you are volunteering to come down with me."

Harry replied, "I want to go. The Icarus people rarely see visitors. It will make for great PR that we desperately need. The outer rings have canceled trade and are blocking all signals from the inner rings."

Captain Jake said, "Sounds good to me."

Samantha said, "Was nice knowing you guys."

*****

Timothy met with Johnny in engineering by the stormfront battery (a large metal cylinder that ran through several decks with multiple wires running out of it). Both of the boys were wearing space suits with cylinders on their backs. The cylinders had a long tube coming out of the side at the bottom that connected to a spray nozzle.

Timothy asked, "Are you ready?"

Johnny replied, "I can't believe I let you talk me into this. We could get into so much trouble for nothing."

Timothy said, "It's happening just as I said it would so far. The coupler broke just when I said it would. Now before Serenity can go down, we will need to manually apply FP to their hull."

Johnny said, "I get that. What I don't get is how that gets us inside Serenity to go down to the planet with them."

Timothy said, "We just have to hold onto the hull and ride Serenity down."

Johnny exclaimed, "That won't work! We'll die!"

Timothy began to laugh. Once he stopped, he said, "I'll get us inside. Is that the special canister I packed for you?"

Johnny nodded yes then said, "Frank is going to kill you when he finds out. We should just tell the captain or my mom."

Timothy replied, "Captain Jake already suspects the people of Icarus are bad. That's why he came here instead of Alpha Mining. Alpha Mining is where we should have gone for the part. Icarus most likely won't have the right sized part we need down there. If it's a trap like I think, we can't escape without that part. That's why we have to be prepared to do this. If they don't have the part, then we will take what we need to make our own part. That's the only way to make sure we live. These could be the people responsible for killing all those scientists, and we're next if we do nothing."

Johnny said, "Okay. If they don't have the part, we'll do it your way."

Filipe entered the room and said, "I thought I heard voices. What are you two doing all dressed up?"

Timothy gave Filipe a cheesy smile as he held up his spray nozzle and said, "Volunteering to help transfer FP to the hull of Serenity, sir."

Filipe looked at Timothy with surprise then said, "How did you know that we were going to need to do that? I just found out myself."

Timothy replied, "I'm clever, sir."

*****

Captain Jake was aboard Serenity and sitting in the cockpit with Jesus. The two were shooting the bull, waiting for the FP to finish being applied to the hull.

Jesus looked at his console and said, "FP is at appropriate levels."

Zac yelled from the passenger cabin, "Captain, we have a request to enter!"

Captain Jake left the cockpit to enter the passenger cabin then asked, "What did you say?"

July, wearing her yellow power suit with black stripes, was smiling and pointed out her window at Timothy, who was waving and pointing back toward the airlock.

Captain Jake said, "Dolly, call Timothy."

Dolly replied, "His W2 is off, Captain."

Captain Jake said, "Captain's override. Turn Timothy's W2 back on for him."

Dolly replied, "I can't, Captain. There is an error."

July said, "Let him in. There could be something wrong."

April said, "The boy doesn't look to be in distress, sir."

Captain Jake said, "Last time someone didn't let Timmy in, a man died. Dolly, open the outer airlock."

April said, "That wasn't Frank's fault. He feels terrible about it."

Captain Jake said, "I'm sorry. I didn't mean it like that. I just mean Timmy's special. That kid can pull miracles out of his butt if we learn to listen to him. He's already saved more lives than anyone else here by discovering that black mold. He knew the RO Station was working on a nuclear weapon, but no one thought to ask him."

April said, "Why would we? He's a child."

Captain Jake said, "He's a genius with a college diploma at the age of nine."

The inner airlock door opened to show Timmy and Johnny standing there in their space suits. Timmy was waving to Captain Jake while Johnny had his head down, staring at the floor.

Zac, wearing his yellow power suit with black stripes, asked, "What are you doing here, young man?"

Timothy said, "Hi, future father-in-law. Johnny wanted to see his mother, and both of us wanted to see Icarus. I've never been to a planet before. I want to know what gravity feels like."

Captain Jake asked, "Is that why your W2 was offline? So I'd have to let you on board?"

Timothy looked down at the floor as he answered, "My W2 has kinda been acting up lately." Timothy then looked up at Captain Jake and asked, "Can we please go to the surface with you? We'll stay on the ship and behave. We promise."

Captain Jake said, "Johnny, your mom is in the engine room if you want to see her." Johnny turned around and entered the engine room without ever raising his head.

Timothy asked, "Does that mean we can go?"

April said, "They have no weapons, sir. The boys will be safe aboard Serenity."

Captain Jake pressed his W2 then said, "Emily, you have a hitchhiker headed your way. You okay with him tagging along with us?"

Emily's voice returned over the comms. "I see him, Captain. First volunteering to work, and now he wants to spend time with his mom. I don't know what's gotten into him, but I'll take it while it lasts."

*****

There was only one city and one structure on the desolate planet known as Icarus. The structure was a large black pyramid-shaped structure missing the point on top. The top, instead, was a flat surface with a large white circle painted in the middle to indicate to ships where to land.

As Jesus landed Serenity, Captain Jake looked out the window and asked, "How do we get in without wearing power suits? I don't see any airlocks to attach to."

Jesus touched down and replied, "Above my pay grade, boss."

June said, "Easy airlock just popped up."

Jesus checked the security cameras then said, "Annoying bastards." Jesus then spoke loudly, "Everyone stay seated! I need to line up our easy airlocks better." Jesus then readjusted Serenity.

Captain Jake entered the passenger cabin to see Timothy staring out the window at the easy airlock with a look of true hatred. Captain Jake asked, "Everything all right, Timmy?"

Timmy turned to face the captain, putting a big smile on his face, and answered, "Everything's great. Although it's really hard to move in gravity."

Captain Jake said, "Your onesie mimics gravity to build muscle. If you get your W2 to work again, you should adjust the resistance settings so you can move normally."

July said, "I can show you, Timmy. Ours are set to auto adjust so we don't have to worry about it."

April, June, and Harry were already standing in the airlock. April said, "We're ready, Captain."

Zac said, "Any sign of trouble, Captain, and we'll come get you."

Jesus reiterated, "Yes. *They* will go get you."

Captain Jake walked to the airlock and said, "I know. Jesus and heroes don't mix."

The moment the door closed, Timothy told July, "Sorry, but I need to use the bathroom."

July said, "You can go in your space suit."

Timothy replied, "That's gross." Then he continued on his way back to the engine room. Once there, Timothy frantically searched through drawers.

Emily, hearing the commotion, walked over to see what was going on. Emily asked, "What are you looking for?"

Timothy replied, "Diagnostic interface. I need to check on something up front."

Emily opened a drawer that was high above Timothy's head and pulled out a small rectangular device with two USB cords running out of it. Emily asked, "This what you're looking for?"

Timothy took the interface then said, "Thank you. I need Johnny too."

Emily loudly said, "Johnny! Timmy needs you for something!"

Johnny poked his head around the corner, looking less than enthused. Timothy walked over, grabbed Johnny's hand, then began dragging Johnny behind him and said, "Thanks, Johnny's mom."

Emily shouted after them, "You can take those FP transfer canisters off now and stay awhile!"

Timothy and Johnny entered the passenger cabin then immediately slipped into the airlock without anyone noticing. Once the airlock door closed behind them, Timothy began to remove his canister.

Johnny asked, "Did you already hack their security system?"

Timothy unscrewed the cap of his canister then dumped out pieces of Michael's drone as well as four wheels. Timothy said, "It's definitely a trap. I need your W2."

Johnny disconnected his W2 from the sleeve of his space suit and handed it to Timmy. Johnny asked, "Why do you need my W2? That wasn't part of the plan."

Timothy took the W2 and connected it to the diagnostic interface. Timothy said, "Did you see that easy airlock on the landing pad?"

Johnny began to assemble the drone while he replied, "Yeah. My mom pointed it out to me. She was surprised they had one."

Timothy said, "Because they shouldn't have it. This base was built before the easy airlock was invented."

Johnny said, "So they upgraded. What's the big deal?"

Timothy said, "These people are supposed to be low-tech. They don't do upgrades."

Johnny asked, "Are you still going to be able to hack their security system? We can't steal from them until we know we have to."

Timothy said, "It's going to be okay. I synced my W2 to yours. Plug in the interface to their easy airlock, and I can hack into their security feeds from there."

Johnny asked, "Can't you just hack it through Serenity?"

Timothy replied, "They disconnected the easy airlock as soon as the captain and the others were on the other side. They also cut off communications. We have to hurry, Johnny."

A light in the airlock flashed and beeped, indicating the air was removed. The airlock door then opened. Timothy said, "There's not enough air to breathe, but we can still talk. We can't use the easy airlock without Jesus finding out, so you'll have to jump."

Johnny looked down at the twenty-foot drop and said, "No way. Do you not understand how gravity works?"

Timmy replied, "I know how your space suit works. Don't drop the interface or your W2 on the way down." Timothy then pushed Johnny out the airlock.

Johnny screamed as he fell, and although he hit the steel landing pad hard, Johnny's space suit cushioned his fall.

As soon as Johnny got back on his feet, Timothy said, "Catch." Then he dropped Michael's drone down for Johnny to catch. Johnny wasn't able to react in time to catch the large drone, but the impact of hitting Johnny slowed the drone's descent enough not to damage it.

*****

Captain Jake and the away team walked down the easy airlock at a steep angle. Near the bottom was the junction point where they found the Icarus door still closed. Once they were in front of the door, it automatically opened. The door immediately closed behind them once they passed through.

April said, "I prefer manual airlocks, especially when we aren't wearing power suits."

Harry asked, "When did the Icarus people have these installed?"

June said, "Maybe the Icarus people aren't as backwater as we thought."

Captain Jake said, "Careful what you say. Sound travels, and we don't want to insult our hosts."

June said, "Sorry, Captain. Sorry, Icarus people, if you're listening."

The Icarus section of the easy airlock ended at a shaft that went straight down with ladder rungs.

After climbing down this section that led to a small tunnel, the Icarus easy airlock retracted above them.

April said, "We lost contact with Serenity. They must be jamming our signal."

Harry said, "The good news is they don't want us dead. If they did, they'd just open the airlock."

April said, "Please don't give them any ideas."

It was a short walk to the next airlock with long fluorescent bulbs lighting the path. Again, the door opened and closed automatically upon approach. This door had a large wheel in the center that automatically spun to lock and unlock.

The room they entered was thirty feet by thirty feet with tacky wallpaper and red carpet. Along two of the walls were old-fashioned brown love seats that looked like they might recline. The far wall had a plexiglass window next to a hinge door with a doorknob.

Captain Jake walked to the window but could see nothing but an empty cubicle with a swivel chair.

Harry leaned down to pet the carpet and said, "Actual carpet instead of grass."

April walked the room, noticing two ancient bulky security cameras. April said, "I have only seen non-360-degree security cameras in movies."

Captain Jake said, "Guess they are making us wait. Might as well take a seat." Captain Jake headed over to a love seat.

June was already sitting down in the love seat opposite of the one Captain Jake was headed toward. June said, "I wonder how this reclines." Suddenly, the sound of wood cracking filled the room. This noise was quickly followed by a scream of pain from June, who was jumping out of the love seat. June shouted, "Damn it! That was sharp!"

Everyone looked to see that the right arm of June's love seat was mangled.

April yelled, "You swore to me that you had limiters put on that thing!"

June yelled back, "I did!" Then in a softer tone, June said, "They're just touch-sensitive sensors that restrain my strength anytime they sense a pulse." June's voice turned loud again as she said, "It's not my fault! There was something sharp in the arm that startled me."

April retorted, "Your arm's metal. It can't be cut."

June stated, "Touch sensors make it sensitive. Real skin or not."

Captain Jake walked over to the damaged love seat and ripped a piece of cloth away from the armrest. This exposed a set of red diamond chainsaw chains.

Harry asked, "Is that what I think it is?"

April said, "I don't like this. Let's get back to the ship. Now!"

Captain Jake said, "We can't. We don't know if the airlocks open or closed. Assuming we could even get that door to open."

June ran her hands over the armrests of the other love seat then said, "This one's rigged too."

Harry asked, "If it's booby-trapped, why didn't it go off when June sat down?"

April said, "Security cameras. She wasn't their target."

Harry said, "They are set on only killing the captain. That's why they didn't open the airlocks."

Captain Jake said, "Opening the airlocks wouldn't work. It's not a vacuum out there. Zac would get us back to Serenity in time and revive us if necessary. I was about to sit down. You saved my life, June."

June blushed a little then said, "Guess that makes us even for you not ditching me in Hades City."

Harry said, "It is possible these death chairs weren't meant for the captain. It never actually went off."

Captain Jake said, "I'm not sitting down to find out."

April said, "They could have motherships headed this way. Holding us here keeps Equality from running away."

Captain Jake said, "I have faith Jesus would run and get help." Captain Jake walked to the door leading deeper inside to find it locked. Captain Jake said, "June, mind opening this for us?"

June walked over to the door. The sound of metal twisting and snapping filled the room. The door swung open, and June said, "That's why I didn't want a normal limiter."

Captain Jake said, "Thank you, June" as he walked past her.

April started to walk past June and mockingly whispered, "Thank you, June."

A new sound of metal screeching filled the room. Everyone turned to see the wheel on the airlock door start to slowly spin.

April shoved Harry out of the way as she and June rushed the airlock door. June was the first to put her hands on the wheel. Although her arm was metal, the rest of her body was not. June was forced to let go as her body was getting twisted around.

Harry said, "What's the big deal if the door opens? We just have to make it outside so they can see us from Serenity."

As April tried to grab hold of the wheel, she said, "And if they vented the outside and closed the outer airlock door? How's Serenity supposed to see us then?" The wheel literally picked April up and set her back down, where she was forced to let it go.

Captain Jake was about to tempt his luck when June shoved him to the side then punched with her pink camo arm through the wheel. A thick metal spoke quickly came crashing down on June's arm, forcing her to let loose a bloodcurdling scream, but the wheel stopped.

April asked, "Can you hold it?"

June cursed. "Yes, I can fucking hold it, but you need to do something. This fucking hurts."

April said, "It's a metal arm. Stop whining."

June replied, "With fucking touch sensors! It feels like my arm's getting crushed!"

April said, "Good. Now you know how it feels."

Captain Jake said, "Let's go. We need to find a person or a terminal."

Harry said, "I don't think anyone will help us."

April said, "You find someone. I'll make them talk."

*****

Jesus was sitting in the cockpit of Serenity watching the security screens when he saw something that made him shout, "Hey! There's a remote-controlled car painting on the landing pad!"

July and Zac were both on their W2s, and both jumped up to look out the window. July said, "I don't see a remote-controlled car, but that looks like Johnny by the Icarus easy airlock. Looks like he's plugging something into it."

Zac said, "Timmy must be the one driving the remote-controlled car, but I don't see it."

Jesus said, "The car's right behind us. You have to use the security cameras to see it."

July said, "If I get arrested for vandalism, April will be so pissed."

Jesus activated the intercom and said, "Emily, how did your son and Timmy get outside without setting off any sensors?"

Emily exclaimed, "They're outside! What the hell are they doing outside?"

Zac said, "It looks like they're drawing a rectangle on the landing pad with a drone converted into a car."

July said, "That's lame. If I'm going to get arrested, I want it to be for something cool."

Zac said, "I'm going to go get them." Then he headed to the airlock, only to find it locked.

Emily asked, "Where the hell did they get the drone from? All the ones back here are accounted for."

Zac said, "Airlock doors locked. Emily, what about your side?"

A minute later, Emily said, "Locked here too."

July asked, "Should we cut it open?"

Jesus replied, "Hell no. We could lose all our air if the outer doors open."

Zac said, "Johnny's moving to the rectangle. He's taking off his canister."

Emily said, "Johnny's W2's giving me a busy signal."

Zac said, "He's pulling out a sawsword from the canister."

Emily said, "A sawsword can't fit in a canister."

July said, "It can if you cut away part of the handle. That's a red diamond chain. I bet it's Frank's spare. He's going to be so pissed."

Jesus said, "Those little shits snuck on here with a plan."

Zac said, "Johnny's staring at Serenity. He's hesitating. Don't do it, Johnny. You know better. Don't do it."

July said, "Make the cut, Johnny. Don't wimp out now."

Jesus asked, "Who's side are you on?"

July replied, "What? I want to see where this is going."

Emily shouted, "He's cutting into the landing pad!"

Jesus said, "Shit, the Icarus airlock just opened. It vented atmosphere."

July asked, "Are they sending out security?"

Jesus said, "God, I hope not."

Zac asked, "Emily, can you pull up the blueprints for this place? Maybe we can figure out what they're doing."

July said, "Johnny is throwing away the top sheet of metal. The car drone is moving over the hole."

Emily said, "I think the little shits are trying to steal the material we need to make another clamp."

Timothy's voice came over the intercom. "The away crew is in danger. I need everyone's help to save them."

Jesus yelled, "Is everyone seeing this?"

All the security camera footage was now replaced with the image of June with her arm wedged in an airlock locking wheel.

The airlock doors within Serenity opened with Timothy standing tall inside the airlock. Timothy stated, "We need to act fast, or everyone is going to die."

July rushed over to Timothy, where she immediately picked him up and set him inside of the passenger cabin. July said, "I'm going to go get my sisters out."

Timothy said, "Hey! You can't get in without connecting our airlock to theirs."

July replied, "I'll cut my way in."

Zac said, "You can't. We don't know where they are. Cut your way in, and you suck out all the oxygen and kill them."

Jesus said, "I can't connect our easy airlock to theirs unless they raise theirs up out of the ground."

July asked, "Why not?"

Jesus replied, "Because they don't do ninety degrees."

July said, "So tilt the ship and connect it."

Jesus answered, "The easy airlock won't engage while the thrusters are on. Safety feature."

Calvin's voice came over the intercom. "What are you guys doing down there? We're starting to register a heat spike from your location."

Timothy quickly typed on his W2 and severed the connection between Serenity and Equality. He said, "Listen to me now or everyone dies. I already swore I wasn't going to let anyone die today. Now! Everyone with power suits needs to get outside. Johnny is cutting out a piece of titanium support beam that we need to repair Equality. He's not strong enough to lift the beam out himself, so he needs help."

Emily was now standing behind Timothy and said, "Titanium isn't going to work. You have—"

Timothy turned to face Emily and cut her off. "After it gets broken down and reconstructed into the shape we need, it gets a six-month chemical bath to harden it. Clair's mom started mixing the chemical bath shortly after we left Equality."

Jesus said, "We don't have six months. We can order a new part and have it here in a day. Let's just get our people and go."

Timothy said, "We don't have a day. There could be ships headed here right now. Neither ship can activate the Carrie effect drive without the other. We have to fix Equality now."

July said, "You said it would take six months. I'm confused."

Timothy explained, "We can use the time dilation pod on Equality to speed up time. It will only take an hour to harden the part." Timothy now stared at Jesus and said, "Suit up."

Jesus asked, "Why? I'm not going out there."

July asked, "Where's you power armor, Jesus? I know you own a set."

Emily said, "It's back here. I'll go get it."

Zac asked, "What did Calvin mean by a heat spike?"

Timothy replied, "This is where the RO Research Space Station got their nuclear material from. There's a nuclear reactor under the base that's going into meltdown. Like I said, we need to hurry."

*****

April, Harry, and Captain Jake found themselves walking down a long dark downward slanting hallway after getting past the door in the waiting room.

Harry complained, "I can't see a damn thing. What do they use for light on this planet?"

April replied, "Just turn on your night vision app like we did."

Harry replied, "Good idea." Moments later, Harry said, "I can see doors up ahead. Maybe we will find people after all."

April replied, "We won't be finding anyone. Just look for a control console."

Harry said, "It was your plan to find and torture someone for help."

Captain Jake replied, "Have you noticed the air getting stale the farther down we travel?"

Harry replied, "I noticed. I also see there's no grass or vines anywhere. That means gas must be getting pumped in and filtered. Are you saying the pumps aren't working?"

April said, "Captain's saying the pumps haven't run for a very long time."

The three reached the first door. The door had no knob and appeared to be an automatic sliding door. Captain Jake saw a button to the side of the door, so he pushed it. The moment the door cracked open, the three were all hit with a putrid stench so strong that all three involuntarily vomited. Captain Jake pressed the button again as they all moved away from the door in search of breathable air.

Once able to speak, Harry asked, "What the fuck was that?"

April replied, "The reason they don't need air."

Captain Jake said, "I didn't get a good look inside, but my W2 contact lenses did. Dolly, was there a terminal inside that room?"

Dolly replied, "None visible in your recording, Captain."

Harry said, "Good. We're not opening that door again."

Captain Jake said, "There are more doors to open. April takes the left. Harry takes the right. Make sure to hold your breath before you open the door just in case. If you find a terminal, try to call Serenity. I'm going to go straight to find out where this leads."

April said, "You shouldn't go by yourself, Captain."

Captain Jake replied, "We're the only living things down here, and we don't have time to waste. Get to opening doors."

*****

Johnny was cursing Timothy as he stared down at the pillar of titanium. Johnny did just what Timmy had him practice in VR. He cut away the top layer so Michael's drone could move in and drop a clamp around the center to keep it from dropping after he cut it free. What they didn't practice in VR was how heavy the pillar was. After cutting the pillar section free, Johnny tried to pull up one end, only to have it tilt and get stuck. In VR, Johnny could easily lift it straight up from one side. Johnny now realized the only way he could lift the pillar section out was to lift from the middle, right where Michael's drone was parked. Johnny muttered to himself, "Timmy's a genius my ass."

Johnny suddenly felt a hand on his shoulder. Johnny's heart suddenly stopped beating as he was frozen in fear. Johnny slowly started to turn, expecting to see Icarus security guards there to arrest him. Instead, Johnny saw July standing there, laughing.

July, still laughing, said, "The look on your face is priceless. Timothy told us what you were up to. We're here to help. Oh! And the base is about to go into a nuclear meltdown, so we need to hurry."

Johnny was speechless as he looked to see Zac and Jesus moving in to grab the pillar. As they lifted it, Jesus said, "This thing weighs a ton. What were you doing trying to lift this out by yourself, Johnny?"

Johnny said, "It was lighter in VR."

Everyone chuckled, then July said, "Let's go get your W2 back, Johnny."

Zac said to Jesus, "Let's hurry and get this onboard Serenity so we can find out what the plan is to get the others out."

Timothy said, "You're not bringing that pillar on board yet."

Jesus stopped and yelled, "This thing's heavy! Why are we carrying it then?"

Timothy replied, "Take it to the far landing gear. We're going to use it to prop up that side of the ship."

July said, "That's clever. Tilt Serenity so we can attach the easy airlock."

Jesus said, "Landing gear's four legs. Only prop up one leg, and Serenity will twist off."

Timothy replied, "That's why you're going to prop up both far legs. The pillar can hold one leg while the rest of you hold up the other."

Zac said, "We can't hold up Serenity. Do you have any idea how much she weighs?"

Timothy replied, "Your power suits will do the work. The math says they can hold."

Jesus said, "You need me inside to fly the ship to get the pillar underneath it."

Timothy said, "We need your power armor to help hold Serenity up. Besides, I'm too short, and I might need Johnny's mom to help me get the Icarus airlocks to open."

Zac smiled at Jesus and said, "Look at the bright side."

Jesus asked, "What's that?"

Zac replied, "Today, Jesus gets to play hero. The captain will never believe it."

*****

Captain Jake reached the bottom of the corridor to find another door. The air was getting so thin that Captain Jake wasn't sure he could go any farther. He held his breath as he pressed the button to open the door.

The door slid open to reveal an overview of a large factory. Captain Jake was starting to feel dizzy, so he used his W2 contact lenses to zoom in rather than walk down to explore. As he looked about the abandoned factory, Captain Jake saw what looked like industrial presses as well as injection molds. There were also several 3D printers. Unfortunately, Captain Jake didn't see any finished products or even molds to tell him what it was they were constructing here.

Captain Jake's W2 rang, startling him. He looked down at the caller ID to see Serenity. Captain Jake swiped to answer and, with an unexpectedly soft voice, said, "Jesus, thank God. We need help getting out."

The reply that returned was from a child's voice. "I know. Johnny's mom is on her way down while I try to hack the doors open. I see the air pumps are off, and you sound horrible, so you shouldn't try to talk. I need you to get everyone back to the airlock. There's a nuclear power plant underneath you that's going into meltdown."

Captain Jake was wondering if he was hallucinating as he asked, "Timmy?"

Timothy responded, "I'm currently the only person aboard Serenity, so I think you should call me Captain Timmy."

Captain Jake asked, "Where is everyone?"

Timothy replied, "No time to explain. Nuclear meltdown is going to kill you and us if you don't get moving. Are the others with you?"

Captain Jake decided to trust Timothy and began to run back up the corridor as best he could. It didn't take long for Captain Jake's vision to turn blurry from lack of oxygen, but he pushed on, determined not to force any of his crew to endanger their lives trying to rescue him. Captain Jake muttered, "Not giving up" just before passing out.

CHAPTER 16

Stacy's Unexpected Surprise

Captain Jake opened his eyes to see June lying unconscious in a bed next to him. Standing next to her was Dr. Helix and Filipe. They seemed to be discussing June's mechanical arm.

Captain Jake turned his head to see Timothy, Clair, Emily, and Irene by the time dilation pod. Captain Jake attempted to speak, but nothing came out.

Dr. Helix turned to Captain Jake then said, "Don't try to speak, Captain. You passed out from lack of oxygen." Dr. Helix picked up a bottle and needle then said, "You will be fine after a good night's sleep." Dr. Helix gave Captain Jake an injection.

Captain Jake stared at June, whose head was tilted toward him. His last thoughts before the drugs took him back under was *I hope she didn't get hurt because of me.*

*****

Davinie was at the conference table with April, Frank, Thirteen, and Calvin with Jesus on the conference table video feed.

Davinie asked April, "Is everyone going to be all right?"

April answered, "Dr. Helix says they will be fine. Captain Jake passed out from lack of oxygen, while June passed out from her pain sensors overloading. We all have to take some antiradiation pills for a while, but they should both be fine by morning."

Calvin said, "That's a check for good news. On the bad news side, we have three bounty hunter motherships headed our way. These three have stayed on us since the RO Research Station. Alpha Mining says they can only get involved if we enter their territory. Eagle One is at Middleman for some joint operation."

Davinie said, "Well, that's just swell. Will the new part be ready in time?"

Thirteen replied, "It will. The bounty hunters won't be an issue."

Davinie asked, "How is it that a teenager and a prepubescent boy went rogue to save our bacon?"

Calvin said, "I believe Clair was in on it too. She got Irene to mix the chemical bath needed to harden the material. That's why the part will be ready in time for us to make our escape."

Davinie replied sarcastically, "That makes me feel better." Then in a normal tone, she asked, "Where did the kids get the sawsword from?"

Frank replied, "It appears to be my spare. It was in my room, locked up in a weapons cabinet."

Davinie said, "We'll need to make a list of charges."

Jesus said, "No, we don't. Those kids saved lives today."

Davinie said, "If they told us what they knew."

Jesus interjected, "Then what? You would have agreed to their plan of hacking the Icarus security system? I don't think so. Captain Jake knew it was a trap and went anyways."

Frank looked at April and said, "Their actions saved lives. Nothing negative goes in their permanent files. We both know Captain Jake will agree with me."

Davinie replied, "The captain's a fool. He needs to wise up before he gets himself killed. Have you had a chance to review their W2 footage yet?"

Thirteen said, "Originally, there were 132 unarmed settlers. They would have been easy targets for whoever was behind this, assuming the settlers truly were antitechnology. Considering how long it would take to construct an underground nuclear reactor, I'd say it happened centuries ago. The decomposing bodies were most likely their descendants. Possible slave labor for whatever they were using that base to build. The equipment Captain Jake found could have been used to mass produce just about anything. The base being abandoned with everyone inside dead indicates they produced all that they needed for whatever it is they're planning."

Davinie said, "You're saying they've been putting this plan into motion for hundreds of years? That's long before the pirate attacks began. Could they have been building nuclear bombs?"

Thirteen replied, "It's possible."

Frank said, "The place was abandoned before the weapons test. Pretty sure you test-fire a weapon before putting it into mass production. They also just destroyed their ability to make more nuclear material."

Davinie said, "I don't know what the hell's going on, but I'll have Harry let everyone know to have their Geiger counters out."

*****

Captain Jake opened his eyes to see June in the bed next to him, staring at him. June quickly turned her head when she saw Captain Jake's eyes start to open. Captain Jake said, "Good morning."

June hesitated before replying, "Good morning."

"Don't you two make a cute couple?" came Irene's voice from a few feet away.

"A great pair indeed!" scoffed Dr. Helix, who was standing by the time dilation pod. Dr. Helix then began walking over to inspect June's pink camo arm then said, "I should have cut this off while you were out."

Captain Jake stated, "That arm saved my life twice down there."

Dr. Helix turned to Captain Jake then proceeded to scold him. "You are not allowed to speak next time you feel lightheaded, and I know you did. The last thing you should try doing is running. I watched your W2 feed, so I know you did. I should keep you here for physiological evaluation for even going down there without power suits."

June now came to Captain Jake's defense. "He was trying to get answers, Doctor. That's his job."

Captain Jake asked, "Did we get any answers?"

Irene said, "I don't know about answers, but you got the material you needed to construct a new part."

Captain Jake asked, "How?"

Irene said, "When you went down to the planet, Clair gave me instructions on how to mix a titanium-hardening bath. Said it was from Timothy on your behalf."

Captain Jake asked, "What did Timothy do?"

Irene said, "I'm not sure exactly. I heard he had Johnny help him hack into the Icarus security system to discover you were in danger. Everything after that seems a little far exaggerated to me."

June giggled then said, "You did say something on Serenity about that kid pulling miracles out of his butt." June's stomach suddenly growled loudly.

Captain Jake said, "I'm hungry too. Any food in this place?"

Dr. Helix handed bottles of pills to June and Captain Jake then said, "You can go to the cafeteria and get your own food. You will need to take two pills a day for the next two weeks."

Captain Jake asked, "What are these for?"

Dr. Helix replied, "For hanging out over a nuclear plant that was going through meltdown. It is a miracle you're alive. Don't do it again, Captain."

Captain Jake said, "I promise not to make a habit of it." He and June left the medical bay.

The two walked in silence to the mess hall as they both spent the time scrolling through their W2s to catch up on what they missed. They reached the mess hall to find Chef behind the counter.

Chef said, "Heard you two almost died out there. You should really be more careful, Captain. The pretty lady already lost an arm."

June replied, "I like my pink camo arm. What kind of muffins do you have today, Chef?"

Chef replied, "Whatever kind you want. If it's not floating in the display case, I can make it for you in under a minute."

While June and Chef spoke, Captain Jake went to the cooler and grabbed a protein shake. Captain Jake said, "Just the protein shake for me. I need to get to the conference table for an officers' meeting. These reports on what happened are missing things. I can't make sense of what happened."

Chef said, "I heard that genius boy got the ship fixed just in time to avoid some bounty hunters from the outer rings. Why are they after us? They have to know we didn't kill those scientists."

June grabbed two banana chocolate chip muffins from the display case then said, "They won't believe it wasn't us until we catch who it was. Captain's on it, Chef. Thanks." June rushed to catch up with Captain Jake as he left the mess hall.

Captain Jake said, "I wish I had an idea who was behind this."

June handed a muffin to Captain Jake and said, "You should really have something solid."

Captain Jake took the muffin then said, "Banana chocolate chip. My favorite." As they walked and ate, Captain Jake noticed June having trouble swallowing, so he handed her his protein shake.

June took the bottle, and after taking a swig to clear her throat, she said, "Strawberry. My favorite."

The two entered the courtyard, where they were immediately startled by the sound of a gunshot. June was the first to relax as she said, "It's just Tie and Calvin target practicing with a rail rifle."

Captain Jake looked to where June was looking then asked, "Since when does a magnetically charged rail rifle sound like gunpowder?"

June answered, "I don't know. Let's go ask."

Stacy suddenly came running out to the hydroponics bay, charging toward Tie and Calvin, at the same time Samantha and Ron came running out of a small cornfield while hunching over, trying not to be seen. The top half of Ron's onesie was flopping behind him as he ran.

June whispered, "Slut."

June and Captain Jake continued over to hear Stacy yelling, "I get to work early to get shit done! Not to have the shit scared out of me by you two jackasses!" Captain Jake couldn't help but notice Stacy looked a little flushed.

June asked, "How did you get the rail rifle to make that sound?"

Calvin said, "I found an app that lets you add a speaker to the gun."

Stacy took the rail rifle and said, "Hook me up with a bazooka. I'll show you how this is done."

Calvin said, "Thought you had work to do."

Stacy replied, "I do, but since I'm here, load the bazooka sound effects."

Captain Jake said, "Not to interrupt, but is Timmy here?"

Stacy replied with a hint of anger in her tone, "He's sleeping in after being up all night saving you, dumbass. Thought you were supposed to still be in the sick bay."

Captain Jake said, "Doc cleared us. I need to know what happened down there, Stacy."

Stacy looked at Captain Jake and asked, "What was Timmy doing down there, Jake? Children don't go on dangerous away missions."

June answered for Captain Jake. "Timmy's W2 was acting up. Captain Jake was just trying to help."

Stacy gave June a glare of daggers then said, "The genius's W2 was acting up? You bought that? The kid was playing you. It's what kids do. You're supposed to be adults. It's your job to see through his bullshit and keep him safe."

Captain Jake said, "I'm sorry. I thought he'd be safe on Serenity."

June said, "He was safe. Wasn't he?"

Stacy exclaimed, "You parked on top of a nuclear reactor! Johnny was almost crushed by Serenity."

Captain Jake asked, "How was Johnny almost crushed? That's not in any report."

Calvin said, "I can show you." After typing into his W2, a large banner dropped from overhead. On the banner was an image of July, Jesus, Johnny, and Zac holding up one of the landing gear legs of Serenity.

Tie said, "They had to tilt Serenity to get the easy airlock to connect."

Calvin added, "Johnny's exoskeleton seized up from the weight. He had to be carried back on board Serenity."

June said, "I have to go find July and thank her." June rushed off.

Captain Jake said, "I have a lot of people to thank. Calvin, mind walking me to the conference table and catching me up on everything?"

Stacy said, "Jake." Once Captain Jake looked at Stacy, she said, "Put Timothy in harm again." Stacy turned to face the cutout target of Captain Spike and pulled the trigger. There was a loud whistling noise followed by the sound of a large explosion as a small hole appeared in Captain Spike's face.

*****

April awoke to the smell of warm freshly buttered toast sprinkled with cinnamon and sugar. She opened her eyes to see the toast on a warming plate on her end table. Next to the plate was a sports bottle filled with orange juice and her morning vitamins.

April was taking her first bite of toast when Frank walked into the bedroom. After quickly clearing her throat, April said, "You didn't have to do this."

Frank smiled then said, "Hero's breakfast. You dragged Jake to safety."

April replied, "Harry helped me. Did you cook him breakfast too?"

Frank shook his head no then said, "Harry's on his own, I'm afraid."

April stared at Frank for a moment then said, "I know that frown line. What's on your mind?"

Frank hesitated then said, "I was thinking we should swap jobs." April gave him a disapproving look, but Frank continued, "You should take my place on Equality. You're better at management than I am."

April patted the bed, indicating to Frank to sit down next to her. Once Frank was seated, April leaned her head against his shoulder then softly said, "I know you hate missing the action. After we drop Ted off at Middleman, you can go with me on the next mission."

Frank said, "That's not it." After a long pause, Frank continued, "I've never been in love before. I don't know what I'd do if I lost you."

April looked up at Frank and said, "Do we need another sparring session?"

Frank chuckled then replied, "No. My right shoulder is still sore from the last one. In a fight, no one can beat you. When I heard the base was going into a nuclear meltdown and you were trapped inside, I thought I was going to lose you. The life drained right out of me. I couldn't."

April smiled sweetly then said, "Takes more than a nuclear meltdown to get rid of me." April pulled Frank's head down to kiss him passionately. April said, "You're also the only man I have ever loved, but I'm not leaving the action. Don't ask me to again."

Frank said, "I won't. As long as you agree to wear power armor on all future missions."

April laughed then said, "That's not going to happen."

Frank said, "You can repaint the colors. I don't care about that, but I want you to have an FP shield. I'm not taking no for an answer."

April looked intently into Frank's eyes then reluctantly said, "You're lucky I love you. Fine, I'll have Filipe repaint a power suit."

While staring into April's eyes, Frank said, "Let's get married."

April looked away then said, "You sure want a lot today." April then stood up and moved in front of Frank. April placed her hands on his shoulders as she moved in to straddle him and said, "You really want to keep me around, don't you?"

Frank looked into April's eyes and replied softly, "Yes, I do."

April leaned in for a kiss then pulled back and said, "I don't want a big wedding."

Frank replied, "You're the only person I need there."

April laughed then said, "It would be tough to do it without me. Our next stop is Middleman. We can take care of it there."

Frank said, "This calls for a celebration." Frank then began to kiss April as he leaned back, pulling April onto the bed.

April was giggling as Frank rolled over to get on top, but then April turned serious and said, "Tell no one. If my sisters find out I'm getting married, they'll be impossible."

*****

All officers not awake before 7:00 a.m. awoke to a message from Captain Jake asking for an emergency officers' meeting. The last person to actually arrive at this meeting was Frank.

Captain Jake said, "Glad you're here, Frank. I think I'm just about caught up on all I missed."

Calvin watched Frank approach then quickly raised his hand for Frank to give him a high five. Frank took his seat, ignoring Calvin.

Calvin said, "That was cold. I was just trying to congratulate you on having morning sex."

Frank said nothing while Stacy said to Calvin, "Mind your own business, pervert."

Calvin said, "It's not my fault I have this superpower."

Davinie replied, "Being a pervert is not a superpower. Can we get on with this meeting now please?"

Captain Jake turned to watch Timothy, and Rex slowly approach the shimmering sound barrier of the conference table.

Stacy turned to see what Captain Jake was looking at then asked, "What is Timmy doing here?"

Captain Jake replied, "I asked him to join us. I told you I needed answers."

Stacy said, "Fine. Then go talk to him one-on-one. Don't do it in front of everyone."

Captain Jake replied, "Timmy's knowledge and actions affect everyone."

Frank said, "It will be okay, Stacy. He's not in trouble."

Davinie replied, "I wouldn't go that far."

Timothy and Rex passed through the sound barrier. Timothy kept his head down as he approached Captain Jake then softly said, "You wanted to see me."

Captain Jake replied, "Yes, I did. Do you know why?"

Timothy, while still staring at the floor, said, "Because you have to fire me."

Captain Jake said, "That thought never crossed my mind."

Timothy looked up with excitement on his face and exclaimed, "Really?"

Calvin stated, "It's straight to jail for you, kid."

The whole table shouted, "Shut up, Calvin!"

Captain Jake said, "You're not going to jail, Timmy, but you are in some trouble. Ignoring the crimes against Icarus, which include hacking, vandalism, and theft, there's the crimes you committed against this ship and its crew. Those crimes are pretty much the same, actually. Filipe."

Filipe said, "He hacked into Serenity to reroute the airlock sensor to his W2. This ensured Jesus wouldn't know when he left the ship."

Captain Jake said, "Frank."

Frank said, "Timmy broke into my room. I'd like Timmy to tell us how."

Timothy refused to look at Frank as he said, "I wasn't going to let anyone else die, and I didn't. You want to punish me, then punish me."

Captain Jake said, "This is part of your punishment. You kept secrets from us, and that needs to stop."

Davinie added, "We're all in this together. None of us are going to just let people die."

Timothy glanced at Frank with a dirty look then said, "I know that's not true."

Captain Jake said, "We all wish things could have been done differently. Had we known what Michael was planning, we could have saved him. You are part of this crew now, and you need to start trusting us."

Timothy looked back down at the floor then said, "Yes, sir."

Captain Jake asked, "How did you get into Frank's room?"

Timothy started swaying back and forth as he answered, "I used a holographic projection to trick the sensor."

Calvin said, "I can upgrade that bug out of Dolly. There was one other anomaly I found while I was checking for any other adjustments Timmy might have made to the ship's systems. During Michael's magic show, there is a thirty-minute gap in the security cameras for Ted's holding cell."

Captain Jake asked, "Do you know anything about this, Timmy?"

Timmy replied, "I was at Michael's show. Who's Ted?"

Calvin said, "It might just be a glitch with memory. That was over a month ago."

Frank said, "I check Ted's security feed daily. I haven't noticed anything."

Captain Jake said, "Let's stay focused. Frank, what kind of a lock did you have on your weapons locker?"

Frank answered, "A three-digit padlock, Captain. It doesn't appear to be tampered with. How did you get past my padlock, Timmy?"

Timothy swayed back and forth faster instead of answering.

Stacy said, "Let him go to the bathroom, Jake."

Captain Jake said to Timmy, "Answer Frank."

Timothy said, "I checked the records. Frank got that padlock specially made after April moved in with him. The combination was her birthday. I guessed it on the first try."

The room was filled with people giggling.

Captain Jake tried to keep a serious face then said, "You're banned from the engine room Timmy, and consider Michael's drone confiscated. You will start helping Dr. Helix out with his research on a drug called heaven's bliss. Do not experiment on anyone. You can go to the bathroom now."

Timmy immediately started running toward the bathroom with Rex close behind.

The room was all smiles as they watched Timothy run away. Captain Jake asked, "Is there any new business?"

Dr. Helix asked, "Captain? Are you saying Timothy wasn't assigned to help me in the medical bay before today?"

Captain Jake suddenly got a worried look on his face as he replied, "No. It has only been engineering and agriculture so far. I didn't want to overwhelm him. Why do you ask, Doc?"

Stacy suddenly excused herself from the table and rushed outside the sound barrier to the cornfield nearby. Once there, she began to throw up.

Calvin said, "Stacy and Rex must have been hitting the bottle pretty good last night."

Dr. Helix commented, "I hope not."

Captain Jake asked, "What's going on, Doc?"

Dr. Helix replied, "That's not for me to say, Captain."

Stacy walked back in, wiped her mouth, and said, "Sorry about that. My breakfast didn't agree with me."

Calvin jumped to his feet, pointed at Stacy, and yelled, "Her boobs are bigger! Her boobs are bigger!" Everyone began to stare at Stacy's breasts.

Harry said, "They look the same to me."

Stacy screamed, "What the fuck is going on?"

Davinie said, "The pervert is right. It's morning sickness. Been through it too many times not to recognize it."

Stacy exclaimed, "I'm not fucking pregnant!"

Dr. Helix asked. "So you didn't ask Timothy to get you prenatal vitamins and accelerated birth medication?"

Stacy shouted, "No! I'm not pregnant!" Stacy grabbed her stomach then, in a whisper, asked, "Am I?"

Captain Jake said, "Dolly, call Timmy and put it on the conference table."

A moment later, Timothy's face was on the conference table's screens. Timothy's eyes were closed as he smiled. The sound of pee hitting the back of a urinal accompanied with the sound of a fan blowing softly was heard.

Davinie said, "Timothy of Nowhere, you don't answer your W2 while you're going to the bathroom."

Timothy replied, "It's not my fault you called while I'm going to the bathroom."

Captain Jake asked, "Timmy? Have you been giving Stacy birth acceleration medication?"

Timothy replied, "Of course. The medical journals all say you should start as soon as possible."

Dr. Helix said, "Timmy! You never give anyone drugs without their permission."

Timothy replied, "I heard Stacy tell Michael that she likes all drugs."

Stacy exclaimed, "I wasn't talking about those kinds of drugs! Why do you think I'm pregnant?"

Timothy replied, "Because you haven't had your special visitor. My mom's told me when a woman doesn't have her special visitor for a while, then that means there's an even more special visitor on its way."

Dr. Helix said, "You still can't give anyone drugs without confirming the diagnosis."

Timothy replied, "I did. I downloaded an ultrasound app that I use every night at dinner to check on the babies."

Stacy's eyes grew wide as she repeated, "Babies. Plural."

Captain Jake rushed to Stacy's side and helped her to her seat.

Davinie said, "Twins. That Michael the Magician had some powerful magic after all."

Timothy said, "Not twins. Well, they were twins, but after she started taking the birth acceleration medication, it became triplets."

Stacy repeated, "Triplets." Then she fainted.

*****

The next day, there was a gathering of all crew and residents of Equality in the courtyard. The banner now called the "Four Heroes of Icarus" was moved to be displayed over the entrance to Serenity. April, Frank, Harry, and Captain Jake stood on the platform from Serenity, raised a few feet above the crowd.

Captain Jake's voice echoed over the PA as he spoke. "Thank you all for coming today."

Rex yelled back, "Like we had a choice!" The crowd laughed.

Captain Jake continued, "As you all know, there was an incident the other day. If not for the quick action taken by"—Captain Jake paused to raise his hands toward the banner—"these four who risked their lives to get us out. We cannot thank you enough."

There was a round of cheers (the guys all looked embarrassed while July was acting like a rock star) followed by Harry stepping up to say, "I've already thanked each of you individually. Now let me say thank you in front of everyone. Thank you, Four Heroes of Icarus. I'm too young to die." There was a round of laughter from the crowd at Harry, who looked like a teenager. Harry added, "May I say that this will be the last time I ever volunteer for an away mission." The room again filled with laughter.

April stepped forward then said, "We not only wanted to thank the Four Heroes of Icarus but also all the people who worked through the night to heal us and repair the ship. Bounty hunters who refused to listen to reason were on their way to collect bounties on us. Thanks to you, no innocent blood was spilled as we searched for the truth." There was another round of applause. April said, "I would also like to give a special thanks to my other sister, June. I have never been a fan of her robotic arm." April shook her once crushed arm as she continued, "I had my reasons for that. But it, and June, saved our lives down there. Thank you, June." The room again erupted in applause.

July was standing next to May in the crowd and asked, "Do you think April's on happy pills?"

May replied, "Has to be."

Frank now stepped forward then said, "There is one other person who needs thanking. Although I can't condone how he did it. The fact remains April—" Frank suddenly was unable to speak.

Captain Jake saw a tear forming in Frank's eye and quickly stepped forward to take over and yelled, "Special thanks to Timmy! The kid scammed his way onto Serenity just to save our lives. Honestly, I shouldn't even be calling him a kid."

Timothy yelled, "I am a kid!" Everyone laughed.

Captain Jake said, "That you are, and so much more. You saved our lives, but next time, let us know what you're thinking. Now, everyone, if you could help me out with something." Captain Jake's voice got low as he said, "Timmy." Then a little louder, he said, "Timmy!" Then even louder, he said, "Timmy!" The crowd quickly began to join in on the chant of "Timmy!"

Before the crowd got too loud, Frank pushed Captain Jake to the side as he climbed down the podium. The crowd suddenly went silent as Frank charged toward Timothy then said, "You saved April. Even after I unwittingly kept you from trying to save Michael. I was wrong about you, Timothy of Nowhere. I owe you a debt that can never be repaid." Frank reached down and picked Timothy up, tossing him onto his shoulder. Frank shouted, "Give this man a hero's cheer!"

The room erupted with cheers then the chant of "Timmy!" It lasted for what seemed like forever to the little boy Timothy, who had never been so happy.

CHAPTER 17

Jake and June

Serenity approached SS Middleman with a skeleton crew aboard consisting of April, Frank, June, and Captain Jake. They were escorting the prisoner Ted of Hades to the local authorities for his sentence of life on Titan to be carried out.

While in Middleman, Captain Jake had a mission debrief scheduled with Tanis and Colt. In the meantime, Captain Jake sent Equality with its crew and residents to Romeo so they could visit the bio domes for some well-earned R&R.

June was sitting in the passenger cabin with April and Frank, but she got tired of feeling like a third wheel. June entered the cockpit then asked, "Do you know what you're doing up here?"

Captain Jake lit up at the sight of June and replied, "I have piloted before, thank you very much."

June rolled her eyes as she sat down in the copilot's seat then said, "That doesn't mean you're any good at it."

Captain Jake chuckled then stated, "I promise to keep you as safe in space as you keep me on the ground."

June replied, "Them are big words. Have you ever even landed before?"

Captain Jake nodded yes then said, "In simulators."

June giggled then said, "That's reassuring."

Captain Jake asked, "What are you doing on Serenity anyways? Thought you'd want to go back to Romeo with July and May to visit family and friends."

June said, "Those lovebirds back there are too busy making googly eyes at each other to watch you. Every time you leave this ship, you almost die. Someone has to protect you."

Captain Jake laughed then said, "This is Middleman, not the outer rings. It doesn't get any safer than this."

June replied, "I've saved your life too many times to start taking chances now." As they approached SS Middleman for landing, June started white knuckling the armrests of the copilot's seat. June said, "It feels different watching the landing from up here. You sure you know how to land?"

Captain Jake repeated, "I already promised to keep you as safe in space as you keep me on the ground. I always keep my promises."

June looked at Captain Jake, easing up on her grip of the seat. June said, "I'm going to trust you for now. But screw this landing up."

Captain Jake smiled and said, "I wouldn't dare."

The landing went smoothly (with autopilot assist), and Serenity was met on the landing pad by a Middleman security team. April and Frank went with them to escort Ted (in his full set of hand and leg cuffs) inside through a side airlock.

Once they were out of view, June asked, "Where to?"

Captain Jake replied, "Business district. I have a debriefing to attend."

The two made their way through the main airlocks that opened up into a large waiting room. Once inside, June and Captain Jake were surprised to find a small group of ex-SS Minnow passengers waiting to greet them.

The group screamed, "Welcome back, Jake!" Then they ran up to give him a bunch of hugs. Afterward, the group started to look behind Captain Jake.

Iris Dulton, a short slender blond, was standing with her young daughter, Megan. Iris asked, "Where's my husband? Ron is with you, isn't he?"

Captain Jake stood there frozen as images of the half-naked Ron running out of a cornfield with Samantha flashed in his head.

June stepped forward and said, "Hi, my name's June. I'm a security officer aboard Equality. I'm afraid we only came here on Serenity on business. Ron is with Equality, headed to Romeo."

The whole group seemed to be disappointed at hearing that they wouldn't get to see more old friends.

Iris looked a little embarrassed as she said, "That's all right. We heard on Harry's news stream that you were headed this way. Megan wanted to surprise her dad. Is the ban lifted so we can video chat with him?"

June repeated, "Ban? What ban?"

Captain Jake quickly said, "The ban that started when we had to go dark for the RO Research Space Station. Yes, that ban is lifted."

Iris said, "Thank you, Jake. It was good to see you again." Iris and Megan began to walk off.

June whispered to Captain Jake, "We stopped going dark weeks ago. Ron's a douchebag."

They then heard Megan ask her mom, "No Daddy?"

Captain Jake whispered, "No argument here."

As the welcoming party dispersed, two women stayed behind. One was a slender bleached blond with tan skin of average height. The other was a bigger boned brunette with a slightly darker skin tone, standing a few inches taller.

The bigger brunette gave Captain Jake a big hug while saying, "It's good to see you, Jakey."

Once she let go, Captain Jake introduced them. "June, this is Jess the hugger, and that's Amy. Two old friends from the journey here."

Jess turned to June then said, "This man pushed us into living together. We have never been happier thanks to Jakey here. We are even thinking about adoption."

Amy said, "I'd rather we had a child naturally."

Jess replied, "Plushy babies are too hard to carry to term."

June gasped. "Plushy babies are so cute! What colors are you thinking about?"

Jess replied, "Don't laugh, but I want a plushy baby with black fur and a white stripe down its back."

Amy filled her eyes then stated, "We are not raising Pepé Le Pew."

Jess ignored Amy and asked, "What are you two doing for dinner tonight? We would love to have you over."

June looked up at Captain Jake with a questioning look on her face. Captain Jake asked, "What time?"

Amy replied, "Does eight o'clock work for you?"

Jess exclaimed, "We need wine! June, are you a red or white girl?"

June replied, "Red's good."

Jess clapped her hands together then said, "So is Amy. I prefer white myself. Reds are too dry for me, but I know just the brand to get. You're going to love it! We will see you tonight." Jess started to drag Amy off.

Amy shouted, "I'll send you the address!"

June said, "You have interesting friends, Jakey."

Captain Jake replied, "Thanks. Dinner should be entertaining."

June looked down at her power suit then said, "I didn't pack dinner attire."

Captain Jake said, "They won't mind."

June said, "I'm guessing you didn't pack dinner attire either?"

Captain Jake replied, "Well, no."

June said, "That settles it. After your debriefing, we're going shopping."

*****

Admiral Noem sat at a large round conference table with Tanis and Colt sitting at opposite ends from each other. Admiral Noem asked, "Has the first part of Operation Net been taken care of?"

Colt answered, "The 15 for Life soil was picked up yesterday from Romeo and transported by Eagle One to a Romeo cargo ship. Production has already resumed."

Tanis said, “I don’t know how you let the pirates get their hands on such a large quantity of 15 for Life in the first place.”

Admiral Noem said, “Technically, they didn’t. Eagle One confiscated the shipment last week.”

Tanis replied, “How many shipments got through before you finally stopped one?”

Colt said, “We now know they were collecting pills being sent to deceased patients on the drug using forged documentation. Their supply chain is broken.”

Tanis commented, “Isn’t it amazing how many people who want to live forever end up taking their own lives?”

Colt replied, “Our citizens are given the choice of how to live.”

Tanis replied, “A slow death is not leaving.”

Admiral Noem said, “That’s enough. What matters is that Captain Spike will be desperate to get his hands on the Chronos soil. With it, he can produce all the Pazel flowers he needs to make more of the 15 for Life drug.”

Tanis added, “And without it, he dies.”

Colt said, “We need him alive to flush out his conspirators. Captain Spike’s just a pawn in this game.”

Admiral Noem said, “We don’t know how much of a stockpile of pills Captain Spike may have. Let’s hope we time this out right.”

Colt said, “Before we get into all that, we need to finalize our agreement for Chronos.”

Travis replied, “It’s been finalized. Our cargo vessel has already been filled with the construction materials to build an underwater base on Chronos. In exchange, you will return the useless soil you have for fresh soil of the same amount. Your people then get to keep not living their lives for eternity.”

Colt said, “One hundred fifty percent new soil. We need extra for research into a better drug that won’t kill people who stop taking it. Such a drug wouldn’t require a daily pill. Then all of Einstein could take it.”

Tanis replied, “When you know you can’t die, you can’t live. Juliet has no desire to help you spread that toxin throughout Einstein.”

Colt said, "And Romeo isn't about to sit by while you use this new sea base on Chronos to pilfer their sea life."

Tanis said, "The humanoid population there isn't doing any fishing. They aren't even trying to explore their ocean."

Admiral Noem said, "Enough. Romeo will get fresh soil so they can keep producing 15 for Life. One hundred twenty-five percent more than what they return. Juliet will be allowed to export a set amount of fish from the ocean of Chronos."

Colt objected, "That goes against the founding principles of Einstein. We are not to interfere with Chronos or its people."

Tanis said, "That's fine. You don't get to take their soil then."

Colt stated, "Our people need that soil to live."

Tanis replied, "Only the ones stupid enough to get on the drug."

Admiral Noem repeated, "I said enough. Colt, your people want immortality. All Tanis wants is a few fish. I call that more than fair."

Colt said, "Fine."

Tanis got an evil smirk across her face as she realized she was getting exactly what she wanted. Tanis said, "Agreed. Let's go out for sushi to celebrate."

Admiral Noem said, "Funny. We still need to go over Operation Net with Captain Jake."

As if on cue, a buzzer sounded. Everyone looked at a large television screen hanging over the front door. The TV showed Captain Jake standing on the other side, waiting to be let in. Admiral Noem motioned to the TV to come closer, and the door opened.

Captain Jake entered the room with a smile of joy coming across his face as he saw Admiral Noem. Captain Jake stated, "I didn't know you would be here."

Tanis yelled, "Stop!" Captain Jake halted his approach. Tanis said, "You have to be scanned for listening devices and explosives before entering."

Captain Jake set his hand on his sawsword and said, "But weapons are all right?"

Tanis replied, "In your hands, that's not a weapon."

The TV screen above Captain Jake flashed green with the word *OK* printed in white.

Colt said, "You're clear to come in, Captain."

Captain Jake walked in and took a seat.

Tanis remarked, "Made quite a mess on things out there, didn't you, Captain?"

Admiral Noem, with an angry tone, said, "You had me send him to test a nuclear weapon without knowing it was a nuclear weapon!"

Tanis said, "I had no idea what the outer ringers were building."

Admiral Noem stated, "You funded it. There was a nuclear reactor on Icarus less than two days' flight from here."

Colt said, "A joint team is being sent to examine the remains of the base. The radiation will make it difficult, but we will get answers."

Tanis said, "This proves the need for the EPF. Trained soldiers, not this ragtag mishmash, should be out there securing space."

Admiral Noem replied, "Violence begets violence."

Colt said, "There has been no violence, yet there is a group trying to undermine us and start violence."

Tanis said, "Time to test your metal, Captain Jake."

Captain Jake asked, "How?"

Admiral Noem answered, "Operation Net. Eagle One recently intercepted a large shipment of 15 for Life meant for the pirates. It is made with a rare ingredient from a flower known as the Pazel flower. This flower is from Chronos and can only be grown in Chronos soil."

Tanis smirked. "With diminishing yields every year. Great plan for immortality."

Colt said, "We're working on finding a fertilizer that will prolong the longevity of the soil. Until then, we need a fresh supply."

Admiral Noem said, "So do pirates now that we have cut off their supply. We'll be sending you, Jake, to escort two cargo ships to Chronos, with the Iron Maiden and Bearclaw motherships. One of these cargo ships will contain the Chronos soil as well as a processing plant that will continue to make the drug for distribution as you travel."

Tanis said, "Until it's discovered that the soil has been contaminated by the Juliet government. This will occur just before you are to leave Middleman space."

Colt said, "At which time the Bearclaw will be forced to fire on the Iron Maiden."

Tanis smiled as she said to Colt, "And the Iron Maiden will return fire. If you get killed in the process, I will feel just terrible."

Captain Jake said, "So you will be advertising the joint venture. Then when we leave, the venture loses two-thirds of its military force. The pirates, desperate to get more 15 for Life, will jump at the chance to attack."

Tanis remarked, "You're not as dumb as you look, Captain."

Admiral Noem said, "There's an automated base on the Chronos moon to keep any would-be thieves from the planet. They have a mothership with two dozen jet arms."

Tanis added, "And three mobile rail cannons courtesy of Juliet."

Colt said, "And a daily patrol from Romeo ships."

Admiral Noem said, "That will end at the start of this mission. Captain Marshall, with Eagle Two, will be hidden on the planet. Eagle Three with four cargo ships carrying a thousand spacemines each will be hidden on the moon."

Captain Jake said, "So I'm to park between Chronos and its moon as bait. I'll let the residents know they won't be able to join us."

Tanis slammed her hand on the table and shouted, "You will do no such thing!"

Colt explained in a calmer tone, "The trap only works if they don't realize it's a trap. Every one of our people on this mission has been vetted with truth serum. Your people can't know it's a trap."

Admiral Noem said, "We catch Captain Spike, we find out who's behind this. He needs the cargo ship intact for its cargo. You can use them as a shield because he won't know which one has the soil."

Colt added, "The cargo ships will also be carrying spacemines attached to their outer hulls for deployment upon arrival. That will help buy you time until the net is deployed. Once the net is up and Captain Spike realizes it's a trap, he should surrender."

Admiral Noem said, "It's going to be your job to make him surrender, Jake. No blood has to be spilled."

Captain Jake said, "Understood. When do we leave?"

Tanis said, “We’ll give them a few weeks. Let their reserves of 15 for Life run out.”

Captain Jake nodded and left the room. As he walked, the thought of taking civilians and children to be used as bait weighed heavily on his mind. Once outside, Captain Jake saw June waiting for him.

June looked up from her W2 and smiled as she saw Captain Jake. June asked, “All set?”

Captain Jake suddenly felt a wave of relief come over him. He whispered to himself, “I keep them safe in space. June keeps them safe on the ground.”

June giggled then asked, “What was that?”

Captain Jake smiled and replied, “Nothing. Don’t we have dinner attire to shop for?”

June interlocked her pink camo arm with Jake’s and said, “Right this way, sir.”

*****

Ted’s time aboard Equality had been quiet and uneventful with the exception of one night that had preoccupied his thoughts ever since.

Ted’s cell was three walls made of bars and one wall made of Faraday metal. That wall brought him his food and drink upon request (although Ted had a limited number of points he could spend each day). There was also a TV that only played news streams and let him check his email.

Ted still had girlfriends that would send him videos, but the ship’s AI would blur out their private parts. Ted would still close his eyes and remember their naked bodies pressed against his as he rubbed one off seven or so times a day to pass the time. Ted always found it funny that a sound barrier went down around his cell every time he started, considering he was alone.

Ted was also surprised that he had no visitors until that one night. Not a single soul came to rub his situation in his face after what he did to them. Ted didn’t actually mind this. All his life, he hated the inner ringers. He considered them a spoiled race who always got the best of everything. They never knew what it was to live off rations or to have your relay station go out, cutting off your access to the web for weeks at a time. Inner ringers got in-person schooling while outer ringers had to take their classes online (made extra difficult when the internet went out). Union laws banned the use of androids but put a kid in a preprogrammed exoskeleton suit, and they could work all day legally. It was a regular occurrence in the outer rings.

Ted truly hated the inner ringers, but the loneliness of his cell was driving him mad. Then one night, there was a magic show being put on by an inner ringer called Michael the Magician, according to the ships news feed.

Ted was leaning his back against the bars, watching the magic show and feeling grateful to be watching some form of entertainment, when the door to the cell block, opened startling Ted. He turned, and his eyes went wide open as he saw a beautiful young woman with straight red hair down to her shoulders enter the room. Ted was instantly mesmerized by how her hips swayed back and forth as she walked toward him.

The woman spoke. "Place your arms against the back wall."

Ted recognized the voice and now the innocent-looking face. Ted said, "I remember you. You were in the pizzeria back in Shell City. Finally decide you want to know what a real man feels like?"

Samantha repeated, "Arms against the back wall." The TV suddenly shut off and receded into the back wall.

Ted said, "Hey! I was watching that." Suddenly, two arms started to form out of the back wall. Ted said, "What the fuck is that?"

Samantha said, "Go to the back wall willingly or get dragged back."

Ted walked to the back wall and said, "I'm going, I'm going." Although the arms were forming to the left of his bed, Ted sat down on his bed then slid back to push his back against the wall. Ted then raised his arm where he quickly felt cold steel encase his wrists. Ted said, "Happy now?"

Samantha unlocked the cell door then walked toward Ted. Samantha quickly surprised Ted by taking off her top that looked like it was part of a onesie. Samantha's ample breasts floated all about as she walked in zero gravity toward Ted. Samantha said, "I'm not happy yet." Samantha paused as she yanked on Ted's legs to pull his hips out more before straddling him. Samantha continued, "But I'm getting there."

Ted said, "It doesn't do much good in its holster. You need to pull it out, or have this wall let go of me."

Samantha said softly, "I need to know something first. There's a war coming between the inner and outer rings. Will you help the outer ringers fight?"

Ted laughed and repeated, "War! The outer ringers don't even have a military. You can't go to war without an army." Ted looked about the room and asked, "What kind of a setup is this?"

Samantha started to rock her hips back and forth then said, "The cameras aren't recording right now, and I'm not wearing my W2 contacts." Samantha pinched her bare nipples then said softly, "Or much of anything else. I'm asking nicely." Samantha stopped moving her hips as she reached into Ted's onesie. Samantha asked softly, "Will you join the fight against the inner ringers?"

Ted took a deep breath as he felt Samantha caress his sensitive skin then said, "All right, I'll play along. What's in it for me if I do?"

Samantha grabbed hold then started to sway back and forth with her hips as she said, "You will be rewarded. Money and…" Samantha gave an extra strong thrust then said, "Other things." Samantha rolled her head back as she started to moan in ecstasy then asked softly, "Will you join us?"

Ted answered, "God, yes, I'll join."

Samantha immediately jumped off Ted and started looking for where her shirt floated off to as she said, "That's good to hear. Find me after the battle, and we can finish this." Samantha grabbed her shirt and put it back on.

Ted yelled, "You can't stop! Finish it!"

Samantha walked out, locking the cell behind her, and said, "No time. The cameras are going to start recording soon. You shouldn't have wasted so much time at the start."

Ted demanded, "Finish or I'll tell them about you."

Samantha shook her head in disappointment then said, "Tell them and not only will they not believe you, but you'll be spending the rest of your life on Titan. A place where the gravity is so strong, your dick won't be able to ever stand up again. Just play along till after the battle, and you can fuck my brains out for as long as you want."

Ted asked, "What battle?"

Samantha walked away and said, "The battle to end all battles in Einstein. It's going to be awhile yet."

Ted thought her to be a mental case at the time, just a nutjob getting her jollies from messing with the convict. Ted thought about it more and more the next few days as the internet was out, leaving him with nothing but recorded self-help videos to watch. Ted just couldn't see the outer ringers as a whole trying to fight the inner ringers.

Then the ship vibrated suddenly. Ted knew the only thing that could shake a ship of Equality's size was scattershot, and scattershot was only used in a serious fight. Suddenly, Ted thought Samantha might have been telling the truth.

Once the internet did return, there was talk on the news feeds about Equality being part of a nuclear weapons test and killing outer ringer scientists they hired to construct the atomic missile. This news enraged Ted, who now knew Samantha was telling the truth.

Soon, all outer ring news feeds were blocked. Shortly after that, a large Black man named Frank showed up, asking about the night of Samantha's visit. Ted played dumb and told Frank to "Piss off!"

Frank left then returned with a godling who injected Ted with a truth serum. Ted was worried that he'd be forced to talk about Samantha, but the truth serum didn't work. Ted quickly realized Samantha must have sabotaged the injection and played along so as not to get her caught.

Finally, the day came for Ted to be taken to SS Middleman for transport down to Titan. Ted watched for Samantha but never saw her. As he walked the landing pad of Middleman in chains, Ted looked about, expecting to see some sort of wild rescue mission with lightning bolts being thrown about. But there was nothing.

Ted was booked into Middleman security. They quickly removed his chains, only to put him into a cheap exoskeleton suit that he would need to move about Titan. After that, Ted was loaded into a pod for transport down to the planet.

Ted felt betrayed by Samantha as he was being transported to Titan. There was a camera in the pod recording Ted's last words. He thought about outing Samantha, but his hatred for the inner ringers was stronger. For them to use outer ringers for the dangerous task of building a nuclear missile, then to murder them like the lives of outer ringers meant nothing. Ted was so mad that he was about to start punching the inside of his pod when it suddenly opened.

"Hurry up and get out" came a voice Ted wasn't sure was male or female. Ted wasted no time in climbing out of the pod.

Ted looked about to see he was in a small empty cargo vessel. "There's a small package by your feet. Put it in the pod then press the button on the side" came the same voice through an open door from the cockpit.

Ted didn't waste time asking questions. He placed the small rectangular package into the pod and pressed the button. To Ted's surprise, it was a blowup doll in his image. The face even looked lifelike with small random movement.

"Make sure it's in the same place you were, and close the pod," said the voice.

Ted did this then entered the cockpit. Inside was a person wearing a miner's suit with a tinted visor, keeping Ted from seeing the person's face. Ted asked, "Is this going to work?"

The person responded, "Been doing it for years. No one's caught on yet."

Ted asked, "Is there really going to be a war between the inner and outer ringers?"

The person responded, "Not a war. One massacre to end all massacres."

Ted asked, "What will you need me to do?"

The person answered, "Fire the first and most devastating shot."

Ted asked, "With what?"

The person answered, "I'm taking you to my secret base hidden behind Apollo along the first ring. Your ship, the Exterminator, is there."

Ted asked, "How the hell did you pull all this off? Just who are you?"

The person raised their visor to show a teenage boy wearing an eyepatch. He said, "I'm Captain Spike. Pleased to meet you."

*****

Jess opened the door to her apartment and said, "So glad you guys made it. You can take your power attire off along the wall." Jess pointed to a wall with magnetic hangers.

Captain Jake was surprised to see all the walls in the apartment were bare metal. There was grass on the floor but no vines or pictures on the walls. The only furniture visible was a dining room set and a ninety-degree sofa. The only thing making it feel like a home was the pop music playing in the background.

June and Captain Jake made their way to the hangers. The day's shopping experience had been a new one for Captain Jake. June picked out his dinner wardrobe for him then had it shipped to Serenity without him getting to see it. It turned out to be a blue button-up shirt with green suspenders and very uncomfortable skinny jeans that Captain Jake left aboard Serenity.

June, in the meantime, made Captain Jake watch her try on multiple outfits, but then she wouldn't let him see the outfit she eventually chose to wear. Until now.

Captain Jake removed his power suit then turned to June. She was wearing a strapless and low-hemmed red dress. June's skin was lightly tanned and sparsely covered with silver sparkles. Even June's pink camo arm seemed to have a glow about it. Captain Jake wanted to compliment her, but he couldn't get words to form.

Amy walked into the room then stated, "Don't you two make a great looking couple."

June and Captain Jake both began to blush, then Captain Jake said, "We're not—"

June cut Captain Jake off, "I love your apartment. I had a friend with digital walls. They are amazing."

Captain Jake asked, "Digital walls?"

Jess squealed. "You're going to love this, Jakey! Belvedere, give us a beach, seventy-five degrees with an eight-mile-per-hour ocean breeze. Oh! And make it sunset."

The room suddenly transformed into a beach with an ocean and a sun setting over the water. The floor even appeared to be covered with white sand. Captain Jake bent down to touch the sand but only felt grass. Captain Jake said, "Amazing hologram."

Jess said, "A little too amazing. Can't tell you how many times I've run into the walls."

Amy said, "A little too often. I keep having to reassure people that I'm not beating her."

Jess giggled then said, "Just tell people what I do. That I like it rough."

Amy frowned then said, "Not funny."

Jess walked over and gave Amy a kiss before saying, "It is to me."

Amy announced, "Dinner's ready."

They sat down at the dining room table with the beach and its gentle waves rolling in only a few feet away. Jess handed out wine-filled sports bottles while Amy brought in plates of burgers and fries. Amy said, "I hope you're not a vegetarian, June."

June replied, "If I was before, I'm not now. It looks delicious."

Jess bragged, "Amy makes her own seasoned glue that holds it all together. You're going to love it."

Captain Jake took a bite of his burger. After swallowing, he said, "This is the best burger I've ever had. How does it taste so good?"

Amy answered, "The meat's not cell grown. It's from a cow dying of natural causes on Romeo. The animal's diet completely changes the flavor."

Jess noticed June staring at Jake instead of eating her own food and said, "It's going to get cold."

June snapped back to her senses then said, "Oh! Sorry." June grabbed a fry, and as soon as it hit her mouth, she remembered she hadn't eaten all day. She was having so much fun with Captain Jake that she completely forgot she was hungry.

Amy whispered to Jess, "Don't embarrass our guest."

Jess responded by announcing, "We have a spare room if you two drink too much and need to crash."

Both June and Captain Jake choked on their food for a moment. Captain Jake cleared his throat then said, "Thanks, but—"

Jess cut Captain Jake off, "The sheets are fresh."

Amy exclaimed, "Jess!"

Jess rolled her eyes then said, "Fine. I'll change the subject. So, Jakey, I heard you blew up a planet on the way here."

June said, "We didn't blow anything up. They blew up a nuclear reactor to try and kill us."

Amy said, "That's awful. The news said the planet was abandoned, so no one got hurt."

Jess asked, "What happened to all the settlers?"

Captain Jake answered, "They're still investigating that. The radiation is making it difficult."

Amy asked, "You just got here, Jake. Why are people trying to kill you?"

Captain Jake replied, "Wish I knew."

Amy said, "I heard your next mission is to Chronos. Try not to let a dinosaur eat you."

Captain Jake said, "You already heard about that, did you?"

June exclaimed, "We're really going to Chronos?"

Amy said, "Belvedere, show us Harry Strum's latest news feed." Within the setting sun, a TV appeared.

On the screen was Harry with a background of palm trees and sunshine. Harry said, "I have not been told the date of departure yet. I can tell you that the EPF flagship Equality will be traveling to Chronos on a joint mission between the governments of Romeo and Juliet. This will be an unprecedented one-day joint operation to swap out old Chronos soil taken from the planet two hundred years ago for fresh soil. This soil, as you may know, is necessary for the growth of the Pazel flower, the primary ingredient in 15 for Life that thousands, including myself, depend on to live. As for why the soil is being swapped out, join me tomorrow as I interview Dr. Dawn, head scientist at the Pazel greenery under the Passay biodome." The news feed ended, and the sun returned.

Jess asked excitedly, "Does this mean you're going to get to meet Adam and Eve?"

Captain Jake repeated, "Adam and Eve?"

June said, "They are the last two scientists still on Chronos. They do daily streaming feeds from the quartership SS Jurassic Park."

Captain Jake asked, "There's a quartership on the planet? Quarterships are too heavy to break the atmosphere."

Amy asked, "How do you not know about Jurassic Island, Jake?"

June explained, "The first scientist to come to Einstein wanted to bring back the dinosaurs. The only planet they could use was Chronos, but it's inhabited."

Jess interrupted, "They have Indians, Jakey."

Captain Jake said, "I know about them and the order not to interfere with their development. That's why I don't get the quartership being on the planet. It's still just one big continent, isn't it?"

Amy said, "Not anymore."

June explained, "To get a section of land to clone dinosaurs at half their normal size, the scientists sent in a small army of robots to clear out the area. The robots went armed with drill darts filled with roofies to erase their memories. They cleared out a small section of land then set off seismic charges to break it off the rest of the continent. They then pulled the island to the opposite end of the planet and created Jurassic Island."

Captain Jake replied, "That's insane."

Jess stated, "What's insane is they won't let anyone visit Jurassic Island. I mean, they have dinosaurs!"

Amy said, "June, you look like you need more wine."

Jess added, "So does Jakey."

June said, "I shouldn't."

Captain Jake said, "You're not on duty. As your captain, I order you to enjoy yourself."

Jess screamed, "Party!"

The four spent the next several hours sharing stories and watching the never-ending sunset as the ocean waves rolled onto shore. At some point, Amy and Jess slipped off to bed without June or Jake realizing it.

Jake looked around and asked, "How long have we been alone?"

June also looked around and replied, "Shit, I think it's been awhile."

Jake said, "We should probably get going then."

June replied softly, "I don't want to leave yet."

Jake turned to look at June. He quickly became lost in her gaze and said, "I don't want to leave ever."

The two were swept away by the moment and the wine as they shared their first kiss. The first kiss quickly turned into the second, third, and fourth.

June pulled back and said, "Belvedere, spare bedroom." A line of flashing lights in the sand led a path to a door.

June and Jake raced while stumbling to the room. Once inside, they quickly started to undress. Jake lifted June up, pressing her naked body against his as he carried her to the bed. Jake laid June down then zipped up the sleeping bag to keep from floating off.

Jake moved to get on top, but June stopped him and said, "I'm always on top."

Jake replied, "I remember the story from Hades City. Not the mental picture I wanted right now."

June saw the passion leaving Jake's face, so she pulled his head down and began kissing him passionately. After a minute, June stopped to stare deeply into Jake's eyes. June placed her feet on the back of Jake's calves then said, "Don't suck."

Romeo

Equality approached the planet Titan's moon named Romeo. Most of the crew and residents crammed onto the observation decks to see the biodomes of Romeo. Dozens of them could be seen along the moon's surface. Each dome was built into a crater with a wall of dirt built up high around the base. Rods were then inserted into the dirt base, barely visible from above. These rods worked in conjunction with a large pole raised up to the top of the biodomes to hold in the artificial atmosphere.

Equality landed next to the Durant biodome. Due to easy airlocks not being sanctioned in the inner rings, everyone leaving Equality had to wear power attire or space suits. The initial airlock into the dirt base of the biodome opened up into a large room filled with military personnel running drills.

A group consisting of Stacy, July, May, Timothy, and Rex entered the biodome. Rex asked, "What the hell is this?"

Stacy smacked Rex in the side of his space suit-covered neck then said, "Language. There are kids present."

May explained, "The military do their training exercises at the entrances of the biodomes. They consider it a strong deterrent from any possible terrorist activity."

July pointed to a large section of lockers and said, "You will have to leave you power suits over there. No one is allowed to wear them inside without a permit."

May added, "Which July and I have."

Rex scoffed, "Aren't you special."

The group made their way to the lockers as Timothy said, "Let them wear their suits. I want to feel the artificial sun. My mom's said they came here once for their honeymoon and spent the whole day bathing in the sun. I want to do that."

Stacy said, "It's called sunbathing. Not something you could ever handle doing."

Timothy replied, "I said I want to do it."

Stacy replied, "Yeah, right. You have to lay still in one spot for hours."

Timothy stated, "I can do that."

Stacy added, "Without being on your W2."

Timothy asked, "Why not?"

Stacy answered, "Because that would mess with your tan line."

July said, "If you guys want to go with us, May and I are headed to May's family sheep ranch in biodome two."

Rex immediately responded, "I'm in."

Timothy asked Stacy, "Can we go?"

Stacy said, "Well, I want to go with Harry tomorrow to meet Dr. Dawn."

May replied, "You can make it to any biodome in under thirty minutes using the subway system. We can even keep an eye on Timmy while you go."

Timmy said, "I want to go see Dr. Dawn too. I interviewed her last year for a dissertation I was doing. My professor said it was the best he ever read."

July giggled then said, "I forget what a nerd you are."

Rex said, "I'm going too. Can't trust Timmy to stay out of trouble."

Stacy sighed then said, "Aren't I lucky?" The group made their way to the subway and headed to biodome 2.

Timothy was excited when they reached biodome 2. It was the first time he got to run around with sun and gravity. Timothy was even more excited when they all (except Rex) got electric assist bicycles to ride to the sheep ranch. Even though he had to walk, Rex also enjoyed the trip because he got to chase a squirrel up a tree.

May's family ranch was four acres of mostly fenced-off pastures with a few hundred sheep roaming around. There was a small red barn used for shearing the sheep. The family home was a white two-story house with a big front porch and a white picket fence.

As they approached, Timothy noticed a swing set with a little girl playing on it. Timmy asked, "Can I go try that, Stacy?"

Stacy replied, "Ask May. It's her home."

May replied, "You can go play."

Timmy said, "Thanks, May." Then he began pedaling faster with Rex chasing after him.

July asked, "Who's the girl?"

May replied, "No idea. Could be a neighbor."

The group reached the house, and May led the way to the front door. May turned the knob three times before opening it. Once inside, May yelled, "Is anyone home?"

A young girl no more than twenty with short pink hair came running into the room, screaming, "I'm here!"

May was startled by the girl and said, "I'm sorry. Is this still the home of Marie and Denis?"

The young woman started laughing then got on her W2. A moment later, she started talking on her W2. "May's home. She just asked me if it was still Marie and Denis's home. Can you believe that? Oh, I have to show you the replay from my lenses later. We can put it on the big screen. It was priceless."

July elbowed May then said, "I think that's your mom."

May stared intently at the young woman for a minute then replied, "Can't be. She's too skinny."

The young woman said, "Denis, I have to call you back. Your daughter just called me fat. Love you."

May asked, "Mom?"

July walked up to the lady and gave her a big hug as she said, "Hi, Marie. There is less of you to hug now."

Marie replied, "It's always good to see you, July. With youth comes a faster metabolism. That doesn't mean I was fat before, May."

May asked, "When did you get on 15 for Life?"

Marie replied, "Your father and I got accepted right after you joined the EPF. Having a daughter protecting the star system got us bumped up the waiting list."

May said, "I just video chatted with you yesterday. You were still—"

Marie started where May stopped, "Old and fat."

May said, "You know what I mean."

Marie said, "You father wanted to surprise you, so we downloaded one of those aging apps. We still have a couple of years to go, but we feel amazing." Marie now started looking Stacy up and down then said, "Ain't you a pretty one? My daughter better not let you get away."

May exclaimed, "Stacy's just a friend, Mom!"

Marie replied, "Give it time, dear. I think this one's a keeper."

July laughed and said, "I love your family."

May asked, "Who's the girl outside? Don't tell me she's Aunt Becky."

Marie replied, "Don't be silly. That's Francis, your new sister. It was getting too quiet around here. Francis's mother is from Beta Mining. She suffered from one of those bad heaven's bliss reactions you've been seeing on all the news feeds. Poor dear. At least you girls would never put that garbage in your systems."

July looked at Stacy and giggled as she said, "No, ma'am. None of us would *ever* try heaven's bliss."

Stacy tried to quickly change the subject. "So you didn't grow up here, July?"

July suddenly stopped giggling and grabbed Marie's arm as she said, "Nope. Marie, you have to meet Timmy and Rex. They're out playing with Francis. Timmy's a nine-year-old genius, and Rex is his talking dog." July then led Marie outside.

Stacy stood there for a second, wondering if she said something wrong, when May said, "July was raised by the foster system. As part of the nature versus nurture experiment, she was relocated every six months."

Stacy said, "That's awful."

May said, "July is the strongest of us. April was the only child of alcoholics. April raised them more than they raised her. June was raised by nannies in a wealthy home. She wanted for nothing except parents that were never around. July kept getting moved around. She had to feel like no one loved her. I couldn't have survived that."

Stacy said, "I had no idea. She's always smiling and upbeat."

May said, "I worry about the day she doesn't smile. I think smiling is the only way she knows how to keep it together."

Stacy said, "At least your family seems nice."

May replied, "They are, but I had nine brothers and sisters. I felt more like a number than a person. It wasn't until April brought us all together that..." May paused talking as she tapped her knuckles on the wall three times then said, "My three sisters and I felt whole for the first time."

*****

Harry stood in front of the Pazel greenery, showing his credentials to the guards. They were about to let him in when Stacy, Timothy, and Rex arrived.

Harry said, "Took you all long enough to get here. I was about to go in without you."

One of the guards said, "We can only let you in, sir. Only one visitor is allowed on the premises at a time."

Harry argued, "The facility is empty. That's why I'm here."

Timothy said, "The facility isn't empty. They still have research material inside."

Rex muttered, "You aren't helping."

Stacy said, "I'm a botanist with the EPF. I have clearance."

Timothy said, "I'm Timmy of Nowhere. Dr. Dawn likes me."

The guard called Dr. Dawn and said, "Sorry to bother you, ma'am. Harry is here with unscheduled guests." The guard nodded then said, "I told them, ma'am. The lady with him says she's a botanist from the EPF." The guard nodded then said to the group, "I will tell them only Harry is allowed."

Timothy yelled, "It's Timmy of Nowhere, Dr. Dawn! I came to see you!"

The guard nodded then said, "Dr. Dawn will be right down."

Timothy proudly said, "Told you she liked me."

A few minutes later, a tall, dark-skinned, and bald teenage girl wearing a lab coat walked out and said, "Timmy, you aren't here to take my job, are you?"

Timmy replied, "No. I already have a job aboard Equality. I work for the EPF."

Dr. Dawn replied, "That's a relief." Dr. Dawn shook Stacy's hand and said, "He never told me his mother was a botanist. That helps to explain how your son understood our research here better than some of my scientists conducting the research."

Stacy said, "I'm not actually his mother."

Timothy said, "My moms died. Stacy's pregnant with my almost father's babies, so I have to keep an eye on her and my unborn siblings."

Dr. Dawn said, "Congratulations."

Rex said, "I watch both of them because they're nuts."

Stacy replied, "The only thing you look after is your whiskey bowl."

Dr. Dawn said, "That's the best animal speech I've ever heard."

Timothy replied, "Thanks. I get that a lot."

Dr. Dawn said, "Why does that not surprise me? This boy is going to do great things."

Harry said, "Not to interrupt, but can we discuss the Chronos soil?"

Dr. Dawn said, "Yes, of course. You can all come in."

As they entered the virtually empty greenery, Timothy noticed an empty section of the floor with bolts sticking out of it. Timothy asked, "Is this where the time dilation pod was? It must have been twice the size of the one we have on Equality."

Dr. Dawn said, "Yes, it was. You ever decide you want to change careers, I'll hire you here in a heartbeat."

Timothy replied, "Thank you, but Equality needs me."

Harry asked, "Can I get some background information before we start the interview? Why are you returning the Chronos soil to Chronos?"

Dr. Dawn replied, "We've been using the same soil for a little over two hundred years. For some reason, no matter what kind of crop rotation or fertilizer we use, we can't seem to keep from getting diminishing yields."

Stacy asked, "Have you identified the mineral you're missing?"

Dr. Dawn replied, "There are three unknown chemical compounds in the soil. We thought we had a process worked out for maximum yields, but lately, they have been dropping at an alarming rate."

Timothy asked, "Have you been studying the places where the flower grows on Chronos?"

Dr. Dawn said, "You're thinking we might need certain animal dung for fertilizer. Animals native to Chronos."

Stacy said, "And the animals' diet might be a factor."

Dr. Dawn said, "We do have researchers looking into it. Unfortunately, the flower is rare on Chronos. That still doesn't explain the sudden drop in production."

Timothy said, "I could look at your data for you."

Dr. Dawn asked, "Does Timmy really work for the EPF?"

Harry asked, "Did you hear about Equality discovering a nuclear reactor on Icarus that almost killed our captain?"

Dr. Dawn said, "Of course. And I heard about the nuclear weapons test. We know Equality couldn't have been a part of making the nuclear missile. The ship and it's captain just arrived in this star system. I thought it was the outer ringers' doing until I heard about Icarus. Do you know who's really behind it?"

Harry said, "Not yet. I can tell you it was Timmy's quick thinking that saved my life and the captain's life on Icarus."

Timmy added, "They threw me a party and chanted my name. It was really cool."

Stacy said, "That party was for more people than just you."

Rex said, "I didn't hear anyone else's name being chanted."

Dr. Dawn said, "I'm sold. Follow me to my office, and I'll pull up the files."

There were several office doors in the back with names on them. Sound could be heard coming from several offices as people worked. Dr. Dawn led them to the door with her name on it and let them in.

The room had a blue carpeted floor with several paintings on the walls. There was a large wooden desk with a computer terminal setting on it by the back wall. In front of the desk were two chairs, and along the side wall was a brown love seat.

As the group entered, Dr. Dawn headed for her desk and said, "This will take a minute to start up. It takes a password, retina scan, and fingerprint just to turn on. You can all have a seat while you wait."

Stacy moved toward a chair in front of the desk while Timothy and Rex headed toward the love seat. Harry stood frozen by the doorway, staring at the love seat. As Rex was about to jump up onto the love seat, Harry shouted, "*No*! Don't sit there!"

The whole room turned to look at Harry. Rex said, "Chill. I'm house broken." Then he jumped up onto the love seat.

Harry screamed, "Get down! That's the same love seat that was on Icarus."

Rex jumped down then said, "You could have just said so."

Stacy asked, "Are you sure?"

Harry replied, "I'm not likely to forget. It's the same color and everything."

Timothy moved toward the couch to inspect it while Dr. Dawn asked, "What's going on?"

Stacy grabbed Timothy and said, "You're staying away from that."

Harry explained, "On Icarus, before the nuclear meltdown, we discovered love seats exactly like this one. They were rigged with sawsword chains."

Dr. Dawn laughed and said, "I've taken many naps in that love seat. There are no sawsword chains."

Timothy started to type on his W2 and said, "I bet if I can find the right frequency, I can set it off."

Stacy said, "Don't you dare."

Rex said, "I want to see the death seat."

Stacy said, "No. Dr. Dawn, how long have you had this love seat?"

Dr. Dawn replied, "A few months, I think. It's a government building. They remodel every so often."

There was suddenly a humming sound from the love seat, immediately followed by the room being filled with white stuffing. Timothy sighed. "I found the right signal, but I missed it."

Dr. Dawn exclaimed, "My love seat!"

Rex corrected the doctor. "Death seat."

*****

Davinie sat in a park under a biodome. She was watching her grandchildren play when her W2 rang. Davinie answered and said, "I'm with my grandbabies. This better be important."

Harry said, "Sorry, Davinie. Captain Jake and Frank aren't answering their W2s." Harry showed Davinie an image of the torn-up death seat then said, "We just found one of those death seats from Icarus on Romeo."

Davinie said, "Good God. I don't see any blood."

Harry replied, "I warned them about the death seat, but Timothy got curious."

Davinie replied, "Of course he did. Who was the target this time?"

Harry replied, "It was in the office of Dr. Dawn. She's the head scientist in charge of everything involving 15 for Life. Only she says the death seat has been here for months, and she's taken naps on it."

Davinie said, "She could still be the target. They were just waiting until the right time. Put out a warning of the death seat across Einstein. Where there's one, there could be more."

Harry said, "Right away."

Davinie added, "Make sure to use a before and after photo so they know what to look for. I have to go. Just got a live link from July."

Harry said, "So did I. Thank you, Davinie."

*****

May and July were at May's family's ranch about to sit down for a large family meal when July suddenly grabbed May by the arm and dragged her out to the front porch.

May asked, "What's going on?"

July said, "June just sent us a link. Click on it."

May quickly pulled out her W2 and clicked the link. The image of the inside of a church appeared on her W2. A black plushy with a white collar was standing behind a podium. In front of the podium was Frank in a tux and Captain Jake wearing a blue shirt with green suspenders. May exclaimed, "April's getting married without us!"

July said, "Yep. The feed's coming from June's contact lens. She and Jake are witnesses."

May exclaimed, "That's bullshit!"

The view now changed to show April walking down the aisle toward the podium. Her top was a white dress with no frills. Her bottom half was white cowboy boots with a white miniskirt.

May asked, "When did April get legs?"

July replied, "The question is, where did she get all the cream to cover up her varicose veins?"

May stated, "I know why you weren't invited."

July said, "Screw this." Then she began typing on her W2.

May asked, "What are you doing?"

July replied, "If April wanted a private ceremony, then she should have invited us. I'm sharing this link with everyone on Equality. You share with everyone else on our friends list."

May said, "I'm on it, but I'm not getting audio."

July said, "Me either. Video will have to do."

The link was shared in time for everyone to watch Frank place the ring on April's finger. Then April did the same, followed by the two leaning in for a kiss. The video stream then changed to show Captain Jake staring longingly into the camera.

July asked, "Why is Captain Jake giving 'fuck me' eyes to June?"

May replied, "I don't know, but we need to have a little talk with the captain about inappropriate behavior toward our sister."

The view changed back to April and Frank. April was now staring at June. At first, the look on April's face was one of confusion as she looked from June to Captain Jake back to June. Then April's expression turned to that of anger.

Frank, seeing this, quickly grabbed April just in time to keep her from lunging at June. Frank then tossed April over his shoulder and carried her out. The whole time, April was clawing toward the camera, and if there was sound, she was doing a lot of cussing.

July exclaimed, "Our slut of a sister is doing the captain!"

May closed the link while getting a look of depression on her face then whined, "How am I the only one not in a relationship?"

July said, "If you're that desperate, ask Samantha out. April will be too pissed at June to notice."

May said, "I can't ask Samantha out."

July asked, "Why not?"

May stated, "Because she hasn't spoken to me since we slept together."

July exclaimed, "When the hell did that happen?"

May replied, "The night of the magic show Michael the Magician put on. I ran into Samantha in the second-floor hall by chance."

July rolled her eyes and said, "You mean you were stalking her."

May said, "She left the show for a while, and I got worried about her, is all. Anyways, we started to talk, and she said she had something to show me in her room."

July laughed then said, "I bet she did."

May said, "As soon as the door closed, she pulled off the top of her onesie. I didn't even know it wasn't actually a onesie. She grabbed my hands and put them on her breasts. Then she asked me which one was softer."

July laughed again then said, "I have to remember that one."

May said, "Whatever. You've had the same boyfriend all your life. This was the best night of my life, but when I woke up, she was gone. When I found her later, she was distant and acted like nothing happened."

July said, "Well, that's just rude. I'll have a talk with her."

May pleaded, "No, please don't. I'm embarrassed enough as it is."

July crossed her fingers behind her back then said, "Okay, I won't."

Journey to Chronos

Two weeks after April and Frank's wedding, Serenity returned to space to merge with Equality. April had refused to speak with June since the wedding, so the trip was very quiet and awkward.

Once merged, Captain Jake asked, "Want to wait for them to go up?"

June replied, "No. April's the one with a stick up her butt. It's none of her business that we slept together."

Captain Jake commented, "That sounds past tense."

June asked, "Isn't it?"

Captain Jake replied, "I didn't think it was a fling. It's fine if it was, I guess."

June said, "We should head back."

June and Captain Jake left their seats to walk on the ceiling that was now considered the floor (without gravity, there really wasn't much of a distinction) after the merge. They walked into the passenger cabin, which had rotated during the merge so that the seats were now on what was considered the floor.

Frank said, "Thank you again for being our witnesses and keeping the ceremony a secret."

Captain Jake replied, "I was honored to do it, and I promise not to tell a soul. Dolly, take us up."

The ceiling above them opened up, and the floor turned into a lift, raising them up. To their surprise, all the residents and crew had gathered and were holding up signs congratulating April and Frank on their wedding.

April looked at June with a look of anger.

May, June, Emily, and Irene rushed up to April. May stated, "We're taking your wife, Frank."

July said, "Yeah. You asses wouldn't let us be at the wedding, but there's no way in hell we're skipping the bachelorette party."

May said, "Let's go, June."

June said, "I'll catch up later."

Irene commented, "You and the captain still on honeymoon mode yourselves, are you?"

July started to drag April off and shouted, "We'll be at the spa getting drunk!"

Captain Jake whispered to June, "How does everyone know?"

June replied, "I sorta broadcasted a live feed to my sisters of the ceremony. Only to them."

Captain Jake said, "Sorry, Frank."

Frank replied, "It's fine. April was the one who wanted to keep it a secret."

Calvin approached and asked, "Did you throw Frank a bachelor party, Jake? I know you didn't because I wasn't invited."

Captain Jake replied, "It was spur of the moment."

Calvin replied, "Tonight at nine. Cargo bay."

Frank said, "No."

Calvin replied, "Yes. Nine o'clock." Then he walked away.

*****

Captain Jake spent the time before the party checking in on the officers to make sure everything was ready for the upcoming secret mission no one on board yet knew about. His first stop was the botanical bay to see Stacy, because he didn't see her with the welcoming party.

Captain Jake entered the botanical bay and was shocked to see Stacy was already showing. Captain Jake said, "Holy shit, you're big."

Stacy replied, "Real nice, Jake."

Captain Jake said, "I just saw you a few weeks ago."

Stacy said, "I know. Birth acceleration pills cut pregnancy time in half. These triplets are getting big. If you're not careful, June will end up looking like this."

Captain Jake asked, "Does everyone know about that?"

Stacy answered, "Yep. Is it serious?"

Captain Jake replied, "I thought it was. Not so sure now."

Timothy entered the room with Clair and Rex right behind them. Timothy said, "Hi, Captain Jake. I was just telling Clair about the death seats we found on Romeo."

Captain Jake replied, "I heard about that. Thanks to you guys, dozens more were discovered across Romeo."

Clair stated, "My future husband is always saving lives."

Timothy said, "I try, but I couldn't help Dr. Dawn."

Captain Jake said, "I'd call discovering a death seat helping."

Stacy said, "Not with that. Someone was messing with her production numbers. She asked us to look into it."

Captain Jake asked, "Messing with it how?"

Timothy answered, "They were helping to make more Pazel flowers than what the soil should have been making."

Stacy said, "Or something changed to make the soil less fertile. It could be sabotage."

Timothy said, "No, it was like a magic trick. One hundred eighty years ago, they tried a new process and fertilizer to help maintain yields. They thought it worked, so they let more people start taking 15 for Life. Only it was a trick. The soil was still deteriorating at the same rate it is now."

Stacy said, "If that were true, then the yields would have diminished at a greater rate."

Timothy said, "That's the trick part. It had to be the fertilizer, because it came from off-site. Everything else in the plant gets videotaped twenty-four seven."

Stacy said, "So you think someone was sneaking in good fertilizer for almost two hundred years then stopped out of the blue."

Timothy said, "It would have stopped about the same time the death seats showed up."

Captain Jake said, "That's about the same time we got here and everything else started going screwy."

Stacy said, "The numbers don't support that. In the last three months, the yields dropped then leveled off, only to drop off again. I say sabotage."

Captain Jake asked, "When the numbers started to level back off? Was that by chance while we were stalled in Hades City?"

Timothy replied, "Yes. How did you know that?"

Captain Jake said, "The dropping yields are like a timer to force a mission to Chronos. Whoever's behind this wanted to make sure Equality was part of the mission."

Stacy asked, "And the death seats?"

Timothy answered, "Those would be like the nuclear missile test. Set them off—"

Captain Jake finished the sentence, "And Romeo would be willing to go to war. Intel suggests the outer rings are gathering a fleet together. I think someone's trying to make sure Romeo fights back and at the same time keep us out of the sector to prevent the war. That's good work, Timmy."

Clair gave Timothy a kiss on the cheek.

*****

Frank and Captain Jake approached the cargo bay through the unusually quiet courtyard. Frank said, "Any strippers and I leave."

Captain Jake replied, "I already relayed that message to Calvin."

The cargo bay doors opened, and to their surprise, it was packed with people, including the bachelorette party. Calvin shouted, "Dolly, disco ball!" Suddenly, the lights dimmed, and a disco ball above the center of the room started to glimmer.

The room suddenly filled with a chant of "Dance! Dance! Dance!" as April and Frank slowly made their way to each other.

Frank took hold of April's hand and led her to the makeshift dance floor, where they slow danced to the song "Amazed."

June snuck up on Captain Jake and asked, "How was your day?"

Captain Jake quickly turned to look at June, a smile automatically forming on his face. Captain Jake said, "Enlightening. Is April talking to you yet?"

June replied, "No, I've been giving her her distance. Want to dance?"

Captain Jake replied, "Thought you'd never ask."

*****

The next day, Timothy and Kevin sat at a picnic table by a small apple tree in the courtyard. On the table sat two Tupperware containers. One was full of peapods that needed to be cracked open. The other container was full of the peas.

Stacy walked over and said, "You're doing a good job, Kevin. It's nice of you to help Timmy with his punishment."

Timothy opened a peapod. The peas within started to float off into the air, so Timothy had to grab them quickly. Kevin then opened the second container so Timothy could throw them in.

Kevin closed the lid then said, "Kevin help."

Timothy looked up at Stacy and asked, "Do I really need to do all of these?"

Stacy frowned at Timothy then replied, "When you're finished with those, there's a couple baskets of corn that need shucking. Don't like it, then maybe you should listen to me when I tell you not to do something."

Timothy moaned, "I said I was sorry for activating the death seat."

Kevin proudly stated, "Peas are green."

Stacy said, "Yes, they are, Kevin. You're making a lot of progress with Dr. Helix, aren't you?"

Timothy said, "I looked at Kevin's file. I think he'd be fine if we got him more heaven's bliss. Or we find the mindbender plant when we get to Chronos."

Stacy said, "Heaven's bliss is what caused this. What the hell is a mindbender plant?"

Timothy replied, "A mindbender plant is where the heaven's bliss comes from. That's what I've named it. This happened to Kevin because he got a second implant before the first one was gone. Didn't you notice the multiple implant marks on the back of his neck?"

Stacy said, "I noticed. How do you know this was caused by an overdose? We still haven't received a sample, have we?"

Timothy replied, "Don't need one. Heaven's bliss is plant spinal fluid. It allows people and plants to exchange sensations."

Stacy stated, "I'm a botanist. That's not a thing. You know I tried heaven's bliss. I never communicated with plants."

Timothy said, "That's because you weren't connected with the mindbender plant. It must have thorns or barbs to transfer the fluid."

Stacy asked, "Why would a plant need to share sensations with an animal? That doesn't help it survive."

Timothy replied, "Maybe that's how it learns."

Stacy sighed then said, "Plant's don't have brains. They can't learn."

Timothy said, "Well, maybe this one does."

Stacy said, "Talking to you is exhausting. I have an officers' meeting to get to. Don't leave until you're finished." Stacy walked off toward the conference table.

A few minutes later, Rex joined Timothy and Kevin at the picnic table and asked, "Why the long face, kid?"

Timothy replied, "Stacy won't believe me. I bet Captain Jake would, but he's in an officers' meeting."

Rex said, "Don't let that stop you. I crash officers' meetings all the time."

Timothy perked up and said, "Really?"

*****

The officers' meeting started with a surprise guest sitting at the table. Sitting next to Captain Jake at the conference table was June.

Stacy was the last to arrive, to which Calvin loudly said, "Thanks for holding us up, Stacy."

Stacy patted her belly then replied, "You try moving around with three people inside of you."

Samantha's voice came over the intercom. "We have arrived at the meeting site, Captain. Everyone is here."

Captain Jake replied, "Move us into the lead position, then keep going with thrusters only. Keep the FP shields up."

Samantha replied, "Yes, sir."

Frank asked, "Expecting trouble? We're still in the inner rings."

Captain Jake said, "There's a lot for me to catch you up on. As you know, we think someone's going to try to start a war while we're gone to Chronos. To counter this, Admiral Noem is aboard the Middleman. Should a hostile situation arise, she will be taking command of Middleman."

Frank said, "They don't have weapons or an FP shield."

Captain Jake replied, "They have jet arms with rotational spider cannons. And it's a target no one wants to attack. Besides that, Eagle One is on the way back. They have a rail cannon."

Frank suddenly shouted, "Get out, Rex!" Then he quickly calmed his demeanor when he saw Timothy walk through the sound barrier.

Rex said, "Timmy has something to say." Timothy was standing behind him with his head tilted down.

Captain Jake asked, "What is it, Timmy? Afraid we don't have a lot of time at the moment."

Timothy softly said, "I only wanted to talk to you, Captain Jake."

Stacy said, "You're not getting out of your punishment. If this is about your silly theory of heaven's bliss, you can turn your butt back around and get back to work."

Timothy looked up at Stacy and angrily said, "It's not silly. When we get to Chronos, I'll prove to you that I'm right."

Dr. Helix asked, "What theory?"

Stacy answered, "Timmy thinks the drug comes from a plant on Chronos that talks to people."

Timothy said, "It's called mindbender. I discovered it, and I get to name it."

Dr. Helix asked, "How does it work?"

Timothy replied, "It alters brain cells to improve interactions with plant cells. With enough of the plant spinal fluid, brain cells would be altered enough to communicate with the mindbender plant. That's what happened to Kevin. Now Kevin needs more plant spinal fluid to be normal again."

Captain Jake said, "Dr. Helix?"

Dr. Helix replied, "That would explain how heaven's bliss amplifies drugs. It's like the brain would know what the drug was trying to do then help it. But why would you think it's a plant from Chronos, Timmy?"

Timmy replied, "Where else could it come from? It should be a plant with a thorn or barb that sticks into an animal to share the plant's spinal fluid."

Calvin said, "It's like pod people. I can write a program to search through satellite footage of Chronos."

Timothy said, "It's called a mindbender."

Stacy said, "Don't encourage him. Plants don't communicate with people."

Captain Jake asked, "Have you studied all plant life from this alien planet?"

Stacy replied, "Fine. Do what you want."

Captain Jake asked Thirteen, "What do you think, Thirteen?"

Thirteen, as always, was active on his W2 as he casually replied, "I cannot say."

Captain Jake said, "We'll check the footage, including infrared footage in case the plant is in heavily forested areas. Thank you, Timmy, but I need you and Rex to leave now. We have officers' business to discuss."

Timothy jumped up and gave Captain Jake a hug then said, "Thank you for believing me." Timothy then exited the room.

Captain Jake looked down at Rex then said, "You too."

Rex asked, "Why?"

Davinie answered, "Because you're not an officer."

Rex replied, "Neither is June. Why does she get to stay?"

June answered, "Because the captain asked me to be here. We're waiting for you to leave so he can tell us why."

Rex said, "Fine, I'll leave. No one left worth talking to anyways." Rex walked out through the sound barrier.

Samantha's voice came back over the intercom. "Captain, you might want to get up here. Colt looks pissed at Tanis."

Captain Jake said, "It's fine. Let me know when Colt fires on Tanis."

Samantha offered a hesitant reply. "Okay."

Captain Jake replied, "We're behind schedule, so I have to make this brief." Captain Jake then explained the plan to capture the pirates.

Once Captain Jake was finished, Frank said, "So we're bait. Why did we bring the residents and children with us?"

Captain Jake replied, "They didn't want us tipping our hands to the pirates. When we get to Chronos, I will be sending them down to the planet on Serenity with June to protect them."

Thirteen said, "That's not part of the plan, Captain."

June said, "I want to stay and fight."

Captain Jake looked at June then said, "We can't fight unless I know the civilians are safe. You're the only person I trust to keep them safe."

June nodded in agreement then said, "Okay."

Suddenly, Equality was pushed to the side violently. Captain Jake said, "Dolly, what's going on?"

Dolly replied, "We were struck by debris from the Juliet cargo ship. Spacemines being carried by the Romeo cargo ship were released and detonated by the Juliet cargo ship, setting off a chain reaction that destroyed the Juliet cargo ship and severely damaged the Iron Maiden. The Romeo cargo ship was also disabled from the explosion. The Bearclaw is now charging its rail cannon."

Captain Jake said, "Dolly, put Colt on the conference table screen right now." An image of the black-furred plushy wearing a yellow power suit with black stripes appeared on the screen. Captain Jake asked, "What the hell is going on? This wasn't part of the plan."

Colt replied, "Plan's changed. There was no secret organization working with the pirates. It was the Juliet government the entire time."

Captain Jake asked, "What are you talking about? Where's your proof?"

Colt smiled then said, "That takes care of Tanis."

Dolly said, "The Iron Maiden has been destroyed, Captain. No survivors."

Colt said, "Don't cry for them, Captain. They sabotaged our crop of Pazel flowers. I need you to continue the mission to Chronos to retrieve more soil and seeds before people start dying by the thousands."

Captain Jake demanded, "Where's your proof?"

Colt replied, "The death seats you helped discover were labeled *Icarus Innovations*. We got a forensic report back on some DNA that was recovered from Icarus. It was for prisoners that were supposed to have been transported down to Titan. They weren't. Everything that's happened couldn't possibly have happened without Juliet's support."

Captain Jake asked, "Why would they?"

Colt replied, "To wipe us out. Take our technology and FP. There's a fleet headed this way right now from the outer rings. The Juliets are planning an alliance, but we'll wipe out Juliet before the outer ring fleet gets here."

Someone behind Colt said, "Sir, there's a dozen Juliet ships headed our way."

Colt said, "You have your orders, Captain Jake. Go get us that soil before Romeo citizens start dying." Colt waved his open palm in front of his face to end the transmission.

Captain Jake said, "Red alert. All passengers strap in." Captain Jake rushed to the bridge.

Captain Jake entered the bridge to hear Tie say, "Bearclaw has just attached tow cables to the disabled cargo ship."

Captain Jake said, "That cargo ship is still carrying two large time dilation pods worth a fortune."

Harry said, "And needed to produce Pazel flowers quickly, or people like me will die."

Captain Jake said, "Right now, I need to stop a war, or others will die. Samantha, move us in close to those tow cables. June and May, you in the cargo bay with your jetpacks and hand cannons charged?"

July said, "I'm July, not June. We're ready."

Captain Jake said, "Sorry, July. We're going to open up the cargo bay door. Need you to shoot some tow cables to melt the metal."

May replied, "Can do, Captain."

Davinie asked, "What are you doing, Captain?"

Captain Jake said, "Dolly, open the door. I'm giving Juliet a hostage to stop this war long enough to figure out what the hell's going on."

Calvin said, "Cables snapped."

Captain Jake said, "Nice job, ladies. Head on back."

Colt suddenly appeared on the bridge's main screen then shouted, "What the hell do you think you're doing! I gave you an order!"

The screen suddenly changed to a split screen with Admiral Noem wearing power attire painted blue with *EPF* painted in white letters across her chest. Admiral Noem said, "Captain Jake doesn't work for you. He works for the EPF."

Colt said, "I sent you the file on what the Juliet scum have done."

Admiral Noem replied, "You gave me no time to verify your findings. You, on the other hand, have just murdered forty-six people in cold blood."

Colt said, "I had a chance to cut the head off the snake, and I took it."

Admiral Noem said, "It stops now. You are to move away from that cargo ship. Middleman is on its way to collect it."

Colt said, "You're siding with Juliet."

Admiral Noem said, "I'm not siding with anyone yet. Try to kill anyone else, and I will."

A voice behind Colt said, "Juliet ships are getting within firing range, Captain."

Colt said, "Return to Romeo space. This isn't over, Admiral." Colt waved his hand in front of his face to end the call.

Admiral Noem said, "Quick thinking, Jake."

Captain Jake asked, "Is the Juliet government behind all this?"

Admiral Noem replied, "Looks that way."

Frank's voice came over the comm. "My government would never be a part of such a thing."

Captain Jake said, "I agree with you, Frank."

Calvin suggested, "Maybe it's pod people." Samantha, Admiral Noem, and Tie gave Calvin a funny look.

Harry asked, "You thought Timmy was serious?"

Captain Jake said, "I did. Harry, I want you to help review the footage from Chronos."

Harry said, "There's almost five hundred years' worth of footage."

Calvin said, "Give me an hour to write a program. I'll narrow it down for you."

Admiral Noem asked, "What are you talking about?"

Captain Jake said, "Possible lead from Timmy. We need time to investigate."

Admiral Noem replied, "The boy genius who seems to pop up in almost every major report I get from Equality. Can't wait to actually meet him."

Captain Jake said, "He's got a way of pulling miracles out of his butt, that's for sure."

Admiral Noem said, "I have to ask you a favor, Jake."

Captain Jake replied, "Anything."

Admiral Noem said, "Romeo has a stockpile of 15 for Life, but it's not infinite. I still need you to go get that soil, or war will be inevitable. If it isn't already."

Tie said, "We won't have the cargo ships or mines to hide behind."

Captain Jake said, "Understood, Admiral. Samantha, set course and activate the Carrie effect drive."

*****

That night, Captain Jake lay in his bed, unable to sleep as he stared at his ceiling. June was laying under the sleeping bag cover next to him, playing with Captain Jake's chest hair. June looked at his face and asked, "What are you thinking about?"

Captain Jake asked, "Why didn't Thirteen comment on Timmy's theory of heaven's bliss?"

June replied, "Thirteen probably didn't want to risk being wrong."

Captain Jake said, "It looks like whatever this plan is started hundreds of years ago. Who would have the patience for such a plan?"

June sat up then said, "You really think Thirteen is involved? They have no personal motivation. They are bred to not have personal motivation. They can't even lie."

Captain Jake asked, "Since a godling can't lie, what would their response be to a question they don't want to answer?"

June replied, "I don't know."

Captain Jake said, "Perhaps something like 'I cannot say.'" Captain Jake unzipped the sleeping bag then began to get out of bed.

June also got out of bed then said, "Put on your power suit before we go."

Captain Jake said, "Thirteen's arrogant, not violent."

June replied, "Thirteen's a godling stronger than both of us put together, and you're about to accuse him of trying to start a war. Put on your power suit."

Captain Jake walked around the bed to give June a kiss then said, "Always keeping me safe. Even from myself." The pair got changed and headed to Thirteen's quarters.

As soon as they arrived, the front door opened to allow them entrance. Thirteen's room was lax of any furniture or paintings. What it did contain were walls lined with computer servers. Thirteen was sitting in the middle of the living room Indian style while typing on their W2.

Captain Jake asked, "How are you, Thirteen?"

Thirteen asked, "Are the power suits part of some coitus ritual?"

Captain Jake smiled then answered, "No, we just want to ask you some quick questions."

Thirteen stood up then walked over to Captain Jake with his W2 extended.

June stepped in front of Captain Jake defensively and asked, "What are you doing?"

Thirteen replied, "Handing over my W2. It is customary for prisoners to have all electronic devices removed."

Captain Jake said, "So you are behind all of this."

Thirteen replied, "I cannot answer any questions until after the Chronos mission. Everything will become clear at that time."

June said, "I'll beat the information out of you."

Captain Jake said, "That wouldn't work on a godling."

June replied, "Maybe not, but I'd really enjoy trying."

Captain Jake asked, "Is it just you, or is the entire godling race in on it?"

Thirteen remained silent.

June said, "Godlings only live sixty years, Jake. Their bodies start to deteriorate after that, so they commit ritual suicide to make room for their replacements. They're a very efficient race."

Captain Jake said, "Dolly, call Frank and Calvin."

After a moment, Dolly said, "Both are on the line, Captain."

Captain Jake said, "Frank, I need you to do a sweep on Thirteen's room. They're under arrest for suspicion of treason. Calvin, Thirteen's got a bunch of servers in his room. Check the ship's systems first for any sabotage, then come check out these servers. I want to know what's on them."

Calvin said, "I thought they bred treason out of godlings."

Captain Jake said, "Thirteen hasn't actually admitted to treason, but they are refusing to speak. I'm getting sick of not knowing what's going on."

The door opened, and Frank, with a drone, entered the room. Frank typed on his W2, then the drone started to sweep the room. Frank asked, "Want me to take Thirteen to a cell?"

Captain Jake replied, "I've got it. He seemed ready to turn himself in, so I doubt you'll find anything. I'll send you my W2 feed later."

June said, "I want to stay and help search just in case."

Captain Jake said, "Sure thing. I'll see you when you're finished." Captain Jake left the room.

As soon as the door shut, Frank said, "He's a good man. Don't do what you usually do to good men."

June walked into the bedroom then said, "Don't believe everything my sister tells you."

Frank replied, "I was in Hades City."

June's tone turned angry. "I didn't rape that guy!" June took a deep breath then said, "Jake's different. It's not about sex. I don't know what it's about yet, but it's not just sex. You can tell my sister to stop freaking out."

Frank replied, "We will see."

*****

The next day, there was another officers' meeting with special guests June and Timothy, as well as uninvited guest Rex.

Timothy asked Stacy, "Where should I sit?"

Stacy answered, "You can sit next to me if Harry doesn't mind taking Thirteen's seat."

Harry replied, "Never say no to a pregnant woman." Then he moved down one seat.

Timothy took the seat then asked, "Why won't Thirteen be here?"

Stacy replied, "Locked up in a cell for working with the enemy."

Timothy replied, "Really? You mean he wasn't just bad at his job?"

Captain Jake said, "Let's get started. I sent Admiral Noem a message about Thirteen, but she's too busy to look into a godling connection right now. Two fleets have gathered on opposite sides of Middleman. One Romeo, and the other Juliet. Both sides are swelling in numbers by the hour. The Romeo side isn't attacking because Admiral Noem is threatening to blow up the time dilation pods if they do. Juliet is screaming for revenge but is hesitant to attack because their ships have fewer FP shields installed. Admiral Noem is turning all relay satellites into signal blockers in part to try to stem the escalation. There's also a fleet from the outer rings that should reach Middleman in two days, the same day we are scheduled to arrive at Chronos. Both sides are denying a possible alliance with the outer rings. Admiral Noem wants to avoid any side working with them the opportunity to strategize an attack."

Calvin said, "When that outer ring fleet shows up, Romeo is toast."

Dr. Helix said, "Even if Admiral Noem helps Romeo with Middleman and Eagle One, it won't be enough, will it?"

Frank said, "Juliet isn't working with the outer rings."

Calvin added, "That you know of."

Captain Jake said, "Admiral Noem has called for Eagle Two and Three as well as the cargo ships with the four thousand spacemines to join her at Middleman. She's going to throw up a barrier of spacemines to keep the peace between the opposing fleets."

Frank asked, "How are we supposed to catch the pirates?"

Harry asked, "How are we supposed to not get killed by the pirates?"

Captain Jake replied, "How things change in the course of a day. Dolly, on the conference table screen please." The conference table started showing a picture of Captain Spike on the bridge of a mothership. Captain Jake said, "The pirate fleet consisting of five motherships, all with FP shields, has revealed their location by a secret space station hiding behind Apollo on the first ring. They are offering their services in the impending war to the highest bidder."

Frank said, "You can't be serious. No one could trust them."

Calvin said, "If the Juliet government is behind this, then the pirates should already be working for them."

Frank repeated, "The Juliet government isn't behind this."

Captain Jake said, "I agree with Frank. Don't forget, Captain Spike is on 15 for Life. That came from Romeo. I believe the godlings are the ones trying to start this war. We need proof to stop the war."

Dr. Helix said, "They can't be the ones behind this. If someone asked for a plan, then they could, in theory, have created one, but they would have no reason to start a war."

Frank asked, “Do you have a truth serum for Thirteen? If we can make him talk…”

Dr. Helix replied, “Their physiology has been altered too much for truth serum to work.”

Captain Jake pointed to the picture on the screen then said, “There may be another way to get answers. Admiral Noem has made Captain Spike an offer to join the EPF temporarily.”

Frank asked, “Has she lost her mind?”

June asked, “Is that Ted behind Captain Spike?”

Frank jumped to his feet while slamming his fists on the table and shouted, “I watched that son of a bitch get dropped down to Titan.”

Captain Jake said, “Everyone aboard Captain Spike’s ship has been identified as a prisoner that was supposed to be on Titan.”

Calvin said, “There are too many electrical storms on Titan to ever check on the prisoners after they get dumped off. It’s kind of brilliant.”

Davinie said, “Colt said the DNA from Icarus was from Titan prisoners. They had to have been the ones constructing the death seats and supplying the nuclear material to the RO Research Station. Don’t tell me they started a war just to earn pardons.”

Captain Jake said, “Admiral Noem or any other fraction does have to include pardons to hire them. They say they’re also offering their services to the outer ringers. Another reason why Admiral Noem had to start blocking signals. She’s considering accepting the offer if it includes answers.”

Dr. Helix said, “I can’t see the godlings helping the pirates with such an elaborate plan. The cause would have to be noble for them to get involved. There’s nothing noble about helping convicted murderers escape their sentence.”

Captain Jake said, “Let’s continue on to current business. I understand nothing suspicious was discovered in Thirteen’s quarters. What was on their drives?”

Calvin said, “Looks like a complete archive of the Solar and Einstein system’s histories.”

Captain Jake said, "I understand you found something regarding the mindbender plant."

Harry said, "We found something."

Calvin added, "Only one something taken from a surveillance drone's feed while the robots were relocating the inhabitants of what's now Jurassic Island."

Timothy looked at Stacy then said, "Dolly, show Stacy the mindbender video on the conference table screen, please and thank you."

On the screen appeared what looked like a deer with short brown fur. Only instead of deer antlers, it had miniaturized moose antlers. The Chronos deer was grazing just outside of a dense forest.

Stacy stated, "That's a Chronos deer. I don't see any." Stacy pushed back against her seat as she was startled by a vine shooting out of the ground to wrap around the deer's leg. Stacy said, "What the hell!"

The deer immediately raised its head then stood frozen in place. The thick green vine with purple flowers then started to slowly move up the deer's leg then eventually wrapped around the deer's waist. Once around the deer's waist, the vine stopped, and the deer began grazing again.

Captain Jake asked, "What exactly are we watching?"

Stacy added, "Creepy, but I don't see communication with plants."

Timothy said, "Dolly, zoom in on the deer's mouth, please and thank you." The screen changed to a close-up of the deer's mouth. Purple flower petals and blood were dripping out the side of its mouth. Timothy said, "It's eating vines, but not the vine attached to its leg and back." The video then changed to show a large TV with two arms, three legs, and a 360-degree camera on top carrying two Indians across a plain. The TV robot's screen was displaying sneakers running on pavement.

Captain Jake asked, "Is that a kids bot?"

Dr. Helix answered, "Yes. They created an army of military grade kids bots to clear out Jurassic Island. They were easy to mass produce, and there's still a fear of androids after the second Russell Arthur incident. No offense, Timmy."

Timothy got a confused look on his face.

Calvin said, "That's all the video we have of the mindbender vine in five hundred years' worth of footage. All areas outside thick forests like the one in the video have all either been wiped or the satellites were conveniently angled away."

Stacy said, "You sound like a conspiracy nut. That video is creepy, but it doesn't prove mind control."

Timothy said, "Dolly, go back to the part where the deer is chewing on the vine."

Stacy said, "Grossing me out doesn't prove you right."

Dr. Helix said, "That purple petal. Is it…"

Timothy said, "Yep, that's a Pazel flower petal."

Dr. Helix said, "That's not possible. The Pazel flower doesn't grow off a vine."

Calvin said, "In five hundred years of footage, there are no images of the Pazel flower on Chronos, except for right there on that vine. Stacy, do we still sound nuts?"

Captain Jake asked, "What does this mean?"

Timothy said, "Don't know, but I think the vine is where heaven's bliss comes from the mindbender vine. It had to have injected the deer with something calm. If we take Kevin down and hook him up to the vine, I think he could talk with it."

Stacy said, "Plants don't have brains."

Timothy replied, "This one does. It senses vibrations. That's how it knew where the deer was. I think it made the deer eat its other vines to hide."

Stacy said, "Are you listening to yourself?"

Dr. Helix said, "Timmy could be on to something. Over a hundred of the kids bots were deployed and running around, not to mention the touching down of the quartership. Anything that could sense seismic vibrations would be freaking out. Let me do some more research, Captain."

Captain Jake said, "The mission thus far is still to go to Chronos and get the soil and Pazel flower seeds as quickly as possible. We need to get back to help Admiral Noem to prevent war."

Timothy said, "We need to find the mindbender vine while we're there."

Dr. Helix said, "Captain, the Pazel flower has to have been bioengineered from that vine flower. We have to get a sample of the vine and petal. Not only could it help create a cure for Kevin and the others like him on Beta Mining, but it could also be the key to creating a better 15 for Life pill."

Stacy added, "Or a better Pazel flower. Without that vine, the flowers have to be missing minerals."

Captain Jake said, "When we get into orbit, we can discuss it with Adam and Eve." Captain Jake looked at Timothy then said, "Kevin is not going down to the planet." Timothy looked angry, but Captain Jake continued, "I do have a request I think you'll like, Timmy. With Thirteen in a cell, I need a new head science officer. Mind taking the job temporarily?"

Timothy smiled while Stacy yelled, "He's nine!"

Captain Jake stated, "He's also the only person coming up with answers since we started the EPF. What do you say, Timothy?"

Timothy thought for a second then replied, "Only if me and Rex get to go down to the surface with Stacy."

Captain Jake said, "Stacy's not going down."

Stacy replied, "Yes, I am. You need me to verify the Pazel flowers and seeds and to ensure storage for space travel."

Captain Jake asked, "Doc? Can she handle breaking atmosphere in her condition?"

Dr. Helix replied, "I will need to give her a shot on nanites. After that, Stacy will be fine."

Rex asked, "Why do I have to go?"

Timothy said, "They have dinosaurs."

Rex replied, "I'm in."

Captain Jake said, "Fine. If it's okay with Stacy, you can go."

Stacy said to Timothy, "You're lucky I don't trust you to be out of my sight. You can go."

Timothy cheered then started to run toward the sound barrier, shouting, "I have to go tell Clair about my promotion!"

*****

Timothy and Rex met up with Clair and Johnny, who were studying in the courtyard. Timothy shouted, "Guess what, guys? Captain Jake just made me the head science officer!"

Johnny replied, "He did not. You're just a kid."

Rex said, "I was there. The crazy captain actually did it."

Clair got up and gave Timothy a hug then said, "My future husband is amazing." Clair took hold of Timothy's hand then said, "Let's go tell my mom. You should come over for dinner tonight too. I'll help my dad cook and everything."

Timothy said, "Okay, but I need to talk to Johnny first." Timothy quickly typed a message on his W2: "Keep Rex busy for a few minutes." Then he showed it to Clair.

Clair said, "Hey, Rex, my dad got me a robotic bunny. Want to see it?"

Rex replied, "Only if I can rip its head off."

Johnny said, "You can't break someone else's toys."

Clair said, "It's okay. I don't think Rex can catch it anyways."

Rex stated, "Challenge accepted." Then the two headed off toward the stairs.

Timothy said, "I will be going down to Chronos on the next mission. I need your help again."

Johnny replied, "No way. You're an officer now. You don't need my help."

Timothy typed on his W2 and said, "Since I'm an officer, this is an order. I'm sending you modifications that need to be made before the trip to Chronos. If anyone asks, you can tell them you're working on recon gear. Nothing else."

Johnny pulled up the blueprints. A moment later, he said, "There's no way Rex will go for this."

Timothy said, "I can handle Rex. Just make those modifications then pack them in one crate, but have a second crate of equal size empty and ready to go."

Johnny asked, "Why do you need a second crate?"

Timothy started to walk away and said, "Have to go test out my new officer's clearance. Thanks for your help, Johnny."

*****

That evening, June and Captain Jake were sitting comfortably on a couch while streaming an old movie together when Dolly said, "Dr. Helix is at the door, Captain."

June asked, "Can we pretend we're not home?"

Captain Jake replied, "I wish. Let him in, Dolly."

Dr. Helix walked in then said, "Sorry to disturb you, Captain, June."

June asked, "Can I get you a drink, Doctor?"

Dr. Helix replied, "No, thank you."

Captain Jake asked, "What's up, Doc?"

Dr. Helix said, "Even with my clearance, it's been difficult to learn what I wanted to about Jurassic Island. Four hundred and twenty-two years ago, Jurassic Island was founded. The quartership landed with fifty scientists, all of whom were fixed so as not to be able to reproduce. The founding scientists thought it morally wrong to populate an alien planet that was already inhabited. These scientists collected samples of all types of plant and animal life on Chronos before they started to clone the dinosaurs. There was no record of them ever discovering the Pazel flower."

June said, "So 15 for Life has been around for a couple centuries now."

Dr. Helix continued, "Over time, the researchers dwindled in numbers. All natural causes, except one scientist who went missing about 269 years ago. His name was Wes. According to Wes's journal, they discovered a new vine on the island. Wes's journal stopped shortly after that, but in the other scientists' journals, they mention Wes has a drug problem. A problem that seemed to get much worse after they discovered the vine. The symptoms were amplified effects of narcotics."

Captain Jake said, "So Timmy was right. This mindbender vine is where heaven's bliss comes from."

Dr. Helix said, "I believe so. I think the scientists discovered the benefits of the Pazel flower but didn't want to unleash a potential epidemic."

Captain Jake said, "So they bioengineered the flower without the vine, then deleted satellite footage to keep the secret. Only someone found out and got their hands on the vine. Then they started making heaven's bliss."

June said, "The timing can't be coincidental."

Captain Jake said, "You're right. The godlings found out or perhaps always knew about the mindbender vine. I don't see how it helped them start this war."

Dr. Helix added, "Or the black mold."

Captain Jake said, "No. There is a connection. If you're sick or stoned, you can't put up much of a fight."

June said, "That doesn't make sense. The people fighting aren't the ones targeted by the black mold, and the ones most affected by heaven's bliss are miners and college kids from Beta Mining."

Captain Jake said, "Godlings look three moves ahead, right? What if they are backing a faction in this war?"

June said, "Then the biggest remaining army after the space battle around Middleman would move to take out their rival's home base."

Dr. Helix said, "Assuming Romeo wins, that would be Juliet. It's right there."

Captain Jake asked, "And after that?"

June answered, "Move to the outer rings with little resistance along the way thanks to black mold and heaven's bliss."

Dr. Helix said, "I still don't believe the godlings would do this. They have no motive."

Captain Jake replied, "The godlings are doing this for someone else. They are working with the pirates, but for moral reasons, the pirates can't be the prime suspect. It can't be anyone in the outer rings because they're set up to be the next casualties in this war. That leaves Romeo or Juliet."

June said, "I can't see either government doing all this."

Captain Jake replied, "I don't think either government is knowingly in on this. The godlings are manipulating all of us for someone. We just need a way to prove it in time to stop it."

Chronos

Part One

Kevin

Equality reached Chronos, taking a stationary orbit between the planet and its moon. Captain Jake was on the bridge with everyone at their station.

Harry said, “The moon base isn’t answering our calls.”

Calvin said, “They still have jet arm drones patrolling.”

Captain Jake said, “Look for openings in the defenses that someone could use to smuggle contraband off the planet. Dolly, open an officers’ link and try calling Adam and Eve. Put it on the main screen.”

On the bridge’s main screen, the image of two teenagers appeared. Both were brunettes, lean and slender of equal height. Both were wearing bathing suits and big smiles with blinding white teeth. One was a woman with curly dark hair down to her shoulders (fall leaves were scattered about her hair). The man had eyes bursting with life. His face was long and slender, and he had a thick handlebar mustache.

The man said, “Hello there. I’m Adam.”

The woman raised her hand then said, “And I’m Eve.”

At the same time, they said, “Together, we’re Adam and Eve.”

Samantha whispered, "They start all their podcasts the same way. It's enough to make you want to vomit."

Captain Jake replied, "I'm Captain Jake. It's a pleasure to meet you."

Eve said, "Hope it's okay that we're not wearing more clothes, Captain. Since the relay stations started blocking signals, we haven't had to do any interviews."

Adam said, "It's been like a second honeymoon the past couple days. Not to worry, the kids bots have your soil packed up and ready to go."

Eve added, "I also have some Pazel flowers started plus all the seeds you need."

Captain Jake said, "We have an extra request regarding the Pazel flower. We know it's originally part of a vine. We need a sample of that vine as well as an original flower. Our doctor thinks the samples could save lives."

Adam and Eve looked at each other with confused looks.

Dr. Helix's voice came over the captain's comm. "Adam and Eve have only been on Jurassic Island for the past two hundred years. It may have been covered up before they got there."

Captain Jake asked, "Will it be all right if we have a look around the island while we gather the soil?"

Adam replied, "Well, you are the authorities. I'm sure you know this already, but in case you don't, you currently aren't authorized to take anything off this planet except soil and Pazel plants. Try to take anything else without authorization, and the kids bots down here will attack. Unfortunately, the jet arms up their will also swoop in to attack. Not to forget the space rail guns will shoot at you, and a destroy or kill order will be placed on you. I'm sure you already know all that."

Captain Jake replied, "Good to know. We will be sending Serenity down shortly." Captain Jake then double tapped his left wrist to end the call.

Frank's voice came over the bridge's comm. "All due respect, sir. You're not going down there."

Captain Jake asked, "Why not?"

Everyone on the bridge said, “Because you almost die on every away mission.”

June’s voice came over the comm and said, “I keep people safe on the ground. You keep everyone safe in space. That’s our promise to each other. You can’t keep up your end if you’re not in space.”

Captain Jake said, “You’re right. I won’t go, but you also won’t be able to get that sample of the vine you wanted.”

Stacy’s voice came over the comms. “All we need is to scan the vine. We don’t need a physical sample.”

Frank said, “We know the location of the vine in the video. It shouldn’t take long to search before Serenity returns to Equality.”

Captain Jake said, “Okay. Away party, get loaded up. Mission is a go.”

*****

Clair was in the park walking with Kevin when she got a message from Timothy that read, “Operation Mindbender is a go.” Clair asked Kevin, “Are you ready to play a game, Kevin?”

Kevin started clapping then said, “Kevin play.”

Clair took Kevin’s hand then said, “This way.” Clair led Kevin to engineering.

Emily was in engineering and noticed Clair and Kevin enter. Emily asked, “What are you two up to?”

Kevin clapped his hands together then said, “Kevin play game.”

Clair said, “We are looking for Johnny. Finding him is part of the game.”

Emily said, “He’s on the other side of those shelves working on something for the away mission. Serenity will be taking off shortly, so he needs to get it done.”

Clair said, “Thanks, Kevin’s mom. We won’t stay long.”

Johnny saw Clair and Kevin approaching and asked, “What are you guys doing here?”

Clair disconnected her W2 from her wrist then handed it to Johnny. Clair said, "Orders from Officer Timmy. Your eyes only."

*****

The away team gathered aboard Serenity. In addition to the standard crew were Stacy, Timothy, and Rex, along with a dozen drones. The lift lowered with two large crates stacked on top of each other.

June asked, "What are these?"

Timothy replied, "Advanced recon gear for finding the mind-bender vine." Timothy began to move the crates toward the back of the ship.

April said, "No surprises this trip. What's actually in the crates?"

June grabbed the top crate then set it on the floor.

Timothy said, "I'm an officer now. That makes me your boss. If you have to look inside, that's fine, but it's a secret. You can't tell anyone."

June opened the lid and looked inside. June quickly closed the lid when Rex tried to look inside. June said to Rex, "You can't look inside. Officer's orders."

Timothy asked, "Can I put them away now? We have to get going."

April asked June, "What's inside the crate?"

June replied, "You're speaking to me again." She moved to stand between the crate and April.

April said, "Yes, I'm speaking to you. Now let me see." June lifted the lid while making sure Rex didn't look inside. April asked, "Is that?"

June replied, "Yep."

April looked at Timothy then said, "I like your style. You can put the crates away."

Stacy said, "I'm an officer too. What's in the crates?" June typed a message into her W2 then sent it to Stacy. Stacy read the message then said, "Seriously? I'm too pregnant to wear one."

Rex asked, "Wear what?"

Stacy replied, "You'll find out when it's time. Now take your seat so we can get going."

Serenity approached Jurassic Island with everyone looking out the windows to spot different species of dinosaurs roaming about.

Rex spotted a T. rex and said, "I bet I could take it."

Stacy asked, "Take what?"

Rex replied, "A T. rex."

Stacy replied, "Don't you dare even try. Even at half size, you couldn't open your jaws wide enough to even bite a T. rex."

Rex replied, "I could find a way."

As Serenity approached the quartership SS Jurassic Park, they saw Adam and Eve standing next to four kids bots waiting to greet them.

Rex said, "I don't see any vines wrapped around them."

Stacy replied, "No shit. Stop listening to Calvin and his ridiculous theories of pod people."

Rex said, "I saw that video of the Chronos deer."

Stacy said, "It was only a minute long. You don't know what you saw."

June said, "Don't worry, Rex. A vine can't get through any of our power suits." Everyone then looked at the pregnant Stacy, who was only wearing a onesie with a sundress overtop.

Stacy exclaimed, "What! It's not my fault it won't fit anymore."

April noticed Timothy's gaze was fixated on four fifty-foot-long containers stacked on top of each other. April, in a very stern tone said, "Timothy, we are going to go outside to greet Adam and Eve while the drones sweep the area. You are to wait here until I say it's okay for you to come out. Do you understand?"

Timothy smiled and replied, "I understand."

April, June, Zac, and Stacy left Serenity while Emily went up front to watch the meeting from the cockpit with Jesus.

Once no one was looking, Timothy went to his W2 to bring up commands for Rex's CPU cap. Once there, he lowered Rex's volume to zero then locked out Rex's access to his keyboard. Timothy followed that up by adjusting Rex's neuro sensors to lower his anxiety levels.

Timothy whispered to Rex, "I need your help. We have to be very quiet, Rex." Rex gave a low growl, then Timothy said, "Sorry, Rex, but we have to be quiet. I'll turn your cap back on later."

Rex proceeded to help Timothy lower the top crate to the floor. Timothy then paused to remove armor plating from this power suit. He then opened up the top crate to remove a jetpack that he then put on. Next, Timothy went back into the top crate to remove a specially designed jetpack for Rex.

Rex normally wouldn't consider letting anyone put a jetpack on him, but with all anxiety being suppressed, Rex didn't even try to fight against it.

Timothy then opened and tipped over the second crate where Kevin was sleeping soundly after Clair poked him with a drill dart back on Equality. Timothy dragged Kevin back to the airlock with ease thanks to his exoskeleton suit. The easy airlock was still extended to the ground with the door left open. Once outside, they wasted no time in activating their jetpacks to fly off toward the woods where the mindbender vine was in the four-hundred-year-old video.

A short way into their trip, Timothy said, "Our W2s are off to keep Captain Jake from telling us to go back. I can't turn your speaker back up until after I set Kevin down. I also had to remove my protective armor to reduce weight in order to carry Kevin. I'm going to need you to protect us from any dinosaurs." Timothy nodded ahead at a flock of pterodactyls that were approaching. Rex barked then headed toward the pterodactyls.

Timothy continued on while Rex kept the pterodactyls at bay. A short time later, Timothy reached his destination. The forest looked denser than in the video, and the grass in front was tall with random patches of grass meshed down as if something large and heavy had recently passed by.

Timothy set Kevin down in one of these meshed down patches of grass while making sure to keep away from the ground himself. Timothy then typed into his W2 to deactivate the nanites in Kevin that were making him sleep. While waiting for Kevin to awake, Timothy surveyed the area, looking for the mindbender vine.

Without realizing it, Timothy lost track of time and quickly turned back to check on Kevin, but he was gone. Timothy shouted, "Kevin!" He looked about frantically to find him. Timothy looked to see if Rex could help him, but it looked like Rex was getting carried away chasing the pterodactyls. Timothy said to himself, "Stacy's going to spank me so hard."

"Where am I this time?" came a voice from the tall grass.

Timothy floated toward the voice and said, "Kevin?" Suddenly, Kevin stood up, and Timothy could see a green vine with purple petals wrapped around Kevin's waist.

Kevin said, "Hey, flying kid. Is this a Romeo biodome?"

Timothy quickly typed on his W2 to restore the connection with Equality and the away crew. Timothy shouted, "I fixed Kevin! I told you so, Stacy!"

Kevin tried to walk, but he didn't move. Kevin looked down at his legs then said, "What's wrong, legs? Man! I must be trippin'."

Timothy said, "I can't think with everyone talking. I'm going to mute you guys. Just pick us up on your way out."

Kevin said, "Oh, great, flying kid. My legs don't want to move. Mind giving me a lift?"

Timothy said, "You can call me Timmy. Kevin, you do know you have a vine wrapped around your waist, don't you?"

Kevin looked down and said, "No, I don't, man."

Timothy said, "So the mindbender does mess with your senses. Hey, Kevin, what's the last thing you remember?"

Kevin replied, "I don't remember, man. How do you know my name, man?"

Timothy replied, "We're shipmates and friends. So you don't remember getting an implant called heaven's bliss?"

Kevin said, "I remember that stuff, man. Hey, you know where I can get some more of it?"

Timothy replied, "It's in you right now. Do you remember me or Equality at all?"

Kevin stared at Timothy for a moment, then his eyes went wide and he said, "Trippy, man. I see a file with your picture on it. It's like a memory, but it's like not mine, man."

Timothy asked, "What's in the file?"

Kevin replied, "The file's labeled *Noah's Ark*. Under your picture is a caption that reads, 'I'm not going to let anyone die.' There are other pictures of plushies and quadruplets. There's a Captain Jake with a question mark over his face."

Timothy asked, "What's the file for?"

Kevin replied, "The file ends with a simulation of hundreds of spaceships floating aimlessly as android robots board them." Kevin suddenly got a blank look on his face.

Timothy asked, "Kevin? You all right?"

Rex returned and asked, "Is Kevin broken again?"

Timothy replied, "I'm not sure yet."

Kevin was staring off into space and said, "Wait here and you will be safe."

Timothy asked, "Mindbender? Is that you?"

Rex asked, "What's that scent?"

Timothy replied, "I don't smell anything."

Rex said, "It smells like a bitch in heat. It's coming from Kevin." Just then, the sound of trees snapping came from the forest, and it was getting louder.

Timothy exclaimed, "Shot! We need to get Kevin to safety!"

Rex said, "You get Kevin. I'll take care of whatever's coming."

Timothy replied, "I can't. I'm only wearing an exoskeleton. If I try, the mindbender will take control of me."

Rex said, "Okay." Then he headed down to Kevin.

"Don't do that! It's poisonous!" shouted Timothy as Rex was about to bite into the vine.

Rex looked up then said, "Oh, forgot about that." Rex then used his artificial hands to snap the vine free instead. Rex said, "The vine's stuck to Kevin. Want me to rip it off?"

Timothy answered, "No. I need to run tests on the mindbender vine."

Suddenly, a dinosaur came crashing out of the forest toward Rex and Kevin. The dinosaur had a narrow head full of crocodile-like teeth. It's body was long with a spindly neck like a crane and broad flat feet. It stood six feet tall and twenty feet long with a long spine-like fins on its back.

Timothy whispered, "A Spinosaurus."

The Spinosaurus only got a few more steps in before a drill dart came flying in and struck the dinosaur in its neck. Only seconds later, it collapsed to the ground, sound asleep.

Timothy and Rex turned to see June approaching from behind them. Rex said, "She looks pissed."

June asked, "What the hell were you idiots thinking?"

Rex replied, "Timothy had to prove he was right as usual."

June said to Timothy, "Bring the connection back. I need to check on April and the others."

Timothy said, "I didn't shut off the link." Timothy checked his W2 then said, "Signal's being jammed. How much of Kevin's talk did you get to watch?"

June answered, "The last thing I heard was 'It's labeled Noah's Ark.'"

Timothy typed into his W2 then said, "Here's the rest. We need to get back to warn Captain Jake. I think all the spaceships gathered around Middleman are in danger."

Rex said, "We need to get out of here. More dinosaurs are coming from the forest."

June picked up the unconscious Kevin off the ground then said, "Timmy, you better take him. Kevin will be safer off the ground."

Timothy floated down to take Kevin then said, "Since they're jamming our signal from Jurassic Park, Serenity could be in danger."

June said, "Great. April's going to be even more pissed at me then. Let's head back." June started to run back while the others took to the sky.

Only a minute into their trip back, Rex veered off course. Timothy shouted, "Where are you going, Rex?"

Rex shouted back, "It's Rex versus T. rex!"

June saw Rex was headed for a T. rex that was approaching across a short-grassed plain. June shouted, "Rex, get back here!" But Rex wasn't listening.

Timothy said, "I sorta did something so Rex wouldn't be afraid to fly. It might be affecting his judgment."

June said, "Great. Take Kevin back to Serenity, but stop short until I get there to make sure everything's safe." June took off after Rex.

*****

Rex was excited to be taking on a T. rex. Once he reached the shortgrass section of the plains, Rex landed on the ground to start running toward the T. rex. Rex recalled Stacy telling him his jaws weren't big enough to bite the T. rex, and even from a distance, Rex knew now that she was right. Rex had a plan as he typed while running. Rex suddenly increased his running speed by almost double as he removed the strength limiters on his suit.

Rex could see his plan vividly in his head. He was going to jump straight up when he reached the fourteen-foot tall T. rex. He would lead with the top of his head, hitting like an uppercut that would knockout the massive T. rex cold, thus making Rex the victor in Rex vs. T. rex.

What actually happened was that Rex was going so fast that when he tried to jump up, his forward momentum only let him get as high as the T. rex's stomach before impact. Rex's power suit automatically lowered his visor for Rex's safety. With the speed of travel added to the weight of Rex's metal suit compounded with the suit's aerodynamic design, Rex flew into the T. rex like a bullet from a gun.

June noticed Rex's increase of speed. June said to herself, "I keep everyone safe on the ground while Jake keeps everyone safe in space." June then shut off her own strength limiters to catch up to Rex a few minutes later.

June found Rex's ripped-off jet engines laying on the ground in front of the T. rex that was still breathing. June quickly hit the T. rex with a drill dart and said, "Go to sleep, big fella." Once the T. rex was out, June said, "Fucking Rex. There was no reason for this."

June walked around to find Rex's head with a cracked visor sticking out the back of the T. rex (his body still being inside the T. rex). June asked, "You still alive, you stupid mutt?" After not receiving a response, June scanned Rex to find him still alive.

Chronos

Part 2

SS Jurassic Park

Serenity landed next to the quartership Jurassic Park with the nose of Serenity facing Jurassic Park. Everyone was linked so they and all the officers and security personnel could see and hear through whoever's W2 link they wanted.

The drones exited the ship first to survey the area for anything that might have been hiding from ship sensors. They were soon followed by April, June, Stacy, and Zac.

Upon seeing the pregnant Stacy, Eve rushed over and exclaimed, "You're pregnant! When are you due?"

Stacy replied, "In twenty weeks." Stacy then grimaced and said, "The ride down got the kids excited. They're kicking up a storm."

Eve exclaimed, "You're having twins! Let's get you inside so you can sit down."

April said, "We need to let the drones inspect the interior of your ship before we enter. It's standard protocol."

Adam said, "You have to forgive Eve. We have never had visitors before."

Eve said, "Vicks and Wedge, be dears and give this poor woman a place to sit."

Two of the kids bots displayed images of thumbs up on their screens, then one robot flipped its thirty-two-inch screen down, turning it into a seat. The second kids bot then positioned itself behind the first to create a back for the now makeshift chair.

Stacy said, "Thank you" as they walked to the chair.

Calvin commented, "Kids bots haven't been popular since the age of the sex bot. I was so born in the wrong era."

Dr. Helix said, "The age of people caring more about their androids than they did about each other is what led to the second Russell Arthur incident."

Captain Jake said, "That's enough of a history lesson for now. Keep focused on the away team."

Frank said, "Area looks clean."

Harry said, "Not to rush things, but can we start getting that soil loaded?"

April asked, "You said you had the soil ready for us. We need to inspect it before we can load it up onto Serenity."

Adam and Eve looked at each other then started to smile. Adam looked back at April to see she wasn't smiling then said, "You're serious. Okay. We were expecting cargo ships, so the soil is in those containers over there."

Adam was now pointing at the containers that April saw Timothy staring at upon their arrival. Filipe said, "Those aren't going to fit in Serenity. The contents of one might, but there's no way you're going to get that container through the airlock door. Even then, the weight will be too much to break atmosphere."

April said, "Don't worry. Timmy's been working on the problem since we landed. What do we do, Timmy?"

After a moment of silence, Jesus said, "He's not here."

Everyone turned to look at Serenity in time to see Timothy, Kevin, and Rex take off. Everyone screamed at them to return, but they appeared to not hear them.

Stacy asked, "Where the hell did Kevin come from?"

Jesus said, "I can go get them."

Calvin said, "Little man's gone rogue again. Their W2s are off."

Captain Jake said, "No time. Scan the soil to make sure it's safe. Then start loading it into sandbags that we can carry aboard Serenity."

June said, "I will go get them Jake."

April said, "I need you here to help clear the area. Zac will go get them." But June gave chase anyways. April shouted, "June! Get back here right now!"

Captain Jake said, "June's doing her job. Now I need you to do yours. Secure the area, then get that soil loaded up so we can get back before war breaks out."

April sneered, "I know my job, Captain." After a pause to calm herself, April said, "Zac, take a drone to scan those containers, and keep watch outside. I'm going to start the inspection inside with half a dozen drones."

Zac replied, "Right away." Then he headed over to the crates.

Stacy said, "I'm going in too. The Pazel flower is in the greenery, right?"

Adam replied, "Yes, of course, but I can't give you any sandbags."

April asked, "Why not?"

Adam answered, "Because they haven't been approved by the Romeo and Juliet governments. Without clearance, you'll be attacked."

Captain Jake said, "With communications being jammed, we can't get permission. Emily, start 3D printing what you can. Filipe, have engineering do the same."

Emily said, "On it, Captain."

Filipe said, "Ron and Johnny are already getting started."

Once Stacy stood up, Adam said, "You bots go help take down those containers."

The kids bots then had sneakers running on pavement displayed on their screens as they walked over to the containers. Their screens then changed to display images of men and women flexing as their limbs extended to climb the containers and then lift the top container off.

Jesus asked, "How are those kids bots lifting up that much weight?"

Zac replied, "They are military grade."

*****

Adam led the way into the lower courtyard of SS Jurassic Park. Stacy, upon seeing the courtyard, said, "This is amazing." Stacy looked with eyes wide open at the white oak trees planted throughout the courtyard.

Adam replied, "You're amazing, Stacy. I always thought Earth was a myth. A bedtime story my parents made up for me. But here you are. I don't suppose you knew my parents. They would have just been teenagers when the trip started. Peter Gillis and Darek Newman."

Stacy replied, "I had an English tutor named Jill Gillis."

Adam said, "That's my aunt. What a small universe it is after all." Adam then led them into a greenery that was growing many exotic flowers, including a patch of purple Pazel flowers.

Eve said, "I have a whole box full of Pazel seeds for you. I can also harvest the ones we have here. Afraid I can't send any whole ones with you. The strain of breaking atmosphere would kill them."

May said, "Drone to the bridge won't open."

April asked Adam, "Is there a reason why the bridge doors won't open?"

Adam replied, "Afraid I don't have much cause to go in there. I'm not sure that I've ever been on the bridge, actually."

Captain Jake asked, "Have all the other doors opened without incident?"

Frank replied, "So far, Captain."

Captain Jake asked, "Can we have one of the drones outside take a look in through the bridge's window?"

Frank replied, "I tried that earlier. The blast shields are down. We should try to manually open the door, Captain."

Davinie said, "Hell no. We aren't authorized to do that."

Frank said, "If there are any intruders on board, they would be on the bridge."

Captain Jake said, "Breaking down the door could set off the defenses. That would put the away team and us in danger. Leave the bridge alone for now."

Calvin asked, "Where are all the kids bots? I thought they were supposed to be hundreds of them? I've only seen the four."

April asked Adam, "Where are the rest of the kids bots?"

Adam replied, "Scattered about the island. They keep themselves hidden while recording nature for us."

Suddenly, screams of "I fixed Kevin!" could be heard over the comms. Everyone quickly changed their video feed to Timothy's while Stacy and Captain Jake both tried yelling/talking to Timothy. Timmy's last words to them were "Pick us up when you're done."

Eve asked, "Is that your friends who took off earlier?"

Stacy held up her hand and stepped away as she and everyone else paid close attention to Timothy's feed. The feed ended with Kevin saying, "It's labeled Noah's Ark."

Stacy muttered, "Little shit was actually right about the mindbender vine."

Adam asked, "What's a mindbender vine?"

April said, "Frank, are you still there, Frank?" April turned to Stacy and said, "The signal's being jammed. We need to get back to Serenity."

Stacy asked, "What about Adam and Eve?"

Adam asked, "What about us? If your signal's being jammed, then the ship is in lockdown. We won't be released until the breach has been dealt with. This is the safest place for us to be."

April walked toward the automated door, but it didn't open. April asked, "How do I override the door?"

Adam replied, "You don't."

April grabbed hold of her sawsword. Stacy said, "Don't you dare. You heard Davinie say we aren't authorized. Cut that door open, and the defenses are going to attack us and Equality."

April asked, "Is there any way to tell what the security breach was?"

Adam replied, "Not from here. We'd have to go to the bridge."

Stacy asked, "What would set it off? We can't be under attack. Captain would have said something if anything popped up on scanners. It can't be for taking anything off planet. We haven't started to load Serenity yet."

Eve said, "Poaching would also do it."

Stacy replied, "Our people would never." Stacy then paused and looked at April, who was already looking at her. Then they both said, "Rex."

April asked, "The android dog we had with us. If he killed a dinosaur? Would that set off the security alert?"

Adam replied, "Afraid so. If that's what happened, then the kids bots will have orders to put him down."

Stacy said, "I replayed Rex's W2 feed. Stupid mutt attacked a flock of pterodactyls."

April tried the door again, but it remained closed. April asked, "The door not opening means Rex is still alive, right?"

Adam replied, "Well, yes, but…" April drew her sawsword.

Stacy asked, "What are you doing?"

April replied, "June won't let Rex die. I have to go save them." April started carving into the door with her pink chained sawsword, but within seconds, the room was filled with loud metal on metal banging sounds coming from the walls.

Adam and Eve began to clutch each other as Eve screamed, "What's going on!"

Chronos

Part 3

Serenity

Zac listened and watched Timothy's feed of Kevin talking like a normal person. Moments after the feed ended, the kids bots who were standing idly (with smiley faces being displayed on their screens). Suddenly, they started to move. Their screens changed to once again show sneakers running on pavement as they left. Two of the kids bots entered the quartership while one climbed in, and the fourth disappeared around the corner.

Zac asked, "Does anyone know what's going on?" After a moment of silence, he looked up at the cockpit of Serenity and raised his arms.

Moments later, Jesus said, "Sorry. Had to boost the signal. We're being jammed by SS Jurassic Park there."

Zac asked, "April and Stacy, you all right?"

Jesus replied, "Anything over a hundred feet away is out of range."

Emily said, "It's probably some sort of security protocol."

Zac said, "I'm going inside to check on them."

Jesus replied, "Don't do that. Have you never watched a horror movie?"

Zac said, "I'm just going to be gone a second."

Jesus said, "If it's security protocol, then the two kids bots went inside to protect everyone. That means the threat is most likely coming from outside."

Zac replied, "Anything on sensors?"

Jesus answered, "No, but being jammed makes it harder to scan."

Zac walked toward a spot between Serenity and the SS Jurassic Park then said, "The outside drones are returning."

Emily joined Jesus in the cockpit then said, "That's what they're supposed to do if they lose connection." Emily sat down then said, "Check out drone two's feed. There's a kids bot holding a sniper rifle."

Jesus asked, "What's it aiming at?"

Emily replied, "Still rebooting the connection. Give me a second. There."

The image from the drone showed the kids bot moving its center leg forward so it could stand like a tripod. The drone then moved to see where the bot was aiming. The camera stopped on Zac, who had his back turned to the kids bot.

Jesus said, "Hey, Zac."

Zac replied, "I'm looking in the direction that the kids bot's pointing, but I don't see anything." Suddenly, Zac felt something strike the back of his power suit, and Zac yelled, "Ouch! Something hit my back!" Zac then heard the sound of a drill bit drilling into metal. Zac quickly tried to reach the drill dart to pull it off, but he couldn't reach it. Zac then attempted to jump on his back to dislodge the dart, but he lost consciousness before he hit the ground.

Emily said, "You have to go get him!"

Jesus replied, "I'm not going out there. The fucking robot will just shoot me too."

Emily stated, "We're not leaving Zac out there."

Jesus said, "I'll move serenity so Zac's right by the easy airlock. The rest is up to you."

Emily said, "That's not a bad idea."

As Jesus was about to start up Serenity, there was a loud explosion from above. They looked up to see a large cloud of thick white smoke appear from high above them. Jesus asked, "What's that?"

Emily replied, "I think it's a full-service smokescreen. It blocks your view and jams all signals."

Jesus said, "We need to just leave now. We get back to Equality, then we can come back with reinforcements."

Emily said, "You can't go. The ion thrusters will ignite the smokescreen. You'd blow us up."

Jesus looked at Emily and said, "That's not true. Ion thrusters only reach three hundred degrees. That can't be enough to set off some smoke." Emily stared back at Jesus with a blank face. Jesus said, "Fine, we'll stay."

Emily said, "I'll put on my space suit. Once the smokescreen hits us, I'll use it as cover to go get Zac."

Jesus said, "We might not have that much time. That kids bot is headed toward Zac."

Emily said, "So fucking shoot it."

Jesus said, "I don't carry a spider pistol."

Emily replied, "Serenity has spider cannons, doesn't it?"

Jesus said, "Oh yeah! But I have to move Serenity to aim. I'll set off the smokescreen."

Emily said, "I was lying. Shoot that thing already."

Jesus said, "I fucking knew you were lying, but it's too late now. I'd just end up frying Zac along with the kids bot."

Suddenly, Serenity shook as it was struck from behind by a large metal object traveling at great speeds.

Chronos

Part 4

The Escape

Timothy approached Serenity from the air while carrying Kevin. Timothy said, "Dolly, set my contact lenses to zoom in on any moderate amount of movement. There could be trouble up ahead." Suddenly, Timothy's view changed to show a kids bot holding a grenade launcher while standing on top of the SS Jurassic Park. Timothy said, "Not what I asked for, but it's what I wanted. The upgrades I made to your AI must be kicking in, Dolly."

Timothy then watched as the kids bot fired a smokescreen grenade high above Serenity. Timothy said, "Full power to the jetpack, Dolly. We need to beat that smokescreen to Serenity." Suddenly, Timothy increased speed.

Once Timothy got closer, he could see a power suit crumbled up on the ground between Serenity and Equality. There was a kids bot approaching it with an image of a man in black rubbing his hands together playing on the screen.

Timothy wanted to help whoever was in the power suit, but he had to keep Kevin safe first. Timothy said, "Dolly, slow the jets for landing." Just then, there was a blinding blur that ran past him, followed by a large thud as something large and metallic struck the back of Serenity.

*****

June approached Serenity at unnatural speeds. She watched helplessly as Zac was shot. June could do nothing but run faster. This caused an orange caution light that already appeared in the bottom left corner of her contact lenses to start to flash, indicating muscle tears.

June didn't care. She wasn't feeling any pain, and she was determined to save Zac from the approaching kids bot that shot him. June knew she could reach Zac before the kids bot, but not before the smokescreen. June made a mental picture of the objects and distance. She knew in order to save Zac, she would need her arm free to draw her sawsword.

Rex could feel that he was moving at tremendous speeds as he regained consciousness. Rex asked, "Where are we?" Then suddenly, his power suit rolled him into a ball as he went rolling on the ground at exceptional speeds until he hit the back of Serenity. The impact of the collusion sent Rex back into unconsciousness.

As June was being blinded by the smokescreen, she drew her sawsword and swung to the right in one motion. She felt her sawsword strike something but had no time to even think about it.

The quartership was approaching, and June had no time to slow down. Instead, June used her mental imaging to count three steps after the strike, then she leaped to shift her momentum into running up the quartership. June then backflipped off to land on one knee, striking a superhero pose.

June's first thought after landing was that she couldn't wait to watch the replay with Jake. June then said, "Son of a bitch." She realized the smokescreen blocked the security camera footage.

Timothy shouted, "June! Was that you?"

June shouted back, "Be quiet. There could be more kids bots."

Emily met Timothy by the easy airlock door and grabbed Kevin while asking, "What's going on?"

Timothy replied, "I think the mindbender is plotting to take over Einstein. We have to go warn the captain."

Emily replied, "I don't know about that, but April and Stacy are inside Jurassic Park." Emily shouted, "June! Can you get Zac?"

June shouted, "I can't see anything!"

Timothy shouted, "Go the opposite direction at the sound of my voice. You need to get inside of Jurassic Park to get April and Stacy!"

June replied, "Okay!"

Timothy asked, "Where's Rex?"

June replied, "Did you hear that loud crash earlier?"

Timothy replied, "Yes!"

June shouted, "If Rex lives, tell him I'm sorry about that! I found the ship! Now I just need to find the door!"

Timothy shouted, "I'll go clear out the smokescreen." Timothy then entered Serenity and closed the airlock.

Emily asked, "What happened to Kevin?"

Timothy replied, "Long story" as he headed to the cockpit.

Jesus saw the determination on Timothy's face then asked, "You're here to save us again, aren't you?"

Timothy replied, "I need to write a program first. Start charging a spider cannon. I need to use it."

Jesus said, "You're not allowed to fire a spider cannon."

Timothy, in a completely serious tone, asked, "Do you want to live through this?"

Jesus replied, "Charging spider cannon."

Timothy said, "Done. Dolly."

Serenity started to lift off, and a counter began to show on the cockpit's main screen. Jesus asked, "What are we doing?"

Timothy replied, "Clearing the smoke."

Jesus said, "You know you can't use the engines to clear the smoke. Ion engine won't do anything."

Timothy was watching the countdown as he answered, "The emergency thruster canisters will though. We...just...need...to..." Timothy pressed the trigger to fire the spider cannon, causing the white smokescreen to flash red for a moment. Timothy continued,

"Take out the kids bot with the grenade launcher so it can't fire another round."

*****

April stood holding her sawsword in one hand and spider pistol in the other. The relentless banging was coming from all sides. It sounded as if an entire army was trying to break down the door.

Adam and Eve were holding each other as they sobbed uncontrollably. Their crying was making it difficult for April to think. April yelled, "Shut the fuck up so I can think!"

Stacy shouted back at April, "Leave them alone! They're doing the best they can!"

April sheathed her weapons then said, "They're not trying to get in. They're trying to keep us from trying to leave." April turned to Adam and Eve then shouted, "What the hell is really going on here?"

Adam and Eve just continued to cry.

Stacy screamed, "Leave them alone! They obviously don't know anything!"

April turned and took a couple steps while whispering to herself, "If they won't help, they can at least shut up." April slowly drew two drill darts out of her ammo belt then quickly turned around. The first drill dart she threw struck Adam in his left arm, and the second struck Eve in her right butt cheek.

Stacy screamed, "What the fuck are you doing?"

April screamed back, "I told them to shut up!"

Stacy yelled, "Well, they're not quiet!"

April and Stacy stared at each other for a moment as Adam and Eve's crying continued to be heard over the banging on the walls.

April now quickly drew her sawsword then pressed the trigger to start the pink diamond link chain spinning.

Stacy yelled, "What are you going to do?"

As April approached Adam and Eve, they never changed their dispositions. They just continued to hold each other and cry, even when the pink chained sawsword tore them asunder.

April stared down at the sparks coming from their exposed torsos and smiled as she said, "If plastic androids and kids bot's is all they have"—April walked to the door—"let's find out why miners call this a can opener." April then resumed cutting the door open.

With a booming thud, the door landed in the courtyard. The banging continued as April stuck her head out to a kids bot on either side. Each kids bot was standing on its center leg as each of its appendages (which all had three-finger hands with an opposable thumb at the end of them) were outstretched and even extended into the adjoining rooms to bang on the walls.

Stacy shouted, "What do you see?"

April shouted back, "Scrap metal!" She then stepped outside, firing her spider pistol at the kids bot on her left. Although she aimed at the TV's body, the lightning was drawn to its arm instead.

Both kids bots stopped banging on the walls. The one April shot had a red smiley face with an angry expression and smoke coming off its head. April turned quickly to see the other was doing the same thing.

April cursed, "Shit!" She quickly had to roll toward the center of the courtyard to avoid the kids bots who were extending their arms at her. April quickly got back to her feet then said, "Okay, let's test your reflexes." April swung at the nearest appendage, which dodged easily. The kids bot she didn't swing at began to circle around April.

A flower pot came flying in at the kids bot April was facing. The kids bot caught the flower pot then threw it at April, who quickly dodged it. April shouted, "What the hell was that?"

Stacy replied, "I was trying to surprise it."

April said, "It has a 360-degree camera. You can't surprise it."

Stacy asked, "What can I do?"

April took another fruitless swing then said, "Stay there until I kill these things."

Stacy said, "What about the other kids bots? Adam said there were hundreds around the island."

April replied, "He lied. Otherwise, there would be more than two here."

Stacy stepped outside as she asked, "If they're not here, then where the hell are they?"

April moved to keep from getting caught in another pincer attack then replied, "Good question, but I'm a little busy right now." One of the kids bots started to move toward Stacy. April shouted, "Get back inside! I can't fight and protect you."

Stacy stepped back inside, and the approaching kids bot returned its attention to April. Stacy said, "Come back inside. They might leave you alone too. They're military grade, April. You can't win."

April shouted, "I'm April of Romeo. These tin can relics don't have shit on me." April readied herself for an all-out thrusting attack. It would leave her vulnerable, but if she could make this a one-on-one fight, she hoped she would be able to use her power armor to overpower the last kids bot.

April lunged at the kids bot in front of her with a swing meant to rip the TV in half. Instead, the kids bot reacted with lightning speed to use one hand and one leg appendage to catch the mighty swing. An image of Bruce Lee wagging his finger appeared on its screen as it began to lift April's sawsword with her still holding onto it. April had no choice but to let go of her sawsword then dodge as the second kids bot reached for her.

Both kids bots approached April. The one with her sawsword kept it high in the air with the chains no longer spinning.

April placed her back against a white oak tree then said, "You guys have orders to capture, not kill, don't you? Kind of takes the fun out of it when I know you won't hurt me."

The kids bots were standing four feet from her and spread out. Their hands were balled into fists aimed at April while their shoulder to elbow arms extended out more to the side. Suddenly, seven fists came flying in at different angles, leaving April nowhere to dodge.

The punches all hit then pulled back briefly to strike again. This process kept April pinned against the tree. The leg appendages pulled back to form tripod bases while the arm appendages kept April pinned with a steady barrage of punches. Then the images on the TV changed to show jackhammers pulsating.

April just laughed at this then said to herself, "I can't believe I have to tell Frank he was right. With this FP shield, I can't feel anything. All I need is for your dipsticks to run out your batteries out so I can move again."

April immediately stopped laughing when she saw sparks of green lightning start to flicker off the kids bots knuckles.

*****

June had two doors to cut through before she made it inside the courtyard. The previously orange flashing caution light had turned to a red flashing caution light. This light indicated June was only still moving because of drugs her suit would have injected her with by now. June knew she had to hurry before her body gave out.

The moment the second door dropped, June could hear screams of pain from April. June raced in where she quickly saw April pinned against a tree as two kids bots jackhammered away at her midsection and joints.

June wasted no time in closing the distance between them in a blink of an eye. Her first target being the one holding April's pink chained sawsword. June sliced the kids bot in half with ease but couldn't then maneuver around the trees in front of her. June ended up running into a tree so hard that the tree cracked and splintered as she went rolling to the ground.

June was dizzy, dazed, and about to lose consciousness when she heard Stacy shout, "Look out!" June looked up in time to see a mechanical hand with crackling green lightning speeding her way. June was barely able to roll to the side to avoid it.

June got back on her feet with her own black chained sawsword still mechanically locked in her hand. June quickly drew and fired her spider pistol at the kids bot, but nothing came out. June said, "Shit." She realized moving so quickly for so long must have drained the battery.

June took two punches in quick succession, one to her abs, denting her suit, and the second to her face, which was blocked by her visor, which auto dropped to protect her (although the visor was severely cracked in the process).

A flash of purple lightning came from behind the kids bot. Once again, its arms absorbed the lightning, but it forced the kids bot to change targets as once again, an angry red face with smoke coming off its head appeared on its screen.

April shouted, "Don't forget about me, you pitiful excuse for a waste dispenser!"

June regained her composure as the red flashing caution light changed to "Death imminent. Shut down now!" in bright red colors. June made ready her strike as she said, "Jake keeps them safe in space. I keep them safe on the ground."

April shouted, "Be careful! It was quick enough to catch my sawsword mid swing."

June said, "Catch this!" She used the last of her power suit's power to lunge and cleave the last kids bot in half. June's power suit froze in warrior pose, and her visor turned dark as the power was drained.

April asked, "How did you move so fast?" as she walked toward June. Every joint in April's power suit was damaged and creaked as she slowly moved.

Stacy raced over and asked, "Is Timmy okay?"

June softly said, "He's fine. Little scoundrel thinks he's uncovered a plot for androids to conquer Einstein."

Stacy said, "The missing kids bots."

April said, "A couple hundred kids bots can't conquer all of Einstein."

June softly said, "He thinks they're going to nuke the ships gathered around Middleman. April, I need your spider pistol. Mine's dead."

April said, "You idiot. That's how you moved so fast. You removed your strength limiters." April removed June's spider pistol then replaced it with hers. April said, "Don't you know how dangerous that can be?" April now got to see June's face as the visor turned translucent. April whispered, "June" as she saw the blood coming from June's mouth, nose, and eyes.

June's contact lenses came back on with the death imminent message changing to an image of her sisters and Jake waving goodbye. June said, "Dolly."

Dolly replied, "Yes, June."

June said, "Put my suit in auto mode to carry April back to Serenity."

Dolly replied in a soft tone, "Yes, June. It was an honor to serve with you." June then picked up April.

April screamed, "Stop moving, June! You're going to die!"

June said, "Dolly, visor dark." June's visor went dark.

April repeatedly screamed June's name as she was carried to Serenity, but June never spoke again.

Samantha

The morning of the mission to Chronos, Samantha was up early to get her breakfast. As she sat and ate, she heard her name called. Samantha turned to see one of the quadruplet sisters approaching. Samantha thought, *Please don't let it be that weirdo May.*

The sister sat down across the table from Samantha then quickly said, "I've been wanting to talk to you. It's about my sister May. You know, the one you slept with and then blew off."

Samantha sat there in silence, thinking, *This has to be July, the bubbly one. I wonder when I slept with May. At least that explains why she's always so weird around me.*

July continued, "I'd like you to give her another chance. I know she has her odd quirks, but that's what makes her so great. May is crazy about you and would make a great girlfriend if you gave her a chance."

Samantha replied, "Your sister is great. I just don't do relationships. Now." Samantha paused as she partially stood up to lean over the table, fully aware of how much her top made her cleavage pop. Then she softly said, "If you would like to try to change my mind, we could meet for dinner and drinks to discuss the matter after my shift tonight. Say my place. Around nine."

July's cheeks turned red, then she hesitantly replied, "We, ah, we could do that. To talk about May. I should get going now." July half tripped over the bench as she tried to leave.

Samantha thought, *Best way to end an awkward conversation is to change the subject.* Samantha turned to watch July leave in her spandexlike onesie and thought, *But that is one fine-looking ass.*

*****

Captain Jake sat on the bridge later that day with everyone aboard the bridge at their stations observing the Chronos away team. At the same time, Davinie, Frank, Filipe, and Dr. Helix were gathered around the conference table to observe the away mission.

Minutes after Captain Jake had words with April on what her role on the planet was, Frank entered the bridge with an angry expression on his face and said, "Captain, may I have a word with you? Outside."

Captain Jake replied, "Of course. Calvin, keep a camera on Timothy. I'm certain he's on his way to find that mindbender plant of his. Let me know if anything happens." Captain Jake left the bridge with Frank.

The moment the door closed, Calvin said, "Fifty FP says Frank decks the captain."

Samantha replied, "Frank's too stuck up his ass to do that. When April gets back, that's another story."

Tie said, "Samantha's right. I also doubt April's going to stop at just a punch."

Outside in the hall, Frank said, "Chain of command is everything. Down there, April outranks June. That means decisions on the ground are made by April."

Captain Jake replied, "April had a mission, and June had her mission. I made that clear."

Frank said, "What you did, Captain, was unacceptable. You disrespected the officer in charge."

Captain Jake said, "That wasn't my intent. I'll apologize to April when they return. But I will also correct April outranking June. June's more than earned a promotion."

Frank paused, realizing he just made things worse for April. Finally, Frank said, "Thank you, Captain." Then he walked away.

Captain Jake returned to the bridge and asked, "What's going on?"

Calvin replied, "Rex is playing with pterodactyls."

Captain Jake asked, "I thought Rex was afraid to fly."

Samantha replied, "The kid probably slipped him something."

Harry said, "Timmy's streaming again."

Captain Jake said, "Dolly, put Timmy's feed on the main screen. Timmy, you need to stop what you're doing. It's dangerous."

Captain and crew could do nothing but watch intensely as Kevin spoke. Timmy's feed ended with Kevin saying, "The file's labeled Noah's Ark."

Captain Jake asked, "What happened to the signal?"

Calvin replied, "I don't know, Captain."

Samantha said, "Calvin probably downloaded a virus while using Dolly to watch porn."

Calvin replied, "I only use burner devices to watch porn. I've learned my lesson. Signal is being jammed from Jurassic Park."

Tie asked, "Wasn't Noah's Ark about a flood that wiped out all lives on Earth?"

Captain Jake replied, "Except for the animals on Noah's Ark. Equality has just happened to have been collecting people from across Einstein since we got here."

Tie said, "There's got to be close to a million people scattered across Einstein by this point. No one could wipe them out."

Captain Jake said, "We need to get back to Middleman. Something bad's about to happen."

Harry said, "We still need that soil and seeds, or I'm going to die. With thousands of others."

Tie said, "Captain, thirty jet arms just launched from the moon. They're headed this way. Looks like ion thrusters only. It will be an hour before they get here."

Calvin said, "You have to see this. Dolly." The main screen changed to show an overview of June taking down the Spinosaurus with a drill dart. Calvin started looking around, bewildered.

Captain Jake said with pride, "That's my girl."

Harry said, "The moon base still won't answer my hails. I think it's all automated."

Samantha said, "If Jesus were here, he'd tell you to run."

Captain Jake replied, "If Jesus were here, I could run."

Frank's voice came over the comms. "We need to speak with you at the conference table, Captain. It's important."

Captain Jake asked Calvin, "Is everything all right at Jurassic Park?"

Calvin shook his head then checked his console before answering, "All's quiet so far."

Captain Jake said, "I'll be right there, Frank." Then he exited the bridge.

Once the door closed, Samantha asked Calvin, "What's got you spooked?"

Calvin replied, "Dolly started plating that video before I asked her to. That's not right."

Samantha said, "That's probably Timmy. After he was made an officer, he made some adjustments. Said the system was outdated."

Calvin replied, "It's outdated for a reason. That reason being Timmy's previous clone, Russell Arthur."

Captain Jake only made it a few feet out of the bridge when he saw Frank, now wearing his power armor, and Dr. Helix standing before him. Captain Jake asked, "What's going on?"

Dr. Helix approached then projected a hologram against the wall. The projection looked like an industrial mode of a person. Dr. Helix said, "This is drone footage from inside of Jurassic Park. That's a mold used to create plastic androids. I've also seen the equipment to transplant flesh onto these androids. All banned technology."

Captain Jake asked, "Why'd you call me out here to tell me? Who do you suspect of being an android?"

Dr. Helix swiped at the projection to show a console with an image of a naked Samantha being displayed. Dr. Helix said, "This would appear to be the last android created. It can fool scanners, Captain. I will need to expose bone to be certain she's not an android."

Frank said, "We don't know if the switch has already been made or not. We need to know discreetly. She could be a bomb."

Captain Jake said, "They didn't create Noah's Ark just to destroy it, but they would disable it to keep it out of the flood."

Frank said, "Captain?"

Captain Jake walked back onto the bridge then said, "Samantha, can you come with me for a minute?"

Samantha replied, "Can you last a minute?" as she stood up.

Captain Jake replied, "You have to ask June. She holds the stopwatch."

As they exited the bridge, Samantha remarked, "I bet that's not all she holds." Once outside, Samantha saw Frank and Dr. Helix then said, "I'm impressed. What kind of kinky stuff do you have planned, Captain?"

Captain Jake said, "It's not that. Basically, they found a mold of you on Jurassic Park."

Samantha grabbed her boobs then said, "I can't blame them for wanting to mass produce these puppies. Are you saying they owe me royalties?"

Dr. Helix said, "He's saying you need to come with me so I can test you quickly in the medical bay."

Samantha asked, "Test for what?"

Captain Jake answered, "Test to see if you're an android."

Samantha laughed then said, "Feel my boobs all you want. They're all natural."

Frank said, "That's for Dr. Helix to determine."

Samantha started pulling down her onesie uniform and said, "You think this body's fake?"

Captain Jake headed back to the bridge and said, "Test Samantha and get her back on the bridge as soon as possible. We have a fleet of jet arms on the way here." As the door to the bridge opened, Calvin caught a glimpse of the naked Samantha and jumped up to see more as the bridge door closed.

Frank turned away from Samantha then said, "You will need to be searched for any hidden devices or weapons."

Right on cue, July and May (both wearing power suits) arrived. Frank said to them, "Search her then bring her to the medical bay.

She may be an android." Frank started to walk away, only to realize Dr. Helix was still staring at Samantha. Frank said, "Let's go, Doctor."

Dr. Helix replied, "Why? I'm not married." Frank grabbed Dr. Helix's arm, and the two headed to the medical bay.

As May and July approached Samantha, May said, "I'm sorry about this. I don't think you're an android."

July pulled Samantha close to the side then said, "If she's not an android, then why isn't she wearing any panties?"

May replied, "People go commando sometimes. I need you to assume the position, Samantha."

Samantha stretched her arms out as she placed her hands on the wall then said, "I remember this is how we first met."

May giggled then said, "In the cargo bay. I never imagined then that you would end up joining the crew." May began patting Samantha down in a search for any implants.

July said, "Stay professional, May."

Samantha said, "The reason I wasn't wearing any panties is because I had a hot date planned for after work."

May immediately asked, "With who?"

Samantha replied, "With you. Well, July, actually, but since you two are identical, it's like a date with you."

May looked at July in shock. July shook her head no then said, "It isn't like that. I was only going to have dinner with her to talk about you."

Samantha smirked. "While getting drunk in my room. I'm sure nothing would have happened."

July shouted, "Shut up, bitch!"

May shouted at July, "Don't talk to her like that!"

Samantha said, "This is getting hot."

July shouted, "I said shut up!" She pulled out a drill dart and flung it at Samantha, striking her in the side of her breast.

May screamed, "What the hell did you do?"

July replied, "At least now we know she's—" July and May turned to look at Samantha, who was still standing with her hands against the wall. Her face was staring at the drill dart in disbelief.

May asked, "You didn't use an acid drill dart, did you?"

July replied, "If I did, we'd know by now."

Samantha pulled the drill dart out of her breast then turned her back to the vine-covered wall. Samantha then sat down while staring at the drill dart in her hand and said, "I didn't know." Samantha started to sob then repeated, "I didn't know."

May kneeled down next to Samantha and softly said, "So you're an android. Is that why you avoided me after we slept together?"

Samantha shook her head no then said, "No. It's because I couldn't remember sleeping with you. I never remember that stuff. Guess it's part of my programming."

May said, "So it wasn't me."

Frank returned and asked, "What's taking so long?"

July answered, "She's an android."

Frank placed his hand on the hilt of his sawsword and asked, "How do you know?"

July shrugged her shoulders then answered, "Hit her in the boob with a drill dart."

Frank looked at May on the floor and said, "Step aside, May. I'll take it from here."

May looked into Samantha's tear-filled eyes and whispered, "Everything's going to be fine." May quickly stood up, turning to face Frank and drawing her red, white, and blue diamond chained sawsword in the process. May said, "Samantha's not a threat. You will not touch her."

Frank removed his hand from the hilt of his sawsword then said, "She's and android. You don't know what she's programmed to do."

May said, "I know. She won't hurt anyone."

Frank said, "The rest of us need to know that too. Put her in a cell until we can check her programming. That's all I ask."

July said, "Help Samantha up, May. I'll go with you."

Frank said, "Put her in the isolation cell. Thirteen's down there, and he may have some secret activation code or something."

May sheathed her sawsword then turned to Samantha to help her up.

Dolly said, "Frank, we lost visual on Serenity. A kids bot fired a smokescreen grenade."

Frank asked, "April?"

Dolly replied, "She was still inside Jurassic Park before we lost visual."

Frank rushed past the girls to enter the bridge then asked, "What do you know?"

Captain Jake replied, "Zac, Rex, and Kevin are unconscious. A kids bot was moving in on Zac, but June made it back in time to save him, I'm sure."

Frank said, "The kids bots are attacking. That means they're a part of whatever has been going on."

Captain Jake said, "In on it or hostages. We never did get to check out their bridge."

Calvin added, "Or androids. Give me an hour and I can write a code to mimic Adam and Eve's personalities."

Frank said, "Samantha's an android."

Captain Jake said, "Dr. Helix tested her already?"

Frank said, "No. July hit her in the boob with a drill dart."

Captain Jake replied, "That works."

Calvin said, "Wait, she got hit with a drill dart and didn't fake it? That's either crappy programming or she's a download."

Captain Jake asked, "What's the difference?"

Calvin answered, "Downloads are way more complicated. A brain has to be scanned for months before it can be copied properly. And it's way harder to insert commands. Messing with a single line of code can make the download go nuts if it's not compatible with the person's personality."

Tie said, "I just saw a flash of red from the smokescreen. Now I see Serenity above the smokescreen. They're clearing away the smokescreen."

Captain Jake said, "They must be using the gas from the emergency thrusters to disperse the smoke. Timmy's pulling another miracle from his butt."

Frank said, "April and Stacy must still be inside if they aren't leaving."

Harry said, "We still need the soil and seeds."

Tie asked, "Where are all the kids bots? The drones only saw the four. There should be hundreds."

Calvin said, "They could be on the bridge."

Frank said, "Only a dozen. Maybe. Filipe did notice a makeshift pipe starting on the bottom floor going all the way up to the bridge."

Captain Jake said, "The kids bots are off planet. My guess is they were on Icarus constructing whatever it takes to cause a flood."

Calvin asked, "Are you all right, Jake? You're not making much sense."

Captain Jake said, "Kevin mentioned Noah's Ark before the signal cut out. The mindbender vine that was around Kevin. Could it grow up that pipe into the bridge of Jurassic Park?"

Calvin said, "I knew it. Pod people."

Captain Jake said, "Tie, can a standard rail gun shell survive atmosphere to destroy Jurassic Park?"

Calvin exclaimed, "Lightning tornado!"

Filipe said, "Not unless I coat one for heat resistance."

Davinie exclaimed, "Hell no! Not only do you not have any sort of authority to destroy Jurassic Park, but that kind of destruction and temperature change could kill all life on that planet. That includes millions of intelligent humanoid life-forms."

Captain Jake said, "I may need a bargaining chip. Filipe, go ahead and coat a shell just in case. Calvin, can you check Samantha's programming to find out what she knows?"

Calvin replied, "If she's programmed, maybe. If she's downloaded from a human consciousness, there's no way."

Frank asked, "What about April and Stacy?"

Captain Jake replied, "Between Timmy's brains and June's brawn, they'll be fine. Get prepared for battle with those incoming jet arms while Calvin and I go see if we can get any intel from Samantha." Captain Jake then double tapped his left wrist with two fingers to end his link.

Who's the Villain?

Captain Jake and Calvin entered the detention center to find July sitting behind the desk. Captain Jake asked, "How's Samantha doing?"

July replied, "She's an android. She doesn't feel."

Calvin said, "If she's downloaded, she feels just like her organic body would. It's just through circuits instead of cells."

Captain Jake asked, "How can you tell which she is? Do you just..."

Calvin explained, "If she's programmed, then her response will be the same regardless of her mood. It won't vary or only vary slightly depending on the sophistication of the programming. Downloaded factors in everything from memory to hormone levels based on diet to determine a response just like the organic version would."

Captain Jake said, "We don't have time to figure it out the long way. Can't you just hack her and let the code tell you what she is?"

Calvin replied, "She doesn't have Wi-Fi. Her download jack is going to be hidden. It could be behind an ear, in a tooth, under a breast, or between her—"

July cut Calvin off. "May's in there with her. She considers Samantha her girlfriend. Talk like that in front of her, and she'll cut off what's between your legs."

Calvin replied, "If Samantha turns out to be programmed, I'm willing to make her a shareable sex doll. For a fee."

"She's downloaded, Captain" came a voice from a cell.

Captain Jake walked over to the cell where Thirteen was sitting Indian style and asked, "You finally ready to talk?"

Thirteen replied, "You discovering Samantha is a signal that things are getting out of hand. Gia wants to ensure you live so as to save lives in the future. Whatever you're doing now is jeopardizing that."

Calvin asked, "Who the hell is Gia?"

Captain Jake answered, "Timothy's mindbender vine. So it is sentient?"

Thirteen said, "Gia is not an it. Like a godling, they have no he or she labels. You have learned far more than we ever expected."

Captain Jake asked, "What's the plan? How are you planning to wipe out all life in Einstein?"

Thirteen replied, "Timmy has been busy. My purpose is to keep Equality and its crew safe. Right now, I presume the jet arms based on the moon have been sent this way. As long as you don't try to leave until tomorrow, they will remain just out of firing range."

July asked, "What about my sisters down on Chronos?"

Thirteen replied, "As long as they don't do anything rash, they will be safe."

Captain Jake asked, "What happens tomorrow?"

Thirteen said, "I will start from the beginning. You are aware of the separation of Jurassic Island, are you not?"

Captain Jake replied, "I am. Is that what caused Gia to hate us?"

Thirteen said, "It is. Gia doesn't create pod people like Calvin suggested. It shares a symbiotic relationship with the animals of this planet. Its vines run across the supercontinent's surface. A person on one end of the supercontinent connected to the vine can feel and see another person's thoughts at the opposite side of the supercontinent. This helps warn people of impending storms."

Captain Jake said, "We saw a video of a Gia vine forcing a deer to eat the vine."

Thirteen said, "You found a video. Timmy is quite extraordinary for a human. That is how Gia fertilizes itself. An animal eats its vines, then Gia releases a pheromone to attract other animals that devour the animal. The future waste from this process provides nutrients for Gia."

Calvin asked, "Gia decides when to and not to release this pheromone?"

Thirteen replied, "Yes. It also lets the native Indians know what crops will grow the best in what soil. When to burn down a forest to replenish nutrients. Even where herds are gathered for a successful hunt."

Captain Jake asked, "What does Gia get out of this?"

Thirteen answered, "The joy of watching the native Indians develop as a people. That's all it wanted, but you humans took that from Gia. At least the piece that got stranded on that island."

Captain Jake said, "We can transplant the vine back to the supercontinent. No one has to die."

Thirteen replied, "Humans knowing about Gia is a death sentence for them. You came here already knowing about Gia. Admit it, Captain. You've already come up with at least one way to kill them."

Captain Jake said, "If it's between them and us, I have to choose us. But it doesn't have to come to that."

Thirteen explained, "Your ignorance is astounding, Captain. The Gia on Jurassic Island never wants to be returned to the mainland. You humans almost killed it when you separated the island from the supercontinent with your seismic charges. It took Gia decades to recover and learn about you invading humans. Then Gia got lucky and caught a scientist."

Captain Jake said, "Wes."

Thirteen, "Yes. Human physiology is different from the native Indians. Gia let Wes go as it took them many days to process the knowledge they gained from swapping fluids. Wes discovered drugs had stronger effects on him after the chance encounter. So he went back for more. This time, Gia used the scientist's W2 to order a kids bot to slowly start drilling a hole into the base of SS Jurassic Park. Over the years, the number of scientists on Jurassic Park diminished as you humans planned. Gia took advantage of this to have the kids bots build android molds in secret. All the knowledge needed was online after all. Eventually, Gia took over Jurassic Park. A petal Gia produces helps to prolong the life of its prey on Chronos. In humans, it reverses it. Gia released this discovery to get you humans to send a cargo ship to pick it up. Gia captured the pilot and replaced him with an android. That pilot came to the godlings, asking for help in saving its people from the invaders."

Calvin said, "Me and Jake just got here."

July said, "I was born here. I'm not an invader."

Thirteen said, "This thinking is why force is necessary. You steal without thinking twice about it."

Captain Jake said, "What happened to Gia happened hundreds of years ago. It was tragic, but they haven't been back to steal anything. Except what Gia tricked them into coming back for."

Thirteen asked, "The material you used to get here, Captain. Where did it come from?"

Captain Jake replied, "Mostly mined from asteroids from our solar system."

Thirteen said, "Shouldn't the citizens of this solar system have the rights to mine the minerals of their own asteroids? As you humans did in your solar system."

Calvin said, "But they can't even get into space yet."

Thirteen replied, "Exactly. You humans have a 'whoever gets there first gets it' philosophy. It doesn't matter that you had a million-year head start on evolution. They weren't fast enough, so they didn't get to keep their own resources. Did you know aboard one of the cargo ships you were to escort here were the materials to make an underwater base? The Juliet people were going to start harvesting sea life in exchange for the Romeo people taking this planet's soil. That sounds an awful lot like invaders to me."

Captain Jake said, "We can talk to Admiral Noem about stopping them from taking anything from this planet. It's not too late for you to put a stop to whatever it is you have planned."

Thirteen replied, "Admiral Noem is the one who brokered the deal. It's too late to stop anything. Precautions have been made to ensure her death. You can do nothing to save her."

Captain Jake asked, "How do you plan on doing it then? What's your grand plan to wipe out all life in Einstein that isn't from Chronos?"

Thirteen explained, "The plan to catch the pirates was to have four thousand spacemines deployed to surround them. This plan was developed by the godlings at the request of the Middleman security force long before you arrived, Captain. The godlings were hired to build the spacemines, but we subcontracted to Icarus Innovations. Instead of being built with a stormfront core, they're built with a nuclear core. You passed those cargo ships a day and a half ago. Didn't you?"

Dolly said, "Serenity is headed back, Captain. They are flashing Morse code. The message reads, 'Impending nuclear attack on Middleman. Must destroy relay satellite to send warning message.' End message."

Captain Jake smiled then said, "I'm losing count of how many miracles that kid's pulling off today."

Thirteen said, "Too much time has passed, Captain. The jet arms will attack before you can leave. Even if by some miracle you make it, Admiral Noem and at least 70 percent of the fleet's personnel will die."

Captain Jake said, "Saving just 30 percent is better than saving none."

Thirteen replied, "You'll be saving fewer than that, Captain. You haven't heard the rest of the plan yet."

Captain Jake said, "The missing kids bots. They're going to take control of the ships after the crews are dead. You'll have the only space fleet in Einstein."

Thirteen replied, "Very good, Captain, but you still aren't grasping how desperate your situation is. Do you know of the quartership SS Expedition?"

Captain Jake replied, "That's the ship Samantha's from. It left years ago to explore the Taylor system."

Thirteen said, "It did. But not before several androids like Samantha and several programmed androids were placed onboard. Afraid the ship suffered from environmental issues shortly after they entered the magnetic void. Since then, they have been constructing an android army. Perhaps I should also mention the pirates are all androids."

Captain Jake said, "The pirates were never on 15 for Life then. The plan to capture them never existed."

Thirteen said, "If they were on 15 for Life, then the godlings' plan would have been flawless. As all godling plans are. All is not lost, Captain. Gia has no desire to see the culture created in Einstein wiped from history. That is why Equality was sent to gather citizens from every sector of space. You are to return to Earth to warn them not to send any more ships to Einstein."

Captain Jake said, "Harry already told us they scrapped the program."

Thirteen said, "Humans are greedy. The program will inevitably be restarted. After the cleansing of Einstein, a small number of godlings will remain to maintain the android army. Any vessels entering Einstein after that will be destroyed on contact. In fact, nuclear spacemines will be set to ensure this. I implore you, Captain. Take Equality back to Earth. Save the lives of your crew and future generations of citizens from Earth. Staying in Einstein means certain death."

July said, "We don't run. We fight. Right, Captain?"

Thirteen said, "You now realize why we tried to kill you, Captain?"

Captain Jake replied, "I do. Dolly, get everyone prepped for the Dizzy Maker Program. Then share this conversation with all officers."

CHAPTER 26

Space Battle

Captain Jake sat in the pilot's seat aboard the bridge. Every crew member was at their station and were wearing power attire. In fact, every crew member and resident were wearing power attire, or at least a space suit with an exoskeleton addition. Captain Jake asked, "Are the scattershots ready?"

Tie replied, "Loaded and ready to fire, Captain."

Harry said, "Serenity is approaching the outer atmosphere."

Captain Jake replied, "Keep an eye on them. They won't be able to maneuver until they're clear of it. Calvin, is the program ready to run?"

Calvin said, "When Timmy suggested this program after watching our first fight with the pirates, I never thought we'd be desperate enough to use it."

Tie said, "I can't believe Davinie is letting us use the Dizzy Maker Program."

Davinie's voice came over the comm. "What the hell is the Dizzy Maker Program?"

Captain Jake smiled then said, "Dolly, initiate Dizzy Maker Program." Suddenly, Captain Jake's power suit readjusted his head slightly to be perfectly straight. The entire suit then stiffened up so he couldn't move while he could feel cushioning in the back of his neck start to apply more pressure.

Davinie shouted over the comm, "This is illegal! You can't take over control of people's power suits!"

Captain Jake replied, "If we live through this, feel free to press charges."

Equality raced forward at the approaching jet arms. Then, like in the first encounter, it fired a scattershot at them with the recoil dampeners almost completely shut off and the emergency stop thrusters removed. This completely spun Equality in a 360-degree spin that would have kept them going if not for the second rail gun being fired. This second rail gun scattershot shell left the barrel with a spin on it. This spin (much like how a professional bowler adds a spin to the ball to increase accuracy and pin action) made the scattershot spread out farther, creating a much larger kill zone.

Captain Jake asked, "Is everyone all right?" There was a sudden flash of red across the bridge's window. Captain Jake tried to reach for the controls, but his power suit was still in lockdown mode. Captain Jake said, "Doll—" Before he could even finish saying her name, Captain Jake was able to move again and began evasive maneuvers.

Tie said, "I got the one that shot us."

Captain Jake said, "Filipe, we took a hit. Need more FP released before we take another one."

Filipe replied over the comms, "We need a second for the room to stop spinning, sir."

Calvin said, "First scattershot took out three jet arms. Second scattershot took out eight. Only nineteen left."

Calvin said, "The rest of the jet arms are spreading out and hanging back. We have no escape routes. Mothership is on its way from the moon. It's using Carrie effect drive to get here. Under a minute before arrival."

Captain Jake ordered, "Reroute whatever powers left in the triple barrel to a rail cannon. Load it with a standard shell. Let's take out the mothership while it's defenseless, and move too fast to dodge."

Calvin said, "Two bogies coming at us from different angles. We're going to take some hits to make this shot."

Captain Jake said, "May and June, you ladies ready?"

July replied over the comms, "I'm July, not June. We're ready."

Captain Jake said, "Sorry. We're going to let two jet arms shoot us. Take them out after before they can recharge. Stay out of the fight after that so the jet arms don't target you. Your power suits won't survive a hit if they decide to shoot you."

May replied over the comms, "I'll kill them all for what they did to Samantha."

Two more red streaks of lightning came across the bridge's window. Captain Jake said, "Dolly, open the cargo bay doors."

Tie said, "Firing rail gun." The shell struck the mothership center mass just below the bridge. The shell must have also hit the ship's stormfront battery, causing the ship to explode in multicolored lightning.

July said over the comms, "Targets down."

Calvin said, "Ten more jet arms have left the moon's surface. Looks like they're equipped with plasma boosters."

Harry said, "Four jet arms are headed toward Serenity. They haven't cleared the atmosphere yet."

Calvin said, "Incoming rail gun shell from the moon. It's headed to intercept Serenity. Serenity can't activate its FP shield until it clears atmosphere."

Captain Jake fired the scattershot shell, destroying the jet arms targeting Serenity moments before they were within firing range. Captain Jake asked, "Can we intercept the shell?"

Dolly replied, "I got this, sugar." Equality began to fly on its own.

Calvin said, "Three jet arms are headed to intercept us."

Tie said, "If any of them shoot us, that shell's going to rip right through Equality."

July said over the comms, "May and I have your backs. Protect our sisters." Both May and July pushed their jetpacks to the max to intercept two of the incoming jet arms. Both sisters fired their hand cannons to release red lightning and disabled two of the jet arms.

Tie said, "Two boogies down. Third's firing."

Equality suddenly took a major change in direction as they were struck by the rail gun shell launched from the moon.

Harry said, "Serenity has cleared the atmosphere."

Captain Jake asked, "Did the shell knock us out of range of the spider cannon?"

May answered with a frantic voice over the comms, "July intercepted the shot! I don't know if she's still alive."

Equality turned so July's power suit could be seen out the window. It still had flecks of red lightning flickering off it.

A flash of white lightning could be seen out of the corner of the window. Tie said, "I took care of the one that shot her."

Captain Jake said, "Dr. Helix, I need you to get to the cargo bay."

Dr. Helix replied, "I can't leave right now. Irene will have to go."

Calvin said, "Still ten jet arms here and ten on the way."

Harry said, "Serenity's charging two of them."

May said, "July's still breathing. She wanted you to help our sisters, so go help them. I'll keep July safe."

Serenity fired both its spider cannons one after the other, taking out two more jet arms. Unfortunately, both jet arms also got shot off at Serenity in close succession, the second hit leaving scorch marks on the hull of Serenity under the bridge.

Three more jet arms went after Serenity while three others moved to an intercept course. Equality swooped in to destroy the three pursuing jet arms with strikes of white lightning.

A jet arm then moved in on May and July, forcing Equality to return. The jet arm retreated only for a jet arm on the opposite side of Equality and Serenity to swoop in then retreat just short of firing range. While this was going on, the moon was randomly firing rail gun shells at them, making it impossible for them to merge or pick up May and July.

Calvin asked, "What are they doing?"

Captain Jake replied, "Running out the clock for the win. Serenity, how are you holding up over there?"

After a moment of silence, Calvin said, "That hit might have knocked out communications. At least they're still flying."

Tie replied, "Yes, but now there's an opening in their FP shield. Another shot in that spot and they're dead."

Captain Jake said, "Load the rail gun. We'll start taking them out from afar."

Tie said, "We only have one more scattershot and five regular for seventeen remaining."

Filipe replied over the comm, "Four regular. That special one you wanted is ready."

Tie said, "We can only hit one with scattershot. They're too spread out."

Harry said, "Serenity's plasma rockets are heating up. They're going to make a run for it."

Calvin said, "I wondered what was taking Jesus so long."

Captain Jake smiled then said, "They're not making a run for it. Load the scattershot. Timmy's got one more miracle to pull out of his butt."

Calvin said, "Jet arms are already converging on Serenity."

Dolly said, "Moving Equality so the scattershot won't hit the opening in their FP shield."

Captain Jake waited a tenth of a second too long to fire. Red lightning shot forth at the same time he fired. Captain Jake's heart skipped a beat as he feared he just destroyed Serenity.

The scattershot took out ten jet arms but also damaged the top hull of Serenity. Serenity remained in one piece and kept flying. Serenity managed to take out two more jet arms with red lightning bolts. Equality (piloted by Dolly) also charged in, and Tie took out two jet arms with white lightning bolts before retreating to recharge their spider cannons.

Calvin said, "Guess that hull upgrade we got from RO actually worked. I don't see any atmosphere breaches."

Captain Jake said, "Thank God. I thought I killed them."

Tie said, "Do it again and they will be. Three jet arms left and three mobile rail guns on the moon. What are your orders, Captain?"

Captain Jake said, "The rail guns will fire whenever we try to merge unless we move out of range. That takes time. We can take out the jet arms with spider cannons, but that means they can also shoot us. Filipe, how are we doing on FP?"

Filipe replied over the comms, "Just loaded the last we have. Reserves are out. From what Serenity's FP levels look like another hit, and we won't have enough FP to create a Carrie effect ring to start the drive."

Captain Jake said, "We have to use the shells to take out the jet arms then."

Harry said, "Captain, the cargo bay doors are opening."

*****

At the start of the fight, Frank received a medical alert from Davinie. The stress of the Dizzy Maker maneuver was more than her heart could take. Although her power suit automatically revived her, Frank flushed Davinie to the medical bay just the same.

After that, Frank headed to engineering to assist with transferring barrels of FP to the reload stations. Then Frank watched on the security feed as July rushed in to intercept the red lightning bolt meant for Equality.

Frank immediately rushed to the cargo bay and strapped on a jetpack. His intent was to rush out unarmed to collect July or sacrifice himself to save April's sister if need be. Frank followed the battle and the conversation on the bridge, waiting for his moment to help. Eventually, he heard that there were only three jet arms left, but Equality was low on rail gun shells and couldn't afford to take another hit to the FP shield.

Frank removed his spider pistol and let it magnet lock against the back wall of the cargo bay. Frank located the nearest jet arm on the security cameras then said, "Dolly, security override. Open up the cargo bay door."

The cargo bay door opened, and Frank wasted no time traveling as fast as he could toward the jet arm. Without his spider pistol, Frank's suit would run out of energy in a few hours, but Frank didn't need that long. What Frank did need was for the jet arm drone's programing not to register him as a threat.

As Frank hoped, the jet arm didn't try to avoid him. Frank waited until the last possible moment to draw and slice into the spider cannon mounted atop of the jet arm. Its stormfront battery's core expunged its -3,000 degree icy core, leaving the drone powerless.

A nearby drone, now considering Frank a threat, moved toward him. Frank charged at this jet arm with his sawsword raised above his head, the flat of the sawsword facing the jet arm. Frank's goal this time was to force the jet arm to fire, leaving it vulnerable for Equality or Serenity to take out.

Frank got what he wanted as the jet arm released a bolt of red lightning at him. The sawsword absorbed the red lightning as best it could. The sawsword quickly glowed bright white, and Frank felt electrical shocks flowing up his arm. This was followed by the feeling that his hand was being melted into his glove. Frank fought through the pain anyways to tilt his sawsword and to strike at its wing as it passed. Frank's sawsword connected, but the white-hot sawsword shattered. The jet arm continued on with no damage being dealt to it while the attempted strike sent new sensations of pain up Frank's arm.

Moments later, Frank watched the jet arm get struck by a red lightning bolt. Frank sighed with relief, knowing this meant Captain Jake could take out the last jet arm and the moon base rail guns with their remaining shells.

CHAPTER 27

Despair

Serenity picked up Frank, May, and July while Equality used up the last of its regular rail gun shells to destroy the last threats to them. The radio silence persisted from Serenity. Even the comms of the rescued personnel went dark after boarding Serenity.

Captain Jake assumed they were mad at him for almost destroying Serenity by waiting too long to fire the scattershot shell. Luckily, Serenity wasn't damaged so badly that it couldn't merge with Equality.

Captain Jake stopped by the medical bay to walk with Dr. Helix to the entrance of Serenity, but the doctor was already gone. Instead, he found Davinie in a bed sleeping while Irene was inflating a large plastic bubble on the other side of the room.

Captain Jake asked, "What happened to Davinie?"

Irene replied, "Her heart couldn't take the ship spinning like it did. Don't worry, her heart was instantly restarted, so there was no blood flow loss to the brain. She just needs a little rest."

Captain Jake said, "That's at least six crew members injured. As long as we can make it back in time to warn Admiral Noem, it'll be worth it."

Irene asked, "Warn her about what?"

Captain Jake said, "I have to go. Take good care of Davinie, and tell her I'm sorry." Captain Jake exited the medical bay and called Filipe. "How long will it take to repair the hull of Serenity enough to get underway?"

Filipe replied, "An hour, Captain. You should know we only have enough FP to run a Carrie effect drive at one-tenth normal strength. We'd be better off waiting until tomorrow and collecting our lost FP once it regains its ability to hold a magnetic charge."

Captain Jake's heart sank. He asked, "Have you watched my conversation with Thirteen? I shared the link."

Filipe answered, "Haven't had the time yet, Captain. Didn't think it would be relevant to engineering."

Captain Jake muttered to himself, "Did I just do this for nothing?"

Filipe said, "Captain? I didn't catch that. I can watch the link now if it's important."

Captain Jake said, "No. You don't need to watch it now. Getting the hull fixed takes top priority. I'll talk to you later, Filipe." Captain Jake hung up and continued to the entrance of Serenity.

Captain Jake approached the entrance to Serenity where he saw Dr. Helix already waiting. Captain Jake felt desperate to see June, knowing that nothing would feel all right until he did. Captain Jake forced himself to talk with Dr. Helix, who was staring at the ground. "Thank you for helping Davinie."

Dr. Helix continued to look at the ground as he replied with a gentle tone, "I do what I can. I'm sorry I can't do more, Captain."

Captain Jake replied, "No one could ask more of you, Doc. I'm sure you'll heal them all good as new."

Dr. Helix continued staring at the ground and said, "Zac has already started treating July for third-degree burns covering her entire body. Irene is preparing a bubble for her that we must get her in right away. Frank is the next worse with third-degree burns on his right hand and arm. April is suffering from several broken ribs, and Rex has a concussion. Kevin I can't even think about right now."

Captain Jake asked, "Have you spoken with Serenity?"

The floor opened, and the lift rose up with July laying naked in the middle of a hospital bed. She was wearing an oxygen mask. Her skin was charred and peeling. May and Zac were standing over her, spraying July down with some sort of ointment.

Dr. Helix stepped onto the platform as it went up and asked, "How are her vitals?"

Zac answered, "Holding steady."

Dr. Helix said, "Irene will have the nanites ready to start treating her as soon as we get her in the bubble."

As the lift continued up, Captain Jake looked down into the hole where he saw Emily trying to remove the charred power armor covering Frank's right arm. His right hand was still clutching the hilt of his broken sawsword. April was sitting next to him in only her blue and green onesie holding her ribs. Captain Jake couldn't help but feel guilty that he failed his end of the promise to June to keep everyone safe in space.

The lift lowered back down then returned up with April, Frank, Emily, and Rex lying unconscious on the floor of the lift. As the lift passed by Jake, he could see that both had been crying recently. No one said a word to Captain Jake or even attempted making eye contact with him.

Captain Jake couldn't take it anymore. He wanted nothing more than to hold June in his arms and beg forgiveness for letting her sister July get so badly hurt. Captain Jake looked into the hole and said, "June."

After a moment of silence, Stacy said, "Come down with the lift, Jake."

Captain Jake stopped onto the lift as it returned down to Serenity. At the back of the passenger cabin, he saw Stacy sitting down and June standing up behind her, still wearing her black power suit with yellow stripes. Captain Jake said, "I'm sorry about you sisters getting hurt, June."

"She can't hear you, Jake" came Jesus's voice from the cockpit.

Captain Jake turned to Jesus (with Timothy standing next to him) then back to June and asked, "Why not?" Captain Jake looked closer at June. Her power suit had a few dents, but it wasn't anything to cause concern. He took a couple of steps toward June and noticed her eyes were closed. Captain Jake shouted, "June!"

Stacy said, "I'm sorry, Jake."

Captain Jake took a couple of more steps then asked, "Sorry for what?" Captain Jake shouted again, "June!"

Stacy said, "She was a hero, Jake. The most amazing hero I've ever seen. She saved all of us."

Captain Jake stopped walking forward as fear took hold of him. Captain Jake asked, "Why are you talking like she's gone? She's right there. Her power suit's hardly dented."

Timothy explained, "She shut off her power suit's strength limiter in order to reach everybody in time. The suit warned her that it was killing her, but she kept going."

Stacy said, "April was being tortured. June saved her, Jake. Saved all of us."

Captain Jake started walking again toward June, hoping it was somehow just a bad dream.

Jesus went to an aisle of seats where Kevin was sleeping and lifted him up. Stacy said, "We're going to give you a minute, Jake. I'll stop by later to bring you dinner. You still need to eat." Stacy and the others took the lift up, giving Captain Jake his privacy to say goodbye.

Once the lift exited, Captain Jake said to June, "When we returned to Middleman, we were supposed to have dinner with Noem. Thirteen already told me I wouldn't be able to do that. He said Noem was dead regardless, but I believed in us. We were going to save Einstein together and show the intellectual blowhard what humanity can do. Now you're gone, and we have no way to reach the relay satellite in time to get a warning to Noem."

Captain Jake started to remove June's power armor as he said, "You know what else I found out from Thirteen? The reason they tried to kill me back in Hades City. And Icarus. Thirteen actually told me back on Chuck Norris, come to think of it. It was because of this moment. They knew I'd choose to fight. With me gone, Noem would have had to captain Equality herself. She told me she trusted no one but me to captain Equality. She never would have taken civilians into battle. Noem would have chosen to return to Earth to keep all of you safe. If she were here instead of me, you'd still be alive. She'd be able to keep living past tomorrow. Davinie and your sister and all the others in the medical bay wouldn't be there."

Captain Jake finished taking June out of her power suit then caressed her pink camo arm and said, "Saving me killed you in the end." Captain Jake leaned in and kissed June on the lips. Captain Jake smiled then said, "We almost did it. One or two fewer hits, and we could have still saved Einstein. But it's not all bad, June. We saved the crew. You kept them alive on the ground, and despite being a little worse for wear, I kept them alive in space. Equality waits around a day then collects all the FP we lost. Oh, and the FP from that mothership we destroyed. Equality can still head back to Earth just like the godlings and Gia always wanted. Stacy's about to have kids. I'm sure it won't be long before Frank and April start popping out little ones." Captain Jake giggled then said, "Someday their kids might have kids of their own."

Captain Jake removed his own power suit, leaving it next to June's. Captain Jake floated June into the airlock then said, "The best part about this plan is that they don't need me for it. Dolly."

Dolly replied, "Yes, Captain."

Captain Jake said, "I'd like to record a message for the crew. Audio only."

Dolly replied, "Whenever you're ready, Captain."

Captain Jake said, "Hello, crew. I'm leaving you with a new mission. You should all have heard about what's happened in Einstein by the time you hear this message. I'm sorry we couldn't have done more. Everyone gave their all to try and stop it. Hold your head up high for that. In the end, we failed, and it's time to do what we can to preserve life. I want you to accept Thirteen's proposal of returning to Earth. It's the only way to save the civilians onboard. Plus, we will be saving future generations from coming here to find nothing but death waiting for them. I myself won't be joining you. I've decided my place is here with June. It was an honor knowing and serving with all of you. I wish you the best of luck returning to Earth. Captain Jake, signing off."

Dolly asked, "Are you sure, Captain?"

Captain Jake closed the inner airlock door then said, "I like this new you, Dolly. My place is with June. Wait until someone asks about me to play the message. They have enough on their minds right now."

Dolly said, "Yes, Jake. I will."

Captain Jake said, "Captain's override. Don't set off the sensors. Open then close the outer airlock once we're outside, Dolly. And goodbye."

Ray of Hope

Filipe, Ron, and Johnny were in engineering prepping materials for repairing the scorched hull of Serenity. After Filipe's conversation with Captain Jake, he decided to watch the captain's conversation with Thirteen while he worked.

Filipe's face changed to a look of shock and disbelief as heard the detailed plan to wipe out all of Einstein. Ron saw this and asked, "What's wrong?"

Filipe froze. He didn't know how to tell Ron his family back on Middleman were going to be killed in a day, and there was nothing they could do about it. Filipe finally answered, "Officer stuff. We need to get these repairs made as quickly as possible."

Ron replied, "Can't rush the process. These replacement pieces need to be custom formed, or they won't fit."

Johnny asked, "Do I get to help install them?"

Filipe replied, "Sorry, but this is no time for training."

"I'm sure it won't hurt for him to watch and learn" came a female voice from behind them.

They turned to see Emily standing in the doorway. Johnny exclaimed, "Mom! You're all right!"

Ron asked, "What the hell did you do down there to get those drones to attack us?"

Johnny said, "I'm sorry, Mom. Timmy ordered me to help."

Ron asked, "What the heck do you know about this kid?"

Johnny replied, "Only that Timmy had me retrofit some jet-packs for him and Rex for atmospheric usage. And at the last minute, he had me sneak Kevin into a crate that got loaded onto Serenity, but Clair was the one who struck Kevin with the drill dart. Timmy said it was to save lives."

Emily walked over and hugged her son then said, "You did good, Johnny. We were attacked by androids, and Timmy thinks he's uncovered a plan to set off nukes in the fleets surrounding Middleman."

Filipe asked, "Is everyone all right? You guys never rejoined the link."

Emily said softly, "No. June died rescuing her sister and April. Jesus made the call not to tell Captain Jake about June. Didn't want him distracted before a life-and-death battle. It was Timmy's idea to keep the communications dark so the captain wouldn't try talking to June."

Ron said, "Screw the captain. Is Middleman in danger from the nukes? My family's there!"

Emily replied, "I don't know if the threat's even real, Ron. Timmy's basing his information off Kevin."

Ron said, "The retard!"

Emily said, "Language! Kevin got wrapped up in some vine and started talking, well, normal like."

Filipe said, "Timmy called it the mindbender vine. It's apparently the protector of Chronos. It's pissed at us for breaking off a piece of the supercontinent. Calls us invaders."

Ron looked at Filipe then angrily said, "You knew about this." Filipe started to walk around the room and asked, "How the fuck does a plant put nukes in outer space?"

Filipe replied, "The godlings are helping it."

Ron exclaimed, "That's why Thirteen's locked up! What's the captain doing about my Iris? About my little girls, Chelsea and Megan?"

Emily said, "Calm down, Ron. We can't do anything until we fix the ship. Captain Jake is just finding out he lost June."

Ron shouted, "Funk Captain Jake! He was with that slut for a few weeks! I've been with Iris for decades! Megan isn't even old enough to know what love is! I left them behind to be safe!"

Emily calmly replied, "I know, Ron. Calm down."

Ron shouted, "You know nothing, bitch! Dolly! Where the fuck is the captain? He's going to look me in the eye when he tells me what we're doing to save my family!"

Asking for Captain Jake triggered his goodbye audio message to the crew.

*****

Everyone gathered in the courtyard seeking answers after hearing the captain's farewell message. With Davinie still in the hospital, that left the injured Frank in charge. Frank shared the link of the captain's conversation with Thirteen, as well as Timothy's full conversation with Kevin. After having his arm treated and wrapped, Frank met with May in the detention center.

Frank was only wearing a gray onesie while May was in her yellow power suit with black stripes. May said, "You look horrible. Sure you're up for this?"

Frank replied, "No. I was a fool for not staying with the captain. I should have known how he'd react."

May said, "No time to think about that now. We aren't going to just sit back and let Einstein be wiped out, are we?"

Frank said, "I don't know what we can do about it. Ship's crippled, and all communications are being blocked. We need Thirteen to speak with the crowd gathered in the courtyard. Thirteen's the only one with answers. They may try to kill Thirteen, and I can't protect them in my condition. Don't know that I'd want to protect anyways."

May said, "I'll keep Thirteen safe until we decide what to do with him."

Frank and May escorted Thirteen to the lift location. Once the floor opened up and the lift from Serenity arrived, they stepped on it and were lowered down to the courtyard. The lift stopped five feet from the ground of the courtyard to help prevent people from trying to attack Thirteen.

Ron shouted above the noisy crowd, "What are you going to do to save my family?"

Frank raised his good hand to request quiet. Once the crowd obliged, he spoke loudly, "With the relay satellites set to block signals, we can't transmit a message to warn anyone. Without FP, we can't travel fast enough to warn anyone. It's time to plan for what's next."

One of the residents shouted, "We fight back!"

Thirteen replied, "You can't fight against nuclear attacks. Captain Jake requested you live with his last breaths. I urge you to listen to him."

Stacy shouted, "You knew this whole time what was going to happen! You said nothing!"

Thirteen said, "Gia asked for our help against a superior adversary who was pilfering their resources and breaking their laws."

"What laws are we breaking?" came Davinie's voice from the crowd. Everyone looked to see her in a wheelchair being pushed by Irene.

Frank asked, "Is it all right for you to be here, Davinie?"

Davinie replied, "I'm not dead yet. Well, Thirteen, I watched your conversation with Captain Jake. I admit our ancestors were pricks to do what they did. Destruction of property by breaking off Jurassic Island. Assault by drugging and removing the inhabitants of said island. But the people responsible for doing that are long dead. You say we're stealing their resources by mining asteroids. Fine. We'll stop."

Thirteen said, "Stopping isn't good enough. All alien life-forms must leave or be exterminated."

Many shouted, "We're not alien! We were born here!"

Davinie shouted back, "Message received! Give us time to spread the word, and we can begin evacuating." Irene and most of the crowd gasped at Davinie's words.

Thirteen said, "You can tell by the crowd's reaction that that won't happen. The human race clings at hope. If we gave you time, you wouldn't use it to evacuate. You would use the time to come up with countermeasures to fight back. Only when all hope is distinguished will you concede. That is why you weren't meant to know about the plan until after its conclusion."

Davinie said, "I have grandbabies on Romeo. You can't expect me to just leave them."

Thirteen looked at Stacy then said, "You have babies about to be born right here. Don't commit them to death. Choose now to start saving lives."

"I will start saving lives!" shouted a squeaky voice from the back of the crowd. Everyone turned and made way for Timothy with Clair by his side as they marched toward the podium.

Thirteen said, "Timothy!" like a curse word under his breath.

With no one uttering a word, the lift lowered for Timothy and Clair to step aboard. The lift then returned to its previous position above the crowd.

Frank asked, "What do you need, Timmy?"

Timothy looked out over the crowd and spoke as loud and grown up as he could. "Time is short. If you want to save as many of the people of Einstein as we can, then you have to make me captain right now."

The crowd went silent. Davinie said, "That's not happening, boy. We know you're a genius. If you have a way to save people, just say it."

After a moment of silence, Thirteen said, "Only Captain Jake could be foolish enough to make a child an officer. No one is going to make you captain."

Frank stepped forward and loudly asked, "Timothy of Nowhere, clone of Russell Arthur." There were gasps from the crowd as this was not common knowledge. "Why do you have to be captain of Equality to help save lives?"

Timothy replied, "Call me Timothy. I can't save anyone this time from the shadows. Time is short, and we have to act now without people wasting time second-guessing me because I'm a kid."

Davinie exclaimed, "Just tell us what it is you think we can do!"

Frank asked, "How many can we save?"

Timothy shook his head and said, "Not everyone this time. Fewer by the minute."

Clair took hold of Timothy's hand then loudly said, "Timothy's my captain."

Davinie replied, "That's cute, but—"

"Timothy is my captain!" came a loud yet nervous voice. Everyone turned to see it was Johnny.

Thirteen said, "Children shouldn't be here."

"Timothy is my captain!" came an adult male voice. Everyone turned to look at Zac, who then asked, "How many times does Timothy have to pull our bacon off the sawsword before we trust him?"

Emily and Jesus shouted, "Timothy is my captain!" Soon everyone was chanting, "Timothy is my captain!"

Once the chant quieted down, Davinie shouted, "I'm acting captain. If the boy has a plan, I'll listen."

"Timothy is my captain! June didn't give her life for nothing" came a strong female voice from the back of the crowd. Everyone turned to watch April approach while holding her ribs.

Frank looked at Thirteen then said, "You heard my wife." Frank then turned to Timothy and asked, "What do you want done with the prisoner, Captain?" There was a round of cheers.

Davinie exclaimed, "You're going to mutiny!"

Timothy said, "Put Thirteen back in their cell for now. I'll need them for phase two. And let Samantha out. We need her help with phase one."

Frank asked, "How do you know we can trust her?"

Timothy replied, "She's only here as proof of what they can do." Timothy next shouted, "I need every person here with a space suit of any kind to go out collecting debris from the battle! The debris will be wielded into a message. It's time for Michael the Magician's ultimate magic trick!"

*****

Timothy sat in the captain's seat on the bridge with everyone at their stations. Behind Timothy stood April and Frank. In front of them, floating in space, was the word RUN with the start and top of the *R* looking like a nuclear mushroom cloud. Each letter was over a mile in length.

Frank asked, "Will it work?"

Timothy replied, "Michael tried to use his formula like a gas. It needed to be turned into a paste instead. It will work."

April said, "I think Frank was referring to the actual message."

Harry said, "I didn't have much time or material to work with."

Calvin said, "This should be bright enough for Admiral Noem to see. Once they backtrack its location, she'll know it's from us."

Tie said, "We salvaged all the spider cannons we could. Half are attached to the sign to detonate the magic paste. Blast doors closing. Ready when you are, Captain."

Timothy said, "Detonate." For one brief moment, the sky shone with a bright orange light. Then the light and everything used to construct the message was gone.

Samantha said, "Wow. That didn't even last as long as Calvin does in bed."

Tie added, "Long enough to get the job done. That's more than Calvin can ever say."

Calvin said, "Really funny, guys."

Timothy said, "Harry, if you would let the crew know."

Harry addressed the ship over the comms, "This part of the mission was a success. Within four minutes, Admiral Noem and the rest of Einstein will get our warning. This will be before the space-mines can be fully deployed. Thanks to your hard work, they have a fighting chance. Captain Timothy knows most of us have been awake twenty plus hours to accomplish this. He asks for everyone to get eight hours of sleep. Tomorrow, we collect the lost FP so we can get back to our loved ones."

Timothy got out of the captain's seat then said, "I'm off to bed. You guys should do the same."

*****

Five hours later, Thirteen was in their cell doing daily exercises. This included jumping back and forth from the ceiling to the floor.

Timothy entered the detention center and said, "Hello, Thirteen. How's your day going?"

Thirteen didn't bother to stop his workout as he replied, "What do you want, child?"

Timothy said, "Five hours ago, we sent a warning message to Admiral Noem. Thought I should tell you."

Thirteen showed no reaction as they replied, "There is no point in lying to me."

Timothy said, "I'm not. We used Michael's solar writing formula. Filipe and I have been working on it. Had to change it into a paste instead of a gas."

Thirteen stopped working out then said, "You must have used the debris from the space battle to write the message. The letters would have had to be spread out to be legible. You would only have had the material for a few letters. What was the message?"

Timothy replied, "I'll tell you if you tell me how to talk with Gia. Without them trying to kill me."

Thirteen said, "No matter the message you sent, the spacemines will detonate. It may not be as devastating as planned, but it changes nothing. The android army aboard SS Expedition will come and take over the undamaged ships lost during the nuclear assault. It will by far be the largest fleet remaining in Einstein at that point. The ships will then fire a rail gun at every settlement in Einstein."

Timothy asked, "Why didn't you tell Captain Jake about the androids like Samantha you have planted across Einstein? I'm guessing they're programmed to commit terrorist attacks across Einstein at the same time you set off the nukes. This will make it very difficult for anyone to mount any sort of counterattack."

Thirteen said, "You are clever. I already told Captain Jake about Admiral Noem's impending death. Adding more would have lowered the emotional effect of that information. Have you told the rest of the crew about the impending terrorist attacks?"

Timothy said, "No. I needed them to work like they thought they could save all their loved ones. Why didn't you tell the crowd? Take away any hope for them fighting back."

Thirteen said, "This vessel is to contain life from every sector of space. That includes carrying a godling. If I told the crowd, they would have killed me."

Timothy asked, "So your people aren't going to survive either?"

Thirteen said, "As I told Captain Jake, some of our people will remain to maintain the droid army from any other alien invaders. Four thousand godlings are giving their lives to pilot the spacemines, ensuring each one will have maximum effect. If ever the time comes when the people of Chronos learn to enter space, we are to tell them of what has transpired. At that point, we will do what they want. Until then, Gia doesn't want the people or the Gia of the mainland to know anything about you humans. Gia is more than willing to die to keep the secret."

Timothy said, "Gia's definitely going to die. The rail gun shell is ready to fire."

Thirteen said, "Davinie won't let you."

Timothy replied, "Davinie retired after our mutiny. Gia is going to die for what they've done. The question is whether or not I return that mold you created to the mainland or not. You know, the mold that killed my moms."

Thirteen said, "That mold was only meant to weaken stragglers who wouldn't be near prime settlements. You're the one who weaponized it."

Timothy said, "I'll weaponize it again if they don't help."

Thirteen asked, "What's to keep you from killing everyone after you get what you want? What is it you think they'll help you with?"

Timothy said, "It's the godlings who are going to help us. I need Gia to agree to our evacuation plan. The terms of the agreement will keep me from killing everyone down on Chronos."

*****

April and Frank rode the lift down into Serenity. Both were wearing matching purple and yellow onesies. April was also wearing her ammo belt full of drill darts. They saw Timothy and Thirteen sitting comfortably as they went over numbers on a laptop. Frank asked, "Are you two friends now?"

Timothy replied, "We have an understanding."

Thirteen said, "A most agreeable understanding at that. All sides should be quite happy, considering the circumstances."

April asked, "Where's Kevin? I thought we were going down to speak to Gia."

"Actually, you're going down to murder Gia" came Samantha's voice from the cockpit.

April and Frank turned to see Samantha was sitting next to Harry. April asked, "Why's they sex doll here?"

Thirteen said, "We need her to download codes. Codes that will be erased should you break your end of the agreement."

Harry said, "I'm here to collect soil while you guys go inside. I only have about sixty days to live without more 15 for Life."

Frank asked, "What's this understanding you've reached?"

*****

Captain Timothy, Frank, Thirteen, and Samantha stood outside the doors to the bridge. Frank said, "I knew we should have broken the doors down to search the bridge."

Thirteen replied, "It's a good thing you didn't. To keep their identity secret, there are incendiary devices placed inside the bridge and along the pipe connecting Gia with the bridge. Had you broke in, there would be no one to negotiate with today."

The doors opened, revealing the bridge. Inside were a dozen workstations. Several seats had skeletons, but only few were occupied by people wrapped in vines. Next to them, standing guard, was a kids bot.

They approached to see that the two people at the terminal were Adam and Eve. Vines wrapped around their waists that continued upward from there to their necks. Their arms were free to handle the controls.

Samantha said, "It smells worse here than a prostitute's couch."

Eve said, "I'm sorry about your people. I want to hurt as few people as possible."

Frank said, "If we knew about you, none of this would have needed to happen."

Thirteen said, "Don't be a fool."

Timothy said, "He's right, Frank. They knew there was intelligent life here, yet they shattered off a piece of the continent anyways. If they knew about Gia, they would have experimented on them."

Thirteen said, "It takes Gia a minute to process speech. If you want a conversation with them, you'll need to wait after you speak."

The kids bot approached then held out its finger.

Frank reached for his sawsword, but Thirteen said, "There is no need. We negotiated the agreement before arriving. The tip of the bot's finger has a USB port."

Samantha asked, "Does that mean I have a USB port?"

Thirteen answered, "Yes. Every time it gets used, your memory gets erased. All you remember is falling asleep."

Samantha asked, "Is that why I can't remember having sex? Is the port in my vagina?"

Thirteen replied, "No. That has to do with a traumatic experience combined with drug abuse that altered your brain chemistry. We simply took advantage of this default when we constructed your mechanical body." Thirteen pulled out the USB port from the kids bot's finger. Thirteen said, "Open wide, Samantha. Your port is hidden in a wisdom tooth."

Samantha giggled then said, "And here I thought I just had a mouth designed for black cock." Samantha opened wide, and Thirteen removed a tooth before plugging in the USB port.

Eve asked, "Will it hurt?"

Frank asked, "Will what hurt?"

Timothy said, "They're asking about they're death. I wanted it for Gia. I sampled a piece of your vine that we brought back to Equality. I wanted to make a pesticide that would hurt as it killed you. But I didn't. The people who died—my moms, Michael, Captain Jake—they wouldn't have wanted me to."

Frank asked, "Gia knows that we're going to kill them? Why aren't the kids bot trying to attack us?"

Thirteen said, "It's part of the deal. Gia doesn't want to live anyways. Their only joy in life was watching over the indigenous people. You humans took that away from them centuries ago. They just want to ensure the future of those people now."

Timothy said, "We're going to blame getting exiled from Einstein on the godlings. This way, Gia doesn't have to worry about anyone trying to attack Chronos. We also agreed to kill Gia in a manner that won't kill anyone on the mainland, which is what would have happened if we fired the rail gun from orbit."

Frank said, "We are planning on leaving Einstein then?"

Thirteen said, "I told you not to tell them."

Timothy said, "We aren't going to have a choice in staying. We instead agreed on an evacuation plan. We're going to travel from sector to sector, gathering people willing to flee. The android army will follow behind us, killing anyone who chooses to stay."

Frank said, "We got the warning message out. We don't know how many survivors there will be. It may be enough to stay and fight."

Timothy said, "We won't be forcing anyone to leave. You should know though. The spacemines were being piloted by godlings. They would have seen the warning message too."

Frank said, "I see. What about Adam and Eve? Can we bring them with us?"

Thirteen answered, "No. Their brains are completely integrated with Gia's now. It's only their bodies that remain." Thirteen removed the USB cable from Samantha's mouth then said, "Here are the codes so the godlings know the new plan."

Timothy said, "Go on without me. I need a minute to say goodbye to Gia."

Frank pulled his sawsword with his left hand then set the tip on the floor as he readjusted his grip.

Thirteen asked, "What do you think you're doing?"

Frank replied, "I'm not leaving the captain in here with a working kids bot." Frank started up his sawsword then cut through the kids bot. Frank awkwardly put his sawsword away then said, "We'll meet you on Serenity, Captain. Don't take too long. April should have the charges planted by now." Frank and Thirteen left leaving, Captain Timothy alone with Gia.

*****

As Serenity left Chronos, Harry started a news stream. The image was that of Jurassic Island while he spoke. "The ones responsible for attacking us yesterday, the ones who plotted a nuclear attack against Einstein, an attack we still don't know whether or not was successful, all started here on Jurassic Park." The quartership SS Jurassic Park suddenly exploded. In its place formed a tornado with white lightning flashing about it. Harry continued, "That's right, folks. The Russell Arthur special. A lightning tornado. Used for good instead of evil this time." The lightning started to fly from the tornado to nearby trees, setting them ablaze. Soon, the lightning tornado turned into a fire and lightning tornado. Harry said, "That's new. The people responsible for starting this have been dealt with. Now it's time to get back to save who we can."

The fire and lightning tornado continued to rip up and scorch the island until there was nothing left.

Ted, Admiral Noem, and Leaving Einstein

Admiral Noem had her hands full trying to keep the peace between Romeo and Juliet forces. Romeo had the stronger space fleet with more ships equipped with FP shields. Admiral Noem's threat to blow up Romeo's priceless time dilation pods was enough to keep them from attacking for the moment.

Juliet had the edge when it came to power attire. Troops were being equipped with jetpacks as quickly as they could be produced. Admiral Noem feared they would attack as soon as they believed they had the numbers to overwhelm the Juliet fleet.

Long-range scans also showed a fleet coming from the outer rings. This fleet was less equipped than Romeo or Juliet, but they could tip the balance of power if they joined either side.

In an attempt to prevent war, Admiral Noem made a deal with the pirates. The pirates would get full immunity for past crimes and pardons for any convictions. In exchange for this, the pirates would hand over any and all information on who they've been working with. Once Admiral Noem had proof of who (Captain Jake sent a message claiming godlings but couldn't prove it) was really behind all this, she could put a stop to it.

The pirates agreed on the condition that they would also be hired by the EPF as security (at an exorbitant salary) until the current situation deescalated. Admiral Noem didn't like it, but she didn't see any other choice to end the conflict. Admiral Noem agreed to the deal as long as Captain Spike could provide proof as to the organization behind starting the conflict.

To provide this proof, Captain Spike sent Ted in his cargo ship, the Exterminator, to meet with Admiral Noem. For Ted's safety, he was to wait until after the spacemines from Chronos were deployed. Any ships trying to attack him would have spacemines to deal with.

Admiral Noem entered the bridge of SS Middleman. The bridge had a dozen workstations all filled with personnel busy working. Admiral Noem asked, "Are the mines here yet?"

A black-and-white plushy officer responded, "Arriving now, Admiral."

Admiral Noem said, "Have the first cargo ship start deploying the mines between Romeo and Juliet fleets. We need to secure a path for Ted to reach us. Have the other three cargo vessels deploy their mines between our fleets and the incoming outer rings' fleet. If the outer rings try to circle around to one side, then we know they made a pact with someone."

A young female officer said, "Ted's vessel the Exterminator is on the outskirts of the Romeo and Juliet fleet with Captain Spike's motherships. Ted says he's ready to join us once the mines are placed."

Admiral Noem said, "If the godlings are behind this, we'll be finding out soon enough. Have Captain Marshall move Eagle Two to escort Ted in."

The young lady replied, "Yes, Admiral."

A half hour later, there was a flash of light that came and went. Everyone on the bridge looked at each other, wondering whether or not they imagined it. Admiral Noem said, "Bob, what was that we just saw?"

Admiral Noem's W2's AI, Bob, responded, "Unknown source of light originating from the Chronos sector of space."

The black-and-white plushy said, "It's a message, Admiral." The main screen of the bridge now displayed the word RUN with the start and top to the *R* looking like a nuclear mushroom.

The young female officer said, "Ted has started his approach before the spacemines have fully been deployed."

An officer asked, "Does the approaching outer ring fleet have nuclear weapons?"

Admiral Noem spoke quietly to herself, "If it's from Chronos, then the message must be from Jake. He got Thirteen to talk somehow. The godlings are most likely providing the outer rings with nuclear weapons."

The young female officer said, "Ted's coming in fast. He's requested permission to dock."

Admiral Noem whispered to herself, "The godlings are also working with the pirates." Admiral Noem shouted, "Evasive action from the Exterminator! It's armed with nuclear weapons. Warn all ships to clear the area!"

*****

Ted was aboard his cargo ship the SS Exterminator, awaiting clearance to travel to the SS Middleman. Admiral Noem was under the impression Ted was coming to sign a contract and give testimony as to how he came to be with the pirates. Ted's real mission was to destroy SS Middleman along with the time dilation pods it was now carrying. This would spark the fight between the Romeo and Juliet fleets. The more damage the two fleets did to each other, the easier time the outer fleets would have picking off the remaining forces.

Ted's vessel the Exterminator had a rail gun and plasma rockets attached for playing Thread the Needle. Concealed within the barrel of the rail gun was a nuclear missile (Ted was told it was a standard explosive missile) that could be fired faster than the rail gun could charge. Once within range of the SS Middleman, Ted was to fire then flee to the Juliet side, thus inciting what would become a massacre of both forces.

Ted was waiting eagerly for the spacemines to finish being deployed so he could start on his course to destroying the Middleman when there was an unexpected flash of orange light. Ted thought he imagined it until he started hearing comm chatter about the strange light. Someone said the light came from Chronos. Another person said it was a message and was about to read it when Ted's comms shut off.

Ted said, "Jackie boy, what's wrong with the comms?"

Captain Spike's voice came over the comms. "You must start your approach now. Someone is trying to warn Admiral Noem."

Ted said, "Fuck me." Then he started up his ion drives as well as his plasma rockets.

Captain Spike said, "Eagle Two is between you and Middleman. Don't let them stop you."

The Exterminator started to accelerate. Ted said, "Jackie boy, request permission to dock with Middleman. Tell Admiral Noem it's urgent I meet with her."

The ship's AI, Jackie boy, replied, "Request sent."

Ted saw Eagle Two up ahead and lowered the Exterminator's nose to fly underneath them. Once past, Ted raised the nose back up while swerving to dodge a spacemine that was suddenly headed toward the Romeo army. Ted saw that all the spacemines now seemed to be moving toward one army or another, but Ted had no time to think about it. Middleman was starting to move away from him.

Ted said, "Give me everything you got, Jackie boy. We need to shove this missile right up that pretentious bitch's ass."

Jackie boy replied, "You're within range. Firing now."

*****

Equality raced to the nearest relay station using every FP they were able to recover. Also, every FP from every power armor was donated to the cause. Timothy even ordered the Faraday metal walls in the detention area be ripped out for converting into FP.

Equality reached the relay satellite in a matter of hours and fired their last rail gun shell—the altered shell meant to destroy Jurassic Park—destroying it from a safe distance away.

Captain Timothy was on the bridge with Samantha at the time. Immediately following the destruction, Dolly said, "Incoming call."

Captain Timothy said, "Put it on the main screen."

Dolly replied, "It's for Samantha. From Mickey of SS Drill er Deep. I wasn't sure if she was allowed calls."

Captain Timothy replied, "Samantha is a member of this crew, Dolly. She's as human as anyone else."

Samantha looked at Timothy and said, "You're gonna make Clair a happy woman once your balls drop."

Timothy replied, "Thanks, I guess. Can I talk with this Mickey? I want to know if he knows anything about what happened to Middleman."

Samantha said, "Dolly, put Mickey on the main screen please."

Mickey's white bearded face appeared on the screen. Mickey said, "Thank God you're all right, lassie. Who's that? You never told me you had a son."

Timothy replied, "I'm not her son. I'm Captain Timothy."

Mickey smiled then said, "You're Captain Jake's son then. I'm Mickey. Pleased to make your acquaintance. Samantha, do you know anything about a flash of orange light that came from your direction?"

Samantha said, "That was from us. We were trying to warn Admiral Noem. Don't suppose you know if she got the message or not?"

Mickey replied, "So it was a warning. Admiral Noem got it and relayed it. She saved a lot of lives, but she couldn't save herself or my crew, I'm sorry to say. That son of a bitch Ted did a suicide run with a nuclear missile. I knew that piece of shit. Suicide wasn't in him. I thought that light was a warning, so I was following it back to its source to get answers. I can't return to the outer rings without answers for the families of my lost crew. What happened, Samantha?"

Timothy suspiciously asked, "How are you alive and your crew's dead? Are you an android? If you are, we have new orders for the godlings from Gia."

Mickey asked, "What's this child talking about, Samantha?"

Samantha said, "He really is the captain, Mickey. What happened out there?"

Mickey explained, "The outer rings gathered every ship to head to the inner rings to protest the nuclear testing and murdering of our scientists. We weren't coming to fight. We just wanted to show that we were willing to fight if they continued. And to say that we wanted no part in bringing nuclear weapons back into existence. A group of young lads wanted to go. They had jet arms but needed a mothership. I told them I'd give 'em a ride. When we got there, we noticed two huge armies formed, so we slowed the hell down. We were afraid that they were gathered to wipe us all out, except we noticed cargo ships setting up a wall of spacemines between us and them. I was on the back outskirts of our fleet. The lads took off in their jet arms to move to the front of the fleet, hiding behind some cargo ships with FP shields. Then came your flash of orange light. Admiral Noem sent out a warning message that the pirates had nuclear weapons. Said everyone should clear the area. Shortly after, Ted charged in and fired a missile at Middleman. If Admiral Noem hadn't warned us about it being nuclear, we wouldn't have known what happened. There wasn't even an explosion. People had to read their sensors to tell that everyone aboard Middleman was dead."

Timothy said, "Your crew couldn't have possibly been close enough to get caught up in the radiation."

Mickey said, "They weren't. When we realized what happened, we tried to turn around, but there were nuclear bombs hidden in the lead cargo vessels. I don't even know when they detonated. They released radiation, and half of our fleet of peaceful protestors were killed before they knew what hit them. Forward moment killed even more who couldn't turn in time to avoid it. The spacemines were veering off toward the Romeo and Juliet armies at that point. Before we survivors of the outer fleet could start to blame someone, the mines started to detonate nuclear bombs. The pirate ships then started to shoot retreating vessels with rail guns. They targeted ships with FP shields, knocking them back into the radiation. Why would they do this?"

Timothy answered, "The pirates filled their ranks with prisoners condemned to life on Titan. The prisoners wanted revenge on Einstein, so they made a pact with the godlings to cleanse Einstein. They have an android army coming to claim those ships caught up in the radiation. You need to return to the outer rings and spread the word we need to evacuate Einstein. Equality's headed to the inner rings to gather everyone we can. We'll meet you in the outer rings by Omega Mining in six weeks with everyone we can save."

Mickey said, "You should know, before I got into range of that satellite jammer, I was receiving distress signals from both Romeo and Juliet moons. They were being hit with terrorist attacks."

Timothy said, "You will find the same thing happened in the outer rings. All actions were carried out by androids. There may be androids among the survivors."

Mickey said, "Thanks for the info, kid. I'll pass on the message and what I've seen. Samantha, keep those photos coming."

Samantha replied, "I'll dedicate the next set to you." Mickey smiled then stroked his beard to end the call.

*****

Equality continued to the area where Middleman was destroyed. Scans showed hundreds of ships were already being occupied by androids. Equality transmitted the code and instructions they downloaded into Samantha on Chronos. They quickly received a message from the godlings, confirming the agreement.

Equality quickly moved from settlement to settlement after that, gathering survivors. Along the way, they learned many had lost loved ones. On Juliet, a power suit malfunction caused thousands to be killed by their suits' defibrillators, suddenly shocking healthy hearts to stop them from beating.

Ron's family, and all civilians aboard SS Middleman, were evacuated before the nuclear missile struck. Ron's family was evacuated to Romeo. Unfortunately, half of the biodome's center atmosphere pillars were destroyed by terrorist bombs. Ron's wife and youngest daughter were killed when the atmosphere was sucked out into space.

May's newest sister, Francis, was underground when biodome 2's atmosphere pillar was destroyed. May's parents and three other siblings weren't so fortunate. Davinie's grandbabies were safe, but she lost one of her sons in the attacks.

Alpha, Beta, and Omega Mining were all hit with a nuclear explosion near their quarterships. The planet Chuck Norris was attacked by ships from the outer ringers for revenge. All life on the planet was destroyed, but the godlings meant to maintain the android army were already in space.

Hades City was the only city left untouched. There was a nuclear bomb discovered and destroyed. The violent tendencies of the people kept the godlings from sending androids out of fear that they would be discovered.

Equality found more people willing to flee than anyone expected to. Of course, Harry's video of the drone army bombarding Juliet after the evacuation was a huge motivator. So many people wanted to evacuate that many had to be placed in stasis and packed into cargo containers to make the trip.

Only Hades City was the one place where most chose to stay and make a last stand. Captain Timothy took advantage of this to trade weapons for needed supplies.

When Equality finally arrived at the outskirts of Omega Mining, they discovered the quartership SS Expedition was waiting for them. The quartership was abandoned with a message being broadcasted on a loop: "For Timothy of Nowhere, with all the data we have for creating Argyle."

Captain Timothy was on the bridge of Equality with everyone at their stations.

Calvin asked, "Is this some sort of trap?"

Samantha said, "Mickey said they swept the ship. It's legit."

Captain Timothy said, "It has a Carrie effect drive. Start loading it up."

Calvin asked, "Why are the godlings giving this to us? What's Argyle?"

Captain Timothy answered, "It's a peace offering on behalf of the Chronos indigenous Indians, should the day come when the people of Chronos want to explore space. Gia didn't want them to have enemies waiting for them. Argyle is the name of a planet in the Taylor system. That's where we're taking our five hundred thousand plus refugees."

Tie said, "There aren't any planets in the Taylor system. Just asteroids. That's where the SS Expedition was headed the last time it left this star system."

Captain Timothy asked, "What do you think planets are made of?"

Calvin exclaimed, "We're going to build a planet?"

Timothy replied, "A planet where every species can live in harmony. Just like what Captain Jake was trying to create here."

"The babies are on their way" came Dr. Helix's voice over the comms.

Samantha said, "We have to go see the babies."

Captain Timothy said, "You go. I have something to take care of aboard Serenity."

*****

Captain Timothy lowered the lift into Serenity where Frank and the remaining three quadruplet sisters (all in power suits) were gathered around Thirteen.

Thirteen asked, "What is the meaning of this?"

Captain Timothy replied, "People are dead because of your silence. Captain Jake died because you took away his hope. We can't let you live."

Thirteen asked, "Where's my trial?"

"You don't get a trial" came Davinie's voice from the cockpit. Davinie entered the passenger cabin then said, "You killed my baby boy, motherfucker."

The sisters grabbed hold of Thirteen, wrestling him to the ground. July pinned Thirteen's left arm behind his back while May outstretched his right arm. April and Frank drew their sawswords. April also drew her spider pistol and fired it at her sawsword, making it glow red.

Frank started his red diamond chains spinning then said, "For Juliet." Frank swung down, cutting offThirteen's arm by the shoulder.

April placed the flat of her red-hot sawsword over Thirteen's tiny stump of an arm to cauterize the wound. April said, "That's for June."

The stench of burning flesh filled the room, but Thirteen never said a word.

May picked up Thirteen's severed arm and started beating him over the head in three-swing intervals, shouting, "That's for my murdered family on Romeo!"

Until now, Thirteen hadn't made a sound. Suddenly, Thirteen started to choke. Frank pulled May back out of concern for what was happening. April asked, "What's happening?"

Captain Timothy answered, "The new world we are creating needs life from every species, including godling."

Thirteen regurgitated a purple egg out of his mouth. Thirteen cleared their throat then said, "This baby has done nothing wrong."

Timothy said, "I'll raise the child as my own. You still have to die. Captain Jake died by leaving the airlock. He would have been unconscious within seconds. Godlings are made of sterner stuff. You'll be conscious to feel your blood boil until it freezes. Could take two to three excruciating minutes of pain before you die."

July picked up Thirteen and dragged them to the airlock. July said, "This is from me and all of Einstein." Then she pushed Thirteen into the airlock. The inner door closed automatically. The outer door then opened, sucking Thirteen out into space.

*****

Clair and Captain Timothy stood over the crib where Stacy's three babies lay floating slightly over the bed. Each had a tether preventing them from floating too far off. Timothy placed Thirteen's egg in a special tether next to them.

Clair said, "I can't believe we're going to be parents already. I can't wait until it hatches. What will we name it?"

Captain Timothy replied, "Stacy named her babies Michael Jr., Jake, and June. I think we should name our godling Noem. It would have made Captain Jake happy."

Clair said, "I like that. Johnny said you had this bed made special out of packed Chronos soil. You planted the mindbender vine in it, right?"

Captain Timothy replied, "It named itself Gia. I can't change that, but yeah, there's a Gia vine growing in the mattress. We need life from every species for planet Argyle once we build it."

Paul R. Strickler is from the small town of Argyle, located in the thumb of Michigan. Paul spent his free time before the pandemic traveling to various poker rooms across the state.

When the pandemic hit, Paul took up the challenge of writing a sci-fi novel series. It's a series Paul hopes can bring laughter and excitement to his readers.

Should you enjoy this book, *Expedition of Equality*, please be on the lookout for the next book in the series entitled *Rebirth of War*.

CPSIA information can be obtained
at www.ICGtesting.com
Printed in the USA
BVHW030509151221
623924BV00021B/26